My thanks to Joseph Hubchenko
and Marie-Claire Blais
and to Joan C.
who helped me enormously

Key West at
THE WATER'S EDGE

Written by

John Serge Hubchenko

third Edition September 2018
ISBN: 978-0-9995613-2-4

Introduction
"Old" Key West

The year is 1973. Tangled coils of trawl wire lie eight feet tall, and boat hulls hauled out for repair still line the shoreline at Key West Harbor. Gritty beige unpaved dirt runs from the harbor shore up to the beaches, seawalls, shrimp houses, and shrimp boat docks. The creosote-soaked pilings and weathered wood of the buildings and docks are everywhere. Beyond the pilings sailboats lay at anchor, but they are not the expensive boats of today. Corrugated buildings comprise the structures in the working areas, galvanized sides blending to rust at their bottoms. The electric plant still belches black soot on the city. Gray wood, brown rust, tan sand. It is Key West before the corporations and condos, funky and coarse, replete with celebrities and fugitives, before the new money and glitterati had driven them out. The reef is not yet dead, the water is still clear. The cycle of boom to bust to boom is currently bust.

Back then there were no cell phones, GPS, laptops or cable TV. It was great.

Freddy is a bit of a screw-up. He is in Key West to escape real life. His attitude is blasé; he is "politically incorrect" (in today's parlance) without realizing it. He is insensitive without being mean or vindictive; he is mocking and mimicking without vituperation, oblivious to any social misstep toward those around him.

The Prologue finds Freddy in dire straits looking back at past transgressions and also forward toward a very uncertain future. But as the story opens in chapter one, he's not serious about anything.

The Water's Edge Prologue

The high Caribbean sun bore down on Freddy halfway through another bright, tropical day. Badly burnt, his skin seemed on fire, but he could do little about it; there was no shade. Freddy considered using the torn canvas as a shelter before realizing there wasn't anything left to rig it to. Also, he considered that he might have to use the canvas as a shroud.

Wayne assumed the blame for every grizzly permutation that brought them to this point. Freddy wasn't sure that this was true, although perhaps if he had known about Wayne's past they might have worked together in averting the calamity that had befallen his friends. Too late in coming, Freddy's best efforts could not keep them from the horrible result.

He became aware of how low the boat sat in the water, felt it lapping at his feet and at the seat of his pants. The end seemed near. If he could get back, perhaps he could set right the balance, to make one side of the equation equal the other. Little towheaded Freddy Taylor - back in Bucks County years ago – out-ran, out-swam, out-thought the others, when it was a game. The game had changed.

Part one

An Easy Way to Live

Chapter one - Cliché Beginnings

"The temperature will be mostly in the lower half of the nineties this afternoon, with overnight lows in the high seventies or around eighty. The forecast for tomorrow, partly cloudy with a thirty percent chance of showers or thundershowers with the high temperature, of course, near ninety. Right now the temperature outside the studio is eighty-nine degrees."

****

"Wanna ride?"

"Sure, that's why I had my thumb out." Freddy had slowed when he saw the raised thumb of the walker in jeans and plaid flannel work shirt. Maybe a rider would help him stay awake. The sleeves of the shirt were rolled up. The shirt was incongruous in the hot weather.

He stopped the truck. The figure bounced oddly and slid jerkily in the loose roadside gravel as it ran. The luggage was a faded blue cloth bag with wooden handles; something an old lady might take shopping. As the cab door of the truck opened the hitchhiker climbed to the bench seat the hand on the hat came away with that piece of top gear and her long, brown hair fell from it. His passenger was a girl of about twenty years with clear brown eyes and a strong, round-shaped face. She settled into the seat and shook her hair out with a quick toss of her head. Her bouncy run to the truck in the flannel shirt had not concealed her striking figure, although she wore it for that purpose. Why else chose such a shirt in 95 degree weather? With a stubbly, grubby smile, he asked the question.

"Where are you headed?" She turned to him, wondering how she should answer.

"Unless I am mistaken, this is the road to Key West, right?

"Uh-huh," he replied, mind dulled by lack of sleep. She paused, wondering if she had to explain further. She decided to give it a try.

"With water on both sides of us, and nothing much around here where else would I be going?"

"That makes sense." Freddy had thought that he might have to stop for a nap, when fortune provided a candidate for conversation for keeping him awake long enough to complete the drive. He was so close to the end of his trip that he did not want to stop now. He was an inch under six feet; he had to scrunch up on the seat to sleep, but it was better than nothing. Falling asleep meant, at least, four hours lost. Then the sun would be set and he would have to drive the very narrow bridges in the dark and he would be unable to hire someone to help him unload, costing him an extra day on the rental truck.

Freddy worked up through the gears and pulled back onto the roadway when he had enough speed to merge the truck, with his car in tow, with the traffic.

From time to time Freddy looked over at the girl and tried to smile. He could see that she was pretty. He could also see that she was wary of him. His hair felt greasy and hung in small blond sweat curls. He turned his half-closed eyes, forced smile, and sagging face with two days of growth, tentatively toward her. After his sixth or so silent invitation for the woman to speak she responded.

"Is there something wrong with you? Maybe you better let me out."

"Don't be scared," said Freddy. It was the wrong thing to say.

"Don't flatter yourself; I'm not afraid of you. I'm just not in the mood for weirdoes."

"I know how I must look. I'm tired, that's all. I just wanted someone to talk to to keep me awake." Freddy explained that he had a rented house waiting for him and needed to get there tonight, if possible. "I'm afraid I'm not gonna make it. I've gotta get some sleep."

"I'll drive," she said. Freddy didn't like that idea.

"I have a car in tow."

"I saw it."

"These bridges are really narrow and---"

"You don't think I can do it."

"It's not that."

"What is it then? Do you want to see my driver's license?" He felt himself being intimidated.

"Have you ever towed anything before?"

"Dump trucks, delivery vans. I drove a flatbed trailer at a construction site. I got a lot of practice backing into tight places." Freddy was sure of that, and of getting out of them, too. They were half-way over a longish bridge somewhere south of Islamorada. "I'll bet I can back this thing right off this bridge." Freddy knew he would jack-knife the combination of truck and car in the first twenty yards if he were to try to do that.

"No need for that." He was too weak to argue about it. He pulled off the bridge and to the side of the road and she climbed over him into the driver's seat which he found embarrassing but exciting. She looked in the side mirror and checked the traffic. There was none. He fell asleep soon after they were under way again, and dreamed of the bumps and the turns of his early days in Pennsylvania.

****

Freddy spent his adolescence in Bucks County, Pennsylvania, running through the woods, chasing trains and swimming in cold, clear, fresh-water, spring-fed ponds. In the summer months he and his friends spent their time at a place known as the Goose Pond. Freddy had never seen a goose there, but he was sure that someone must have.

The boys played tag there all day long, in the water, and occasionally sprinting around the pond and into the woods. He loved those days in the wooded, rolling hills of rural Pennsylvania.

The pond itself was a perilous place. A rectangular raft twenty feet long and half again as wide, made of wood and set on pilings, sat close to the beach on the near side of the pond. Other pilings poked from the water to various heights or were totally submerged with no apparent pattern to their placement. On a high berm to the north of the pond were the railroad tracks. Passenger trains never came through there, but long freights would pass by at long intervals, pulling hundreds of hopper cars, boxcars, flatbeds, and tankers, mostly empty.

The pilings, remnants of collapsed trestle on the bottom of the pond, once supported a line of track running over the pond. The rails had been pulled up long ago. A few old passenger cars languished in the muddy bottom, victims of an accident staged for the making of a silent movie.

****

A shady creek ran into a cove at the far end of the pond. It was narrow enough to jump across, so long as the boy who tried it landed squarely in the coarse grass on the other bank. If he fell short he would hit the steep, slippery sides and slide backward, arms flailing, into the black mud of the creek.

The creek was alive with an awning of tree limbs bearing the leaves of oaks and elms and other broad-leaved trees. They provided a forest-green covering that hung out over the water. Below the branches were ferns and berry bushes. The ferns were lighter greens, almost iridescent; the berry bushes' small round leaves were darker. The place had a green cast, broken by the visible segments of the nearly vertical tree trunks of coarse brown texture. An occasional splash of bright sunlight found its way through the canopy.

The burbling of the creek was punctuated by the croaking of frogs. There were more frogs than the boys knew what to do with. The creek seemed more animated than real life. It was surreal in its vivid colors, made more intense by the creek sounds, animals scurrying, and the way the boys' voices would pierce the air and then die instantly in the echoless labyrinth of vegetation.

Near the creek, at that far end of the pond, a tire swing hung out over the water from the limb of a tree leaning out from the bank of the pond. When not playing tag the boys could divert themselves by swinging out over the water and jumping into a clear spot between the trees fallen from the bank at that end. Gnarled roots, unearthed from the shore, were medusas in the air, victims of the fate which caused their seeds to germinate in the sandy soil at the pond's edge. The trees grew too large for the too-sandy soil on the slope to the water's edge to support them, and so they toppled.

After swinging out on the tire swing the boys would release their hold at the top of its arc and plummet down between the fallen trunks to join the catfish with a splash. The catfish would then lurk in the tree roots until the disturbing phenomenon tired of the tire swing and went back to the other side of the pond to play another game of tag.

The tactics involved in the daily tag games were concerned, for the most part, with hiding from or eluding "it" underwater, under the raft, among the pilings or in the railroad cars. Those underwater obstacles were where the danger lay. One year a boy blacked out and drowned after being unable to find his way out of one of the submerged cars until his breath was nearly gone. He got out too late and lost consciousness four feet from the surface. Occasionally one or another lad would bust his head diving too close to the raft, misjudging the position of one of the pilings while executing the classic primary evasive maneuver, an underwater loop and cut-back after a deep dive. The move was like an inverted Immelmann turn done by fighter pilots with a penchant to prevent being perforated by the projectiles of an adversary. There were several other anfractuous stratagems employed, with varying degrees of difficulty and risk.

The lessons inherent in those accidents were quickly forgotten. These things occurred when the boys were at an age that knows little caution. The games of tag were perpetuated after Freddy left, as they had been before he took part, as smaller boys in the area so inclined grew to an age where they could participate.

Freddy's time there was his training ground, where he went when there was no school and he could either get his chores done or avoid them. He became adept at being nimble and efficient in and under the water, a thing that would stay with him in later years. He wasn't the fastest of surface swimmers; he tended to roll too much on breathing strokes and wouldn't work that out for a few years yet, but even then, he could go on forever. Underwater, he was the undisputed best. Young Freddy Taylor stayed white-haired and sunburned all summer long, bicycling the long trip to and from the pond over wooded country roads.

Freddy was the only child of a carpenter-father and his wife. The family drove to the Jersey shore on weekends in the summer and Freddy came to love the ocean. He would look far-seeing at the horizons, seemingly endless compared to his cozy, comfortable woodlands back home. The vistas took his breath away; the salt air filled his lungs. The salt water seemed to buoy him like a cork compared to the still, fresh water he had become accustomed to. When he stood in the chest-deep water near the shore the swells would lift him and set him down again and the waves would effervesce around him. He learned to body surf. It was swell. He loved the names of the beaches: Seaside Heights, Lavallette, Beach Haven, Margate, Atlantic City.

In the winter Freddy stayed strong hiking to school through the woods in the snow, over fallen trees, through brush and bracken and over hillocks, trudging over the uneven ground.

After his third year in high school Freddy's mother died and the family moved to Camden, New Jersey. His father hoped to find more work than in sleepy Bucks County. He enrolled Freddy in business school. Freddy did not like it but stayed for two years, then got a job with a store selling novelty items for grown-up kids. Soon after, his father died.

Even before the move to the city Freddy had a close feeling for the ocean. Now, in the city with Bucks County behind him forever and his family gone, the ocean was all he had left. He felt he would never be far from it. He may have lacked the convictions and ambition of his city peers, but water, running, swimming, bicycling, were part of his identity. The pattern of his early years would be with him throughout his life.

****

When he awoke, the truck was still. He heard the occasional rush of a passing car. The driver's side cab door was open, and the girl was not there. Freddy forced himself awake and took stock of the situation. The truck was parked in a gas station parking lot. He felt for his wallet. It was gone. He had all of the money in it for his trip and for the rent on the house, money he got by trading his Alfa Romeo in for an old Oldsmobile. He got out, paced a bit and was punching the truck fender when a hand came down hard on his shoulder.

"Looking for me, sport?" She handed him his wallet. "You thought I ripped you off, didn't you? Go ahead, open your wallet and check it." Freddy returned the wallet to his pocket unopened, afraid to offend her further. For the second time. He had again been intimidated by this brash and attractive young woman.

"I'm sorry, I saw the truck was stopped here for no reason, and I jumped to conclusions, I guess."

"We're not here for 'no reason,' we needed gas. I didn't want to wake you up, so I took the wallet out of your pocket and got gas, then I pulled the truck out of the way of the pumps and went to the restroom. How did you expect to get to Key West with the gas gauge on empty?"

"I was so tired I didn't notice. I still have to unload this thing when I get there if I can find someone to help me for a few bucks."

"I'll do it." This time Freddy didn't put up any resistance at all. He wasn't up to it. She took her position behind the wheel and told Freddy to get in. She - Melinda - helped him unload in exchange for a place to stay that night. He was surprised when she came from the bathroom that night wearing just a tee shirt, smelling fresh from the shower, and got into bed with him.

"You didn't think I was going to sleep on that dumb couch, did you?" He had assumed that she would. "This is just a sleeping arrangement," she said, "If I'm interested in anything else, I'll let you know." Within two weeks they were lovers. It was convenient. She stayed for two years.

Freddy came to Key West aspiring to use his savings to start a business of his own. It didn't work out that way. It was a time when the town was not capable of supporting new ventures. The boom had passed and would not come again for a few years, after Freddy's savings had dwindled and he was settled into working when and where he could. Things were much different than they had been as a businessman in Philadelphia. Freddy used to do things; now they happened to him. His life was much different from the one he knew in the north. He didn't know it, but things were about to change again.

****

It had now been three years since Freddy left Philadelphia for Key West in search of adventure. He seldom thought back to his years as one of the young and rising middle management persons for a chain of stores selling fashionable stuff and novelty items to dynamic go-getters - young executives and what have you. You've probably seen the stuff they sell. Genuine replica World War Two leather flight jackets for VPs who fly desks. Oak file cabinets. Trendy things.

So there he was, a brash young and rising person within this prestigious organization. He was - once. By the time of his eventual departure from the land of pizzazz and schmaltz he was not so young anymore and no longer rising. He didn't fit the company image. In the forty stores in his area there were forty other guys doing what he was doing, which was buying, driving a lot to set up grand openings and "Super" promotions, and controlling inventories of all of the inanities they sold. There were two supervisors, and he was not one of them, and not likely to become one of them. In the unlikely event that one of the two died (they were both younger than Freddy) or in some other way demonstrated he was no longer willing to concern himself with the sales of all-brass, hand-tooled, James Bond Walther PPK automatic water pistols, one of the other forty guys with a few fewer miles on him would in all likelihood get the nod. There was already in progress a mad scramble for the boss's Vassar-spoiled, hard boiled two tributes to orthodontia. These Fine Young Ladies and Freddy did not get along famously or in any other way that could be construed as friendly, or even civil. Freddy tended to go for cocktail waitresses; blond and tall (make your own rhymes here) with legs of gold and hearts of bronze, the curvy, tapered sort, the legs, that is. Preferably symmetrical.

The stores were doing well, and the company was expanding. In coming years they would crest on the wave of status-seeking yuppies. The workload was heavy, and the traveling and long hours going from store to store, getting things straightened out and attending grand openings, the stress from internecine competition and minutia attendant to the job were grating on the young managers. Freddy and the others were starting to wear out. One young pup panicked and began to stutter when talking bathroom scales that he had ordered were not working properly. They were not telling the truth. He began talking back to them. Situational irony, that!

There was a real need to keep the troops calm.

One day Freddy was at a stress seminar, something the company had arranged to keep the employees, Freddy surmised, from becoming deranged by the ravages of job-related pressures, like making a serious effort to *look* serious and sell their ridiculous line of products. "This would," Freddy had said, "have made us no longer assets - and I use that term loosely - to the company, rendering us useless, and rendering us unemployed as well if my impression of the compassion of the company is correct." His colleagues smiled their well-practiced smiles and politely moved away from him.

Freddy was in rough shape at the time of the seminar. More cynical than the others at the outset, now his plastic business smile was feeling thick and brittle and was becoming hard to maintain. Perhaps this seminar would be the saddle soap to soften it up.

****

About thirty of them lying around on the rug of a too-small rented room at the Holiday Inn, breathing deeply from their diaphragms in an effort to meld their minds into a mellifluous confluence of persona, relax and forget all the sales hype and guff that the company, in its magnificent munificence, deigned to bestow upon them. They took a cheery quiz which told each of them, based on the number of cigarettes they were smoking and how many liquid lunches of which they were partaking, the approximate date when they were going to snuff it. All that was required to learn this death date was the manipulation of some small numbers and bingo; they got a theoretical idea of when they were going to cash it in.

Freddy didn't like it. He didn't want to know that. Freddy knew he was in trouble when he was penalized seven years on the very first question for not being a girl.

Freddy began to wonder why he should need a seminar like this. He started thinking about some of the subtler aspects of what was going on here. The company was hypnotizing them, mesmerizing and transforming them into automatons with permanent smiles and company tie-tacks in the image of the company logo, a World War One Fokker biplane (a replica, only smaller). They would all look and act much the same as were the near-identical stores they infested like cardboard cut-outs, with the pre-faded, pre-worn (?), jackets and the earthquake-proof earthenware fondue sets impregnated with boron and graphite; (This last item was manufactured in California, land of the free and home of the brave, where earthquakes no doubt have caused many grievous casualties among the many fondue dishes of more mundane origins in that eclectic state.)

Freddy thought the concept of becoming one of these company men was odious.

The seminar was merely the trigger which set Freddy's wheels in motion and began the account of his wending his way southward on a quest for a less structured lifestyle, and of the folks he met there also, folks who (eventually) changed his thinking, folks who made him happy, and folks who took something from him that had been very dear.

Things were looking none too good, and Freddy was not able to find a loophole in this dreary projection unraveling before him. Being unable to find a way to blame the company for his apparently debilitated condition and engage in lengthy and lucrative litigation allowing him to retire rich and early, and being too set in his ways to reform, Freddy gave his notice and left the room. He picked up a few personal items he had at the office. Because he could think of no earthly use for anything in his authentic early American oak desk for whatever he would be doing next, he bequeathed that monster and its contents to the next young champion the company would fetter to that excellent piece of furniture to figure out.

Freddy returned his company car keys to the kiosk in the garage below the building and left. It was raining. So what.

He took the water pistol.

****

There he was, in Key West, three years later, still planning career moves. It is morning, time for a cup of coffee. Last night he had been frequenting some of the local drinking establishments with his buddy, Wayne.

Put on the teapot. Wrong. His "ex" live-in girlfriend (Melinda) took the teapot a year ago. Put some water in a saucepan. Get the coffee out of the refrigerator. Light the stove. It lights with a whoosh - he had turned the gas on earlier. The smell of hair singed off the back of his hand fills the kitchen; there are carbon curlicues on the back of his hand.

Now he gets out a small one cup funnel and a filter sized for a single cup of coffee. The filter goes into the funnel and the funnel goes into the coffee. No, that's not right. He shakes his head to get things organized.

The filter goes into the funnel, and the *coffee* goes into the *filter*. The funnel balances precariously on top of a giant coffee cup which it does not fit. It is a truly great coffee cup, cleverly decorated with hand-painted fornicating bunny rabbits. It matches the decor. He did not buy it, his "ex" did. (She took the teapot, though).

Now the water boils. He waits one minute to ensure the correct brewing temperature and pours the hot liquid from the saucepan over his fingers and down the side of the funnel, which tips, collapsing the filter and allowing a liberal amount of French roast blend coffee grounds into the cup with the hot water that has bypassed the brewing process. He'll drink it anyway. He is awake now, sort of. Now, if he only had a donut.

Chapter two - Key West

The watcher was now half a block away, in the shadows of a building across from a church courtyard, watching a small-fry dealer operate. The dark complected man he was watching was looking for something, furtively shuffling through the leaves that had gathered at the base of a huge, bushy, spreading tree in a walled corner of the courtyard. The tree had fluted and twisted columns forming its base reaching down to the roots on the ground. Wind swirling in the closed corner of the yard had spun the fallen leaves in circles around the massive root arms at the base of the tree, catching and gathering the leaves between those wooden buttresses in great numbers. Earlier the watcher had seen a tall, thin man with a long blonde ponytail down his back pause there to smoke a cigarette. As he feigned to stoop and tie his shoelace he hid a small package in the notch where two of the arms facing the dank walled corner joined the bole at the back of the tree. The first man then went to an old brown van parked several streets away as the watcher tailed him until he drove off. The watcher then returned to the courtyard and updated his notes as he waited for the package to be picked up....

****

Key West is the last of the linked islands, or keys, that extend the arc of the east coast of Florida, curving westward until they point toward the Dry Tortugas. The national park there at Fort Jefferson was home and prison long ago to the hapless Doctor Mudd for his part in the events subsequent to the slaying of Abraham Lincoln. The Maryland doctor set John Wilkes Booth's broken leg.

Key West is the end of the line for those traveling by road. The road is U.S. 1 and is the stretch of pavement whose path begins (or ends) in Fort Kent, Maine, and meanders through small New England towns, stutters through the urban decline and overworked cement of the industrial northeast, and alternately glides through the open areas south of the Jersey sprawl and slows through the detours and detritus of the older, larger southern cities as they grow to regroup and renew themselves for the onslaught of a southward shifting population.

When the roadway leaves the mainland the land mass narrows to form the several larger and many smaller keys. The road runs down Key Largo, Tavernier, Plantation, Islamorada and the Matecumbes, Long Key, Duck Key, Grassy Key and through the city of Marathon, Big Pine, Ramrod, Summerland, Sugarloaf, Big Coppitt and finally terminates near the county courthouse in Key West. Under the bridges between each of the keys there are tidal channels which flow between the Straits of Florida on the Atlantic side and the many mangrove keys and uninhabited islands on the Gulf side, reversing every six hours over vast stretches of shallows cut by swift and tricky currents during these tide changes. These islands, shoals, shallows, and currents comprise the Gulf of Mexico as it exists in its eastern sector, that portion in close proximity to the Florida Keys.

A mere 7500 acres of habitable dry land comprise the populous portion of Monroe County's 1144791 acres. The rest of the county contains part of the Everglades in the area of the mainland south of the Tamiami Trail and opposite the state's westernmost wetlands, the Big Cypress National Preserve.

The road from the mainland to Key West spans 135 miles and 43 bridges bordered by seas in shades of blues and greens, reflecting alternately the light green and aqua of sandy bottom, mottled greens marking rock and coral beneath the surface of the sea, and dark green swatches that are underlain by beds of turtle grass and vegetation. These greens become blues when the sun becomes more horizontal. Far out, past the reef, close to the horizon in the east, is the deep green of deep water, sometimes a smooth convex turned down on each end and sometimes a series of bumps when the wind is up. The water is pushed into humps as that great marine river, the Gulf Stream, pushes north and east against the prevailing northeast wind.

The Atlantic half of the panorama is at its most spectacular in the summer when distant tall white clouds, tops darkened, disgorge their moisture in slanting torrents, isolated storm systems, apart and unto themselves, raining themselves into extinction. They are aloof and alone in their demise. At times, in some summers, several of these lone systems will space themselves in the skies well clear of the thin line of islands, presumably so as not to dampen the zeal of the appreciation of the traveler. Not to worry. If on one of these summer days the procession of showers should err and find itself over the islands the duration of the ride through each small squall is a matter of minutes. It is Freddy's idea of fun; it is what he likes best of all when he drives the keys. His friend Annie tries to make him put the top up. These same summer days find a bright and seldom obscured sun lending specular highlights to each tiny dollop of water oscillating back and forth, like Neptune's children in the sea, holding mirrors and dancing.

The western-side view of the ride is populated by mangroves, bunches of tree-like vegetation standing on the surface of the water. They are fragile in one way; that they are best able to exist in and near shallow salt water and have little tolerance for the intransigent treatment they are given by men questing to squeeze as much money as they can from the profound beauty of the place by bringing this aquatic paradise to market for the masses.

The most striking visual aspect in this western direction is not realized on the sunny days when the eastern counterpart is at its best. On such days the mangroves seem to be shoreless islands of a regular height of about six feet (actually they are taller) and uniform in shape. They are quite pleasant enough in contrast to the water's colors and sometimes-browns of this more shallow side. But on a heavy, hazy, closed in day, when the light of the sun is impossibly flat from its diffusion by the haze, when there is not a breath of a breeze and the horizon is all but invisible, it is on these days when the mangrove islands seem to float in the sky. Their inverted images reflected below them in the silver-black water are in eerie symmetry.

Freddy and Wayne and Annie, Wayne's well-built girlfriend, lived together in Freddy's latest rented house three blocks from the Atlantic Ocean (technically the Straits of Florida at that locale) and not three-quarters of a mile from the Gulf of Mexico. Both were done in those same shades of blue and green that flanks the length of the keys, caused by the various sand, rocks, clouds, corals and reflections contributing to those pleasant colors. It was an easy walk to the beach, and most days the water was gentle and inviting. There were three tennis courts two blocks from the house and Freddy used them regularly. He was a marvel. He did not always win, but he could outlast a siege by Attila the Hun. His best strategy was wearing down his opponent until he was reeling with heat prostration. Freddy developed a taste for beer, a good tennis game (considering the quantity of beer he consumed), was a strong swimmer, freediver and bicyclist, and of late was a lousy but still enthusiastic spear gun fisher.

Wayne liked ping-pong, but there was none to be had. He liked to shoot baskets. He also liked to swim, had been a lifeguard for several summers at Montauk, New York, when he was at school, patrolling the beach for foolhardy swimmers during the not infrequent storms, and was a competent swimmer in any sea. Annie liked to do aerobics. Freddy liked Annie's aerobics also; he could watch them for hours. All the guys liked Annie's aerobics, but they tended to make most women depressed. One Sunday morning in early December shortly after Wayne had moved in to share the rent Freddy was watching the public TV station, waiting for "Fawlty Towers" to come on. National Geographic was doing a story on the Florida Keys:

"The mass of the skeletal remains of marine life,
of millions of long-dead, fossilized sea creatures,
together with accreted Miami oolitic limestone make

up the base rock and rock-like marl from which the land mass of the keys is formed. The last island, Key West, is the 'Isle of the bones'. The name acknowledges the remains of the Calusa Indians left on the beaches after the raiding Seminoles from the mainland pursued them to the sea and slayed them."

"Wayne, what's 'oolitic'?'" Freddy called to Wayne, who was puttering around in the kitchen.

"Small, round granules," was the shouted answer. Wayne knew all kinds of stuff. Freddy's attention returned to the TV:

"In 1827, on February 7, Lieutenant Perry, Captain of the "U.S.S. Shark", hoisted the United States flag over Key West. By 1836 Key West had 400 people living there and it was the largest city in Florida. At the time, there were bridges across salt creeks on Duval, Simonton, Whitehead and Eaton streets, as they are known today in the downtown area. An 1846 hurricane filled the salt creeks with silt and started Key West in on filling other such tidal influxes. Later, as the trend continued, large areas of landfill would considerably increase the island's usable land mass.

"Key West is now one by four miles, has its tourist traps as does any other resort town, and its history of shipwrecks and smugglers, is a home for the legends of Hemingway and Henry Flagler and his overseas railway. The hurricane that ended the railway on Labor Day of 1935 was the biggest storm of its kind on record with winds of two hundred and fifty miles per hour."

****

In Freddy's Key West bicycles and mopeds abounded. A few years before the island was simpler; it was not the clutter of people and traffic which was to be in the next four decades and that now in Freddy's Key West was starting to sift into town. It was not yet as commercial as most of the mainland meccas for those who would escape the ravaging snows and bitter cold in those fell lands to the north. When he left the mainland, riding those limestone links to the Isle of the Bones gave rise in Freddy a feeling of escape, of being sundered from the dark and dreary northern reaches of tedium and despair by blue-green water under balmy southern skies.

The new prosperity of Key West spawned by tourism and development was slow to start, constricted at first by a poor economy, a gas shortage, daily electric outages and a water shortage. Those who did venture forth had to brave all of those skinny bridges converted from the old railroad line. One by one those problems were overcome, and the attractions that the keys had - warm weather, a beautiful setting and a reef five miles offshore at Key West drawing divers from around the world to study and enjoy - were lures that would bring schools of newcomers.

Freddy recalled the city back then, prior to prosperity and progress, just as things started to change. The major political issues included nude sunbathing and the height of a person's fence. The trend in old town was to restore old conch houses - clapboard claptraps; frame structures bedecked with gingerbread - jig-cut balustrades and scroll work trim - and ringed by porches. The city's tourist face was an island paradise that continued to look like the rum smuggling, cigar making, fishing, shrimping, sponging and wreck chasing community it once was, a mixture of one and two story buildings reminiscent of Queen Anne architecture mixed with Victorian, New England, and Bahamian building styles. Some of the older buildings were constructed of materials taken from the shipwrecks on the poorly marked coral reef, when it was rumored that some evil men made a lucrative business of showing false lights to lure ships to their doom. It was the look of these buildings, with their ship's railings and gingerbread, square-posted porches and widow's walks that were unique, evoking a mystical feeling of being in an era of the seagoing past, with just a hint of piracy.

Rum smuggling had given way to drug smuggling. Cement and steel and ideal weather made it possible for a different kind of exploitation of the natural uniqueness of the place. Deleteriously striking physical changes to Key West would beset the nine-to-fivers, retirees, and fisherman living there. The islandy kind of life was inexorably disappearing behind a skyline rising between them and the oceans they could once look upon. But, as Freddy would say, that's the way it goes when there are fortunes to be made.

Big money could be made in the keys, in tourism, in real estate and in drug trafficking. The temptations were great; fortunes can attract a bad element and bring out the worst in people. A well-placed person with a low profile and no past could make a killing. Wayne was such a person.

****

Wayne Talbot arrived in Key West sometime in early October, 1976. Just short of six feet two inches tall and well proportioned, his was not the physique of a weightlifter with those bunchy muscles, nor was it the build of a swimmer with long, powerful muscles with lots of stamina. There are two types of muscle fiber, fast twitch and slow twitch. A sprinter would be described as fast twitch. Slow twitch is more like a jogger. Wayne was like a soccer player, tough and fast and enduring. Slow twitch and fast twitch both. Freddy was a swimmer type but somewhat gone to seed. Only by virtue of a marvelous constitution did Freddy's five-eleven frame retain any of the vestiges of its early promise.

Wayne had curly, reddish-brown hair and ruddy arms with blond, sun-bleached fuzz on them. He had brown, penetrating eyes, a square Scottish jaw and forehead and a set to his shoulders, a confidence in his walk that was neither macho nor pretentious. There was no chip on his shoulder. He would avoid trouble whenever possible, but that was seldom necessary. The presence of assurance he quietly carried about him precluded thoughts of aggression by other males who would otherwise browbeat or bully a less formidable potential adversary. Freddy wasn't much bothered by anyone either. His deep blue eyes were intelligent, when focused, but otherwise vacuous. Often in his cups, he was inconsequential, invisible to the self-centered, self-inflated types that would be his natural enemies. It is hard to stare down de-focused eyes. Although he was cynical, Freddy wasn't mean. He got along with everyone, most of the time. Not always.

Freddy met Wayne in a bar, the Olde Bottle Cap Inn. A holdover from Key West's past, it had been a dry goods store of clapboard over rough-hewn Dade County pine named Rosa's seventy years ago, already an old building at that time. It was added onto in piecemeal sections and converted into a bar with a technically illicit backroom casino if the statutes were to be believed, but actually it was the standard arrangement in those days when Key West was the jumping-off spot for Havana, and high rollers, low rollers, and hard characters were the normal fare. The gambling was tolerated. Those perfunctory shows of enforcement done from time to time were known well in advance - a 1932 raid of twelve known gambling places turned up not a single slot machine. The raid was well publicized. Key West's heyday as Florida's largest city started well before that.

Wrecking became popular soon after the city was settled. It was Key West's first industry. Sailing ships plying their trade of laces, silks, wines, and other precious cargo piled up regularly on the then unlighted, unmarked reef, as treasure-laden Spanish ships returning from the pillage of the new world had done centuries before.

Cigar making started in 1831. By 1868 cigar making was a large industry. With several factories in production the little city was the biggest cigar maker in the country.

By 1911 the cigar industry had moved to Tampa, falling victim to fires and strikes in Key West. With the advent of the steamship, the sailing ship was not as viable a commercial vessel as it had been. Reef markings had improved. It marked the end of the wrecking industry and the end of an era. As those things faded from the scene Key West's interests expanded with the start of the steamer trade, a new railroad, and a bit farther along, commercial aviation. A man named Henry Flagler was a prime mover in the facilitating of the transportation to the keys that would enhance their development. Blind by that time, Henry Flagler rode the first train to Key West on January 22, 1912, on the overseas railway he built, a year before his death in 1913. He had fallen down a flight of steps, from which he did not recover.

Mule drawn street cars were seen in Key West in the early 20's. By '27 there was airmail service to Cuba from Key West International Airport, the first such one in the country with Pan American Airways offering regularly scheduled service to Havana with flight number one lifting off on October 28, fourteen years after Augustin Parla Orduna made the first air international crossing to Cuba, flying the 119 miles to Mariel on May 19, 1913.

The railroad became the link connecting the Keys with the mainland and the port of Key West was soon thriving. Three freight ferries, the *"Flagler"*, the *"Parrott"*, and the *"Palmer"*, worked the waters between Cuba and the end of the railroad, bringing cargo to Cuba and returning with pineapples when they were in season.

All these things ended. There had been rum smugglers. It wasn't worth it anymore. There had been a sponging industry. It was doomed at first by disease and then by the invention of cellulose. It all ended - the cigar industry was no longer rolling, the railroad sunk, destroyed in a hurricane, and the port of Key West went into decline. Navy subs and patrol boats were at Key West during World War Two and for a while after, and the Navy built the original fresh water pipeline to Key West. A roadway was put onto the old railroad bridges reconnecting the keys and the mainland, but eventually the Navy presence was reduced and moved to other ports. After that, in '59 and the early 60's, Cuba was closed to travel.

It was after a hiatus of lean years when Key West was making a gradual resurgence into prosperity through tourism and development that Freddy and Wayne became friends. The town was changing again. A more conservative type of tourist had begun to frequent the island city. The swarthy types in Panama hats and jet-setters (gay blades back then) and the idle rich venturing south to do some slumming were gone, giving way - slowly - to people who for one or two weeks forsook their polyester pants and tapered shirts for their perception of tropical garb. There were people in brush-painted Volkswagen buses moving furtively through the streets. Backpackers started to arrive. Backpack-less ones, traveling light, could be seen smashing coconuts on curbs when they got hungry.

Around the time of Wayne and Freddy's meeting another group began to arrive, the wide-ranging retirees in campers and Winnebagos driving inexpertly on the interstates and scaring the daylights out of bicyclists on the narrow downtown streets, if they managed not to squash the poor souls. Imagine the average local person peddling his way down a blind alley or small lane finding a big, square, sheet metal and glass fronted live-in Leviathan on wheels looming large across his path, straining and groaning to make an impossible turn. A head with two small round glass eyes behind the two big square glass front windows is not even looking in his direction, striking the bicyclist with visceral fear. Next is a detour over the curb by the bicyclist, trying not to get scraped off the bike onto a phone pole by the damn driver of the vacation bus, as he just keeps going, as happy and alert as a conch in its shell, oblivious to the consternation of the hapless bicyclist in his efforts not to wet his shorts. Freddy punched one of the big bruisers once, as he slewed through the curb-and-phone-pole maneuver, just to get the driver's attention. Hitting that vehicle made a nice loud, satisfying noise, the resounding thunderclap of thin sheet metal struck in the center. The girl on the bike behind him, freshly fallen from her own bike (not having learned the proper maneuver yet), merely cursed. But she did it adroitly. Another time, while shooting pictures of the wildlife sunbathing on a nearby beach, Freddy went to the aid of an unfortunate vehicle, an already forlorn and much maligned Vega, being mashed by one of the monsters. Freddy kicked the grill work in on the beast as it was trying to back over the lonely Vega squatting in the middle of an empty parking lot as his camera and telephoto lens swung wildly from the strap around his neck. He drew enthused applause from the string of dirt bags, starved for entertainment, sitting on the nearby sea wall

****

The bicycle was the preferred form of transportation in downtown Key West. Freddy's bike was resting outside the B.C.I. (Bottle Cap Inn) the night he met Wayne. Freddy was perched at the straight, mirror-backed bar on one of the twelve or so stools, his flashlight on the bar before him. (No flashlight on bike at night - $15 fine). Wayne was shooting pool. Nature calls...

"Scuse me."

"Sure, pal, just let me make this shot."

"Hokay," says Freddy, "I will try to contain myself. Jus' wanned to get rid of some of thisss Michelob."

"Thanks." Wayne looks at Freddy sideways. Freddy doesn't notice.

"Thas me, self-contained Freddy. My skin keeps alla Michelob in. Ya missed."

"So I did." Freddy negotiates his way to the men's room. On his return, there is Wayne again, shooting the same ball. Freddy offers his advice.

"Why doen ya try the six? Straight in."

"Because I'm shooting high balls."

"Oh, stripes. High balls. Doen like High Balls much. I'm drinkin' beer." Freddy continues to stand behind Wayne, watching him shoot the ball. Wayne seems pretty even tempered. He looks clean cut, your typical college athlete, a few years out of school. He is not hairy like the rest of the people in the bar. He must be new.

"Missed again. Oh, sorry." Freddy returns to the bar. He feels like singing. It is Wayne's turn to shoot again. "Ya gotta have skin, miles n' miles n' miles a skin, it keeps everything out, and every-thing else in..." Wayne sinks the eight ball, which he was not shooting at, and promptly ends the game. He loses, turns red and looks from Freddy to the bartender, malice in his gaze. The bartender takes exception to Freddy's singing.

"Either knock that off or hit the street."

"Hokay," says Freddy amiably. "I fergot the words anyway." There is only one empty seat at the bar and it is next to Freddy. Wayne returns from the pool table and sits down. Freddy turns to him and says, " Hey buddy, why'er you so red?" That did it.

"I was trying to shoot a friendly game of pool here!" Freddy is sure that for this guy, that was a major breach of calm.

"Calm down. Beertender, get this man a beer." To Wayne: "Whas your name?"

"Wayne"

"You drunk?

"No"

"I am. My girl left me."

Calmer now, politely making conversation, Wayne says, "Oh, that's too bad. When did it happen, recently?"

"'Bout a year ago. Ran off with a Brazilian."

"She left town, huh?"

"She went about three blocks. She took the teapot, too." Wayne is clearly uncomfortable. He is wondering why he is here.

"Why are you here, Wayne?"

"I'm taking a break. Thought I'd work my way around the country before settling down. I'm looking for a job."

"What can you do, besides go to school?" What a nosy drunk he is.

"A little of everything. Did odd jobs through college."

"How odd? Things get pretty weird down here - from what I heard, mine you. Yull probly fit right in."

"Hmmmmmmm..."

****

Wayne turned out to be all right, though, not strange at all. He said that it had taken him seven years to get through school after starting late and alternately working and taking classes. He had amassed a bunch of credits and had earned an actual degree of some sort in things like office biology or corporate history or anal physics - something like that. He was kind of sketchy and reticent when it came to talking about it. Freddy attributed this to Wayne's reserved manner. Because of this belated meticulous blooming Wayne was no spring chicken. No greenhorn rowdy, fresh from school was he. But he was still a bit of a stuffed-shirt.

Despite their differences they got along great, with the exception of Wayne's initial irritation with Freddy over the pool game at the bar. Wayne did not know what had come over him. That was before he knew the effect Freddy's singing had on people. They embarked on several joint undertakings which were supposed to afford them a comfortable living. Of course, all of the good ideas were taken. The town had enough pool halls, pizza places and junk shops for the tourists, and plenty of bars. The dive business was saturated for the time being and charter boat fishing was past its peak, and very competitive. Being a waiter was good money, but it was not to Freddy's liking. As he had said on many occasions, "I've got a bad enough lifestyle already."

One day looking at a trawler being hauled to have its hull cleaned Freddy hit upon an (other) brainstorm. To Wayne...

"How would you like to clean bottoms for a living?"

Wayne looks thoughtful for a moment, then, "Who's bottom? That new girl at the restaurant on South Street has a nice one." You could tell that Wayne was softening up a bit and becoming accustomed to Key West. "I'd work cheap."

"No thilly," (this from Freddy feigning faggotry in a misguided attempt at humor. It is a trait in Freddy that Wayne has been trying to expiate.),

"I mean boats," says Freddy. "Big boats. And little ships."

"We don't have the capital or the equipment to get into that," counters Wayne, so Freddy tells him, "I was thinking we could get one of those air scrubbers and do it by the foot. Leave the boat in the water. Small boat owners might go for it - no yard fees, less hassle and I bet we can beat the shipyard prices by a bunch."

And so they became hull cleaners. Working with air tanks or a hooka rig for breathing and a compressor for the air scrubber they could do a pretty decent job right there in the water. They got the tanks filled for a nominal charge (free) at Billy's dive shop and knew enough people in town to get referrals for the hull service and for a variety of other jobs and minor repairs on small boats, like replacing a prop or mounting a transducer. That is one good thing about working on boats - they are always breaking down. The wiring, the trim, the controls and the fittings, they all break down regularly and that was good for business, even after the first spate of hull jobs had played out and were no longer enough to subsist on.

One Friday morning Freddy was working alone at the marina. He was doing a simple job of mounting an antenna on a 22-foot open fisherman for a friend from one of the local pubs. Wayne had gone into town to pay some bills and start the weekend early. He figured that there was not too much damage that Freddy could do on this particular job.

The boat Freddy was working on was dockside at the cement landing of the marina tied up behind a 43 foot Hatteras, the "*Sea Story*", from Tampa. The "*Sea Story*" was an unusual vessel in that it seemed to be equipped with a decidedly feminine pair of hips without a torso between the two fighting chairs overlooking the stern. Freddy was looking at this comely piece of gear upside down through an access door in the center console of the 22 footer, lying on his back, looking forward while attaching the antenna cable to the radio.

Being naturally curious about all things nautical, he got himself out of that awkward position and sat up in order to better study the situation. Just then he saw what must have been a crew member of the Hatteras, thirty or so, red shorts and a five o'clock shadow, leave the boat and walk in the opposite direction down the dock. He must have been bending over in the back of the boat working on something. There was no other sign of life on the boat. "Eeeaacchh! what is the matter with me," Freddy thinks, "Am I blind, or have I been living down here too long?" He is embarrassed and furtively looks around to see if anyone watching might have guessed that he had just mistakenly developed an interest in someone who pees standing up.

Realizing that no one had seen and that nobody cared anyway, he went back to work. As he was picking up his tools and preparing to leave, sitting hunched over behind the console and dropping the tools into the toolbox, a pair of not-too-shabby ankles went by at eye level up on the dock beside him. Now, he was sure that there was no one down at the end of the dock except the guy who left the boat earlier. Freddy's gaze traveled up slender legs, tapered nicely, the way he likes, and hairless. Did he shave his legs? Red shorts. "Oh-oh, I'm gonna be sick," thought Freddy. "Oh, no he's slowing up to say something." Freddy's face turned upward to be blessed with the vision of the prettiest, cutest lady he had seen in a long time. Naturally, his face was twisted into a mask of disgust in anticipation of having to deal with what he was sure was a degenerate pervert or, at least, an individual with a very confused sense of sexual identity. Her smile melted away as his heart broke and he mentally kicked himself as hard as he could. Freddy saw that she was unsure of his intent and alarmed by his expression. She warily said "excuse me," and walked away, presumably to safety.

The receding figure is in a black one-piece suit with shiny red shorts pulled snugly over the lower half, new foam sandals in layers of rainbow colors, and white, soft looking smooth skin in between, just touched with a tinge of pink from the sun. This cannot be a local girl. Shaved legs, too! In contrast, Freddy's own sandals are leather with the stitches holding the leather foot-part to the bottom pavement pounding part rotted away, giving each sandal a big, wide grin. His tee shirt advertises a bar, has a hole in it and had lateral and diagonal grease lines on it where he has been brushing up against a steering cable. Freddy had been fiberglassing in the shorts, and they were stiff and shiny on the front. He didn't even want to think what that might look like. His only chance to detain the lady, even if he hadn't scowled at her, would have been if the fright response he had generated caused her to faint dead away or go tharn like Fiver in *Watership Down*.

There she was again, thirty yards distant, leaving the marina building and getting into a car. She had arms, too. Short black hair, page boy style, not quite to the shoulder. And now there was the addition of a white shirt with buttons up the front, sleeves rolled up and tied at the waist instead of being buttoned. Sillily, he realized he forgot (ha!) to shave this morning. (As if he had intended to).

Chapter Three - Downtown

She was gone, leaving only the faint, lingering smell of coconut scented suntan oil, which was soon overpowered by the dockside smells of gas and rotting fish. Freddy stood looking at the spot where the car had been (What kind of car was it? He barely noticed. Could have been a rental), wondering where she had come from and where she was going. Then, trying to dismiss the matter with a few bewildered shakes of his bushy blond, untrimmed head, he carried his tools back to the 66 Olds Cutlass convertible that he used as a pickup truck.

At four o'clock the day was still beautiful. It was April and the water was flat and starting to warm up. The tourist season was coming to a close; the best time of the year would soon be upon Key West as the island emptied and the days got long. It would be too warm for the northerners. Some "weekenders" would visit from within the state, predominantly from Miami and environs, but mostly it would be just townies; long-time residents, the crop of replants that got tired of the north, the retirees, and the people who came to work in the tourist industry for a few years and then move on.

Freddy headed for his car. It was a custom car, blotchy forest green. He painted it one midnight with a borrowed compressor and a couple of six packs. A passing taxi added an interesting texture to the job by kicking up a dust cloud while sliding to a stop, eager to let out a tug boat crew returning to their boat. They had delivered a load of bunker 'C' fuel oil earlier in the evening to the electric company's steam generation plant a hundred and fifty yards up the channel from where Freddy was painting the car before they went out and got loaded themselves.

The radiator was out of a Pontiac and it almost fit. The right tail light had been pushed into the trunk by a truck, was subsequently pulled out again with a come-along by Freddy, whereupon he administered to it a cosmetic quick-fix with about fifteen pounds of plastic body filler. His job at the marina finished, Freddy got into his distinctive vehicle and left. Rolling out of the marina lot and onto the road, he turned right, over the bridge spanning the waterway entrance to the marina and set out to join Wayne for a sensible cocktail (this in the vernacular of island folk displaced from foreign, northern regions.)

He first buzzed the Bottle Cap, Wayne and Freddy's usual hangout. It was a two-story wooden sided building framed on unfinished 4 and ¼ inch square Dade County pine with a glass brick front and a neon sign on the metal awning over the front steps, a lush garden on the side with a Key lime tree, an umbrella tree, a mock orange, and Night-blooming cereus. A quick beer later he was back in the Olds heading down Catherine Street. A right turn onto Duval and the car was pointed toward the tourist part of town and the greatest concentration of shops, restaurants and bars. He drove mechanically. After the first few hundred times he made this trip, crawling up Duval Street and waiting for each of the seven traffic lights on the short mile and change between the ocean and the Gulf of Mexico he became inured by the sameness of it all. The only thing of interest to him was the exceptional sighting of a stunning lady.

The density of pedestrians increased as Freddy approached Sloppy Joe's Bar. Presumably Wayne would be there, if the information he gleaned from Joe, the bartender at the B.C.I., was accurate. Wayne had made the bank and bill paying run this week, and as such he had all of the proceeds from the week's work on his person. If Freddy did not catch up with him soon he would have to head back to the house and forgo happy hour. He pulled up in front of the building on the Greene Street side, next to the loading zone sign.

Sloppy's was an old, if not venerable at least a much-touted Hemingway-drank-here bar on the corner of Greene and Duval. The Duval Street side, running roughly north-south, had three gaping double doors. The Greene Street side had four. These were left open from eight a.m. to four a.m., business hours rain or shine, every day of the year except Sunday mornings, to entice customers in from out in the sun for a libation by day and as a beacon leading to a safe anchorage at night for those whose view of security is to be rendered deaf by state-of-the-art Japanese amplifiers rather than risk the rigors of patrolling the pavement and peering into the open doors of other area establishments. Of course, each place was eager to have its share of the formidable number of dollars spent downtown each night. The open-air format was widely used. Tourist traps, beer and wine places, gay garden bars, and a few redneck redoubts spaced at wide intervals, jewelry stores, tee shirt shops and art galleries punctuated the encapsulated community of diverse types of people, all of them trying to lure lookers through their open doors. In its pre-electronic years, Sloppy's was the best place to view the world, either from the horseshoe-shaped bar or from one of the surrounding tables. One could watch the tourists by day and the street people by night.

Sloppy Joe's was the bar in which Freddy served his Key West apprenticeship, weaned on beer and street lore, at a quieter time when there were no bands or concession stands, just townies and shrimpers, fugitives, derelicts, and characters. No more red French wine, no more red Alfa Romeos would he have. Jesus Christ was frequently in the area, and so was Uncle Sam - and both were *en costume*. A few adventurous tourists also. They were tolerated.

****

A cop happened along as Freddy rolled up. Chagrined, he pulled out again to find a more legal location to park the car. He arrived at the doors mumbling an epithet, grumbling to himself because he had to park a block away. For years he could usually pull up and park right in front. Freddy stepped through the doorway out of the glaring sunlight and waited briefly for his eyes to become adjusted to the dimmer light inside.

The motif of the place was islandy/Hemingway/World War II. There were half a dozen fans suspended on long conduit poles from the high ceiling spinning below the level of half a dozen parachutes, one around each fan pole, bellied out upside-down, in a manner inverted from the way they are usually seen in when performing their usual function. Their centers were drawn up around the base of the suspension poles for the fans. The chutes assumed the shapes of giant Bundt cake pans as seen from the bottom of a large oven. Over-large, out of perspective and not-too-good oil paintings of island scenes featuring native girls with bare breasts in grass skirts hung from the walls between the doorways. Photographs, clippings and memorabilia of notable past customers (Hemingway and Tennessee Williams, Hemingway and Stan Smith, Hemingway and Lassie, etc.) decorated the corners and the back wall. A fish with a beer can in its mouth hung over the bar and other game fish were spaced around the place. The only thing missing was Bullwinkle. A large portrait of an American flier, circa World War II, was probably the best thing in the place.

Freddy looked around. Wayne was at the bar. He was with Annie, the lady he was currently seeing, a short blond with short hair, a quick smile and a ready laugh. She was aware that she'd been typed as being a little fruity and air-headed, but it did not bother her. She was a nice person, much too nice for Wayne, according to Freddy. Wayne had gotten lucky again.

Freddy had never seen anything like it before. Wayne, mellowed somewhat by his association with those of Freddy's ilk, was still sober and somber by Key West standards. With his Scottish, red-haired good looks he was in marked contrast with Annie, his present paramour. It was unusual in a town where most of the better-looking ladies, to Freddy's mind, went for the gooniest guys they could find, especially so because Wayne and Annie seemed so different, the introvert and the extrovert; the scientist and the cheerleader. They were sitting close together at the crowded bar. Freddy squeezed in between them, putting one arm on the bar where it was sticky with spilled beer. With his back to Wayne Freddy slid his other arm around Annie and gave her a healthy squeeze. Wayne took his cue:

"Hey, watch that stuff!" said Wayne.

Freddy told him, "I'm tired of watching, I want some, too," looking into Annie's eyes as he said this with the lustiest grin he can muster on his leering face. A couple of tourists at a nearby table pretended not to hear. Freddy takes a quick, admiring look at Annie's figure. She has full, high breasts in a white tee shirt tapered sweetly to where it tucks into her yellow short shorts. No bra. Her hips flare out generously and he likes that also. Annie loves the attention and smiles delightfully.

"Hi, Freddy, nice to see you," she said in her sweet voice. "You look hungry." Annie was hinting that she was ready for dinner.

"If I look hungry it's because you look delicious," said Freddy. "I don't know what you see in Sir Lancelot over there. Why don't you come live with me?"

"Silly," she said. "I already do live with you. You and Wayne. I love you both." The couple at the table reddened. Wait until the congregation back home hears about this.

"So how did we do this week?" asked Freddy. "Where's my money?

"Here it is, Freddy, eighty-five dollars."

"Is that all? Could be better. Annie, you're going to have to start doing tricks." Hearing this Annie barks and tries to balance a coaster on her nose and clap her hands like a seal.

"Freddy, it could also be a hell of a lot worse," Wayne reminded him. The rent is paid. So is the gas, electric, and water, and we still have some fish in the refrigerator from our last spear fishing expedition. All you need is beer money. Remember the months when we barely had enough to eat."

"Yeah, I lost six pounds," Freddy said, ruefully looking down at his recently re-expanded waistline. "Tomorrow is Saturday. What do you want to do about it?"

"Kill big fish!" said Wayne, taking a sloppy swig of beer and using his best macho tones, his shoulders thrown back in Latino-type bravado. There might be hope for Wayne yet.

"Ok, let's do it, then," Freddy rejoined. "You want to go too, Annie?"

"No, Freddy, all I get to do is sit in the boat. I'm afraid of those spear guns, anyway. Besides, you just want to see me with my top off." The eyes of the male component of the couple at the table widen and his gaze goes involuntarily to Annie's wondrous breasts. His wife looks angry, pays the bill and starts putting things in her purse. She rises hurriedly and leaves in a huff, her husband anxiously at her heels.

"Does it show that much?" Freddy asks, peering downward, visibly disappointed.

Despite Annie's affected ways, the girl was no dummy. But then, Freddy knew that already. They shared an affectionate camaraderie and enjoyed their sexy banter. Freddy knew that something more than just a short affair was in the offing for Wayne and Annie, even if Wayne didn't. He was bright and capable; she was already a charmer and would be even more engaging in the coming years as the final touches of poise and maturity manifested itself. Freddy would hate to see them go, but it seemed that their future and fortune would be elsewhere. So far, Annie was on board with this concept but Wayne appeared to be holding back a bit. But even with that, Freddy doubted that they would become two more of the underachievers and escape artists that came to Key West to look for self-gratification and to pursue a hedonistic way of life so that they would not have to cope with the real world. It was not the normal pattern, though, for people in the tourist trade in the timeless resort town to remain there. Most often took their fill of Key West and, disenchanted or disillusioned, moved on, either to another tourist town or to settle down and start their lives. There were exceptions - those who stayed, became couples, and settled down- but they were few.

"So what's for dinner?" Annie asked of them, a smile of ravenous anticipation on her angelic face.

"Fish!" They said in unison.

Annie smiled wanly as her enthusiasm drained from her face.

"S'amatter, Annie?"Freddy asked. Wayne looked up at Annie's face.

"In California we have these things called steers! We eat them!"

"Well, Annie they don't swim in the ocean, and I don't think our yard is big enough to grow one."

Wayne added his two cents: "I don't think that there's enough grass in Key West for one. I'm pretty sure they can't eat marl...."

****

It was broiled grouper. Wayne prepared it with lemon, butter, rosemary, and some onion. He was getting good at it. Annie had no objection to eating fish, but not every night. In lean times it became a staple at their house. When they had nothing else to do they would go spear fishing. Their refrigerator was usually full of fish, so they had fish a lot. More than a lot. Every so often Annie wanted a greasy hamburger or fried chicken, just for a change. Before the start of their boat cleaning and repairing business there had been a good deal of spare time for Wayne and Freddy. They were formerly basically unemployed, with the exception of the odd yard job or day labor at a construction site or cement pour. Spearfishing and lobstering filled much of this time and kept them in shape. It was good exercise and it kept the refrigerator stocked with grouper, hogfish, snapper and lobster and whatever else happened along. They sometimes would barter for those items they did not go out for, king mackerel, yellowtail or shrimp.

Neither Freddy nor Wayne enjoyed fishing with rod and reel. They found it to be a heck of a lot more fun to get into the water themselves and chase after a meal than to sit in the boat dangling a line over the side. Sometimes they would pick up a few conchs they found, in the grass on the bottom, but because they were so slimy and finicky to clean the general attitude the boys shared toward those strange creatures in their calcium spun castles was that they were more trouble than they were worth. It was easier to buy commercial Bahamian conch in the fish store when they had a hankering for some.

Freddy put green beans in a steamer. He sliced mushrooms and put them into a skillet with butter. After a few minutes of concurrent sautéing and steaming he added dry sherry to the mushrooms and dumped the beans into that, and then put sour cream and sliced almonds into the conglomerate mess.

Annie made a basic salad and highlighted it with an avocado and slices of smoked ham, cut up. It was a very good salad, even if the boys failed to tell her so. "Gee, this is fun!" she said sarcastically.

"She is making salad," thought Freddy, "She *always* makes the damn salad, for chrissake, what is there to be so enthused about?" It did not dawn on him that she was bored with that assignment. It was a typical evening for the three of them.

****

Annie had come to town in the first week of November and had met Wayne soon after at the cocktail lounge where she had taken a job. Her arrival in town was about a month after Wayne's. She moved into Freddy's spare bedroom with Wayne not long after that and quickly fitted into the routine of the house. The addition of Wayne and Annie had improved Freddy's life. He had company, and the house was cleaner than it had ever been before, which pleased Freddy, even though he often had to bear Annie's wrath as she fumed at him for doing something ridiculous and creating a mess or for not doing his share of the cleaning. Freddy had been living aimlessly for three years, and his new companions were an improvement in his situation. Freddy often complained that there were never any sexy undies hanging in the shared bathroom for him to peruse. Annie maintained she didn't wear any.

The only other living occupant of the house (Freddy's aquarium didn't qualify) was a narcoleptic cat that Annie had adopted. It was old; no one else would have taken it in, but Annie was a soft touch. The cat slept so much that Freddy sometimes would look at it and think that it finally did die. It was a nondescript gray with white paws and chest, and Annie, a Catholic, had baptized it with a few drops of tap water and christened it "Bootsie", no doubt making the cat's naming the most belated name-giving for any cat in existence. Bootsie had a habit of crawling up on Freddy's chest in the early hours of the morning and falling to sleep there with one paw in Freddy's mouth. Freddy would awaken in the morning wondering what he had been drinking the night before to give him such a disgusting cotton mouth. Finding Bootsie to be the culprit fouling his pallet, he would throw him off the bed. Annie became very protective of Bootsie, fearing that the fragile cat would not bear up to such treatment.

"Freddy," she would say imploringly, "that cat would not hurt a flea!" Unfortunately for Freddy, that proved to be true. That evening, and for some time after, Freddy was itchy until he made the connection and deflead his bed. The cat was not in evidence tonight. It was sleeping in a chair in a dark corner of the living room. Freddy would sit on it later that night.

They dined in the Florida room of their rented two bedroom, one bath house. The others chose a slightly fruity white wine from Italy, from the selection of one in the refrigerator. Freddy opted to have a Michelob, which has a delicate balance and is the perfect complement to any meal. After dinner and the momentary confusion and disturbance of a screeching cat, a gut-wrenching leap from the chair by a startled Freddy and a scolding from Annie to be more careful, they sat watching an old John Wayne movie on TV, sipping an after dinner drink and digesting the jointly prepared meal. It seemed that everyone was satisfied with the service and the quality. To no one in particular Freddy said, "We're almost out of fish." There were a mere nine pounds left in the freezer. "Are we still going spear fishing tomorrow?"

"Sure, why not," Wayne answered. "I think the weather is going to be good for several days yet. Where do you want to go? How about in close, say, Eastern Dry Rocks and work over toward Sand Key? I don't think I want to be out all day tomorrow. I'd like to do something with Annie in the afternoon."

Giving his head an eager affirmative nod with a wide-eyed smile at Annie, Freddy said, "Me, too!" Annie grinned back.

"What am I going to do with you, Freddy? I'll have to find you a nice girl."

"What am I going to do with a nice girl? Find me a tramp with lots of money."

"You don't mean that, you big phony. Gosh, we're your friends, who do you think you're kidding? I think what you really want is someone sweet and pretty from a nice family."

"Annie, you're talkin' about you!" She canted her head and lifted her chin with lips pursed and eyebrows raised, her eyes fixed on some distant point in the enlightened realization that this was probably true. Philosophical Annie. Oh Annie, what's the use in arguing, he thought. The tramp doesn't sound too bad right now, at the end of a Friday night with no other prospects in reach. He then recalled the lady he saw on the dock earlier that day and wondered if she might be at the marina tomorrow. Annie might have something there - perhaps there was some substance in what she said about a sweet and pretty girl. The one haunting his thoughts earlier in the day certainly qualified.

Their attention went to the TV as they all got sleepy and their minds quieted down. Captain John Wayne is in the islands. What islands, Freddy does not know, but he is on a wooden sailing ship and it is probably around the turn of the century. The twentieth. Apparently the natives are trying to dive down and extract something of value from a wreck which rests at the bottom of a cute little cove ringed with palm trees behind a sandy crescent of beach. It seems to be too much for the native islanders. After all, they are only local pearl divers working at depths of over a hundred feet. They cannot be expected to know how to dive for treasure. Captain John Wayne will have to do it. He jumps into the water fully clothed after taking a monstrous breath and out-dives the islanders, stays under for two minutes and forty-five seconds while lifting a heavy treasure chest, wresting it from sucky mud in order to tie a line around it that he has brought from the surface. He goes up. He breathes a couple of breaths and goes right back down a second time. This time he fights an octopus and wins! This is evident by the inky clouds flowing from the mortal wounds he has inflicted on this basically timid beast. "I didn't" know those big ones were so easy to stab," Freddy comments. "The little ones lying dead in the ice in the fish market I used to work in seemed awfully tough to me." Freddy received a rude retort. Still he continued: "I can see that large, Bahamian cook on that schooner saying to himself, 'dis boy gonna be tuff!'"

This disrespectful jibe drew a retort from Wayne: "You jest, but that Bahamian cook probably speaks three or four languages. How many do you speak? And your English sucks, too!" After several commercials, J. Wayne is still fighting the creature. Must be four minutes at least, probably a record for fighting an Octopus while holding your breath. God, Freddy envied him.

Wayne - "Very interesting."

Freddy - "Fuckin' wonderful."

Annie - "Oh, Freddy, such language" she said, heartbroken, the pitch of her voice trailing off in hopeless resignation.

Seeing that he was not appreciated, he went to bed. His last thoughts before going to sleep were of the lady on the dock.

Chapter Four - Spear Fishing

"Scattered showers and isolated thunderstorms continued to the north and east and along the west coast to the keys. Temperature readings were mostly in the mid-eighties to low nineties.

The local marine forecast for the lower and middle keys, east to southeast winds at 10 knots tonight and 10 to 15 knots Saturday and Sunday. Seas beyond the reef 1 to 3 feet increasing to 2 to 4 feet Saturday and Sunday."

****

It was a pale gold morning.

The light of the early sun gave crystal clarity to the colors and contrasts of the beginning day. As the sun got higher, the billowing yellow clouds to the north washing the earth with golden hues vanished and the April sky turned a cool, bright blue. It would be sunny. As usual, Freddy was the last one out of bed and would still be there if someone had not awakened him by waving a cup of coffee under his nose. Annie was making sandwiches and packing them with some nuts and raisins and several beers into a cooler.

"Put some nuts in the lunch, Annie, I like nuts," said Freddy.

"I've got your nuts. I'm in charge of the nuts in this house. Good thing for you that I like nuts."

Freddy had the vague impression that he had been insulted, but he shook it off. He walked out of the door, reappearing 30 minutes later after all of the preparations for the day's boat trip had been completed.

"Where ya been, Freddy?" Wayne asked as Freddy came through the door that morning.

"Out for a walk down to the corner where the road ends. The pelicans were having a good day today," said Freddy. Freddy liked pelicans. "In fact, for several days they've been diving non-stop at the end of Seminole Street. The schoolies are churning up the water, so they're getting chased by something down below. Tarpons maybe. The pelicans are taking advantage of the situation. Boy, can those birds do some crazy aerobatics! You'd never think so to look at them standing on a rock; you'd never think those ungainly looking birds could wheel and dive like they do."

Spear fishing was thirsty work. Annie had elected to go with the boys after all, provided they came in after half a day. And she was determined to become proficient at spear fishing also. Wayne had promised to take her to a play being done by a local theater group that evening. She would make sure that he would not forget.

Wayne was collecting the spear guns and various other items of necessary equipment for the excursion and Freddy was wandering around the house confused by all and sundry that came his way. He knew they couldn't leave without him. Hell, it was his boat, wasn't it? He dodged out of Wayne's path as Wayne hurriedly made his way to the car. He was carrying a load of smelly rubber things, fins and stuff which had not quite dried from the last boat trip they made. In passing Wayne asked, "How you feeling this morning, Fred ole' pal?"

"Not too bad, thank you. How's yerself?"

"Well, at least I don't have a hangover." Wayne and Annie were always needling Freddy about his drinking.

Again with the insults!

"Cretin," said Freddy. Freddy was the better for their concern, but this morning it was undeserved, or so Freddy thought. Annie joined the attack.

"Come on Freddy, hurry up, you hooligan."

She giggled gleefully as Freddy suddenly came to life and chased her out of the door by pursuing her while prodding her pretty butt with the blunt end of an old, spear-less, spear gun." Stop it, you sex maniac!" she squeaked. It is only a matter of time before she actually says "leapin' lizards!" Mrs. Kupcha, the next door neighbor, looked up from trimming her flowers with an expression of dismay.

She liked her young neighbors but feared they were going to burn in hell.

A smattering of small, white clouds, too big for buttermilk curds and too small to worry about were the only things hanging in the sky save for a few gulls, and, of course, the sun. Visibility would be good in the water.

When they arrived at the marina the water was calm and the sun was shining brightly. It would be high in the sky by the time they got to their destination. Freddy had a wet slip at the marina which was very handy when they wanted to jump in the boat on short notice and take off with a minimum of hassle. Less than ten minutes to transfer the gear and snacks to the boat and they were off. Freddy looked for the *"Sea Story"*. It wasn't there.

After clearing the no-wake area and letting the engine warm up Freddy opened the throttle a bit on the 175 horse Johnson in back of them.

"Better be careful," warned Wayne, "those stringers are not as new as they used to be." He was referring to three wooden braces running fore to aft attached to the inside-bottom of the hull. They were strips of plywood five-eighths of an inch thick and four inches high, affixed to the five-eighths inch edge to the fiberglass hull to stop the hull from flexing and to give it strength. There was a central one and two others running parallel to it eighteen inches away on either side. They had broken some months ago.

"This is a ten-year-old hull, Freddy. I know we fiberglassed over those stringers pretty well, but this thing still takes on water through those hairline cracks under the stringers every time the water gets rough. We should pull them out and replace them with two-by-fours set on edge. That would be plenty strong enough." It was a job Freddy knew needed to be done, but he kept putting it off. He would work on other people's boats, but he never seemed to get around to his own.

All of Wayne's speculation on the seaworthiness of Freddy's boat brought a look of concern to the usually angelic face of the only passenger on board wearing a two piece swimsuit. Not for long, Freddy hoped. Still, she was such a sweetie that he could not but try to make an effort to allay the fears that Wayne had caused to be wrought within her...

"Annie, don't listen to that shit. We ain't gonna sink. Not today, anyway. The weather is beautiful." Annie's smile returned.

The cautious Wayne pointed out, "Well, you had better slow down for the spoil area." Freddy dutifully slowed the boat as they passed through the area where a smaller channel met the main channel. Because the tide was running, the water heaved and roiled where the two channels met, as the two streams became confused and combined in dull, rumbling undertones. The water was calmer in the main channel. Twenty minutes later Freddy and Wayne were in the water shopping for seafood while Annie read and worked on her tan, her big brown breasts basking in the sun. She did not as yet have a spear gun. That would change.

****

The day was as good as they thought it would be. The two of them were working in thirty to forty feet of water, Wayne using his Hornet gun with its 60 inch stainless steel shaft, and Freddy with his old standard Canon Arbalette with its 48 inch spear. Wayne suspected a slight bend in Freddy's spear, but he said nothing to Freddy. It amused him to see Freddy's antics after an off-center shot.

Some weeks back Freddy had tried to get a grouper he'd shot out of a hole using the spear for leverage. He had just made a shot through the fish high on the back. A kill shot would have been nice. Freddy didn't like wrestling with groupers - they could hold their own in the water a lot longer than he. John Wayne could probably do better.

Of course, Freddy should not have bent the shaft in the first place. It is not easy to bend a spear shaft. It takes technique. It can occur after a poor shot at a fish, high on the back or through the tail, in an area where there are rocks or caverns nearby so that the fish can wedge itself so tightly as to become inextricable while pulling or prying the fish out to get the spear back. Freddy did this as he washed the copper/adrenalin taste from the snorkel mouthpiece, which is usually rubbery, pasty, gummy flavored, cause by his exertions while making facial contortions while thrashing and flailing and kicking up silt during the spear extraction maneuver, breaking the watertight seal of the mask and allowing a liberal amount of sea water to get into the mouthpiece and under the bottom part of the mask.

With his vision now distorted because his eyeballs are awash is where all of his training comes into play. While kicking to regain the surface, he tilts his head back and breathes some of the precious little air he has left through his nose and into the mask to get the water out of the mask so that he might see whether or not he is about to get his hair parted by a passing sailboat coming at him with deathly silence or a fast-approaching Marine Patrol eager to see if they can catch him doing something wrong. Finally, he regains the surface, but not before his eyes cross and he sees a blackout mist closing in from each side and obscuring not only his vision but the inside his head as well because he was doing the grouper boogaloo for two minutes with nothing but a depleted body without gills to help him. The partial blackout comes at four feet. That is where the pressure differential is greatest between the medium of the beautiful blue unbreathable sea and the oxygen-rich cyan sky. And that was Freddy's method of spear fishing lately. He would get no prizes for it. He and Wayne worked together, one diving and one regained his breath on the surface and they finally extracted the grouper. It would not have been right to leave the wounded fish in the rock to die. They ate what they shot, they did not shoot what they did not want to eat, and they did not waste a fish after shooting it. That was morally wrong. With all of their bravado and play-acting, they were essentially subsistence fishermen.

Before he met Wayne, Freddy would set out on his forays from shore near the house in a thrice-patched Zodiac inflatable boat he owned with a zero horsepower egg beater on the back. Slow, but it beat swimming and stymied the fish-stealing barracudas when the fish they wanted were thrown aboard the little boat. A bleeding fish was sometimes cleaned off a spear shaft by a poaching barracuda. Putting the fish into a mesh game bag suspended from a float or into a laundry basket set into the center of an inner tube only frustrated the attacking fish and resulted in an annoying, sometimes intimidating harassment by the predators. Freddy would get his fish up into the boat right away. He was puzzled these days why he had seemed to be so much more accurate back then.

The whole concept was relatively simple. A boat ride to a place where they know there are some nice rocks and things for fish to congregate and hide and feed around, a swim around, diving down to check under rocks. If they spotted a sizable eating fish they would approach slowly, get close and be still - floating motionless if they could, until they could squeeze off a shot when they thought they could shoot the fish for a merciful kill through the eyes.

Today they were both using three rubbers for propulsion of the shafts on their spear guns, as they usual did, and a light line attaching the end of the shaft to the spear gun to keep the spear from swimming away from them in a fish body, should either of them make the kind of a shot that Freddy usually made lately. It galled Freddy that he was the guy who had initiated Wayne in spear fishing and Wayne could now do it so much better than he. Wayne thought that he would keep the amusing secret of the bent spear shaft a while longer, although he felt conflicted when Freddy made a shot which was not a clean kill. For the present, they were bringing back more fish than they needed, and Wayne still got a kick out of Freddy's travails and his having to wrestle squirming fish back to the boat.

The boys were out near the Eastern Dry Rocks, working toward the east with the current. Annie was helpful by keeping an eye on them, just in case, and letting the boat drift with them, occasionally starting up and adjusting her position when necessary. Wayne soon boated a nineteen pound black grouper, having shot him just behind the gills. The fish was still wriggling after the shot, but this Wayne stopped easily by sticking his thumb and forefinger into each of the fish's eyes immediately after he was shot and still dumbfounded that such a rotten thing could have happened to him. When Wayne pressed the fish's eyes into its head it became sort of paralyzed and was willing to go anywhere Wayne wanted it to. Wayne figured that it must be a very compelling experience, like a hooker leading a john around by the balls.

As the morning wore on Wayne bagged another small grouper and a couple of hogfish, his favorite eating fish. Freddy was sizing up his third snapper, in about twenty-seven feet of water. It was a fairly good sized fish. He'd missed his last shot, a Nassau grouper, by hitting him a glancing blow on his hard snout. As often happens with a shot like that the spear bounced off. The grouper turned and looked impassively at Freddy floating helplessly and looking back at him, and then the fish slowly turned and swam away. Since they were less than six miles from shore, the fish were smart and knew what they could get away with. They would have to travel much farther to find a good spot where the fish were less wary because few humans had ever hunted them before.

The snapper before Freddy now did not want to give Freddy a side shot. It wasn't running, just watching and turning and skitting a mite whenever Freddy tried to flank it. There were a few rocks behind it. Freddy did not want the fish to go in there so he rushed the shot. Wayne would have been stock still, the gun held out in one hand far in front of him so that he could stay as far from the fish as possible, lessening the chances of spooking the fish. He would remain poised and waiting until the fish was in his sights. Freddy was too eager. He wanted to regain his spear fishing prowess which had recently deserted him and not be outdone quite so handily by his former protégé. He was too distant when he made the shot. The snapper darted forward, to Freddy's left, and the spear seemed to veer perhaps four inches to the right. Freddy thought this must be an illusion caused by the fish's sudden movement. The spear went through the fish near the tail. It flapped wildly with the spear through the tail all the way back to the boat, still thinking it might be able to swim off. Freddy could not get a hold of it. He was once again the comic figure at the side of the boat, treading water in the tangle of the spear gun's trailing line, with the fish flapping wildly against his arms and face. Freddy flung it on board. Wayne was already back in the boat pulling off his fins and booties. Annie was tying her top back on. Nothing was going right for Freddy.

"Another of your famous tail shots, Fred?" was the first thing out of Wayne's mouth. Freddy knew that Wayne would have to say something. He seemed to be taking perverse pleasure in Freddy's spear fishing peccadilloes, as though they were some kind of joke. "Uh," Freddy managed to say.

They headed in, beers in hand, tired and feeling satisfied with their catch. Wayne was, anyway. The good feeling of the sun and the salt was on them. The breeze generated by the boat's passage smelled good and drew off the intense heat of the sun. Freddy switched on the bilge pump and several gallons of water spewed over the side from the bottom of the hull. And that was the pattern of their days back then. It did not seem to Freddy that anything was likely to change.

As usual, Freddy was wrong.

****

In a dark, smoky room in a godown in Chaing Mai, Thailand, two men sat facing each other across an oddly canted, weathered, wood plank table. A third man sat in a lone chair off to the side, out of the sightline of the nearest of the two, sending hand signals to the man facing him. He was the broker's man. He had come for Jade, the sea green to pearl white stone prized for centuries in the Orient. Each man had a gun at his side.

At this warehouse and at the others in this most infamous of Jade smuggling cities, jadeite was sold; green Burmese jade boulders in the rough; a black market item carried for fourteen days over mountains and through jungles from Burma into Thailand on human backs.

The covert dealings of the three men here were not for jadeite in the rough, they were for jade in other forms. The man at the table with his back to the broker's man was a Burmese smuggler. He brought stolen jadeite cabochons, highly polished bright green ovals, jewel stones, for sale to the broker. The man facing the broker was in fact a buyer for the People's Republic of China with connections to sellers of high-quality carvings of nephrite - ancient, venerated, almost unbreakable Chinese jade from the Kunlun mountains. This prized jade was the heart of Chinese civilization for five thousand years. He brought with him mutton-fat white nephrite horses, beetles, and dragons, subtly carved and priceless, his greed-inspired ticket to the Western world.

The illicit goods would be shipped with the standard fare of smuggled Burmese jade in the rough by air to Hong Kong, from there through the Philippines as cheap soapstone and low-quality Taiwanese jade. It would mysteriously turn up in Brazil, waiting for a way to arrive at its final marketplace in the United States.

****

Sunday night. Annie finished work and was driving home. The old International Harvester Scout came lumbering down the road, wandering noticeably from side to side, as the pretty driver fed constant corrections to the giant steering wheel. Something was wrong with the screw adjustment that controlled the amount of play in the steering. To tighten up the steering meant also to make the steering wheel so hard to turn that a gorilla's arms would tire if he or she were required to drive the pea-green machine any substantial distance. Because she didn't have and didn't want gorilla arms the girl allowed for the loose setting purposely maintained on the steering adjustment by swinging the wheel through six inches of arc to take up the play each time the Scout felt like weaving to one side of the road or the other. There was a rhythm to it. Riding in the car, a passenger could feel the slight side-to-side pull each time the lady at the wheel tugged the Scout, which was like a big, green wandering pet, back on the course designated by its master.

The thing was an eye catcher. The green paint was streaked by brown rust lines trailing down from the top and from the hood like the boat in the movie *"Sand Pebbles"* and there were several moldering places around the body. The hood was perforated by rust holes, as the white, bolt-on top had been before her Wayne smeared body putty over it in quantity. Now there were stalactites, hundreds of them, hanging from the ceiling inside the vehicle where the putty oozed through. A barely discernible diver's flag license plate was on the front holder, once a red field with a white diagonal stripe, now almost so rust brown that the original paint was more a memory than a thing seen, a subliminal suggestion of a dive flag behind the brown rust.

The Scout smelled like hot grease. Strange, since it neither burned oil nor smoked. It sounded at idle like an industrial fan, mired in dust and nicotine and vibrating with an out of balance spin that had acquired the growl of age. On the road it just roared. It started right up, ran well, and had the personality of a venerable veteran that commanded respect.

The blond, blue-eyed head most often seen behind the wheel was usually smiling and singing with the radio, a happy person driving a car that was happy to have a new lease on life, happy with its owner, and determined to run for her as long as it could. It was a love affair, it was her "Inty", and it didn't mind if she ground the gears constantly.

Annie looked as though she should be driving a Corvette through western mountain passes. She was a beauty, from California, but not so faddishly California-ish as to be objectionably redundant or trite. She did not use the omnipresent "awesomes" or "supers" currently being heavily overused in some quarters in that state until they eventually lost all meaning by being used in countless vague applications (back East short words and guttural sounds were made to suffice). Annie was more apt to say "Oh, my goodness," a-la Little Orphan Annie (no relation) and indeed was wide-eyed with wonder at the world around her. She was happy receptive and sweet. She was one of those individuals that are so nice that it sometimes leaves a person at a loss.

Annie had done two years at UCLA, where she had been a cheerleader, of course, as well as an above average student. Of all things most unseemly, owing to the impression she gave of leading a hopelessly air-headed existence, she had a marked aptitude for organization. She was excellent at cooking as well. And she was beautiful. Once past the unintended vacuous veneer she had developed in resigned response to being always stereotyped as the dumb blond, she was discovered by those who made the effort to know her better to be intelligent, sensitive, and fun to talk to. This revelation made even more desirable. Freddy trying to be discrete in his thoughts surmised that she was probably a particularly gratifying partner in the physical sense. Thinking from the standpoint of someone who sleeps one bedroom away from her, concomitant with the sounds of rapture often heard emanating from that bedroom, giving extra points for endurance (he could only guess at the range of motion), Freddy figured she was great in the sack.

An avid reader was Annie, interested in mainstream fiction and National Geographic, and predictably, people. Grown from a middle-class family, she had a happy childhood and was always good to her folks, ("My goodness, you only have one of each!"). After "wowing" the boys in high school she went to college and wowed them there, more because her parents wanted her to go than because she really wanted to. Two years were enough for her and she set out to see some of the country. As beautiful as California was, there were also other places she wanted to see, and her travels took her to New Mexico, from there to Aspen, to Virginia, and finally to Key West, where she was destined to meet Wayne.

****

Wayne had bought the car for her for a hundred dollars. In its last life it had been used as a dive vehicle, pulling boats out of and putting them into the water, carrying salted gear back from where ever it was asked to, and then sold off when it seemed that there could not be much use left in it.

Wayne resurrected it. He bolted up the body on either side of the bench seat to remove the sway-back condition caused by a sinking of the cab as the rust of the sheet metal supporting the cab fell away into the dusty, riddled pavement of Key West, sinking a bit more with each jolt of a wheel falling into a hole. He rebuilt the alternator, which was obviously not original equipment and returned it to the all-thread and nine-sixteenths socket being used as a spacer that was its mount.

He replaced the shredded throttle cable with a bicycle brake cable, changed the master cylinder, and did a lot other little things. The lower radiator hose was replaced by three hoses of various sizes and shapes from other vehicles at some time before the car's maintenance was Wayne's responsibility. The hoses were a jury rig running in three directions involving two plumbing nipples, a bushing reducer and six hose clamps. But it worked. Even the radio worked, with its triangular coat hanger antenna.

So here she was. She had her wheels, and took her "Inty" to the beach and to the store and "well, gosh, everywhere!" Even when it suffered from some minor malady, she didn't get mad at it. She worried about it. It seemed that she even felt sorry for it.

Annie's Key West life revolved around Wayne, almost from the first moment she met him at the lounge she cocktail-waitressed at, dashing the hopes of the throng of suitors vying for her affection, even before he knew what a fortunate guy he was to have her fall in love with him. He still didn't know.

Annie's other spheres of activity orbited around her job. She was gregarious, and if she wasn't in the company of her two male housemates, she was doing something with the girls from work, shopping or going to the beach and trading stories about their boyfriends that they were not supposed to tell anyone.

At the time she met Pamela, Annie was at the stage where she was being taken for granted by the boys. "Men are sniveling dogs," as Annie would say to Pamela, albeit with a good-humored absence of malice.

****

She pulled up to the curb at the front of the house and shut Inty off. Dapper legs in stockings swung down out of the high bench seat. A passing bum saw them on high and dreamed of better days. The trim figure in small beige vee neck cocktail uniform bounced to the house and went inside. Her Wayne would be waiting.

Chapter Five - Mystery Woman

The weekend had evaporated. It was history, as Freddy would say, and now it is Monday morning and time to get to work. Freddy has to get to the marina early to check the gear stored for an upcoming job.

Freddy senses that the morning is optimistic and promising. He is closer to being optimistic than he has been since he has had a good night's sleep without outside inducement. He got one last night without so much as a single beer; that in itself was unusual, and then he awoke spontaneously this morning with no need of clocks or prompting from his pals.

It is early. It is light although the sun is not yet up over the horizon's rim clouds, and it is quiet at this hour as he drives along the Atlantic. The Olds is running evenly in the damp morning air. Overnight condensation from the front of the car, the hood and fenders, is blowing off and evaporating. Some of it is flying onto the windshield. The convertible top is down and there is the pungent smell of newly festering seaweed on the wind from bottom grass deposited on the coarse grit of the calcium-hard ground marl beach during the night.

The beach is at the southeast corner of the island. It makes a long, sweeping curve that starts with the sunrise on the horizon at Freddy's left and ends with the sun on his right as he turns gradually to the north,making its first tentative pokes through the low clouds, sending exploratory shafts of light to the water's surface. The quiet inactivity at this hour is calming to Freddy. The clouds will burn off soon, or dissipate in showers that never reach the sea's surface.

Left hand on the steering wheel, an oversized cup of coffee, festooned with the ubiquitous and ever-popular fornicating bunny rabbits and filled with French roast with a dash of cinnamon is in his right, the bottom of which is resting on the passenger seat. The faint cinnamon smell is wafting around in the partial vacuum behind the windshield, mixing with that of the seaweed and the other morning smells. The only thing moving on the beach is a solitary earth mover mashing down the mounds of seaweed and sand scraped from the shoreline. It is pushing the gritty mulch around a shallow covelet lapped by wavelets of the incoming tide, like the flapping fins of a beached fish on the margin of wet sand.

Mobile concession stands mounted on truck bodies and poking through the ported sides of vans would vie for the best spots at the curb later in the day. One day soon campers would clog the near lane. Years to come would bring throngs of joggers and walkers in thongs and funny multi-colored running shoes at this early hour. But here and now, the only person Freddy can see is the driver of the plow.

The sulfurous smell of weed piles sitting from the previous day's plowing gives way now as Freddy sails by, replaced by the thick, earthy smell of wet and sandy weed-mulched soil. There is a serenity about the scene. Freddy feels like passing his turn-off and continuing on up the coast, returning maybe in a month or so, if at all. It is a day to forget responsibilities and give in to the wanderlust which sometimes comes upon him. He makes an end to the sweeping turn that brings him off one island and onto the next. His turn to the marina is the next one. The car picks up speed and he stares out ahead, a hundred feet, a hundred miles...

He slows the car and makes the turn. He goes to work.

****

A disgruntled Freddy pulled the Oldsmobile into a parking space near his boat. He noticed that the "Sea Story "is tied up to the dock, just where it had been several days ago. He wondered if this could somehow be linked to his unexplainable optimism earlier. Standing on the deck of the Hatteras and turning at that moment to reveal a beautifully sculptured figure is the object of his affections since Friday, about to leave for another day of fishing. From the set of her shoulders and the scowl on her face, he surmised that she was not happy about it. Such a pretty scowl. Freddy was impressed by the woman. He would like to tell her so. Their initial meeting and the impression that he must have made dictated that he use discretion in attempting to make contact again with the object of a subsequent pairing. He was nervous. Surely he remembered how to talk to beautiful girls from good families from Iowa or where ever. "What's the big deal, right?" he asked himself. Why should he worry about what to say to this girl, he wonders, when he hasn't worried about what has come out of his mouth in the last three years? To add to his anxiety he realized that she is probably rich, too, and he never did get along well with rich girls. She was only twenty-five feet away. Her hands were folded together in front of her and there was a hint of a puzzled frown and a moue on her mouth on her formerly un-tanned, now sunburned, dark-eyed, softly triangular face as she looked at him. She notices me, he thought. Aware that he was sitting in his car dumbfound with the engine running and looking at her with a blank, unfocused expression, Freddy smiled weakly, said "Hello," and shut the engine. He removed himself from the vehicle.

"Hi." The frown was quite fetching, but the beginnings of her amused smile had his heart doing barrel rolls. Or was that his stomach?

"Nice boat," said Freddy. "Are you going fishing?" Good going, bonehead, he thought. Of *course* it's a nice boat, it's a Hatteras! Outriggers, fighting chairs, rods and reels abound. What else would they be doing besides fishing?

"That is *all* we've been doing for days. Actually, I'm just going along for the ride, my father and his business friends are going to try to catch fish. We're going to troll all day long again, I imagine." Her sigh indicated that there are things she would rather be doing.

"I'm very sorry for you," Freddy commiserated. It was evident that she was not enjoying the fishing trips. "I was forced to do it a couple of times myself. Nothing like rocking and rolling around in the Gulf Stream at six knots to make a man feel like a true sport." He felt as though he was laying it on too thick, too sarcastic. She blanched a bit. "Isn't there something else you would rather do? Have you seen the town yet?"

"I've done some shopping," she lamented, "and I've been to some restaurants, but mostly I've just seen lots of water."

"I'd be delighted to show you my town." Delighted? My town? How out of character. Was he actually saying these things?

"But I don't even know you."

"I don't know you either." A friendly smile came to her face. She got out of the boat and extended her hand in polite introduction, smiled again and said, "My name is Pamela Greer. Pam. I came down with my father and his business associate for a short vacation. All they want to do is fish every day. I'm starting to hate it. My dad thinks I'm having a good time and I don't want to disappoint him, but I don't think I can take much more of this."

Freddy thought to himself with pleasant surprise that things weren't going too badly. She actually seemed to like him. At least she was talking to him. He wondered why. "I'm Freddy. Bottle cap Freddy." He had mistakenly used the nickname he was known by on the south side of town.

"What?"

"Ah, Freddy Taylor," Freddy said quickly, "Pleased to meet you, Pamela."

"Thank you."

"Where you from, Iowa or someplace?"

"Ohio. Close enough. Four letters, anyway." He was feeling foolish and running out of things to say.

"Are you a fisherman, Freddy?"

"No, I don't even own a boat. The bank and I have an arrangement worked out, though. If I pay them installments adding up to three times what the boat is worth over the next four years they'll let me keep using it after it's worn out. Then they'll let me have it. I bought it used." That was an unfortunate disclosure - in essence he had told Pamela he was broke most of the time.

Everything looked ready to go aboard the *"Sea Story"*. The boat was loaded and the engine was idling. The Captain and mate with the ponytail (he wasn't that good looking after all) had appeared at the end of the dock and two portly gentlemen had emerged from the chandlery/bait store/snack bar which served the marina at the beginning of the dock. Freddy realized that there was not much time left if this romance he had envisioned was to get off the ground. He must arrange to get Pamela away from these two old and apparently well-meaning but one-tracked gentlemen.

"Well, I have to go now, Freddy. It was nice to have met you." Time had run out.

"Wait! Would you like to do something later?" he blurted. Registering some surprise at the suggestion and a mild amount of amusement, Pamela said, "I don't think I should. What would I tell my dad?"

"Dad" was now there at boat side and time really had run out. He must try something drastically creative. He chanced a guess based on looks on which of the guys was Pamela's pop. Freddy was reasonably sure it wasn't the Chinese guy. In his best approximation of pseudo-Ivy League suavity gleaned from his previous co-workers he said, "Well, hello there, Mr. Greer, sir. So pleased to meet you at last. I was just chatting with Pammy."

Pamela's eyes opened a bit more widely at that in surprise at the familiar Liberty Freddy had taken with her name, but she said nothing. "Haven't seen her in *ever* so long!" He should really have a pipe and a sweater with an "H" on it to do this right. After a pause, the man extended his hand and said, "Ah, yes, pleased to meet you, son." And Freddy past thirty. To his daughter: "Friend of yours. Pam?" He emphasized "Pam." He did not say "Pammy." His tone was wary.

"Uh - yes, Daddy," she said, uncertain of where to go from there. "This is Freddy..."

"Taylor," Freddy interjected, "Freddy Taylor, of the Pennsylvania Taylors." Let him hash that out, there must be some Taylors left in Pennsylvania. "I met Pammy *years* ago at school. We had a mutual friend." Time to cut this conversation short lest he become trapped in the weave of too much fabrication. The future of Pamela and he was already hanging by a thread on this feigned chance reunion he had cut from whole cloth. No need to smother what chance he may have in a blanket of lies. It was up to Pamela now. Either she would play along with this next gambit or it was goodbye Freddy.

"I *say,* Pammy, are we on for later?" She was momentarily frozen with indecision bordering on hilarity which prompted Daddy to ask, "Oh, are you two seeing each other later?" Freddy willed her to snap out of her trance and respond. She did.

"Oh, yes Daddy; Freddy and I are going to get together later and talk about old times." Freddy let his breath out. He had sensed that she had made her decision and saw the conspiratorial flick of her eyes toward him. It was time to make an exit. Then her father protested mildly.

"Well, all right. I thought that we would go out for dinner, but I suppose that there is time for that yet. Where did you say you went to school, Freddy?" Freddy didn't even know what state Pamela went to school in.

"Actually, I came in from out of state on weekends to visit Pammy's friend Susan."

"Susan?" asked Mr. Greer, "Who is Susan?"

Freddy knew he would overdo it. Time to go. "I shouldn't be keeping you any longer. Look what a beautiful day you have, should be fun out there." Freddy saw the comic frown on Pamela's face as she stood behind the two older men. "I really must run myself. Have a lovely day. See you about seven-ish, Pammy?"

"Ok, Freddy," this with a big, amused grin. "Bye - bye for now."

Whew. So far so good. He waved goodbye and said, "Ta-ta," retreating a safe distance as the "*Sea Story's*" stern turned out of the bight and out of sight. There is a problem, though. He did not know where she was staying. Now all he had to do was figure out from where he was supposed to pick her up.

****

A conversation between Pamela and Mr. Greer ensued:

Mr. Greer: "So it appears that you'll be seeing that boy tonight. I think he's a bit of a lightweight in the responsibility department. I hope that fellow didn't think he was fooling anyone with that gambit! Pamela, you're a smart girl with a good education. I don't worry about your judgment as a rule; I just hope you've thought this through."

"Dad, the education was enlightening and school was a good experience and I thank you for paying for it. I had a good time. But there are things I have to work out by myself. My degree in Philosophy won't make me rich, of course. And learning how my instructors and other people view *their* world by the books that *they* have read, by the professors *who taught them* and *to whose principals they adhere,* and by the books *they* have written and the lectures *they* have administered certainly doesn't guarantee that I will make the right choices just because I have been schooled in their view of the world."

Mr. Greer furrowed his brow: "Those men are scholars, Pamela."

"Yes," she said, "They are scholars. And they are mostly men. Their view of the world and the mental state of the world is clearly biased by who they are and into which society they were born; the circle in which they were raised, their class status, income, and their religion. They have a limited perspective. The evolution of their assessment of humanity is like a self-fulfilling prophesy. They believe the world is a certain way and for them it is."

"Yes, Pam, I suppose that could be true."

"Consider this, Dad. In another region, another country, don't you think their teachings, their beliefs, and their sense of right and wrong would be different? Of course they would, because that's the real world, a male world. I have to think for myself."

Mr. Greer smiled. "There is no doubt that you think for yourself, Pamela."

****

Throughout the rest of the day at work Freddy's thoughts strayed to Pamela and the coming evening. His work suffered and they did not get a job done that was contracted to be finished that day. This dismayed the usually redoubtable Wayne.

"Freddy, what in the hell are you doing today?"

"Such language!" Freddy huffed in mock shock. Then he recanted. "Ah, I'm sorry, Wayne. I've got a small problem."

"I know."

"I met this girl the other day."

"Oh no."

"And I don't know what to do with her."

"What did you do with the last one?"

"This is different." Freddy in his ardor did not realize how lame that sounded, especially in the light of what Wayne had seen him bring home in the past.

"What did you latch onto now, Freddy?"

"No, it's not like that at all. It's not a 'what', it's a 'her'," he said as he screwed a storage compartment to the deck they had just repaired. "Actually, she is a very sweet girl, but I don't really know who she is or where she's staying."

Wayne reflected on this dubious piece of information. "That makes sense." He had told Freddy more than once that his relationships with women are like dinghies that pass in the night, some more dingy than others.

"So what else is new, Freddy?" There was sarcasm in his tone. "Started a little early today, did you?" Freddy knew that this last comment was in jest, but, "We are not amused" is his acute reaction. He took umbrage at this undeserved jibe and reacted with haughty injured pride. He grumbled to let Wayne know this. Unfortunately, Wayne was already back to work and absorbed in what he was doing. Puritan work ethic or something. Freddy was left to continue pondering his situation. Should he hang around the marina all day until the "*Sea Story*" pulled in? Should he phone all of the classier motels - he did, after all, have a phone, and her name. In the end he decided that it was unwise to risk another dockside encounter with Pamela's keepers, not wanting the old fellows to catch him working and blow the Freddy Taylor of Princeton (or whatever), routine. He began packing his things. Wayne looked at him, astonished. His face was flushed.

"Where are you going, Fred? We have to get this done!"

"I've got to leave early today, Wayne."

"This is an excellent time to tell me! Why do you have to go?"

"I have to pick up that girl."

"Where?"

"I don't know." And with this Freddy departed, leaving an exasperated and steaming Wayne on the dock to re-fasten all of the trim on the boat and clean up.

Freddy decided to talk his problem over with Annie. She would understand. At least, Annie would listen - she had all of the primarily female traits such as being gossipy and interfering, even if she did get a short ration of cattiness, though why this should be so Freddy was at a loss to understand. Presumably, she read Cosmopolitan, so she should have had the training.

****

"But Freddy, even if you find her, where will you take her?" asked Annie, in the same sing-song high pitch she would have used to say "Gee, whiz, what*ever* will you do!"? Good question.

"Dinner, anyone?" he said. "That would seem to be the thing to do. On the surface, that would appear to be a very necessary evolution, although it actually has its roots set deep in our primordial genetic memories."

"Freddy, you're losing me again," she warned. Freddy had already taken several flights of fancy speculating on the possibilities for the evening. "Besides," she said as she continued to sort the laundry, "where are you going to get a long pair of pants? This girl doesn't sound like the kind that would want you to show up in shorts, not if she's as 'respectable' as you say she is." Annie appeared to have taken Freddy's lofty praise of Pamela, a woman he did not even know, as an indirect slur to herself. It was a sensitive area for her, a personal affront, after all her years being pigeon-holed as the dumb blond. Wrapped up as he was in his own quandary he didn't notice her indignation. Now he had Annie irritated at him as well as Wayne. Annie looked at her watch and then glanced out the window toward the road in anticipation of Wayne's arrival.

"Wayne is awfully late. Freddy, are you *sure* Wayne said it was all right for you to leave work so early?" she asked accusingly. Freddy's sheepish grin was her answer, and Annie turned on her heels and marched off rapidly to another part of the house. Freddy sent an apology in her wake as she left him alone to ruminate on what he might do about tonight.

Freddy's mind, not being occupied by work and having nothing else to do for the next hour and a half, became lost again in fanciful daydreaming about what the night might bring. The thought of lighting Pamela's fire made Freddy woozy. Pamela could send him to incandescence. There was the danger of euphoric self-immolation.

Provided, of course, that he can discern where Pamela is staying.

His flight of fancy ended; he returned to the ground and set to work to locate the woman. Calling all of the better motels on the island brought negative results. Then he tried some of the motels a short distance up the keys. He called the marina in desperation and he got the expected what-in-the-hell-are-you-talking-about routine from the guys working there. He was unreasonable to expect otherwise. There was no way around it, he would have to drive to the marina on the off chance that there was still someone there from the fishing party or crew to direct him to Pamela's whereabouts. The odds of this last course of action were not good as it opened the possibility of discovery that Freddy was not the old friend of Pamela's he had portrayed himself to be. This would lead to the obvious but erroneous conclusion by the senior Greer that Freddy was a ne'er-do-well, up to no good, and not to be trusted with his daughter. Freddy knew that this was only partially true and railed inwardly at such projected proscription of his amorous waxing regarding the lovely and succulent Pamela. So he was a little horny, surely they couldn't shoot him for that, could they? As a matter of fact, they could, it's been done before.

It was six o'clock when he got there. The marina was closing. There was but one thing left to do...

****

Finally in comfortable and familiar surroundings at his local watering hole, assisted by Dottie, the bartender, he assessed what had come to pass. Dottie had brought him a beer. She was slender and personable, smiling and friendly. She conversed with the ease born of practice in this social situation. She was a good listener. Long blond hair. Good figure. She had a boyfriend with a black Brillo pad for a head of hair which went down non-stop around his chin and up the other side to form and equally scraggly beard, framing a small insignificant face of close-set eyes, and a non-distinctive nose. The face was similar to that of a rhesus monkey, with expressions to match. He weighed two hundred and five pounds and was ever in need of a shower. His name was Joe (duh, Joe). There was just no accounting for taste.

"Would you like another beer, Freddy?" she smiled as she swept away the empty and propelled it into the Hefty bag lined trash can with the resounding crash of breaking glass. He was in the Bottle Cap adjusting his attitude in the face of his own ineptitude. That face was looking back at him from the mirror behind the bar.

"Sure, sweetie. How's that guy of yours?"

"Oh, he's all right. He's down watching the sunset at Mallory Square."

Good placed for him, Freddy muses. "Hell of a nice guy," Freddy lied. Probably out looking for someone to mug. The magic of the moment was interrupted by the ringing of the phone.

"Bottle Cap, Dottie speaking. Just a second, I'll check." With this Dottie scans the half dozen people at the bar, all of which are well known to her in that they are relatively reliable patrons of the establishment. It was close to summer and Key West was going into the small town mode it used to assume for that season. The population was comprised of non-seasonal locals and those persons shipped there by law enforcement establishments of northern communities because they were found to be undesirable in said communities. Why those northern cops thought that these villains were ideally suited to Key West was beyond Freddy, and Key West's own police force often found that they had to relocate some of these felonious prize trip recipients back from whence they came, or at least in a generally northerly direction.

Dottie's eyes stopped on Freddy. They narrowed in a pensive way and her head tilted like a dog trying to understand something. She said to the phone, "Yes Bottle Cap Freddy is here. I think that's who you want. Hold on." To Freddy, she explains. "Somebody is calling for Freddy Taylor. Is that you? Sounds like Sears catalog sales or somethin' like that." As compared to what, he wonders. She made the statement as though she were reassuring him that it did not sound like there was an angry creditor on the line, a definite bartending faux pas. She handed the phone to him.

Freddy is a bit loosened up by three libations and feeling witty and possibly even loquacious should the need arise. In his own interpretation of the local idiom, he answers the phone, "Jallow, dees ees Freddy spicken." He is decidedly not witty, nor even nice.

"Hello, Freddy?" It is a hesitant female voice. Realizing who it is, he falls into a nervous silence. He says "Uh." The voice again comes to life. "I'm sorry; I must have the wrong number." Again he says "Uh," then catches himself and shouts "No, wait!" into the receiver just as the phone clicks dead, much to his frustration. But then it just as swiftly comes back to life, catching him in mid-epithet, "Oh, sh... Hello?"

"Hello?" comes back in answer. "Hello, Pamela, is that you?"

"Freddy, is that you? Why did she call you Bottle Cap Freddy?"

"It's a long story, Pamela. How did you find me? I'm not listed. Where are you? I never got the address."

"I know. I remembered you saying something about the Bottle Cap earlier - why, that's what you said, 'I'm Bottle Cap Freddy! - Freddy, are you drunk?"

"Not yet. Uh, I mean no, of course not. Where are you?"

"I'm in the lobby of the Pier House. We're registered in my father's friend's name. It's after seven and my father was wondering why you hadn't picked me up, so I came down to the lobby to try to call you."

"Well, stay right there, don't move. I'll be there in ten minutes. See you in a little bit." She hung up and he handed the phone back to the bartender. To the bartender he said, "Dottie, give me a cup of coffee in a to-go cup. You can dump the rest of this." Looking first at Freddy incredulously and then at the just-opened beer, she said,

"Ya mean you're not gonna finish your beer? sheesh, that never happened before."

****

Driving hunched forward as if to urge the Olds onward, willing the traffic lights not to wait so long, one hand around the coffee and the other on the wheel, he slid the car into the Pier House lot. He made it in eight and one-half minutes, without spilling too much coffee. With a screech of tires he pulled up right in front of the well-appointed lobby in his dirty, dented denizen of the pothole-pocked city streets. Her dad was watching through the glass lobby doors...

****

As it turned out, everything worked out fine. They had an excellent dinner at the Polynesian restaurant, Shrimp Tempura for her, Jade and Pearls for Freddy and a bottle of the Chablis that was the house special for the day. The conversation was relaxed and comfortable, an unusual occurrence on a first evening out, and which sometimes does not happen at all. It turned out that he had not been as effective as he thought at fooling Mr. Greer. Pamela told him that her father was amused by Freddy's performance, even if he was not convinced that his daughter should be seeing the likes of Freddy Taylor. He was lurking in the lobby ready to whisk his daughter away to dinner at the slightest provocation. The arresting sight of Freddy's car had given him pause and gave Pamela enough time to slide through the doors of the lobby before her father could voice an objection. He had realized, however, that his girl was palling at the prospect of doing nothing but fishing for the remaining four days of her vacation. Freddy quickly made plans for Pamela and him to alleviate that situation.

Things were slow at the business and Wayne said he could pick up the slack for the next few days. He really was an all right guy. Freddy found Pamela to be shy in some ways, but not naive, animated, fun to be with. Together they saw the art galleries and the museums at the old lighthouse and at the two small forts, one to the east and one to the west side of the island, called the Martello towers, erected to defend the island against invaders by sea. They learned about Fort Zachary Taylor on the Navy base, which had been occupied by Union soldiers during the Civil War when it was a Northern stronghold against the Confederacy.

They saw Hemingway's house. Pamela even got Freddy to ride the Conch train, a Jeep in tandem with several small, bench-seated, canopied trailers, fashioned in black and orange to simulate Henry Flagler's train that perished in that monster hurricane of Labor Day, 1935.

He took her snorkeling a short distance up the keys where there were some decent spots off the roadside in close to shore in the quieter areas along the convoluted shoreline a short distance from the highway. The week passed.

Freddy had done these things before, some several times, with the advent of each visit by friends, relatives, or visiting dignitaries from the north. This time, it seemed fresh and new again.

Pamela's last day was Friday, tomorrow. She was leaving in the morning and flying back to Ohio and her job. She had to be at work Monday morning. The two older gentlemen would be flying up with her and the Captain and the mate would be taking the "Sea Story" back to Tampa. Freddy convinced Pamela to take a later flight and Wayne took the day off and the four of them - Annie would be going too - were going to catch lobsters and take a boat tour around the island for Pamela's benefit. They would return home and cook and eat the lobsters.

Pamela could catch the late plane out. That was the plan.

"What about tonight, Freddy?" asked Pamela.

"Tonight, we dance!" What a treat for Pamela.

Chapter Six - A Night on the Town

Freddy picked Pamela up at eight o'clock. He had shined his old, black Florshiems, dug a pair of perennial cuff-less, dark blue polyester permanent press double knit dress slacks out of the closet and filched a pair of dark blue socks from Wayne. Sweat socks would not cut it. He had an old Johnny Carson white-on-white shirt on with the long, studded collar and French cuffs. Those he rolled up twice, not being inclined to put on cuff links. Annie trimmed his hair, calmed him down, and doted on him. He loved it. If Wayne didn't marry her, he would.

Carnations in hand, he rang the bell.

She wore a simple shift, islandy, of local origin. It was pale blue, sleeveless, cut low, with a vee front with a zipper from cleavage to the waist. It was currently adjusted to allow a generous amount of quality curvature to be seen.

Her breasts were of an almost perfect roundness, full, firm and high and not too large for her body. A soft smile was on her lips.

Her browned face, arms and chest contrasted the light off white of her dress; the material of her shift was something soft-textured and downy, cut to fit close to her body. He saw a tracery of a button shape beneath the shift at the center of each swell of breast, and the sparkle in her brown eyes.

The softness of her garment seemed to accentuate the softness of her skin. The shift was mid-thigh. Bare, firm, tanned legs instead of stockings. A pair of low-heeled pumps. She spun around for him; there was no back at all. He caught his breath. The skin of her back glowed. It was a deep, warm-blooded red-golden brown. A thin silver chain hung around an elegant throat.

They walked from the Pier House to Mallory Square and watched the jugglers, hawkers, and tourists. The westering sun sent angled beams shooting through wispy bordered gaps in the clouds giving them a religious look like stained glass. After the sun was down, still they stayed, hand in hand, gazing at the sky backlit by the sun beyond the horizon. It played out its colors, yellows to reds, reds to red-limned gray remnants, and a last flash of purple. They had a cocktail at a garden bar a short walk from the square. The spiritual calming effect of the sunset was still upon them, artistry in nature, an ethereal manifestation of the physical workings of the world. They would have been there much longer had not Freddy's eyes drifted to the face of his watch. He got up with a start.

"Time to go, Pamela!"

"Ok," she said, grinning broadly and squeezing his arm. Their reverie broken, they set out to join Wayne and Annie. They were to meet at a resort on the other side of the island to hear the band and do some dancing.

****

Annie and Wayne were seated at a table mid-way down the room. The lounge was carpeted in floral designs and decorated with plants and street lamps hung on the walls from angled brackets. A wall of paired glass doors looked out over the lawn and sand toward the Straits of Florida, the Cuba, and finally the Atlantic Ocean.

"Have you seen this guy dance yet, Pamela?" asked Wayne at their approach.

"No, Wayne, this will be the first time for me."

"You're in for a real treat." Annie looked disapprovingly at him. That Wayne was *so* sarcastic sometimes.

"You better have a drink first, Pamela," Annie warned in a confidential aside, and then she giggled behind her hand. A waitress came by and took their drink order. She wore a short flapper outfit which hinted at the hotel's nascent era. Completed in 1921, it had been planned by Henry Flagler and finished with his money after he passed away in May 1913. The lounge was called the Calabash, and the hotel was the Casa Marina, or House by the Sea.

****

"Oh, my goodness, we're all dressed so differently," Annie chimed. And they were. Wayne wore jeans and a Joe College type button-down pinstripe collar shirt. Annie was in white medium length shorts and a violet blouse. The shorts were pleated, there was a yellow ribbon in her hair and her shoes were expensive-looking yellow loafers. The California girl, the post-grad, the recycled retro Freddy and the sexy tourist lady. Except for Freddy's attire being dated, he and Pamela were the closest to looking like they were a likely pair and had arrived together. Freddy looked good, Annie was pleased with her observation and beamed at everybody, and a small smile crossed Wayne's lips. Annie's ability to generate empathy was infectious. Freddy shuffled self-consciously in his chair and looked dumbly at Pamela.

Soon they were dancing. Again there were vast differences. Someone who had just walked into the lounge would never know they were together to look at them. Wayne did reserved, stuffy steps. Annie was the animated, arm-swinging, high-stepping California girl and Pamela was in the middle of the road there somewhere, true to her Midwestern upbringing. No one knew what it was that Freddy did, Freddy didn't know himself, but it was certainly different, and that didn't seem to worry him. He did it with obvious enthusiasm. It was sort of a swing and a kick done in a half-crouch, knees and elbows going in and out. During the more compelling musical passages the swing would go full-circle, two spins counter-clockwise and then one clockwise. The chicken dance would have been a good name for it - Freddy moved like a chicken on drugs scrambling around in the dust.

As it got later the pace of the music slowed. Pamela and Freddy danced close. The other two were off in their own world, talking at the table. Freddy and Pamela finished dancing and left them in the lounge to take a walk around the grounds and out onto the pier.

They walked along the hedges and between the bushes of the landscaped grounds to the beach with an arm around each other's waist and crossed the lawn to the pier. Their shoes made a slow cadence of hollow wooden sounds on the decking of the pier until they stood at the end. A light breeze caressed them and the sea gurgled from below as it pulsed around the pilings. The moon was nearly full and low in the sky.

A swath of moonlight on the water was wide at the curve of the ocean on the horizon, narrowed in the middle distance, and flared again below them at the foot of the pier. It sent reflected moon glow shimmering up into their faces. It was an hourglass of moonlight, a timely measure in the last hours for Freddy and Pamela, distant light in the sky shining on the ocean from so far away, illuminating the sea from the horizon to the water at their feet. They heard something jump out on the water, likely a fish being sought by another as a meal. They looked in time to see the flash of a fin and a splash as the fish returned to the water. The phosphorescent plume marking its flight was halfway between them and the moon, on the right, just outside the waist of the hourglass's concave dish on that side. Disney could not have done it any better.

They turned toward each other. Pamela searched Freddy's eyes for something, some key to his feelings. Freddy looking back into her eyes was afraid to hold eye contact and afraid to let it go. They kissed softly, for a long while.

"I'm glad I met you, Freddy," she murmured.

"I wish you weren't leaving. Can't you stay a few more days?"

"No, I have to get back to work," she said and smiled. "And why would you want me to? I'm sure that there are a lot of girls coming to Key West who are dying to meet you."

"Not like you. I could like you a lot.

"It is good to hear you say that Freddy, because I like you, too. It makes it harder to go home."

"What time do you have to be back at your hotel?" Freddy asked.

Softly, she said, "I don't have to be back tonight, Freddy, my dad flew back a day early."

****

They walked back through the grounds as gusts started rustling the tops of the palms, then through the lobby and the two blocks to the house. Freddy left the car at the hotel. Wayne and Annie were still there - they would never miss them. If Wayne and Annie needed the car, they knew that the ignition was so worn that it would turn using the screwdriver under the seat.

They arrived at the house and Freddy ushered her in. They went to Freddy's room and closed the door.

****

He stood before her and she looked up at him, her lips slightly parted, her pupils large, her eyes wide open and her senses at peak. She bowed her head modestly and stepped toward him. Slowly, Freddy undid her zipper. Her breathing stopped as he slipped the shift from her shoulders and let it fall to the floor. She stepped out of her only other garment.

They gave themselves to each other, and then they slept.

****

The man slipped through the narrow vertical chink sixty feet high and thirty feet deep in what appeared to be the face of a large rock monolith. The shoulder-width cut was actually in stone which was an integral part of the temple built stone by stone 1500 years ago. Earthed over during the intervening centuries, it now was overgrown with grasses and bushes which had crept up from the encroaching Guatemalan jungle, hiding it from view from above and below.

Once inside the temple he lit his lantern. He dropped down into the tunnel and worked his way down past the bats and crumbling masonry into the tomb below. He ignored the bones on the kapok-covered wooden litter and began to pick up carved jade beads from the chert floor and put them into the pockets of his vest. Into a large cloth sack he put two three-legged ceramic pots, carefully buffering them with strips of toweling. The other man of his team had almost finished loading. He was struggling with a large jade plaque and a fuchsite mask inlaid with shells and colored with cinnabar, packing them into a similar sack with objects of obsidian and turquoise.

Their targets were sculptures and ceramics, gemstones, plaques and carvings for sale to unscrupulous art and antiquity dealers and wealthy private collectors in Miami, New York, and a host of foreign cities. They'd already lost one man in a cave in. They could yet lose more. The government guards that had been alerted and were on their way from the city two and a half days distant were now near. It was likely that there would be gunplay before the plunder ended, but the risk was worth it for so incredible a find as this.

Before he started up the tunnel he reached for one last object that had caught his eye. It was a vase, about 8 inches high, red and brown ochre and painted with Mayan gods and animals, tapered gently at the waist. He packed it into the top of his sack and started to climb. They would soon start for a spot on the Caribbean coast where a broker could be found...

****

Freddy opened his eyes. The sunlight shone in over the crimson trim atop the white cafe curtains on the window in the northeast wall of his bedroom. He could see the tops of the azaleas fluttering outside, hear them stirring slightly in soft susurration with the breeze. He turned to look at her. Her eyes were already open. "Hi," she whispered. She was on her back, smiling demurely, softly and shyly, and had whispered the single word from her pillow beside him. The sheet was drawn up over her body.

Freddy reached for her, putting his hand on her waist and letting it slip around her back. As he started to draw her near, she exploded across the space between them and gave him a hug.

"Freddy, last night was incredible. Where did you learn all of that stuff?" she asked.

"What stuff?"

"You know what I mean."

"Oh, *that* stuff. I didn't. Why? Complaints already?"

"No, Freddy, no complaints." She threw a leg over him and oozed against him contentedly.

"Good, you can stick around for a while." The flip remark reminded him that Pamela would be on the last plane out of Key West that night.

"C'mon, Pammy darlin', get dressed and cleaned up. We've got big things to do today."

At first she frowned at this new familiarity but then dismissed it.

"Goody," she said with enthusiasm. "What are we going to do today? It doesn't really matter, though, whatever it is it will be wonderful. What should I wear?"

"Put on your bathing suit."

"Why, where are we going?"

"Fishing."

At this last declaration, he could have sworn he heard a groan from somewhere. Pamela seemed to deflate a little. But only momentarily. What a trooper.

****

Wayne and Annie were having coffee in the Florida room. As Pamela and Freddy made their ingress somewhat sheepishly, they met knowing grins. Annie's said she approved. Wayne's was more like "You devil, you, what did you do last night?" It was all smiles and cheerful "good mornings" and some subtle hinting that Pamela and Freddy had slept late and they should be getting underway if they were to do anything with this day. "Let's get the gear into the car and grab some breakfast on the way to the marina," said

Wayne, "we can't sit here all day; we have to be macho and kill big fish." And so they put things together as rapidly as they could. After donning a wet and clammy swimsuit reeking of stale sea water Freddy went in search of his other gear. His booties, snorkel and mask were in the bathroom hanging over the bar behind the shower curtain where Freddy was vaguely conscious that they must have irked Annie as he remembered her prim, pursey-tight lips, and the low, throaty rumblings coming from the bathroom earlier last night and then the wet-haired scowl he got from her when she was done with her shower. Speargun and shaft were in a corner of the bedroom near a soft spot in the floor which Freddy carefully avoided. Termites. Gear bag in the closet with the tools and dirty laundry, lobster measure attached to tickler with an old shoelace. Fins standing up in the living room. Dive flag still in the trunk of the trusty, dusty Olds, which Wayne had retrieved last night when it became apparent that Freddy had absconded with Pamela. Annie's efforts to reform Freddy's housekeeping habits had gone a long way toward curbing the squalor the house had been in before she arrived on the scene, but she had not yet been entirely successful.

They were almost ready to go. Freddy summoned Pamela to his bedroom closet where he collected the extra fins and mask Pamela had been using during her stay and he ceremoniously handed then to her. He grabbed up the rest of the gear and realized he was still missing something. "Pamela, my hands are full, would you get my dive watch? I think it's in the top dresser drawer." The drawer was one of Freddy's many catch-alls. Pamela opened the drawer and found the watch. Her gaze was drawn to something brassy and shining at the back of the drawer. She saw the gun. "Freddy?" He peered over her shoulder to see what brought on her puzzled frown. "Oh, that. It's a water pistol. I stole it. Look real, doesn't it? Let's go, we got everything." Relieved but confused, she followed him to the car.

****

They had a hearty breakfast at an old and venerable corner diner known for its generous portions, a colorful clientele, and good coffee. Windows from floor to ceiling faced the intersection on two sides, shaded by Venetian blinds. Stained glass *objet d'art* hung from the ceiling and stained glass trim decorated the tops of the windows. Inside there were conch shells and wooden popsicle stick replica ships, brass and pewter statuary. It was a good place to breakfast, read the paper and watch the world go by.

They made plans for the day over an assortment of eggs and omelets, sausage, bacon, hash browns and fruit cups, orange juice and coffee. They decided (Freddy and Wayne) to take the boat out toward to American Shoals and spend the day on the reef. After they had eaten Wayne excused himself and went to the restroom.

Pamela and Annie had finished appraising each other and were comfortable together. They would be good friends, given time. Pamela waited until Wayne had gone, looked at Annie with a conspiratorial smile and said, "Annie, I like Wayne. He's the strong silent type". Freddy wondered if they had forgotten he was still seated at the table. He looked into the air and spoke to no one in particular.

"OK, here we go...," was his derisive jibe made with unconcealed envy. He did not begrudge Wayne his due respect. Annie continued on as though he'd said nothing.

"I know what you mean. I was attracted the first time I saw him. I like those strong shoulders and cute rear end." Annie was puffed up with pride. Freddy made a face, but Pamela would not be put off by him.

"Where did Wayne go to school, Annie? He seems so smart. Where is he from?" This brought a troubled look to Annie's face and the corner of her mouth twisted. Freddy answered for her. "Wayne doesn't say much about his past," he said as he squeezed Pamela's knee beneath the table, and communicated to her with his eyes that it would be good to leave the subject alone. He could see that she understood, and she changed the subject.

"Where did you meet him, Annie?"

This changed Annie's mood and she warmed again to her favorite subject and told Pamela how she captured Wayne. Freddy followed the story as would a spectator at a tennis match.

Wayne returned, Freddy paid the bill, and they departed for the marina.

Wayne had topped the fuel tanks after their last excursion, so there was little to do at the marina in the way of preparation. They jumped into the boat and set out for the reef. Wayne drove. He pulled out the switch for the bilge pump and a couple of gallons of sea spewed from the discharge port on the side of the boat. Wayne gave Freddy a look as if to say, "Better fix those stringers!"

They set a roughly south-easterly course from the mouth of the channel and headed for American Shoals. Annie and Wayne stood at the center console as Wayne steered, enjoying the wind in their faces on the ride out, knees bent slightly, absorbing the light, rhythmic slap-slap of the hull cutting through the small chop on the water. Sitting on the bench seat behind them Freddy fiddle-faddled with things - screwing on spear tips, changing the odd worn rubber on a spear gun, and storing things into one of the two compartments under the bench seat. The other was a live-bait well which they frequently used to keep their catch in, keeping the fish in salt water until they got around to gutting them.

That being done, Freddy sat, gawked about and looked at Pamela. She sat next to him, her hair swept back by the wind of the boat's motion. She had another frown on her face. Her eyebrows were bunched and she had her lips pressed together indicating a question was forthcoming. She yelled over the engine noise.

"Freddy, how am I going to fish? We don't have any rods and reels."

"I'm gonna show you."

Her lovely mouth made a big "O". He thought of the previous night and smiled a lustful inward smile.

Chapter Seven - The Reef

Swimming and snorkeling close to shore is ok, but the reef back then was a different thing altogether. Instead of isolated groups of coral heads and sea fans, there is mile upon mile of barrier reef, as the outer portion of the reef is commonly thought of, composed of colonies of living organisms growing larger and taking new forms as new generations of the tiny animals grow over the calcareous skeletal remnants of their antecedents. Shapes and sizes of the calcium carbonate, magnesium, and algal formations change to suit the currents. Where each type of coral and marine life tends to occur is according to the depth and temperature of the water which is a function of the slope of the bottom and the distance from shore at the time the organism started to form. The currents influence their shapes and forms. The maximum depths at which reefs can grow are limited by, among other things, first and foremost, the intensity of the light which reaches them. With proper nutrients and temperatures, the limit is about 230 feet. The reef grows outward as debris accumulates on the reef slope. Above 100 to 160 feet the slope is dominated by encrusting calcareous algae, below by fragile, branching gorgonians. In the Pacific, some coral cores extend one mile downward before hitting bedrock. At rates of vertical growth of as much as six-tenths of an inch yearly, they represent perhaps 100,000 years of growth, indicating rising water depths in that area over the period. In Florida, where the shoreline on the broad, shallow continental shelf there and where the water depth has changed radically over the ages, formations sometimes seem oddly placed.

The reef, by geographical definition, not the common parlance, is actually miles wide in Florida, and includes the area from close in to shoreline to the drop off of the last escarpment into deep water, not the more picturesque line of coral and rock outcroppings and bulwarks that parallel the coast at the reef's outer limit.

Stands of Elkhorn and Stag Horn Coral cover large areas. (They are now almost completely gone). In places, they fill the view underwater to the limits of visibility that are imposed by that medium. Orange forests of antlers, bereft of their namesake animals, rise from the sand as though the beasts were buried beneath it, leaving only a strange herd of immobile, headless horns frozen in silent stampede.

There are brain corals. They come in colors. Their convoluted surfaces resemble the texture of the brain, replete with tortuous game-book maze-like paths, twists, turns, and cut-offs, cutbacks and cul-de-sacs. These colonies can be small, or they can be six or eight or ten feet and nearly round, discrete hemispheres or ones with bulbous appendages. They can be gigantic elongated plum tomatoes standing on end in forty-five feet of water and extending upward to within ten feet of the surface. Star corals are similar in texture to these brain corals but their surface pattern is more ordered, the spicules of these animals forming a pattern of points on the members of the colony suggestive of decorative stars.

Sometimes these corals look as though something has gone wrong, when they are concave dishes of shallow incidence, forming a depression on the bottom. Failed soufflés. Cow patties dropped from very large cows, splattering in nine-foot saucers as would be expected of such a substance falling from the great height resulting from anatomical location of an anus high in the air due to the existence of this mythical maritime bovine behemoth.

Then there is fire coral. All coral is abrasive and will remove skin from a careless knee, leg or shoulder should an unwary swimmer fail to notice that he has ventured too close and finally contacts the massed animals. They don't like being touched. They are fragile; human touch and temperature differences may kill them, and their rough texture, whether by design or not, helps keep people away. Fire coral has yet another means of achieving retribution. Besides the ability to abrade a human's tender flesh, this mustard brown coral with small, flat blades burns like hell when it contacts the skin.

All of this and more Freddy imparted to Pamela on the long ride out, lest she mar that perfect skin or cause malaise to the body

Freddy coveted. He felt it deserved the best possible care. It was impossible to make her immune to all things dire lurking in the sea; he felt his lecture was the next best thing. Pamela found it hard to hear Freddy over the engine noise and so had difficulty following his discourse. She did not want to interrupt this scholarly display and hurt Freddy's feelings so she listened most seriously and read his lips as best she could, with nods of the head to indicate when each pearl of wisdom was hoarded away, whether or not she actually had a good grasp of it. She raptly pretended to garner each gem as Wayne looked on skeptically.

Pamela being thusly briefed and having acted suitably impressed, it being a perfect day and all hands ready and raring to go, Freddy went to the bow as Wayne slowed the boat and lowered the Danforth into the sand between two fingers of coral so as not to break any of the creature's colonies and anger the rock-like god's within. It was in this frame of mind that Freddy set about the task of procuring pelagic beasts by violent, brutal means to later sate their pagan palates.

"OK, Pamela, ease on down into the water. Don't make a splash-fest out of it."

"Why, Freddy, in case there's a shark around?"

"Oh heck no. I'm not saying that you shouldn't stay alert for sharks, but that's not really a problem unless you jump in on top of one. But if there's eating fish around we don't want to spook them."

"What's your biggest fear, Freddy?"

He shuddered "Jellyfish..."

Everything was perfect - except - no fish! They looked under every rock they passed and swam through all of the canyons between the palisades of the fingers of coral for long distances all around the boat. Annie and Wayne were off somewhere on the other side of the boat and Freddy suspected they were fooling around.

Pamela was enthralled with the shapes and colors of the underwater terrain and the small tropical fish, rocks, Gorgonia and architecture of the reef. It was all so new to her, very different from those days on the surface without an inkling of what was under it.

Freddy was taking lustful pleasure watching Pamela swim. In water sights are magnified. Gravity does not pull mercilessly on bodies; they look better, more rounded and appealing. This effect on Pamela's already beautiful form was not lost on Freddy.

They came to a shallow area where a boat frame lay sunk in four feet of water. Clusters of tropical fish swam about the old wreck. There Freddy stood Pamela on her fins and hugged her. Standing together in the water as angelfish and neon gobies swam around them, he removed his mask and let it hang around his neck by its strap, then he removed Pamela's and kissed her. Then he playfully pulled her pants down as pairs of curious damselfish hovered around and flitted through their legs. She pulled his down. Then they weren't playing any longer, they were fooling around. He untied the string above and undid her top and braced himself as best he could against the boat frame, and she came to him and wrapped her legs around him as her breasts swayed and moved with their own motion and with the surge of the ocean's swells. Ho, boy, fun in the sun.

****

If that wasn't enough to make Freddy's day, they finally came upon some fish. Three big, silver tarpon swam by with a purpose, as though they were going to be late for an appointment. Sleek and beautiful, but not eating fish. Immediately after, three spotted eagle rays in formation and with wings synchronized cut a diagonal course across the tarpons' path, leading their eyes to where yellow tails and grunts were schooled under the coral. The yellowtails were too small for spear fishing, the grunts too bony and troublesome to suit Freddy. A blue and green parrot fish was browsing below and to their left as they swam out into deeper water. Pamela studied it carefully for a moment. It was crunching up coral in its small, beak-like mouth and eating the animals within. She looked expectantly at Freddy and he motioned her on. The parrot fish was not edible – not by them, anyway. Suddenly there it was. Pamela and Freddy swam over an outcropping and saw the grouper hovering near the mouth of a coral cavern, in about thirty feet of water. Freddy motioned for Pamela to watch. Two good breaths, a perfect surface dive and he floated down toward the grouper. It looked to be about twenty-five pounds.

The grouper waited for Freddy, sidewise to the cavern opening, slack-jawed, round-faced and indolent, curious to see what he was doing. Freddy took careful aim, stayed stock still, fired, and missed. The spear traveled under the grouper and to his right, seeming to arc to the right of where Freddy had aimed. The grouper hardly appeared to notice except for slowly backing into his cavern so that only his hard snout presented itself. Embarrassed, Freddy returned to the surface.

"Let me try!" There was excitement in her voice.

"It's a hard shot, Pamela. My mistake has him on his guard and he's holed up pretty good."

"Please, Freddy?"

How could he refuse? Of course, he had to let her try, even though the water was deeper than any dive she had done in practice. She watched intently as he put the 48 inch steel shaft back in the guides, re-strung the nylon line attaching the end of the shaft to the gun and put the gun butt to his hip, facing away from her, to re-arm the three elastic bands that propelled the shaft forcefully through the water, and hopefully, through a fish, when the trigger was pulled.

As he handed the gun to her he said, "Be careful, Pamela, these things are dangerous." He had spat the mouthpiece of the snorkel out to talk. "Keep the spear pointed away from you and anybody else at all times." Pamela had enough to handle at the moment so she left her mouthpiece in and nodded vigorously that she understood.

"All right, honey, keep your face in the water, keep your eyes on the fish, don't lose sight of him. Breathe slow. Longer breaths. Relax. Remember, it gets easier to equalize the deeper you get, just don't forget to start equalizing as soon as you start down. Ok, Pamela, do an efficient surface dive and glide down." There was Freddy again improvising with a new and unexpected familiarity in his speech.

She prepared to dive on the grouper, which had half emerged from its lair. She didn't have a chance.

She jack-knifed her body and kicked her legs into the air, the weight of her legs driving her body down almost vertically. As soon as she straightened her legs the weight of them above the water and the assist of gravity drove her rapidly deeper. She started kicking a bit too soon, before her fins were fully submerged, wasting a little energy, and she slewed sideways a tiny bit, not being used to the heft of the spear gun. Altogether, it wasn't too bad.

Pamela came up on the fish with both hands on the gun, getting her body closer to the fish than it had to be and increasing the chances of having him bolt deep into his hole. Then she stopped and hung there. Twenty seconds, then thirty, forty-five. Without momentum for stabilization she started to float over on her side involuntarily as the slight current tried to push her parallel to the escarpment. It was close to a minute when the fish finally decided that this latest intrusion was no threat, and he came entirely out of his niche, turning sideways as he did. She pulled the trigger, and still everything remained motionless. There was no flurry of fins, no cloud of silt obscuring what had happened. Pamela still hung there beautifully, diagonally, arched backward and canted slightly toward Freddy allowing him to see the front of her body, breasts and legs in three-quarter profile. She bent one knee, the bent leg now making a near perfect triangle with the straight one, the swept back fins extending the line of her image. The scene could have been a poster. The fish was not swimming away, either. One convulsive jerk and it was done; the spear had passed cleanly through both of the fish's eyes. Freddy grinned from ear to ear as Pamela made for the surface. How about that, folks, she done good. He was tickled. He was proud of his charge. From his vantage point above, it seemed to him that the spear actually curved toward the fish after Pamela had pulled the trigger! Then a sobering thought came to mind. He had missed, and now he had to tell the others who shot the fish. Oh, well, there were worse things.

She surfaced, breathless. "Nice going, Pamela. Let's get it back to the boat."

"You take him," she panted.

"Why?" Freddy asked, puzzled at her distress.

"I killed him. I killed a beautiful fish. I was only playing before, but I actually killed him. You take him back to the boat, *please*, Freddy!"

"All right, Pamela, take it easy, it's all right." He felt that he was wanting in words of wisdom. What else, though, could he say?

Back at the boat, Freddy took the necessary ribbing on being out-done by his student. Annie reveled in the fact that Freddy had been bested by a woman on her first attempt to spear a fish. He remarked that it was beginners luck and countered by asking Annie how many fish she had shot lately. She said none so far, but that, too, would change, Pamela inspired her. Freddy couldn't get over how funny Wayne thought the whole thing was. Wayne was in hysterics. Later that night Wayne sneaked Freddy's spear gun from his room and quietly straightened the shaft.

All the predictable stuff being said, it still being early enough if they hurried and everyone being ready for a change of location, they motored in back in the direction of the marina to work the broken line of isolated coral heads and patches of rocks and coral southeast of Key West in search of lobsters.

****

Florida spiny lobsters are arthropod crustation decapods, crawfish with no claws. Freddy was good at catching the tender-tailed crawlers, barricaded behind coral mounds like French castles in the countryside of turtle grass and sea ferns, with portcullises of gorgonians - sea fans of soft coral with grate-like webs growing perpendicular to the current. Les Cardinaux de la Mer. Sea urchins are the sentries, Beefeater guards with hats so large that they are all that can be seen of them. The battlements may be the mantle of Elkhorn coral - golden yellow Elkhorn coral predominates over Stag Horn at these generally shallower depths - or crenellated with the rock remains of a variety of other invertebrates, or be the rigid leaves of the strange and ruddy sea fans after they have died and been overgrown with fire coral or sponges. They may be the shallow-water finger coral spires of a castle in Brittany or the brain coral cupolas of a Slavic citadel in the Ukraine.

This world they would share for a while with the creatures of the sea. It was similar in many ways to the seaward edge of the fore reef close to deep water from which they had just come. They now were at the back reef, less than a thousand yards from shore. Many of the same types of fish and animals lived here but were more widely spaced. There were not the coral fingers, buttresses of massed animals hundreds of feet long with sand channels between them, found on the edge of the fore reef. Those sconces were the bulwarks between the shallow side of the reef and the deep water. Here coral heads, alone and in groups spread over sand patches were surrounded by expansive plains of turtle grass and sea ferns teeming with small animals, sea slugs, urchins, anemones, and shellfish, disguised in browns and greens and hard for untrained eyes to see, and countless larvae and diatoms. The lobsters were the lords of these domains; spiny armored knights on long-jointed pincers. The coral fortresses were their keeps.

Freddy, an unlikely predator in a sea of predators, comes to this world with an old, broken top of a fishing rod which he calls a tickler. With it he prods his prey into a net on a hoop with a short handle. By fish standards, he cuts an ungainly swath. The fair maiden Pamela swims by his side, similarly equipped. He had noted the length of time that she had been submerged as she dove on and shot the grouper. As they looked under the coral heads now, he was again amazed at her breath control.

The game is to tap and tickle the lobster out from under his rock into the net, a simple trick for those with the feel for it. Tap the lobster on the back end, he goes forward. Tap him in front, he goes back. What could be simpler? Again Pamela was a quick study.

After watching as Freddy made his dives, swept away urchins with his net and caught a few lobsters. Then Pamela had him put her in the proper position and steer lobster into her net. Then she measured him as Freddy instructed and started to put him in the yellow nylon mesh game bag Freddy was carrying. It was the first lobster she had handled. Docile until it knew it was out of the confines of the net, it surprised her with a quick tail thrust and escaped her grasp. Freddy swam it down with a short burst of speed. He brought the lobster back, motioning to Pamela to watch what he was doing. Freddy showed her how to hold the escape artist with its tail tucked under so it couldn't open it for another thrust. Once the lobster was securely ensconced in the nylon bag Freddy spat out his mouthpiece and explained:

"Grab them across the back and squeeze. They're stronger than you think, but they'll be calm as long as they feel the pressure. Then fold the tail under so they can't use it to swim. From now on I want you to spot them. Look for the antennas as you swim; dive down and look if the coral head is big and seems that it might be a good place for lobsters to hide." Pamela considered how she was supposed to know what lobsters thought was a good hiding place. She missed a couple, which Freddy pointed out to her. Soon he had her searching systematically, always moving her gaze from one field of vision to another sequentially, the way a good lookout on a ship does. She was good at it.

Pamela and Freddy swam back to the boat and stored the lobsters. She was pleased with herself; she had had a big day so far.

"Freddy, this is wonderful! I've never done anything like this before. I spearfished, I lobstered..."

"I did something I've never done before, too."

She thought about this for a moment. "What...?" and then she remembered the sunken boat. "Oh, Freddy you liked that, did you?" she asked coyly. He didn't answer - she knew he did. He just smiled and continued putting the lobsters into the storage compartment. "Freddy, why don't we go out and get some more? I'm not tired yet."

"Sure, baby, anytime."

"Freddy! I meant catch lobsters. I may not get a chance to do this again for a long time." The allusion to her departure brought a fleeting grimace to Freddy's face. She caught his facial gesture and made a small empathetic smile. He addressed his next statement to the lobsters.

"We can't get any more, Pamela, the legal limit is six each, and that's what we've got. If you want to catch more you'll have to come back another time."

"I'd like to, Freddy."

Wayne and Annie returned to the boat. They passed up their gear and guns to Pamela as Freddy went up front to pull the anchor. Wayne had shot two mutton snappers.

"How'd you do, big guy?" Freddy called back to Wayne from the bow. Annie looked up at him as though to scold. "Oh, *excuse me*, Annie, how did *you* do, big girl?" he said with his eyes pointedly trained on her chest as she climbed over the transom.

"I do jest fine, thank you." She was hugging Wayne's arm. He puffed out his chest and leaned back, looking down sidewise at Annie as he towered over her. Freddy was about to make a remark about Annie having a lot of positive buoyancy in the chest area when he realized that Pamela was listening. Pamela had her eyebrows raised over Freddy's sheer lustful folly. Wayne and Annie and Freddy had been playing at this sex-banter for a long time; Pamela had not yet been initiated in the sport. Annie, realizing that Freddy had spoken with his genitalia and not his mouth, moved to counter and diffuse his transgression.

"Don't pay any attention to him, Pamela, he flirts *all* the time. He's just a big tease, that's all." Pamela's eyebrows returned to a lower, more reasonable level. It was all right. Freddy realized he got away with it. Wayne, of course, remained implacable as always, except for his fits of laughter during and after Freddy's spear fishing fiascoes, and pointed the boat for home.

****

The boat was up on plane and the wake was spread twenty-five wide feet after a man-high rooster tail on the broad, flat sea. Those two, Wayne and Annie, were once again eyes-front watching the outline of Key West grow larger against the sun-streaked clouds. Pamela and Freddy were again on the bench seat behind them, sea spray salted, sun-browned and bone weary and flushed with the internal fire of their exertions and externally with the outer glow of a day-long exposure to sun and water. Freddy was sitting on Pamela's left. Tall clouds behind them reflected the low sun, pouring soft light through the edges of her black hair, and played on the new sun-bleached red tinted highlights, hot red kindling ready to burst into flame. A catch light of silver sun off the molten water's surface was low in each of her eyes as the fireball burned in its last hour. Thigh against thigh, leaning her body into his, she sighed with the sensuality that comes after such a physical day. Her warm, salty, sea-smelling skin melted into Freddy's as he whispered in her ear, letting his lips work against that delicate sculpture, "Pamela, you're not going to make your plane."

"I know."

****

They headed home with their load of fish and crustaceans. Freddy was sweet-sad and with Pamela pressed against his side. He was too caught up in his emotions to yell as he normally would have at the occasional tourist who did not know where the hell he was going or the bubba parked in the street, blocking traffic while a fellow conch leaned on the car, strutted around and did his look-at-me macho rooster silliness act. Freddy unthinkingly swerved to the inside and passed the preening lothario without slowing down, causing the Latin man to retract his rear lest his pants receive a forty mile per hour Oldsmobile-buffed quick-shine. Annie glanced askew at the dreamy driver from her catty-cornered position in the back seat, worried that Freddy might run into something. Wayne uncharacteristically chortled and looked rearward with glee as a stream of Spanish invective was hurled at the car while the gap widened between the conscious would-be combatant and the unconscious Freddy. "Young love," said Wayne, to no one in particular.

The evening air was redolent with the pre-summer fragrance of a curiously early bloom of thin, white petals on the sweetest smelling, small-leafed jasmine. The lucky thumb-sized flowers with seven-pointed stars were backed by glossy dark green leaves.

Bracts of bougainvillea, red and pink, yellow and purple were standing in bunches and clinging to trellises or reaching from the tops of fences. As the evening advanced and the sun's long rays softened the sharp edges of the world, these omens seemed to auger well. A plane flew overhead as they approached the house. "Bye, Pamela," Freddy called to the plane and waved as it circled into its flight plan for Miami and points north.

****

They were ravenous. "Let's eat," cried Freddy as he jumped from the car. (He rarely used the doors.) Wayne began to organize the dinner preparations.

"Ok, who is going to clean the lobsters?"

"That's me, said Freddy, and he headed outside to remove the tails from the carapaces. Pamela volunteered to do the salad, and Wayne would, of course, cook the fish and lobsters. "Be sure to get some butter melted," Freddy called in, "Lots of butter."

"Freddy," Pamela called back, "Too much butter is no good for you." Freddy ignored the unprecedented piece of advice.

"Freddy will be the first person ever to O.D. on fried food," came Annie's hollow voice from somewhere. She was for some reason rooting around in the kitchen cabinets and had been talking with her head half into one of them. She emerged with a can of condensed chicken broth. "And why do you think Wayne always cooks the fish?" she continued, now more easily heard, standing in the center of the kitchen while hefting the can of chicken broth in one hand, the other hand on her hip, "Freddy uses enough garlic to kill a horse."

"A small horse," Wayne qualified. Freddy came back in with the tails. "I'm done. You guys cook, I'll watch." Freddy noticed Annie and the chicken broth can. "Whaterya gonna do with that, Annie?" She does not answer him but sets the can heavily on the counter. The realization is made that there is no vegetable in the offing. "Who's gonna do that?" asks Freddy, hoping it won't be him.

"*I'm* doing that," chimes Annie. A quizzical look passes between Freddy and Wayne.

"But Annie, honey," Wayne exclaimed, "you always do the salad."

"Pamela's doing the salad."

"Why didn't you ever cook before?" Freddy asked stupidly. Annie's head snaps toward him.

"'Cause no one ever _asked_ me to, that's why. Didn't you think I knew how to cook?" This brought no reply from Wayne as he apparently thought she didn't. "Gosh," was her airy excursion. They worked in silence, all except Freddy. Wayne pretending to watch the fish, Freddy setting the table finally for something to do to be less obvious, Pamela as the neutral observer, all stealing curious glances to see what Annie was up to. She ferreted in the refrigerator and came up with broccoli which she steamed. The boys could accept that. This is what they normally did with broccoli. Placing another saucepan on the stove, looking up and huffing at Wayne to get him to move out of the way, she melted a couple of tablespoons of butter added thyme and flour. Annie was generating quite a bit of interest. Heavy cream went in, and chicken broth. Wayne's hunk of snacking cheddar that kept the munchies in check on TV nights she grated and added slowly while stirring, along with the sandwich Swiss and Parmesan. The lads were now watching openly as Annie's quick, deft hands added things into the mix. The sauce smelled good. She then put the concoction in a square Pyrex dish, grated more cheese over it and browned it in the oven. Then she took the asparagus out and around each group of three wound a piece of prosciutto and that went into the oven as well. It began to dawn on Wayne that he should take Annie more seriously. The discovery made him wonder what else he had failed to see in her.

"We didn't know you could cook," Wayne said. "Were you keeping it a secret?"

"I didn't want to be just the maid around here, and I already do too much cleaning for you louts, but this routine around here was getting ridiculous. I like to cook, and besides, making a salad every day was making me crazy. Golly."

"Good, I was getting tired of doing everything around here anyway," said Freddy.

****

After dinner everyone sat around in front of the television, talking. At first the conversation was about literature and Annie once again caught Wayne by surprise by discussing the works of Tolkien (Knowing Annie as he did Freddy wasn't too shocked by that), H. Rider Haggard, Wodehouse, and Frank Baum with Pamela. The world was changing rapidly for Wayne.

Conversation slowed and segregated, the two couples polarizing as each pair shared their own intimate thoughts. Bootsie, Annie's cat, lay asleep (as usual) in the base of an outsized potted plant on a low table in the corner. Finally, Wayne and Annie went to bed and they were alone.

"Freddy?" said Pamela to get his attention after a long silence

"What?" he answered softly.

"I think Wayne is going to marry Annie."

"Does Wayne know that?"

"Not yet." They were silent again for a moment.

Freddy sat close to Pamela, arm loosely around her shoulders. "Are you in trouble with your boss because of me?"

"Not really, Freddy," she said in low tones. "I'll miss a day's work, but I'm in splendedly with the boss. He's my dad." So here was Freddy with another boss's daughter scenario.

"I guess that means your dad isn't going to be overly fond of me for making you miss that plane. What kind of work do you do?"

"Daddy owns a paper factory, 'Fisher Towels and Paper Products.' `Quality you can count on.'"

Freddy whistled softly. "So you must be a rich kid. What are you, an executrix or something?"

"No," Pamela said as she laughed. "My dad's making me work my way up. I won't have my own office for a year or so."

Freddy pooched out his stomach and assumed his most basso profundo tones. He said, "Someday, little Pamela, ahem, this will all be yours. Oh, yas indeed!"

"Wrong again, darling, I plan to get some experience with Daddy's business but it is not what I want to do for the rest of my life. That I haven't decided yet."

"Pamela, I know what you should do," Freddy said as the widening of his eyes betrayed his emotion, "You should move down here and live with me."

She sat silent for a moment, then: "Freddy, I can't. I've only known you for a few days, that is not enough time to make a decision this important." She saw his face cloud over.

"How much time do you need to know how you feel about me?"

"Freddy, you're kind, you're smart - but you don't seem to care about what is going on around you. I've never believed that ignorance is bliss, but Freddy, you live by it! You're not making any effort."

"Are you asking me to change, Pamela?"

"No, Freddy, I wouldn't ask anyone to do that. And I hardly know you. I do know that any change must come from you, and only if you want to. I've think I've seen the real Freddy, in things you've said, in the way you've been toward me. The Freddy you portray to everyone else is an image."

"Is it?" With the two words, he made it clear he wanted an explanation.

"I think it is. You are living your reputation as a funny vagabond. The reputation is in control now, not you. Don't you see that, Freddy?"

"I'm trying to." He took a breath. "Even if I am doing as you say, I don't have much reason to do anything else, do I?"

"That is for you to decide. You think about it. Give me some time to think also, and sort things out. Don't get ahead of yourself. Go slow." He wondered if he had gotten in over his head. He wanted Pamela to stay, but for what? To cohabitate for a while? He had done that trip before. He didn't think that was all there was to it. Pamela was unsure of what ground she stood on with him, he could see it in her eyes; she searched his face, her mouth tight, neck arched and chin raised toward him. She looked into his heart for answers. Hands on her shoulders, he kissed the furrowed brow until her forehead relaxed and she closed her eyes. Freddy finally spoke.

"Ok Pamela, that's what we'll do. You know I want you here, but I can see why you would be unsure of me." Her hands caressed his lower back; her breasts were against his chest.

"Don't worry, Freddy, you'll see me again, if you want to. If you don't forget about me by next week, that is. Call me in a month or so."

They sat for a while locked in their own thoughts while holding each other. Pamela wondered if Freddy could accept the change in his life a relationship would bring. Freddy's own feeling was that he had heard yet another version of the "famous last words".

They went to bed, and the next day Pamela left on her plane.

Part Two

Things Change

Chapter Eight - Freddy's Tailspin

"A cluster of strong thunderstorms is approaching the lower keys from the southeast. Boaters may expect strong, gusty winds and heavy rains in the area of these storms. At this time we have 85 degrees and a forty percent chance of showers with southeast winds at 10 to 15 knots. Seas outside the reef 3 to 5 feet, 2 to 4 inside, higher in and near thunderstorms. Weather conditions are not considered favorable for tropical storm development. Today might prove to be a day much like yesterday."

****

Thunder! It is the hurricane season again and lightning streaking across the sky is a frequent occurrence. The days are marked by frequent wind changes and storms in the area. The isolated systems don't last long; the squalls come through and are quickly gone or rain themselves out. When a big blow is within a few hundred miles there are days of sustained gray skies and frequent periods of rain.

They are fortunate to be residing in the keys. Dade County to the north is beset by heavy rains at this time of year and will get teeming thunder showers on many days of the season, followed by the cloying steam bath the sun generates afterward, driving the temperature up ten degrees or more when the rains cease and the clouds dissipate.

In Key West, the morning's panorama is filled with an abundance of cumulous clouds. At first light they are tall specters all around the island but rarely overhead. As the half-light becomes daylight the clouds go from black silhouettes to gray, to white cotton columns. They seem to grow and get big heads as the air starts to rise and the sun heats them and inflates their tops. They take shapes. Elephants. Anvils. They are a line of giant poodles walking on their hind quarters, forepaws on each other's backs like circus dogs marching around a giant ring. To Freddy these clouds often appear to be strange four-footed animals with odd appendages or peculiar shapes. Sometimes they are an old man, sometimes with a pipe. These images give way as the clouds burn off or rain themselves out and disappear. Then follow the hot, sunny hours. Freddy has frittered away the entire day.

It is an evening in early June, the start of the hurricane season; six weeks have passed since Pamela has gone. It has been, and promises to continue to be, a stormy year. Freddy sits in his favorite rattan chair on the patio of his favorite ocean front resort contemplating the sky. Now the wind shifts and the picture becomes confused, the upper airs become streaked and wispy as clouds have their tops curled, spiraled, and torn away by high winds aloft. The sky is a maelstrom, mirroring his inner feelings. It is a place where all types of clouds are on display, one kind overlaying another into the distance. Freddy muses on the permutations, the apparent confusion wrought by forces with their own sense of order, a natural result of what has gone before.

The last of the light diffuses through the clouds as he sits and watches the sunset. Color bursts and patterned gradations from red to orange to silver-gray occur across the sky and then to indigo at the edges of the setting sun's corona as Earendil the Mariner steers his gray Elven ship, whose lantern is the fruit of the tree grown in the light of the Simarill, wrested from the crown of the dark lord, out past the edge of the earth, as he has for days uncounted.

Night comes and the clouds recede. They back off from the full rising moon, shrinking from its greenish cast. The glow blends to the deepest blue of India ink at the farthest reaches of the atmosphere. The pull of the big green-white globe on the ocean had the tides high and nocturnal revelers at their rowdiest, but Freddy sits quietly gazing at the sky, morose and moody, and muddled from too much beer.

****

Soon it was two months since he had seen Pamela. He thought back on his attempts to call her. The first phone call, some weeks ago, resulted in a recorded instruction to leave his name, number, and the time he called. He hung up. He hated those things. Next time he tried, again the recording. Three rings and a click. Then the speech. As instructed he gave his name and phone number, feeling foolish, screw the time of the call. Freddy thought of giving his social security number in an attempt at frivolity to assuage his discomfort at the prospect of purporting his admiration for the woman to the device, but then thought, the hell with it, look what happened to Nixon. Annie and Wayne tried to lend him encouragement, but he remained sullen, disgruntled, grumpy, and petulant.

When Pamela returned his call the conversation was about the things she needed to catch up with at work, and the weather up there in Cincinnati and anything else to steer him away from the subject of when and if she would return. That was the way of things, though, to Freddy's mind. Once she was back in familiar surroundings he figured the memory of the vacation trip to Key West was just that - a nice bunch of memories already fading, and nothing more, emotions shared and feelings expressed between them already relegated to the past, something to look back on years from now. Freddy tried being philosophical about it and that made him thirsty, so before long he was comfortably immersed in his old liquid lifestyle. Perhaps there was a touch of malaise to his manner, but that would sort itself out, or drown. For the present he was all gregarioused out. Lugubrious was a state of mind, and probably a hoax at that.

Wayne was looking for a real job and thoughts of settling down were baking in his brain pan. He didn't know yet whether he would stay for another season in Key West and Freddy thought the nesting urge might be upon him. Who could fault him for wanting to find a sensible place to hibernate snug and secure with his cuddly blond California honey bear? And Freddy's behavior lately wasn't likely to make them feel inclined to stay.

In the long term, it was doubtful that there would be enough boat work to get them through the "cold" weather, and Freddy might also have to try his hand at something of an establishment kind of employ. His lachrymosity of late was already affecting his work at the marina. Small things were going wrong, like dropping electrically powered hand tools over the side and stripping screws to fittings he was supposed to be installing. He didn't think that the hangovers improved his work quality, either, but he didn't care. It was putting a strain on Wayne to have to go over and correct Freddy's work and Freddy knew it. Out of respect for their friendship Freddy tried harder to be more efficient on the job.

Hopefully, everything that was going to go wrong did. For a while Freddy did well. He tried staying home nights, but gave that up also when he found himself making cat noises to Bootsie, who was spending a rare night out in the yard caterwauling with others of his ilk. Freddy assumed, correctly, that Bootsie was nearly beyond that sort of thing, but he supposed that the cat had his memories just like he did. Freddy chimed in; trying for quality as well as volume, but his feline friends remained unimpressed. Perhaps Bootsie was getting used to him. The cat was looking much better since its hair was growing back in.

Besides Freddy's regression to his former sodden self, his relationship with Annie's cat was another source of tension in the house, between him and Annie. She couldn't understand why Bootsie gravitated toward Freddy when he treated the cat so poorly. On a recent morning Freddy had cause to propel Bootsie from his bed. The cat's outcry in protest prompted Annie to come to her pet's defense.

"Freddy, you leave my cat alone," Annie warned as she walked purposefully into the living room to confront him later that morning.

Freddy replied, "I woke up again with Bootsie's foot in my mouth again. Yeeach. Tell your cat to sleep with its foot in *your* mouth! I have dreams that I'm suffocating 'cause it's sleeping on my chest. How would you like to sleep with something heavy on *your* chest?" She reddened. He immediately regretted saying that.

"Well, keep your dumb door closed, and then Bootsie can't get in."

"What? And block the air flow? Then I actually *will* suffocate."

Annie got into one of her "Oh, Freddy," looks, the one where she breathes heavily and sighs. She thought of him then as a recalcitrant child who would not understand that he had erred. She worried about Freddy, and she feared for her superannuated somnambulistic cat as well. "Freddy, please don't yell at him or treat him rough anymore," she pleaded, "He's old."

"Annie, all I did was toss him on the floor. I was half asleep, for chrissake! I didn't know what I was doing. The dopey cat scared the wits out of me!"

"*Look* at him, Freddy." Freddy dutifully looked at the cat, catatonic again on the couch, as Annie had bidden him. "He is a *good* cat," said Annie. "He must have had a hard life." She paused here and gazed fondly upon the decrepit animal. "He was so skinny when I found him, and now look how good he looks!" Freddy decided he must be looking at the wrong cat.

"His hair was all falling out, and now he has a nice, fine coat! With his white face and white chest and white feet and gray fur it makes him look like he's dressed formal, like he's wearing a morning suit. He doesn't have long to go, I know, so please let him have a nice time while he's still with us."

He tried to envision the cat's fur as a suit of wedding clothes. It wasn't as absurd as it sounded with Annie's imploring face beaming at him, given her affection for the ever-sleeping feline. Freddy resolved to try to get his air conditioner fixed and keep the door to his room closed. He would be more careful of the numb creature from now on.

The cat, deprived of one of its favorite places to sleep, developed a new gambit. Bootsie would leave the house early in the morning when Annie went out to do her running, climb up onto the roof and jump with a bang onto the top of Freddy's air conditioner, startling him awake. Freddy would try to puzzle out why this was happening each morning to no avail. Bootsie would then settle down, lulled by the air conditioner's vibration, for a nice warm nap in the sun.

****

Due to what Freddy regarded as unprecedented and injurious treatment at the hands of the formerly wonderful and now heartless Pamela, and his pondering and pouting and general disagreeability because of that slight of mind, he got less interested in exercise. He did some swimming, not enough. No tennis and bicycling for bar transportation only. He had increased his gross tonnage by several pounds and until recently was as pasty and pliable as pasta allowed to percolate past its prime. He got back to the *al dente* stage gradually by starting in again with some serious swimming, and the hitting of a few tennis balls. The increase in outdoor activities had turned his epidermis from apple blossom white to cherry pink. "If I wasn't such a well-lubricated individual," he said, "my skin would slough off like a Nevada mudslide."

****

The boat was leaking badly enough to be a nuisance. Freddy had taken to making solo swims from shore, about six hundred yards out, to look for lobsters. Free-swimming and towing a dive flag on a buoy with a Styrofoam float, he took twenty minutes to get out far enough to seriously deplete the lobster population (get his limit). Any closer and there was competition from guys working the easier areas from two-man inflatable Sears's boats and people towing around inner tubes with baskets in their centers. The swim was therapeutic. The drag of the flag and float felt good. Once he got over the anxiety of being out there alone it was lovely and peaceful, with no human sounds to interfere. Anything goes wrong now - heart attack, black-out, bump on the head, and he needn't worry about anything ever again. Swimming past rocks and sand patches well known to him, then over seaweed and grassy areas - always slim pickings - there was a time to think uncluttered thoughts, and the passage of time itself was difficult to judge for lack of a point of reference. His thoughts swam ahead of him in anticipation of the tasty crawlers up ahead. When he got to the scree and rock piles he knew he was over four hundred yards out. He knew a big eel who lived here. Farther ahead were the coral heads.

****

Today the big eel was coiled by its hole, below Freddy and off to the right. Freddy was disposed kindly toward the sea snake, almost as though he had seen and been recognized by an acquaintance. There were a few fish darting and hovering around the rocks. A spear gun would be of little use here today or on most days, the attendant fish being tropicals, a handful of small yellowtail, a few small snappers. Those ubiquitous grunts. A cormorant was paddling along not far from him low in the water, decks awash, its head turning constantly, searching for fish. Freddy admired the birds, black, goose-necked, excellent swimmers but poor flyers. "Hey Cormie," Freddy called, giving the bird a name Annie might have invented, "make a dive." Freddy submerged and watched the bird's webbed feet paddling along beneath the bulk of its body. The bird dove as directed and Freddy kept pace with it as it swam underwater. Aware of Freddy and annoyed, the canny fisher surfaced and then took flight, its feet flapping on the surface half a dozen times at quickening intervals as it flapped its undersized wings frantically for a final push into the air.

Another hundred and fifty yards and he was at the start of a cluster of coral heads, his secret and that of living here now and those before his time, those who long since vacated Key West. His thoughts turned to another, a tender-tailed swimmer. He thought of her black hair floating languorously around her face when she was motionless under the water, fluttering and waving, pulsating like a hydra as she swam. And legs, nice ones, kicking from the base of the two firm double rounds (almost too round!) halves of her behind. The lines of her body all curves and contours most attractive, another kind of feast. The dry-land sybarite is now a philosopher very alone out at sea, thinking back on what has transpired and putting reasons to those things, his mind in a state of calm resignation. Eventually, he knows, he must return to shore where temptations there will dull his senses. The worst was yet to come. For the short term, anyway.

****

Finally, in desperation, Freddy tried writing a letter to Pamela. It was on a Sunday morning after too much Saturday night drinking, the worst kind of all. Annie and Wayne were taking a holiday in Miami. Freddy was taking care of the house. And Bootsie.

****

At about 11:30 in the morning Freddy awoke. The A/C was out of action once again. He was lying in a pool of his sweat; the heat and oppressive humidity combined to break through his drunken stupor and conspired to awaken him.

His first thoughts on waking were of Pamela. It was vexatious. It bothered him that he should be so affected by her, now that she no longer seemed to have an interest in him. He blamed her for the way he was acting, although he knew she was not at fault. He would damn her and then recant, feeling sorry that he had thought such evil thoughts which could add to the hex upon him. He got up. There was no breeze. Belatedly, he turned on the ceiling fan, mad at himself for not doing so last night before he passed out. Now the sheets would have to be changed.

Stumbling and shuffling into the living room, he saw the carnage. He made a mess of it the night before and knew he had better clean it up or Annie would be mad. Both Annie and Wayne were tolerating him too much more of a degree than he deserved, and he knew it. His eyes took in the scene.

Bootsie was sleeping in the corner, at the base of the planter. There was a plastic to-go cup half full of Scotch on the coffee table. The room smelled of the stale alcohol vapor of the Scotch evaporating into the still air and hanging there. He picked up the cup to take to the trash can. A notepad and a pen sat on the table next to where the Scotch had been. He stopped and looked down at it and saw some unintelligible scribblings on it which he knew to be "Dear Pamela," written many times, as though he could not get it down right, to where he was satisfied with it. The muscles around his eyes constricted until his fuzzy mind focused enough to recall that he had tried to write a letter to Pamela last night.

The cushions on the sofa were in disarray. Shoe marks were at the end of it. Apparently he also decided to take a nap on the sofa sometime during the course of the evening. The last thing he remembered was trying to turn the stereo down with the TV remote control. He also had a vague and not-so-fond memory of beer, rum, and chocolate cake, and some black guy giving him a screwdriver he had ordered because he said it wasn't strong enough. Freddy, always the health nut, drank it for the vitamin C.

The memories were out of sequence, jumbled. He remembered where the chocolate cake came in when he saw the clue - crumbs on the rug around the coffee table, brown smudges ground into the fabric of one of the seat cushions on the sofa. Freddy walked into the kitchen, poured the Scotch into the sink and looked into the refrigerator to confirm his fears. Annie's delicious double-chocolate cake with Dutch chocolate almond frosting now looked like Mount Saint Helens after the blast. The remaining half was gouged and angled like the mountain whose side had been blown away. He wondered what he could do about that.

He could try to clean the house, remove the cake and deny any knowledge of its whereabouts, but he could not keep going the way he was. He had to confront the problem, and Freddy saw the problem as resolving the matter of Pamela. Freddy went back to the living room with a glass of orange juice and sat down at the coffee table to write the letter he tried to write the night before.

He tore off the used top sheet and carefully wrote "Dear Pamela." Just then a noise from the corner interrupted him. Bootsie had his mouth open and was going **ACK! ACK!** His eyes were distended and his entire skinny body stiffened enough to see the undulation of his ribs. He evacuated his bowels and bladder and rolled from the planter onto the table, landing on his back. Even Freddy knew that cats were not supposed to do that, they were supposed to land on their feet. Bootsie rolled once again, off the table, and came to rest on the floor. Bootsie the cat was dead. Just before his death Bootsie had lifted his head and turned it to Freddy with an understanding, almost benignly forgiving look on his slender, serious face. At that moment, Freddy knew that Bootsie loved him. But now he had to face reality, and Freddy knew that there was absolutely no way to convince Annie it wasn't his fault. Now, he was in trouble.

Chapter Nine - Freddy's Perigee

Annie and Wayne returned from Miami at three-thirty. Freddy was sitting innocently atop the stain from the chocolate icing on the sofa when they walked in. The sofa was still damp from the upholstery shampoo Freddy used on it and he was feeling uncomfortable but afraid to move, so he sat there suspiciously. He had fared better with the rug - the ground-in cake had come out for the most part, but his scrubbing had been in a heavily trafficked area and now the light beige rug had a lighter beige oval on it at the end of the coffee table. There was a spot on the rug about a foot and a half across that was cleaner than the rest of it. There hadn't been time to clean the whole rug.

Freddy cleaned the kitchen, trimmed the cake into a wedge that tapered from a broad base at the bottom to a small, iced triangle at the top so that it looked like it was distorted and out of perspective like a picture of the flat iron building taken from ground level with a brownie camera. He ate as much of what he trimmed away as he could, not wanting to throw any of Annie's cake away. He felt that that would have been an insult to her cooking. Now he felt sick.

He cleaned up after poor dead Bootsie and put him into his litter box and buried him in the backyard. Now, seated before them gingerly, he waited for the inevitable.

"Hi, Freddy," Annie said sweetly as she came in the Florida room door and spotted him sitting precariously on the wet living room sofa. She was smiling and looked relaxed. She must have had a good time on her holiday.

Annie looked around and knew something was wrong immediately. The place was too clean. Freddy looked as though he had swallowed a mouse.

"Hi, Annie," Freddy said weakly, with a nervous smile on his face. Wayne followed Annie in and he exchanged greetings with Freddy as well. Annie continued to look around keenly. She sniffed the air. It smelled like Lysol. Freddy had used it to mask the alcohol odor.

"Freddy, what is different around here?" asked Annie. "Is everything all right?"

"Actually, Annie, I made a big mess. I only just now finished cleaning it up."

"Oh, Freddy, what *ever* am I going to do with you?" She scrutinized the kitchen, and then the living room. "Gee, Freddy, it doesn't look too bad." She paused as she looked down and spotted the light beige oval on the carpet.

"What did you do to the rug?" she asked as she sat on the sofa beside him on the cushion he had tried to clean. "It's wet!" she said, and stood again quickly. The corner of Freddy's mouth turned up slightly in a timid false smile.

"Freddy, you're hiding something. Get up."

He did, and she saw the stain on the sofa cushion, once a few small spots, now spread of over a much larger area due to Freddy's efforts. Still Freddy said nothing. Wayne looked on. After some heavy thought, Annie said, "My cake!" and went to the refrigerator. She removed the remainder of the cake from the refrigerator and looked at it ruefully.

"Freddy, where's the rest of it? How do you do these things?" The question was asked more in puzzled dismay than in anger.

"I'm sorry, Annie, I had too much to drink, I guess."

"You guess! Freddy, this has to stop. You are making life miserable around here lately. And you make fun of people. I have news for you, mister, people don't think it's funny when you mimic them!" She looked in the corner of the room. She noticed that something was missing. It was Bootsie's litter box. It took her a moment to work herself up before she said anything.

"**Where is my cat**!" she demanded. She turned to face him squarely, shoulders tensed and face coloring. "Freddy, what did you do to my cat?" Her fists were clenched in anger at her sides.

"It wasn't my fault, Annie, honest."

"Where is he?"

Freddy drew a breath and composed himself, let it out and spoke slowly and solemnly. "He died, Annie."

"Oh **no**! What did you do to him?" She was near tears. With red eyes and with her fists clenched she asked, "Freddy, did you throw him?"

"No, Annie, I didn't throw him. I think he had a heart attack. He just rolled out of the planter and died."

"Rolled…?"

"Out of the planter and onto the table." Freddy was gesturing with his hands as he spoke. "And then onto the floor."

"How horrible!" She was beginning to soften. "Where is he? You didn't put him in the garbage, did you Freddy?"

"No, Annie, I wouldn't do that," he said hastily. "I buried him."

"Where?" she said tenderly.

"In the back yard, next to the Christmas palm. The one he used to like to scratch." She broke down in heart-rending sobs.

"Well, thank you for that, Freddy." Bleary eyed and tearful, she came to him and gave him a hug around the neck. She sat again, oblivious to the wetness of the sofa, and wept on his shoulder. She sat up and sniffed. "What did you bury him in?" She asked sadly.

"What?" Freddy was feeling trapped again.

"His coffin. What did you bury him in?" After a pause, she stopped sniffling. Annie thought about the missing litter box and had a horrible thought. Her face became more calm, her cheeks and mouth relaxing some from the doleful expression of a moment before.

"You didn't bury Bootsie in his litter box, did you, Freddy?" She asked, her tone menacing once again, not wanting to believe that this was so. She saw in his face that he did.

"Freddy, you did, didn't you? You buried Bootsie in his litter box! How could you?" She looked in his face, daring him to explain it away. He couldn't. He couldn't tell her, "But Annie, it was only a cat!" Annie walked rapidly to her bedroom and slammed the door. At least Bootsie had his morning suit on, thought Freddy.

Freddy went to his room and got his tennis racket. He had to do something. He would hit tennis balls against a wall and try to work out his frustrations. "Wayne, I gotta get out of here for a while. Tell Annie I'm sorry."

"Ok, Freddy, I understand. Annie will be all right. Just give her some time, that's all." Freddy nodded and left the house.

****

Freddy's personal perigee came later that night in a bar called the Mascot. To imagine this place, you must first see dusty, pot-holed Caroline Street as it was then, before the development started. Caroline runs northeast-southwest from Fort Street to Grinnell.

Whitehead is one of the two sister streets paralleling the main drag, Duval. The other sister is Simonton. These three streets run roughly north to south from ocean to gulf, Whitehead to the west of Duval, Simonton to the east, Duval in the middle. These three streets form the backbone of the downtown area. James Street, near Caroline's opposite end, is one block south of Caroline's eastern limit. It also runs northeast to southwest and is next to the ancient electric company whose six superannuated boilers used to belch black smoke into the sky, raining black carbon particles of sooty grit on the aging surrounding neighborhood.

The Mascot was one-third of the way from the Grinnell Street end on Caroline and two blocks southeast of the shrimp docks. This location on Caroline, the shortest route back to the boats from the downtown bars, made it a convenient and easily accessible last stop for those shrimpers who were returning to their boats after being thrown out of those downtown establishments to which Caroline Street was their link. After fourteen days of backbreaking work at sea, some of the shrimpers tended to drink a bit, and they liked to talk. They did so loudly, as though they were still shouting over a diesel engine whose muffler ceased to function years ago. They liked to party and would brook no interference from those who would keep them from their booze, especially in their own territory. And the Mascot was their territory.

The outside of the building was just as dingy as it seemed - a stuccoed block building with black soot in the tops of the stuccoed ridges, a three step walk-up entrance at the front right corner of the building and a garden of mostly dirt. Oppressively small, the low roof fit it to a tee. Immediately upon entering there was a pool table.

The length of the pool table ran the width of the building plus a little more at each end allowing some space in which to make a shot. There was a small horseshoe-shaped bar set off the back wall and not much else. The long dimension of the bar ran front to back for twelve feet and the short leg at the bottom of the "U" connecting the two longer legs was as long as the eight-foot pool table. Behind the bar was an amazingly small young woman, considering the size and demeanor of her charges.

Someone was saving aluminum. There were hundreds of beer cans, uncollapsed and stacked fairly neatly, in the hall leading to the restroom in the back of the building. The stack was about three feet high, five feet long and two feet out from the wall opposite the restroom door. The windows of the establishment were protected by wrought-iron bars. It is not known whether they were to protect the inmates from an outside threat or to keep those within from injuring passers-by. Some of the windows still had glass in them.

Freddy at his lowest ebb wandered up the steps into this place that night after a warm-up on the tennis court, and another warm-up at Sloppy Joe's. By the time of his arrival at the Mascot Freddy was very warmed up indeed, and still in his tennis clothes. He had a silver lame' scarf - from who knows who or where - tied around his neck. He made it through the door and stood at the entrance foggily scanning the occupants.

The drunks sitting on the right side of the bar were in various states of hairiness and dishevelment. Moving his gaze to the left and downward he saw the little red head of the bartender-pixie. Her hands were flat on the bar and her elbows were up in an authoritative stance. She stared quizzically at Freddy as if to say, "I wonder what this character is doing here." To the left of the bar there was a relatively clean-cut guy sitting next to an enormous black-bearded one in a polo shirt with broad, horizontal black and white stripes.

Two people were playing pool, and of course with Freddy being in the doorway and the pool table being just the other side of the doorway, Freddy was in their way. One of the players glared threateningly, but Freddy was too fogged to notice. Things were looking dark indeed as all eyes turned to Freddy to stare the newcomer down. Freddy was oblivious and could not be stared down. The player whose way Freddy had violated started forward as though he intended to remove the oddly dressed interloper physically from his path without so much so much preamble as a spoken word. The situation was saved, temporarily, as a friendly voice came forth from the other pool player.

"Hey Fred, uh, what 'er you doin' here, tryin' to get yerself killed of somethin'?" It was Cap'n Walter, of the shrimp boat *Southern Lady.* He was one of the farther-ranging shrimp boat captains as to choice and variety of places in town he would visit when not at sea, and was allowed in. A thoroughly nice fellow, one of his most endearing nuances of character was a penchant for catching an adversary unawares from behind with a roundhouse punch to the kidney. He and Freddy had gotten drunk together quite a few times at Sloppy Joe's.

"Walter, ole buddy, goodaseeya."

"Uh, Fred, you better sit down afor ya fall down an' have yerself a drink. Michelob, is it? Peggy, get this guy a drink."

"What'll it be, stranger?" she asks. She emphasizes "Stranger." A voice says, "fruit cup is more like it," Freddy doesn't hear it.

"A Michelob an' a Peach Schnapps, please."

"What? I don't think we got that."

"Michelob?"

"No, Snops." She starts looking.

"I been drinkin' 'em all night," Freddy tells everyone. "Peachalobs, I call 'em. They're great." No one is interested.

Peggy gets a Michelob out of the cooler and she is surprised to find some Peach Schnapps as well. Not knowing the nature of the liquid she pours a few ounces in a rocks glass.

"Gee, Peggy, you're a cute little thing." She decidedly is not, but most anything would look cute to Freddy right now. This is not the right thing to say to this young woman. She responds:

"I might be little but you better not try to give me any shit. I got a lotta friends here and they'll tear you apart." This Freddy forgets instantly and he tries fruitlessly to engage Peggy in conversation since no one else at the bar seems disposed to talk, but she is bored, and wants no part of it. Meanwhile, Cap'n Walter's pool partner has been making some god-awful shots and has finally lost the game despite Walter's good-natured clowning around and taking ridiculously hard shots instead of the obvious ones just to keep the other man in the game. The loser misses what is to be his final shot - Walter runs the balls and ends the game - and the man is amazed that he did not fare better. To vent his frustration and add yet a bit more venting to the establishment he throws his pool cue stick violently through the window, smashing it against the bars outside. It bounces between them and breaks one of the remaining pieces of glass. The cue stick drops to the ground below the window into the sick, sooty bushes outside. The man sits down, disgruntled and grumbling.

"Freddy," Walter says, "Come on n' play some pool, I'm fresh outta partners. All these guys wanna do is drink, and fight." So Freddy makes the effort. He is a comic sight in these surroundings. The back of his white tennis shorts have a black dye stain on them from a new, cheap bicycle seat. Where the bicycle is locked he does not remember. The scarf is dangling from his neck and his shirt is half out. His knees are dirty. Stalking stiff-legged about the table he finds his shot. Bending, he eyes up the angles, takes a couple of test strokes with the cue stick, decides on right english, and strokes the cue ball. Roars of laughter erupt as the cue ball goes off at an oblique angle. With a grimace Freddy picks up the chalk. "Musta forgot to chalk up. Couldn't get any english on the ball." Walter sinks a couple and then it is again Freddy's turn. Same thing. Each subsequent attempt to shoot results in the cue ball scurrying off to one side or the other. Each time it goes skittering off in one direction or another Freddy is met with gales of laughter. The game is soon over and Freddy and Walter return to the bar and sit down. Walter is still laughing.

The momentary diversion of a clatter of cans comes from the rear of the building as the one clean-cut guy knocks down the stack of neatly piled empty cans in the back hall while on his way to try to find the restroom. His navigation and stabilization systems appear to be malfunctioning. The man falls into the pile, passes out, and urinates. He remains lying there in the pile of empties. This is but a temporary distraction for the crowd at the bar because the guy sleeping among the empty beer cans is one of them and Freddy is not. Freddy remains the butt of derision.

From somewhere Wayne has entered unnoticed by the ribald group and he looks around warily. Freddy is as yet unaware of his presence.

"Freddy," Cap'n Walter asks, "didn't anybody ever tell ya to check yer cue tip before ya started shootin'?"

"What are you tryin' to tell me, Walter ole' pal?"

"Uh, the cue tip on the stick you was usin', that little piece a leather on the end? It didn't have none. I mean it wasn't there at all. An' you chalkin' an' chalkin' the wood end like a fool all the while."

The general hubbub of mirth and derision increases as does Freddy's displeasure. The big man in the polo shirt says, "You're a goddam idiot," in the tone of a polar bear. His laughter resounds in a rolling, resonant peal. This is more than Freddy can bear, and he becomes indiscreet.

"You guys don't look like geniuses to me. Your friend is layin' in the back there in his own piss - I'm sure that takes a lotta talent. And you look a big fat bumble bee in that stupid polo shirt. With brains to match, I'll bet." Silence ensues and even the hardened patrons of the place turn to look in awe as the big man starts to stand and continues rising until he is taller by four inches than anyone in the room, or about twice as tall as the bartender. Freddy knows he has committed a breach of etiquette as the bumble bee looms ever larger above him seeking redress. Wayne is still unseen by Freddy and is unlikely to be noticed now by anyone since Goliath has captured everyone's attention. Wayne watches the large man approach Freddy and quietly circles behind him. Good ole' Cap'n Walter has prudently moved aside, allowing the agitated antagonist full access to Freddy.

Wayne is six-two and built well, but no match for the sheer size of the man attacking Freddy. The man now has an outsized hand on Freddy's throat and is throttling him. Still, Wayne comes on, moving to counter the big man's aggression. He raises up on the balls of his feet, reaches over the man's shoulder and grabs the two smallest fingers on the hand on his friend's throat and bends them backward, putting his not insignificant weight into the move. Wayne stays in back of the man and continues to apply pressure, spinning the man around as he bends the fingers backward until they snap. There is a devastatingly fast shuffle of feet as the man stops his spin and Wayne's work shoes come down hard on the flimsily sandaled toes of the still reeling man. He recoils in pain, face contorted. It is all he can do to lean back on the bar and clutch his hurt hand with the other. The fingers seem to be at a disgusting angle. The crowd is bewildered and still too stunned to act.

"Let's go, Freddy," Wayne commands. Freddy is sufficiently sobered by the scuffle to know that this is a prudent course of action. They make for the door and Freddy sees that the Olds is sitting there with the engine running and the top down. The car is parked facing the wrong way and the driver-side door is open at the curb.

They hurry to the car and Wayne jumps behind the wheel after pushing Freddy over the side of the car into the back seat. "Oof!" He exclaims. They speed off in a cloud of dust as the tires screech trying to find traction on the sandy street. From the back seat comes, "The Wayne in Spain, falls mainly in the play-ain, I think he's got it!"

"Freddy, don't sing!"

****

All was peaceful and safe the next morning at the house when the phone rang. Except for Freddy, the house was empty. Freddy assumed that Wayne had gone to work, and Annie was probably out running. The intrusion by the phone required that Freddy leave his bed, find his balance, walk to the phone and lift the receiver to make it stop ringing.

"Uh, Freddy?" It was Cap'n Walter.

"Yeah, this is Freddy," Freddy replied. Walter was upset. He said he was supposed to go shrimping today.

"What are you telling me for?" He is told by Walter that the big bumble bee of last night was his first mate. "So what?" Freddy asks. Well, he wasn't going to go shrimping today because of what happened in the Mascot last night. "Jesus, Walter," Freddy intoned, "All Wayne did was break up a fight. A fight that might have got me killed, I might add."

"Uh, yeah, Fred," came the reply, "but did he have to break the guy's fingers and toes?" he snarled angrily.

"I'm sorry, Walter."

"Oh, he'll be OK; he's got his Masters dee-gree. He'll get a job somewhere, but what about me? I'm stuck without a crew." He hung up.

Sitting blank-faced for a moment and thinking, Freddy wondered what he really knew about Wayne. He was never disposed to speak about his past. How did he learn to fight like that? Freddy recalled the cold, relentless, slightly wild glare in Wayne's eyes last night as he subdued the much larger man. He remembered that look and for a moment that look had penetrated his inebriation and chilled him to the bone. At that moment, he had been frightened. Perhaps there was something in Wayne's past that Freddy didn't want to know about. He decided not to think about it and headed back to bed. Unknown to Wayne or Freddy, a man near the wall in the dark corner of the bar had seen Wayne enter and backed into the shadows. Today he was making a phone call to Colombia.

****

He lifted the last chip carefully from its anti-static foam packaging and inserted it into the circuit board. The boards he had prepared fit the expansion slots for a number of personal computers, but these spare parts would never work in any machine in which they were installed. The chips in the boards were meant for quite a different application; they were key components in highly classified military guidance system radars.

He'd found a man in the heat of the New Jersey summer willing to sell out his country in one of the last areas in which it had technological pre-eminence. For a large cash sum the man had diverted the shipment of chips from a Silicon Valley manufacturer which were to be delivered to a New Jersey systems-engineering firm working under government contract to a computer mail-order warehouse twenty minutes from his Sand Bridge Virginia home. They would soon be bound for Miami to be delivered by the broker there to a Central American government official sympathetic to the country's Soviet military advisors. Soon they would be in the Soviet military equipment they were designed to outsmart.

Chapter Ten - Wayne Takes Charge

Freddy hadn't been lying there for long when whom schud retoin but Vane. Oye Gevalt. And Freddy wid an aching head.

"Good morning, Frederick." It seemed they had reverted to the days of stuffy old Wayne. "You really overdid it last night, Freddy, this has to stop."

"Oye, Gevalt, I'm such a meshuggah...."

"Fred, cut that out, it's insulting. And snap out of it. You can't go on living like this."

"Who's going to stop me?"

"I am. Whether you like it or not."

"Who the hell are you to tell me what to do?"

"I'm the guy who's going to straighten you out." Wayne's tone was ominous. The angry tension drained from Freddy's body. Sapped of the strength to resist, his next words were much more subdued.

"All right, Wayne, what do you want me to do?"

"For a start, take an interest in the work we are doing in order to make a living. Second, start acting like a human being and stop mooning over Pamela. Third, stop making fun of people. You think you're funny, but you're insulting them." Freddy hung his head and said nothing. "I think right now you should get something in your stomach."

"I couldn't keep it down right now, Wayne. My mouth feels like peach fuzz. What I need is a bit of the hair of the dog that bit me."

"Just one." Freddy liked this kind of therapy. Perhaps Wayne's program might not be so bad.

"You got it."

Freddy reeled in the sunlight when they stepped outside. He got into the passenger seat of the Olds. Wayne followed him outside and went around the car and sat in the driver's seat. He started the car.

"Where to?" he asked. "Want to go back to the Mascot?" I'm sure they'd be happy to see you."

"God, no!" Wayne drove to the Bottle Cap. Freddy wore his dark glacier glasses - silver mirrored sunglasses with black leather side panels for cutting off sidelight and stray reflections from the inside surface of the sunglasses when out on the water or during a hangover – Freddy was not about to encounter a glacier, Freddy hadn't seen snow in four years - and he let his eyes rest in the relative darkness and head recline on the back of the seat for the duration of the trip as the sun beat down on his forehead, cheeks, and chin.

Soon they were climbing the two tiled steps at the entrance of the Bottle Cap and passing from the glare of the early sun into the dim interior. The bar lights were not yet on. The bar's illumination at this hour came through the old-fashioned glass-brick front window sections at either side of the entrance. Freddy crinkled his nose. It smelled early. The morning smells of the bar were a blend of several distinct and easily recognizable odors. The windows had just been opened and the fans had not yet been turned on to get the air moving. The atmosphere within was thick with the scents of alcohol and stale beer, nicotine and the septic smell of bar rags soon to be plunged into bleach. In the old bar, in the sub-tropics as it was, there was the cloying odor of old plumbing and open drains allowing sewage smell in from the backed-up sewers in the street. It was an underlying smell. Even when the air started moving the smell hung behind, a faint, background aroma sensed under the other ones even when the sluggish city sewers did manage to get pumped clear of town to an outfall just off shore. The pervasive smell, though barely noticeable, was still there.

The early light was close to horizontal. It revealed wood paneling made nondescript by a thick veneer of nicotine. The floor of broken pieces of Cuban tile was evocative of an imagined bar in a South American country without electricity or running water. The place had an easy, neighborhood feel to it, a comfortable place to conduct a day's business. Wayne and Freddy took seats at the bar.

"Wayne, what time is it?" Freddy asked upon realizing that the bar had just opened.

"Eight o'clock."

"In the morning?" Freddy was incredulous.

"It'll do you good. You deserve it anyway. I'm not going to let you sleep in on workday mornings anymore just because you went out on a bender the night before."

The morning bartender was on, a pleasant older lady. The usual coterie of characters was present. They waited outside the door each morning for the bar to open, a mix of ex-submariners returned to Key West to retire, guys who had lost fortunes, old fellows who were town institutions and existed on odd job and barter system lifestyles with a hint of larceny in the package, and a few ordinary guys, each one of them with a story of his own. Add to these a few vagabonds who did not get to bed the previous night and were having a liquid breakfast and the picture is complete.

The bartender, Ann, was an amiable older lady with gray hair swept up from her neck and neatly piled on top of her head came over to take their order. Her shoes clacked on the wooden duckboard flooring behind the bar. It was damp and swollen from the humid atmosphere and made a wet, hollow sound as her shoes struck the wood. She stopped before them. Through his haze, Freddy smiled back at the tolerant smile on her world-weary face, which was powdered heavily and looked flakier in the light from the open doorway than he remembered.

"What'll it be, guys?" she asked pleasantly.

"Anything but Peach Schnapps." That was Freddy.

"Two Bloody Marys, please," said Wayne.

"Isn't it a bit early for you fellows?"

"You should have seen me a few years back, Ann." She responded to Freddy's statement with a puzzled look.

"What are you doing, breaking Wayne into bad habits? He's such a nice boy, with those brown eyes and curly hair. I am going to be very angry with you, Freddy, if you get Wayne into some of your own mischief."

"Actually, I'm just making a solo comeback."

"That's what you think," said Wayne. They drank in silence and ordered their second Bloody Mary. Ann made them, set them in front of Wayne and Freddy. She then went to see if any of the other clients needed her expertise in making shots and beers. Freddy had some questions for Wayne.

"Where did you go this morning if you didn't go to work?"

"I had something to do."

"Mind telling me what it is? Or is it a secret?"

"Yes to both."

"Ok, then, tell me how you knew to find me at the Mascot last night."

"That one is easy. Carol, the bartender at Sloppy's, gave me a call and told me you were in there soaked to the gills and drinking something ridiculous. I believe she said Michelob and Peach Schnapps. Can that be right?"

"Peachalobs," Freddy corrected.

"Well, she figured that you were going to be sick any minute. By the time I arrived you had already left. She was about to throw you out anyway. It was a simple enough matter to check the few bars that would serve you in that condition. I didn't bother checking the places where you wouldn't get into any trouble."

"Thanks, Wayne."

"Don't make it a habit."

"There's another thing that bothers me, Wayne."

"What would that be, Freddy?"

"Did you have to rough up that shrimper so bad?"

"Yes, it was necessary."

"Why, for God's sake?"

"Do you really think we would have gotten out of there if I had just asked him nicely?" he said sarcastically. "I had to put him out of action as quickly as possible - he was too big and mean to fool around with. I couldn't let him have a shot at me so the sooner I neutralized him, the better my chances were of getting us out. He had the advantage, and he and his friends there would have been all over us if I hadn't hurt him quick and got us out while the others were off guard. We were lucky."

Everything he said was true, Freddy could see that now, but to have Wayne sit there and calmly discuss tactics and what sounded to Freddy like some kind of battle logic made Freddy think that

Wayne had done this sort of thing before. Freddy wondered what kind of odd jobs Wayne had done to work his way through school. It was disconcerting. Wayne clearly was disinclined to talk further about it from the cryptic way he had evaded Freddy's earlier questions. Freddy decided to let the matter drop.

Freddy ordered two more. "No liquor in them, please, all right. Ann?" said Wayne. Freddy started to protest but saw that Wayne was serious. And Freddy had come to realize that Wayne was someone a person should take seriously. Ann made a remark about how unusual it was for her to get orders for virgin Bloody Marys. When they finished their drinks Wayne got up to leave.

"Where are we going, Wayne?"

"To work, of course." An anguished Freddy followed him out the door.

****

For the next week Freddy was permitted a couple of beers a day. Needless to say he did not become a model worker, but the improvement was considerable. If anyone was now neglecting his work, it was Wayne. Wayne and Annie had taken to going off by themselves and making goo-goo eyes and all that horseshit (Freddy's vernacular). Wayne and Annie were growing closer all the time and Freddy felt that it wouldn't be long before they ran off and got married. Not that they could not get a great send-off in Key West. Freddy thought sarcastically that the jaded crowd he knew would celebrate hurricanes, the landing of the Hindenburg, anything. But Wayne's reticence over drawing attention to himself did not seem to lend itself to a major celebration in town. He did not appear to want to be part of the local news. Although Wayne was a bit of a mystery man and kept quiet about his past, Key West was not a town where he was alone in that. People tended to take each other at face value, and Wayne was well thought of and respected in the circles he moved in.

Annie was "allowed" to cook more since the boys found out she was quite the little Home-Ec'er. Well, actually, the Haute Cuisine side of Home Ec. She did a lot of French cooking. This led Freddy to speculate inwardly on those flexible lips, that could turn down in a perfect crescent in disgust, pucker as her eyes lit up and her head tilted when she tasted something good from a cooking spoon, become a thin, hard, bunched line when she was adamant over some issue, or part sensually and seem to puff up as she turned her face upward to meet Wayne's.

Freddy had always been very fond of Annie, and overprotective, though sometimes condescending in the past. Not great qualities, admittedly, but now he had a new-found source of respect for her. He curtailed his suggestive jokes and carrying on. They no longer seemed appropriate. She also took him to task on his habit of mimicking ethnic, regional and national accents and flagrant use of unflattering pantomime:

"Freddie, you should be more careful about how you speak. Don't you know that what you say and who you make fun of can hurt people's feelings?"

"I try to be witty…"

"No, Stop right there! Wit has truth in it. The object of wit is not, or at least should not be, to impugn others. You are a wisecracker. Wisecracking is simply calisthenics with words."

"Ahhh…" was all Freddy could get out.

"Ahhh? What do you mean Ahhh?" Annie was steaming. Now he was feeling the pressure from Annie in addition to Wayne's proscriptions. Freddy slinked off.

Freddy was the better for the exchange, though he was hardly cured of his linguistic bad habits.

Freddy actually approved of the turn of events between Wayne and Annie as they spent more of their time together and less with him. Having more time to think now that he was off on his own most of the time, his thoughts kept coming back to Pamela. He was thinking more clearly with Wayne's help and came to the conclusion that in the state he was in prior to the Mascot incident he was of no use to Pamela or anyone else. More rational now, Freddy realized he had not given the woman the time to sort things out as she had asked him to. Freddy was feeling healthy again and began exercising regularly. Exercise heightens sensual awareness and

Freddy was horny. More than that, he missed Pamela. He decided to try to call her at home on Saturday morning when the rates were low and the effect of the call on the phone bill was less likely to cause Wayne to fume at him. One thing remained unresolved, and it bothered Freddy. Wayne was missing every few days in the early morning. Annie had no idea where he went, nor would he tell her. Freddy worried that he might be in some sort of trouble.

****

Saturday arrived. Freddy had risen early and decided to take a look in the ocean for lobsters. His usual lobster place by their house had been played out for some time. He was returning with lobster now and then, but the swims had been largely therapeutic, a holdover from his period of inebriation, an outlet to work off excess alcohol and frustration and return with some semblance of clarity and order in his mind. Today he was going to hunt lobsters for the fun of it, and as he would say, "You can't catch them where they ain't."

As an alternative spot for the swim he took the short drive to Stock Island. Instead of heading to the marina where the boys still managed to find some work, he turned off about a quarter of a mile before and headed for a point of land where a small fleet of shrimp boats were docked. Beyond that group of trawlers stood the newer of the two power plants that the City owned.

The plant was a single boiler design and had one big turbine, versus the downtown plant on James Street with its six small units. The boiler was a high capacity, high pressure model. The bearings in the turbine wore out as fast as they could put them in. When it did run, it smoked. It was supposed to operate more cleanly than its predecessor. It's the thought that counts.

As Freddy drove by the plant was on the west side of the spit of land as he traveled toward the end of the point. Beyond the plant was a deep channel for the Stock Island-based portion of the shrimp fleet providing access to their dockage. Beyond that channel was another jutting finger of landfill with a junkyard, a commissary store, and a co-op, and at the landward end a dry-dock big enough to haul the seventy-six foot trawlers.

The east side of the land finger Freddy was on faced a shallow bay three hundred fifty yards across and one to two feet deep. Freddy could see a pair of thin, white egrets standing in inches of water near the small, overgrown island at the bay's mouth. Past the bay was the marina where Freddy did some of his work, on the main land mass of Stock Island. A weaving channel cut through the shallow bay which separated the marina from open water.

The channel wove through the bay in esses, sparsely marked by reedy-looking bamboo poles stuck in the shelf at the sides of the channel. A number of the markers were at an angle twenty or thirty degrees off the vertical. Many an errant boat embarrassed its owner by going aground there.

The last structure on the point to the opposite seaward side at the mouth of the channel, past the electric plant, was an old, multi-stage flash evaporator, a desalting plant similar to the type used by the Navy in Gitmo and the Arabs in Arabo, (here, another group of people toward whom the recidivist Freddy were fair game for ridicule for the sake of humor) a place where Freddy pictured lots of "towel-heads" running things frenetically. It was in disuse and sat there decaying while waiting for a scrap metal concern to cut it up and cart it away. The water company retired the old girl when a new thirty-six inch diameter pipeline from the mainland was built to replace the leaky sixteen inch one constructed by the Navy during World War II. Freddy was familiar with this thing because he had worked there frequently for up to six weeks at a time during the many shutdowns for repairs when they hired general laborers for shifts of twelve hours on and twelve hours off. He loaded trucks and did the dirty jobs inside the evaporator. When the plant was re-tubed they removed eighteen thousand old tubes of a five-eights inch in diameter. The tubes were of copper-nickel alloy. Each one was one hundred and ten feet long. They would first cut the tube in half within the evaporator, then working at opposite ends, they would pull out the fifty-five foot halves with hydraulic pullers. True to form, the local paper made a misprint which made the fifty-five foot tube halves fifty-five inches inches long. A gang of coolies including

Freddy would then scamper out to the still writhing snakes and bend them by hand until they were small enough to put on the truck. It was tedious and back-breaking, and a black oxide thoroughly permeated every article of clothing and the skin beneath. Freddy ruined a bunch of clothes on that job, but the money was good. He wore mostly double knit shirts and pants from his previous life and would show up at midnight looking like an executive and leave at noon the next day looking ridiculous, like a black man with sun blond hair. Two good things came from that job. Freddy got to know the security guards who would eventually come to be watching the plant around the clock to prevent looting, which gave him an "in" when he wanted to go out to the point for lobsters, and he learned how beautiful the night sky could be on the end of the point, away from city lights.

He parked the car, saying hello to Steve, the watchman on duty, and walked with his gear past the old evaporator. It was a sorry sight, all open and with broken pipes in varying sizes up to sixty-inch diameters on top of and all around the plant. Beyond the plant there was nothing but a two hundred yard strip of marl landfill contained by a sea wall on all three sides.

The first curious thing Freddy noticed as he walked toward the end of the point was a shrimp boat anchored off the end of the channel fairly close to shore, maybe three miles. When the weather was bad shrimpers sometimes anchored in close and slept during the day, waiting for better weather to shrimp the next night. Lately, the weather had been as good as it gets, and Freddy could see no reason for the boat to be laying over. This boat was too close-in as well, much farther from the shrimping grounds than it needed to be. There was dockage such a short way from its anchorage. If it wasn't shrimping, why was it sitting out there? It didn't make sense for the boat to be anchored at the entrance of the channel.

Freddy thought he'd seen this boat before. He realized he had seen it on previous mornings from the marina. It was curious.

He ruminated on the possibility of the boat's presence being drug related. Surely there were better places than this for it if that was the case. Freddy had seen the Marine patrol and Federal narcotics agents with binoculars out on this point often enough to know that this was not the best spot to be for such an enterprise. Still, you never know.

The Keys were notorious in that drug smuggling went on in major proportions. Often a larger boat would sit offshore during the night and load bales of marijuana onto smaller, fast boats for the run in to shore. Shrimp boats were sometimes used as these mother boats. The smaller boats might be of two types. One is the cigarette hull, long, thin and fast, built to cut the water, relying on sheer speed to out-run pursuing law enforcement agency vessels. Another choice is boats with a flatter bottom that can run on plane in very shallow water, hydroplaning in a few inches where pursuers cannot follow. What with the many secluded inlets and the convoluted, irregular shoreline, there are many miles for the law to patrol and the odds are good that the smuggler can make his drop.

Freddy looked closely at the shrimper. This one looked normal, but something else was wrong. The water line was right; it did not have a fake water line painted on the hull like a mother ship, an easy target for officials when spotted heavily laden and going in the wrong direction from a shrimping standpoint. Those boats were stopped and boarded. Those unlucky boats, however, were expendable, as were the boats that made the drop, an operating expense of boats and material lost now and then in the normal course of business. The runs that did succeed would pay enough to cover those losses and keep the big wheels in business while some of their underlings might have to do some time. Breaking into that business involved taking chances to work your way up.

Freddy realized what was implausible about the boat. At this close range, he saw what had caught his attention. The shrimp boat did not look like a working boat - there were no rust stains on it, no dings in the hull, all of the running gear and rigging looked to be in perfect shape, it didn't even have the traditional automobile tires hung over the sides as fenders. He tried to read the name on the bow. It looked like Big Nick, Turbo, Colombia. What was a trawler from Colombia doing here? Freddy made a mental note of it. If he thought of it later, he would ask around and see if anyone in the boating community knew what the story was on the strange lone trawler.

Freddy was nearly on top of the sea wall when who should he see but Wayne. He was sitting in Freddy's thrice-patched Zodiac inflatable boat, binoculars in hand, looking at the same shrimp boat that held Freddy's curiosity moments before. Freddy stopped dead and ducked behind some scrub brush near the end of the point. Since Wayne was not willing to explain his early morning absences, Freddy was sure that he would not take well to being surprised there at whatever his secret doings were. As Freddy watched, Wayne started the no-horsepower egg beater and motored to the marina. Freddy could see him tie up the rubber boat and head down the pier.

In Philadelphia Freddy used to do things; now they happened to him. He didn't know it, but things were about to start happening again.

Chapter Eleven – Somewhere, Over the Rainbow

"A tropical wave moving west-northwest will bring showers with strong gusty winds that are expected to spread over the southeastern Bahamas, eastern Cuba and Jamaica. Pressure remains high in the vicinity of the wave and there are no signs of tropical storm development. In the marine picture a ridge of high pressure from the Atlantic across South Florida will remain stationary through tonight. The tropical wave in the northern Bahamas will move across the keys by late tomorrow.

It's raining over most of South Florida and the Keys bringing cooler temperatures to the area. At 2 o'clock it is 83 degrees up and down the Keys. In the water it is 84."

****

It is now two o'clock in the afternoon and the phone is ringing somewhere over Kansas. Actually it is ringing in Cincinnati, Ohio, but to Freddy it must be Kansas 'cause where else could Pamela, his Good Witch of the North, be? As Mae West might have said, when she was a wicked witch she was even better. Too bad for Freddy that his particular Witch only chose to do a matinee in Key West instead of an extended engagement. A tropical rain is falling hard and fast outside the window. The drops are in such numbers that they look like they are oscillating up and down. He looks again and imagines the beads of liquid are traveling rapidly down strings like those lamps he used to see in Italian restaurants up north only gone crazy. The palms behind the rain are gray and stippled, as flecked as a grainy photograph.

The phone is ringing. Once, twice, three times and the click of a recording machine. Pools of rainwater are spreading in the street. Reflections of the muddled milk and ashen colors of the clouds and of the muted sprays of curved green combs of fronds crowning bulbous bottomed palms quiver on their surfaces, speckled lodens and curdled shades of gray. The intensity of the downpour increases. The same old message is delivered. Perhaps it is the wrong number and it is the Wizard giving him the runaround. Now the rain outside the window is hitting the ground like bullets; big, elongated heavy gobs of water slapping the surface of the puddles with a crack and splattering in circles of wide, high arced droplets. The pounding has forced a fine mist into the air and it is being borne on the breeze. The curtains stir and lift inward into the room as the wet, cool air blows through the louvered window. The mist in the wet air clings to Freddy's skin, makes a patina of tiny droplets on the hairs of his arms.

Freddy goes into the name, number and time of call song and dance and is about to hang up when a live person comes on the line. "Hello?" says a distant female voice. The curtains start to luff and the window sill gets wet. Freddy pays it no mind.

"Freddy, you called." It is of course Pamela and she sounds happy. "Darling, it's been five weeks since I've talked to you. Why have you waited so long?"

"Pamela, it's good to hear your voice. I missed you."

"I've missed you, too. I thought you gave up on me."

"That's funny; every time we spoke down here and even mentioned that you should come back soon you short-circuited the conversation and started one in another direction. I've called before and all I got was the mechanized voice." He said nothing for a short moment. "Pamela, I want to see you again."

"I'm glad, Freddy. But I had to think. I couldn't just up and leave, now could I?" Freddy recalls that that is what he did, three years ago. He just up and left. "I've been Daddy's little girl for so long it's hard to change. Tell me how you missed me, Freddy."

"I think you know already. First time I saw you smile it made me feel giddy. I don't know what love at first sight is supposed to be, but I know I want you here. This must sound like some syrupy grocery store novel."

"Freddy..."

"I want you to come back. I want you back here if I have to come up there and get you; if I have to tear you from your father's arms."

"Freddy, please wait a minute---"

"We belong together." Was he so sure of that?

"Freddy---"

"I want to share my meals with you, I want to feel your warmth, taste your mouth, smell your perfume and breathe your scent." Now he was going too far.

"Freddy, wait!"

"It's no use trying to put me off any longer. I'm not takin' 'no' for an answer."

"Freddy, now just stop and listen for a minute, will you? I'm coming back. Daddy doesn't like it, but I'm coming anyway."

"Oh, ok," he said lamely. He thinks he may have tipped his hand. He turned enough for something to catch his eye. There were Wayne and Annie standing behind him. Annie was blushing and Wayne was sticking his finger down his throat as if trying to vomit until Annie pulled his arm down. How gauche. Not becoming at all. Too much like something Freddy would do. Annie discreetly led Wayne from the room while Freddy and Pamela finished their conversation.

"Freddy," said Pamela, "I am impressed. That was quite a speech."

"Yeah, well, I guess I have my moments."

"It was nice. I can't wait to get down there and see you."

Freddy felt a flush of anticipation at those words. "Come soon so I can ravish your body."

"That sounds fine, Freddy."

"I can hardly wait." Now Freddy was feeling sheepish at maintaining the ardor of the moment. Always the buffoon, he was compelled to say something to break the spell. "Don't be surprised if I get lost on the way to the airport."

"Freddy..." He sensed her irritation at his frivolous nonsense. He was suddenly afraid again, balking at taking the new turn of events seriously.

"Oh. Must have been the last girl."

"Be serious. I'm the girl with the dark hair and no tan."

"We'll have to work on that. I'll help. I'm anxious to see the bronze version again."

They talked about how long it would be before Pamela could train a replacement for her job and leave Cincinnati, and caught up on getting re-acquainted before hanging up. Once again, the world was all right by Freddy. But there was a haunting unease lurking in his mind as well; his doubts about making a commitment. Freddy's two roommates strolled in from the other room.

"How did it go, ace?" asked Wayne. "What were you doing, auditioning for a soap opera?" Wayne did not like soap operas.

Annie said, "Cut it out, Wayne. I think it's wonderful that Pamela is coming back. And the sides will be more even around here," she said silkily. That last comment brought a slant-eyed look of concern from each of the boys, and Wayne said, "Now, just what is *that* supposed to mean?" Annie's return gesture was a Cheshire-cat smile. Inscrutable Annie. Pleased with herself, with a small shimmy of her squared shoulders, she left the room.

To Freddy, Wayne said, "That was pretty hot stuff, my boy,Were you in heat or what?"

"Wayne, you wouldn't understand, you insensitive dolt," countered Freddy.

"Dolt! Dolt, is it? Ho, ho! Sounds like you might be serious about the lady. Maybe you're going to propose at the airport."

"Come on, Wayne, I'm not crazy, you know. Besides, how would she support me?"

"Just as well. With your attention span you'd get down on your knees and forget what you were down there for. Probably get side-tracked and start fooling with something."

"I like to check out the best parts - bottom round..., flank steak..., the loin..."

Wayne thinks a minute. "There's a guy down at the beach who wears a loin cloth.. Nice guy.

Rents beach chairs"

Wayne, you're off track."

Wayne strove to make some sense of it with his closing query on the matter. "The girls wear 'G' strings, don't they? I mean when they wear anything at all. Is that so different?"

"Only in certain bars."

"It's the same thing, 'covers some of the same territories, but girls tuck them in cause' they're neater."

"Yeah, I always thought they were pretty neat myself."

****

Freddy was a dynamo at work. There was no job too big or too small as he sang his way through the day, working and dancing around the boats. Wayne was amused and glad to finally be getting some output from him. The rest of the guys at the marina assumed that Freddy was merely going through another one of his strange permutations. One week to go and he would be joined by the luscious Pamela. In his over-exuberance and rapture at Pamela's impending return, he overdid it. While running up the four wooden steps leading from the dock to the store he tripped up the steps, falling heavily on his right wrist and jamming it backwards on the top step, hyperextending it up and back. The wrist was painful. He took the rest of the day off and made an appointment at the doctor's for the next day.

****

The trip to the doctor was a pleasant diversion from Freddy's regular activities. It relieved some of the tension he felt waiting for Pamela. The injury was little more than an annoyance, really, unless he tried to do something foolish like tie his shoes. He found his way to the doctor's office and took a seat to watch the people at this change of venue. It soon became his turn for the attractive receptionist's attention. She asked a few questions and handed him a sheaf of papers.

Of course, he had to fill out forms - five or six of them. They were for mostly redundant stuff like medical history and insurance. Freddy was paying cash and there was no history of accidental wrist breaking in his family, his father was a carpenter, after all. Strong wrists. He tried to explain this to the receptionist.

"Excuse me, miss, could we save these forms for someone else? Might save a tree's life somewhere down the line."

She smiled up at him and explained that the routine was a necessity, there were six doctors in the complex and Freddy could be in there to see any one of them at any time. It was good to have his history on record. Freddy thought of clean underwear.

"Ok, I'll do the medical history, although I don't see where it will do anyone any good. But I'll do it." He shuffled through the pages. "How 'bout this one?" He held up a green insurance form. "I'm not going to make a claim for this injury. Do I have to write 'no' in all these spots?" She looked at the page he was holding above her head.

"I'm insulted," she said, "that you don't like my form." She made a little grin. Uh-oh, thought Freddy. That sounded like flirty-talk to him.

She was not a young girl, but neither was she decrepit. Her over-full bosom was nicely arranged in an open-throated blue cotton blouse, with several of the top buttons undone. What the hell, it was hot. As he stood at her desk she had leaned forward to speak with him. Her posture was good, she was trim and her breasts were shaped well, rounded and not droopy despite their size. She was friendly and pleasant. He belabored the conversation to steal another look down the top of her blouse at the two friendly, healthy, pink rounds that seemed to swell up toward him.

He said, "Of course I like your form, it's a very nice form."

"You're just saying that."

"No, really," he assured her.

"Would you like to take it home and work on it?"

"It's a nice thought, but..."

"You don't have to say no, just check it...out." Freddy felt flushed. She sat there looking dreamy, made a shift in her chair, arching the small of her back subtly, making her back straighter and moving the weight of her hips forward. Her shoulders went back a little. Freddy imagined it was for his benefit.

"I think I already did." Finding no further way to extend the flirtatious conversation, and knowing that he should not, Freddy smiled cordially and returned to his seat, receiving a coy, sidewise grin as he left her desk. Whoa, ain't life grand. He sat there filling out forms fast and furious as his throbbing wrist allowed. He hoped she realized the pain he was going through for her. He returned the completed forms. As he turned to go back to his chair and continue waiting, she asked, "Is my form filled out nicely?"

"It sure is, he intoned over his shoulder. "Perfectly."

One of the other occupants of the waiting room was a middle-aged tennis player, overweight and balding, with a suspected pull of his Achilles's tendon. He looked as foolish as he probably felt, limping around in his sweaty shorts. A lady with a cast on her arm sat at the far end of the room. Freddy noticed that the wall was yellow. Music came from somewhere. The Carpenters. No, a Carpenter song, with lots of muted sugar-voices.

Then arrived a limping lady, young and cute and small of build, with a cast on her leg and the attendant crutches. Largish breasts. They all had largish breasts these days. Apparently the frail little bird had injured her right calf. Poor, cute thing, thought Freddy. They waited.

****

Finally it was Freddy's turn and he was in the examination room with the doctor prodding and squeezing and asking Freddy if it hurt, presumably so he could help him. The doctor decided Freddy needed some pictures taken. "What for, the yearbook?" Freddy quipped. Apparently not funny. The girl with the cast was then ushered into the examination room. What, Freddy wondered, was this, co-ed examinations? If so, it was new to Freddy. Unisex, and now this. The doctor says sit down, and Freddy says sure. He had been standing all of the forty seconds since he was told to have his picture taken. Proceeding to the comfy looking exam table that was indicated, Freddy turned to sit on it just as the cute, crippled girl hobbled over did the same thing. Freddy had misunderstood the doctor's ambiguous command. It wouldn't have taken much to knock her down, but she managed to remain standing as she stumbled back onto her injured leg in a reflex reaction and howled. Freddy reeled back onto the table, catching himself with his hurt right hand and joining the ululation. What is she trying to do, take his seat?

It dawns of Freddy that there is nothing in this room resembling an x-ray machine and he has fallen victim to the typically vague directions given by the doctor. Freddy thinks: doctors know what they're thinking and assume everyone else does as well. There is nothing to be done for it. Once again, Freddy is the buffoon and he smiles meekly as he is shown to another room, toward the rear of the building, one with an x-ray machine. He hovers dubiously over the proffered seat, reticence latent still from his inadvertent interloping in the case of the lady with the cast. He sits.

After a short wait, the perky-breasted receptionist comes in to do the picture taking. Goody! She says something sultry that sounds like a greeting, removes the pen from her mouth and shuts the light. How cozy, he thinks. Somehow she finds a small work light above the x-ray machine. Now it is she who is standing and Freddy is sitting. In marked contrast to the doctor's touch she gently adjusts his wrist to the proper position under the machine, letting her fingers and nails trail lightly up his forearm. Her hip touches his arm. He experiences a sensual tingly tremor as her light touch sends shivers of pleasure up his arm.

She steps back out of his vision and pushes a button to set the machine buzzing, then returns and repeats the process. Freddy smells her perfume and senses her body heat again as she stands beside his chair. He turns to see what she is doing and finds that he is staring through the slit in her open-throated blouse at her left breast which is at point blank range. Somehow another button must have come undone. He can see the bottom of her smooth, round breast. It has a gently upward curve. She is back-lit by a small orange lamp near the doorway which gives the scene a warm effect. Thankfully, Freddy's eyes are still good and he can focus at close distances and finds the effect rather nice, pleasing to the eye and very sexy in silhouette. It is, he thinks, a beautiful tit. His lips part unconsciously.

The top of her breast and her smallish pink nipple are highlighted by close proximity to the work light above the machine, since that part of her is out in front ahead of the rest of her body, inches from Freddy's face. He feels stirrings deep down.

Freddy is moved. He does not know how artistically inclined the woman is so he refrains from telling her any of his observations. He then becomes aware that she has been standing there for quite some time, ministering to his wrist for longer than necessary, so he glances up at her face and sees that she is smiling seductively, has engineered the whole display. As he breaks out into a sweat he thinks, "Pamela, get here soon."

Chapter Twelve - Pamela's Return

The first week in October was gone. It had been six days since he had sprained his wrist and he was able to undertake light tasks and generally be of some assistance at the marina. Not that there was much to do - their business was with small, local concerns and was not likely to improve at the onset of the tourist season. Soon business would be down to a trickle. They anticipated at least six slow weeks; they would need to cultivate other alternatives if they wanted to come through the winter chubby and cheerful as squirrels with lots of nuts.

Wayne was often preoccupied with something and Freddy was becoming more concerned with Wayne's early morning absences - still a taboo subject - than looking for another line of work, which had been his previous concern. Of late Wayne had been hinting at the possibility of having to take some time off to make a trip, possibly on short notice. He was hinting at it as if to prepare Annie for his sudden departure. He gave no indication of where he intended to go or what he would be doing there. He bristled when Annie at first tried to find out why he might be leaving, and now she no longer said anything about it to him. Annie was afraid to mention it, afraid to think about it, like doing that would make it happen. She was clearly upset when he made these allusions to leaving, worried that he may not love her anymore. And just when it seemed that the girl had him all ready to propose. For the moment, though, those unspoken worries were suspended. All was in readiness for Pamela's arrival. She had finally tied up all of her loose ends. Her plane would get there tomorrow at one in the afternoon.

"Sit down, Freddy, tomorrow will get here," said Annie.

"I *am* a little nervous," he admitted. "I wonder if I'm doing the right thing having her give up a comfortable career and getting her father mad at her and have her come down here. Hell, who knows, it may not last very long between us. What happens if she gets to know me?"

"That's the chance you'll have to take, Freddy, my lad." She said, and she smiled benevolently.

Next day they all piled into the Olds, Wayne driving, Freddy in the back seat, Annie looking around like a happy puppy in a car and smiling at people, and went to greet Pamela at the airport. The reunion was amid a plethora of hugs and baggage and glistening eyes and heady tingles of sensual antipasto between Pamela and Freddy. Pamela seemed to be the same sweet, demure girl she had been when she left, minus a tan. First on Freddy's agenda was the VIP treatment for her, starting with dinner.

The four of them went straight-away to a restaurant near the water with a tiki bar out back. The bar had a southeastern view of the Atlantic and looked up and down at the piers of other restaurants and hotels radiating out from a shoreline gently arcing out of sight below the horizon in the near distance. Sailboats at their moorings bobbed to and fro, masts swinging out of time with one another. The bar sat on a wooden deck shaded by a very old Banyan tree.

The mixologist on duty was Marty, a tall, thin, acerbic and cynical humorist, a perennial favorite for forty years. Freddy had a Gin and tonic, Annie's drink was a Strawberry Daiquiri and Pamela had a frozen Pina Colada. Wayne had a Scotch and soda. "Good tropical drink, Wayne," said Freddy with a smirk. Wayne smiled wanly.

On this day and befitting the occasion they decided to partake of Marty's acerbic wit only as briefly as decorum required before hieing away to a waterfront table. They had important things to speak of, the paper company in Cincinnati and how-would-they-get-along-without-Pamela, the local Key West news, scandals, and the general chicanery of the police, politicians, and lesser lights burning themselves out around town. It finally came down to...

"Freddy, what have you been doing with yourself?" Pamela had asked the question.

"Generally behaving," (A groan here from Wayne and Annie.) "Wayne has been riding herd on me for the past couple of months.

For a time there I was in rugged shape, but I'm out of that now. I had an elbow problem, but I straightened it out."

"Now that he is willing to work there is no work to be had," was Wayne's dry observation. "He's on light duty anyway since he hurt his wrist." Freddy basked in Pamela's pity. Yes, Freddy had seen a doctor; no, there was nothing broken, but possibly he would get a swollen bursa and have to hit it with a book. Doesn't he hate going to the doctor? Freddy thought of the buxom receptionist. Yes, it's hell, he lied.

"You will notice," Freddy went on, "that my sense of humor is restored and that my mental capacity is in part returning." Freddy was beginning to feel the effects of the gin. "Also note that while I have not been playing Hamlet since your removal from the ranks of the well-rounded gender, neither have I been mincing around playing 'Air on the "G" string.' Which reminds me, do you have a 'G' string, Pamela?"

Pamela was shocked. "Freddy, what for?"

"Oh, just something I had in mind," he said dreamily.

"Maybe I'd better get one, then," Pamela said huskily as she squeezed his right hand.

"Owwwwwwww!"

"I'm sorry, Freddy!"

They all laughed, Freddy while maintaining an injured look and clutching his right wrist away from Pamela with his left. Wayne saw an opportunity to tease Annie, sitting bent forward with both hands on her Strawberry Daiquiri like a little girl with a Sundae, playing now and then in the whipped creaminess of the drink with her straw, in a state of relaxed silence. "Pamela, if you need one of those 'G' string things you can borrow one from Annie. She has a bunch of them in her drawer from her last job here in town."

"I do not!" said Annie, sitting straight up as her voice rose and fell musically. "Gosh, Wayne, sometimes you are impossible," she said as she gave him a prissy slap on his arm. "Jeepers! All this talk is making me hungry!"

Annie was happy. Today she felt good about herself. She had a new best friend — not one of those catty girls who sabotage each other but a real friend. "Geez, how could *that* happen," she wondered, "a California Girl like me and an egghead athlete Ivy-Leaguer like Pammy! The boys in town like me 'cause of the way I look but they don't think that I am very smart 'cause they stereotype me. But that's OK, they can't help themselves, society is the problem, and they tip me really well. They like Pamela 'cause she looks as smart as she is. That's a turn on, too, on an island where there are lots of lonely guys and not many girls. I feel sorry for them, but I like the ratio. Did I say they tip me really well?"

Pamela thought about these developments and permutations and she wondered if she had become that judgmental Philosopher/Psychologist that she strove not to be. She resolved to keep herself on an even keel.

They decided to go back to the house and unpack Pamela enough to let her feel comfortable and let her get cleaned up, and then get ready for dinner. Wayne got up and walked to the railing to stretch his legs. He looked back as Freddy joined him a few moments later.

"Where are the girls?"

"They made a last minute pit stop," said Freddy. He leaned on the railing with Wayne while they waited for Pamela and Annie and saw what Wayne was looking at, the mysterious shrimp boat, the *"Big Nick"*, came into view. It was sailing toward the south. Freddy decided to broach the subject.

"See that shrimp boat, Wayne?" Wayne said nothing. "It has been anchored off the point by the old desalting plant, on and off, mostly on, for the last several weeks."

"Yes, I think I remember seeing it," came the reply. Freddy knew that he had seen it because he had seen Wayne on that morning weeks ago spying on it or waiting for a signal, or something, from the rubber dinghy.

"I've been looking into it and asking about it discreetly. The guys at the packing plant don't remember her and they say she's never come in here with a load of shrimp. She has never even come in to pick up ice. In fact, they've never put in to this port at all. The Coast Guard boarded her, but they found nothing wrong. It has an expensive radio, loran, and radar. They say it looks like she's never been shrimping. They say it's pretty fancy inside her. Completely re-arranged below decks. No place to store shrimp, just staterooms and bunks, a big galley and a lot of radio equipment. Pretty suspicious, huh?"

"There isn't anything illegal in what they are doing that I can see, Freddy."

"But don't you wonder what they are up to?"

"Freddy, let's drop it. I know you know I've been watching that boat. I don't know what else you know, but it doesn't concern you anyway, so stay out of it, ok?"

"Wayne, if you're in trouble or mixed up in something..." Wayne remained steely and adamant in his refusal to divulge his connection with the shrimp boat. The ladies returned and Freddy gave up on the subject so as not to sour the evening. But his concern over the strange goings-on was increasing.

All that business could wait until tomorrow. Tonight was Pamela's. They went home and put on long pants and tropical dresses, and then they went to, in Freddy's parlance, "put on the feed bag," at the Polynesian place in town. On the way out Pamela asked Freddy, "Where's Bootsie?"

"Buried in shit," he said, and rushed her out the door before she could ask what he meant.

****

Under the thatched roof, amid aquariums and soft lantern light, they ate egg rolls, fried shrimp and ribs from the pupu platter. "Oh, Freddy, look at that one," said Pamela as she pointed out one of the colorful fish swimming in their glass display cases. "Maybe we should start an aquarium."

"The ocean is my aquarium," said Freddy with a grand, encompassing gesture with the fork in his hand, as the big shrimp impaled on it dripped cocktail sauce on the tablecloth. The waitress dodged in time not to be skewered. She knew Freddy from past experience, so she took this in stride.

"Pamela, Freddy's being foolish again," said Annie. "Wayne told me about the time Freddy tried to start an aquarium with saltwater fishes before I got here." Her tone implied that her world in Key West had not been created and that nothing existed except chaos in the time before she was with Wayne. "All he could do with it was make green, smelly water with nasty stuff floating in it. When I moved in with those two Freddy had already given up. He cleaned out the aquarium and put paper fishes in it." Pamela was amused by this disclosure. Freddy looked indignant that Annie had made fun of his efforts to beautify the home.

"Where did he get the paper 'fishes,' Annie?" Pamela asked.

"He cut them out of my notebook pad with colored pages with a scissors the day after I moved in. He hung them on the little coral castle and pasted them to the sides. All I did was ask him why he had an empty aquarium." She looked at Freddy and shook her head. Their entrees came and Annie's attention was diverted from her story. She edged forward in her chair looking politely ravenous from plate to plate. She looked at each entree almost gleefully. Freddy couldn't get over how that little girl could eat. She had Shrimp Tempura. Pamela had a Seafood Platter and Freddy had the Sweet and Sour Pork. Wayne had a Teriyaki steak.

Over dinner they spoke of the possibility of getting into a business that would support all of them all of the year round and involve all of them as well. Wayne remained somewhat on the moody side as though his thoughts were straying. Perhaps either the long-range plans the others were speculating on were making him uncomfortable - a conflict with the trips he was dropping hints about, or the movements of the shrimp boat today were on his mind. It occurred to Freddy that perhaps the two things were related. He wondered why he had not thought of that possibility before. Freddy didn't think Wayne would be upsetting Annie by preparing her in advance for his departure if he was thinking of deserting her. It must be something Wayne could not avoid.

It was hard on Annie. She wondered what she had done wrong, did everything she could think of to make Wayne happy, hoping he would stay and fearing that if he left he would never come back.

There was a finality in his manner when he spoke of leaving that Freddy had noticed, and this was not lost on Annie.

Freddy did not wish to poke into Wayne's past, but something must be done. He did not know what to do or how to go about it yet, not discreetly, anyway. Wayne had always been vague and taciturn when anyone asked him about his past. The end result was that no one knew much about him, but everyone liked him and chalked up his reticence as a mannerism of his. Maybe Wayne thought they were all nosey, who knows? Freddy forced himself out of this train of thought and got back into the dinner chatter.

After dinner they listened to the band for a while, over drinks, and then headed home. Wayne was chauffeur; Annie sat straight up and satisfied by his side, a contented, inward smile on her face. Freddy was glad to see it. The top was down and the stars had come out in the clear night sky. Pamela looked up, her head back on Freddy's arm.

"Look at the sky. Freddy, it's so beautiful," said Pamela.

"The sky is my planetarium," said Freddy."

****

Pamela and Freddy were finally alone. They undressed each other.

"Well, it's all still there," Freddy whispered.

"Freddy, can't you ever be serious?" she said as she put her arms around his waist and pulled him close.

"I'm getting serious right now."

"Kiss me, Freddy."

"Where?"

"*All over.*"

So he did.

****

Freddy did not know it until it was all over, but there had been an item in a newspaper in central

New Jersey three weeks before. A body had been found, male, Caucasian, about forty-five years old. It had been bound in a piece of canvas, weighted, and dumped into the deep excavation of a clay pit filled with water where the clay had been mined two decades earlier. The body had broached to the surface after decompositional gasses once again made it positively buoyant and the weights fell through the rotted canvas. The body was floating at the surface when it was found by two little boys, aged eight and six.

The man was tentatively identified, using prison records of dental work, as Walter Clayton. He had turned state's evidence in the trial and subsequent conviction of several members of the Sargento family for their activities in organized crime. Clayton had been released several months before his discovery in the clay pit and must have been killed and deposited there shortly thereafter. There were two bullet wounds in the body, one in the head, and one in the abdomen. It was thought that the shot to the stomach was done first and the man was allowed to live in pain for several hours before being shot in the head. He was already dead by that time. His hands had been tied. Several of his fingers had been cut off.

Another man, a Theodore McLaren, also involved with the Sargento case and responsible for obtaining key evidence against the mobsters, had been released from the state mental hospital in Marlboro five months earlier for the brutal murder of one of the Sargento brothers. It was deemed that the killing was not a matter of self-defense and while the court was sympathetic in the case of Mr. McLaren, who had been instrumental in bringing many of the gang to justice while working at the behest of the police, the brutal murder was unpardonable and Mr. McLaren unfortunately had become mentally aberrated in his dealings with the cruel and vicious mobsters. Mr. McLarens's sentence was lenient under the circumstances - a period of observation at a state mental hospital followed by parole. Mr. McLaren was wanted for questioning in the matter of the death one Mr. Clayton but he could not be found. He had apparently been released through a rear entrance at the facility at Marlboro with the help of an attendant there. His case was being reviewed by the parole board at the time. Why the attendant had done this could not be determined. He was killed in an auto accident shortly thereafter.

****

"Oh, my goodness!" she oozed, as the maple syrup lent its viscous adherence to the glass table top, leaving the apple flapjacks high and dry on their china islands. Soft and warm, they sat there above the syrup as it lapped at the napkin and inundated the flatware and the base of the plate. It was a sticky situation.

They were having breakfast in the Florida room and Annie had toppled the jug of "molasses," as Freddy had called it.

"It's that tricky-shaped bottle," said Wayne. "They shouldn't make them look like grandmas in Vermont."

Freddy mused over this for a moment. "Grandmas in Vermont. Sounds like a song I used to know."

"God, no," said Wayne, "don't sing!"

"Grandmas in Vermont, keep Grandpa's eyes shining..."

"That's 'Moonlight in Vermont' you're thinking of, Freddy," Pamela advised him. "It is either that or 'Autumn in New York.' The way you carry a tune makes it hard to tell."

"Oh, really?" Freddy considered this information carefully, with furrowed brow.

Annie headed for the kitchen for a cloth to wipe up the mess. She called back over her shoulder, "It's Maple syrup you're thinking of - molasses doesn't come from trees, silly."

"You mean there aren't any molasses trees in Vermont?" Freddy asked incredulously.

"No, of course not," said Wayne, joining in the foolishness.

"What happened to them?"

"Molasses comes from sugar," Wayne explained. "Maple syrup comes from trees. In Vermont. Besides that, what we have here is pancake syrup, it's got Maple syrup in it. Molasses is for beans."

"I'll say," was Freddy's rueful remark. "What can you get from Pine trees? We got a few scrubby Australian Pines around here."

"Pine-Sol. And the scrubbier the trees, the better - get it?"

"No, Wayne, explain it to me."

Annie made her way back to the Florida room with a cloth to wipe up the sweet sticky liquid. Freddy held a hand up to bid her to wait. He produced a cake server from the drawer of flatware. Using it as a trowel he removed some of the syrup from the table top and deposited it onto his stack of flapjacks. First the others were dumbfounded, then they follow suit. Freddy was in one of his neat moods. He had considered dumping the flapjacks onto the table and eating them from there.

After breakfast and banter they had coffee and inanities. Another hour of idle chatter had happened before Pamela and Freddy decided to go for a walk. Pamela had not yet finished her coffee.

"Give me a few minutes, Freddy, while I finish this," she said.

"Bring it with you, Pamela. Let's go have a look around." They took a leisurely stroll first to the resort two blocks away. They watched the tennis players there and Freddy made some suitably disparaging critical remarks about the degree of expertise of the milk bottles on the courts. It was typical of Freddy to scoff at tourists in their bumbling quests for fun in the sun. Pamela did not approve of this ungenerous attitude and said as much. First the reproaches on his behavior and deportment from Wayne and then from Annie and now this from Pamela. Freddy grumbled and shuffled a bit before conceding that he might need to re-align his attitude in that respect. It seemed that he was not going to have things all his own way anymore, at least for the duration.

They next walked to the swimming pier at the end of the street, known locally as a gay domain, where women sometimes sunbathed naked when they did not want to be hit upon. They came upon two ladies to whom Freddy had previously become acquainted and with whom he had had a brief flirtation. A light breeze was rolling up the beach towels they were lying on and their movements to adjust the towels caused them to rise on their tummies. All they had on were their bikini bottoms. As Freddy said "Hi" they rolled their ultra-browned bodies toward Freddy and Pamela and gave a cheerful "Hello, Freddy."

He said, "Good to see you, ladies." Wrong thing to say under the circumstances. Freddy introduced them as Karen and Laura, two cocktail waitresses from Marathon forty miles up the keys who came to Key West every chance they got to lay in the sun after a night on the town. "Nice tan, ladies," Freddy said approvingly. They rolled further, onto their sides, allowing Freddy to admire their dark bodies more fully.

"Yes, we're working on it," said Karen.

"Another hard day at the beach," Laura added. Freddy didn't know if Pamela was shocked or embarrassed or indignant at this air of fraternity, with only the air between them and the two luscious young ladies. The girls themselves could not have cared less about their state of near undress, but Pamela had some pointed words on the subject as they walked away and the girls sang "Bye, Freddy," in their wake.

"How well do you know them, Freddy?"

"They're just friends, Pamela. We've had a few drinks together, they've been out on the boat a few times, and that's all. You're shaped better than them anyway." This mollified her somewhat. Why was he feeling so defensive? He'd been bludgeoned with the stamp of ownership. What did he expect, though, after campaigning so hard to pry her loose from her ties in Ohio? It wasn't so bad, though, he liked the sense of stability to it, and perhaps it was a situation that was overdue. There had been individuals living together at his house. First there were two, he and Melinda, then one, himself, then variations on the theme until finally it was three, when Wayne and then sweet Annie moved in. Now instead of individuals there were two couples living in his house. It was a novel concept for him. He wondered how many more changes there would be. He had a thought about the two girls on the pier. "By now both of them were probably going with big, ugly, goons or skinny geeks. You have to be dopey-looking for a good-looking woman to like you in this town."

"Yes, Freddy, I know." Freddy had a vaguely funny feeling that he had been insulted.

****

It was not all one way. Many things changed for the better in the next few weeks. Freddy was overjoyed to think that perhaps never again would his laundry beckon to him from the hamper portal at the closet door. His room smelled better, too, without all of those sweaty tennis clothes fermenting for days on end. He no longer feared that the dust bunnies that used to lurk under the bed would grow to immense proportions, become carnivorous, and attack him during the night. The one-time whirlwind romance had become a domestic couple. The rough patches were not that rough and the good spots were very good indeed. Freddy's transformation into a reasonably civilized person was heartening to Wayne and Annie, but then what do they know about it, thought Freddy, they were too civilized already.

Pamela was undergoing some changes also. She became an avid water person, snorkeling and free-diving at each chance. She did it well. She turned brown, and a body that was already magnificent became legendary. More toned; the muscles of her arms and legs elongated into swimmer's muscles. She was finely contoured. Lean and firm all over. Everything was a little tighter and higher and Pamela looked even better than before although Freddy would not have believed that was possible. She moved with the grace of a princess and the sureness of an athlete. The guys at the marina were wondering what she was doing with a goon like Freddy.

Wayne was doing better also, seldom making his morning spy missions. The shrimp boat was gone and the pre-occupation Wayne had had with it was also gone . Only one minor disconcerting note played upon Freddy, and that occurred as a result of his suggestion that Wayne take a civil service test. The post office was hiring, and Wayne was still seeking another source of income. He had said to Freddy at the time, "I don't want to do that."

"Why not, for God's sake? The pay is decent and the job security is good. Unless you find a way to use your education down here, which I doubt you will, given the 'bubba' system they use here, you can't do a lot better."

"No, Freddy, I don't want anyone snooping around in my past."

****

That evening Annie and Pamela were talking together. They were sitting in Annie's room on her bed. Annie looked troubled. Her brow furrowed and her lips tightened. "It's as if he goes inside himself. Like he has a secret place; a secret place where I can't go. He has a secret cave. Some men get drunk, some are whores, and far too many are aggressive when there is no need. I guess there weren't enough manners to go around when they made the men. That kind of man, I can understand, and that's not the kind of guy I want, but Wayne doesn't do those things. He's kind and gentle, but sometimes he is cut off in a different world and he's cut off from me. It's very hard for me to take." She said this while staring defocused into the bedspread.

"Wayne has excellent manners," said Pamela, for wont of something better to say.

Annie looked up from the bed. "True, Wayne has excellent manners; until I ask him a serious question about his past or about us. Then he's a clam."

Pamela was silent. Now she could find nothing to say. Irrepressible Annie read the concern in Pamela's face and bounced back into a positive attitude to try to alleviate her friend's concern.

"You and Freddy seem very close. How is that going? You majored in Philosophy, what are you doing to bring him along?

"Nothing, Annie, he has to do it himself." Annie nodded sagely that she understood. Another brief silence ensued, and then Pamela asked:

"What did you do in school, Annie?"

"In high school I did sports and the regular stuff and home ec" Then in college I just did a bachelor's degree with wandering majors, - and sports. And then chef school."

"That's sound expensive," said Pamela.

"Scholarship. College, I mean. Chef school, *that* was expensive. My, Pamela, did you think I was just a pretty face?"

"Ah, no, Annie, of course not."

Annie's eyes opened wide and her jaw dropped. **"You mean you don't think I have a pretty face?"**

"Oh, no, Annie..."

"And I thought you were my friend! C'Couldn't you be more tactful? That was brutal!"

Pamela moved to rectify the situation. "Annie, of *course* I think you have a pretty face. Your face is beautiful. You misunderstood me."

"*OK*, then, that's better. One must be *clear* in these matters." The crisis was over. After a pause in the conversation, a question occurred to Pamela.

"I take it you like cooking, is that so, Annie?"

"Love it. That's what I want to do, cook."

"Then why on earth do the guys cook everything?"

"They think that they are great cooks, so I let them."

"Annie, you've got to assert yourself more."

"Should I, and upset the apple cart for them? I guess that's a question for a Philosopher."

"Touché."

"Pamela, tu peux parler français? "C'est magnifique! Maintenant, nous pouvons avoir des conversations françaises ensemble. Combien de la français sait-tu?"

"Touché"

"That much, huh?"

"I have pretty much forgotten what I learned. It didn't stay with me."

"You've got to *use* it, Pamela! No matter, I'll teach you. It will be fun. We'll start with greetings and goodbyes." Before long the first lesson was over. Just then Freddy passed by the doorway and heard:

"Bonne soit, Annie………Bonne soit Pamela, á prochaine!" He thought to himself, "Uh-oh, this can't be good."

****

After that, the guys relinquished their reign in the kitchen over the salad incident and bequeathed the stove to Annie. Wayne would cast a curious eye to see what she was doing as the pretty dynamo seared, sautéed, baked, sauced, fruited, minced, chopped, and mandolined. Pamela watched intently and picked up pointers and techniques. Freddy worried about something, but he didn't know what it was. He was suspicious of change, even though any disquiet he felt over this was clearly irrational. Sure, he was displaced in the kitchen, but there were worse things given the upgrade in culinary expertise which Annie had imparted upon the household. He thought maybe he was merely jealous…! A few nights later Annie was doing her show enthusiastically and loving it.

"So you see, Pammy," Annie explained, "the colors on the plate are not only pleasing to the eye, but they are nutritionally balanced also."

"Wee, zjem bow-koo lay cool-err, ay ee-gal-mohn sah sohn tray bon," said Pamela. Or so it seemed to Freddy sitting on the couch. Freddy rolled his eyes and muttered under his breath, "jeez!"

He got up and poked his nose into the kitchen. Annie scowled, having heard the "Jeez!"

"What do you want Freddy, you pirate you! Avast, you scurvy varlet! Arrgh! We won't be needin' the likes of a churl like you in here" Freddy turned and left silently.

The end result of Annie commandeering the kitchen was that, although they had been eating well prior to this, they were now eating even better.

Annie and Pamela were becoming best friends. Pamela and Annie were downtown shopping for bathing suits. After perusing the counters in one shop, Annie held up a blue two-piece against her body. "How do you think this would look on me, Pamela?"

"Annie, anything in this store would look good on you."

Annie expression to this indicated that that was obvious. She decided an explanation was in order. "I'm looking for something functional and sporty and not slutty." Pamela nodded in accord. Annie looked up suddenly. Her eyes narrowed and she focused sharply on a guy who was looking at the women's bathing suits, an odd thing in itself. He noticed her keen scrutiny and wandered off through the door, out onto the street, and was gone.

"Something wrong, Annie?" asked Pamela.

"That guy, I've seen him before."

"One of your cocktail customer's sans doute."

"No, they *want* to be noticed, they want attention. This guy didn't, Pamela. There's a lot of guys on this island and not many girls like us. This guy wasn't interested 'cause I am obviously a girl, he's up to somethining."

Pamela: "He *was* dressed a bit funny"

Annie: "You mean that mock British outfit? You can't go much on that, people here do what they want. One guy dresses like Uncle Sam, with the high hat, the stars and stripes, the whole rigmarole."

They shrugged off the occurrence and each bought a bathing suit and a rash guard for free diving. The rash guards were tight compression-fitting tops of very thin but tough stretch material designed as a protection layer in the water.

Pamela smiled. "The guys at the marina are going to love seeing you in that."

Annie grinned. "I know! Let's get a beer and go home."

****

They were at the corner bar with their purchases in bags in front of them. Annie looked around the bar. "Freddy likes this place."

"Yes, I know," said Pamela.

"He knows everybody, " Annie went on, "Hi, Harold," she called out to a compact man with a neat, short haircut. He was wearing a well pressed long-sleeved white shirt and long black pants. He grinned at her and said in a gravelly voice through clenched teeth, "Everything is copacetic. Tricks of the trade. Mmmmmm."

Annie explained. "Harold is ex-Navy. There's a lot of retired Navy down here. Quite a few submariners from those old subs – you know, not the nuclear ones. Harold was in Demolition and there was an accident. He doesn't say much, just the same few phrases, but he's a nice old guy. And then there is Ice House, and Sparks, and oh well, I don't know all of them, but Freddy knows them. Like I said, Freddy knows everybody, the fishermen, the Bahama village folks, his group of tennis players down at the beach..."

"Yes, I've seen them when we play down there. It's a well-rounded group. There are the college grads who wait tables and run the cattle boats, some old Key West family locals, the gay guys and girls, and even a tourist now and then." They were done with their beer.

"Time for laundry," said Pamela."

"Don't even bother with Freddy's shorts, Pamela. He got fiberglass resin all over it. It's so stiff you could stand it up in the corner."

****

That scenario was the picture of their multi-dimensional relationship at the present moment, the chemistry of their lives and environs, their general configuration. Whatever Wayne was hiding probably had something to do with the law, as Freddy suspected. But things were going too well to upset the status quo. Pamela was working a few mornings a week at one of the tourist boutiques downtown to keep her in spending money. She was fairly well off, having substantial savings from her two years of executive apprenticeship under her father's tutelage. Wayne and Freddy were getting by, and Annie was doing some cocktail waitressing at one of the resorts and bringing in more money than any of them. She had also taken an interest in working with a catering company. Halloween was close and that was a big holiday in Key West. Everything was fine.

Until the shrimp boat returned.

Chapter Thirteen - A Day Off

"Weather summary at 6:30 this morning, isolated showers over the Florida Straits for the Cay Sal Bank to 10 miles south of Key Largo and southwest to 25 miles south of Cudjoe Key. A few showers were over the south Gulf of Mexico 20 to 35 miles west of Cape Sable, and a few showers were over the Gulf waters west of Fort Myers. Little or no movement is indicated.

Skies will be turning partly cloudy in the Keys, temperatures will be warm throughout the week. We might spot an isolated shower or thundershower though, developing at almost any time of the day or night. Chances of showers are slim at 20 percent today with highs around 91 and overnight lows at around 75. For boaters excellent boating weather. Winds are out of the east-southeast at about 10 miles an hour, waves of about 1 foot inside and about 2 to 3 feet outside the reef."

****

It was a Sunday toward the end of October and they were at the marina. They all had the day off. Different work schedules among them made it increasingly more difficult for them to go out on the boat together. Today the weather was good. They decided to go out to the reef and make a day of it. Now that there were four experienced hands they could get organized and out there in no time at all. Freddy was helping to load the boat.

"Wayne," said Freddy, "do you want me to bring this jug of water? It's been in the boat for a long while."

"Is it potable?"

"Why, shoah, I jes' pick it up n' carry it wif me." Wayne did not respond to his bad taste attempt at humor. Freddy caught the direction of Wayne's gaze. He was moving slowly, not paying attention to what he was doing, and looking out to sea. His eyes were narrowed and there was a hard set to his face. Freddy followed his gaze and saw it. The shrimp boat was back, anchored farther out than it had been on previous sightings, and a fast-looking cigarette hull was tied up alongside.

****

They made their way out of the winding access channel with Wayne at the wheel. Once into the deep water channel marked by red and green channel markers Wayne gave the other two craft a much wider berth than was necessary, actually going outside the channel markers to do so. He said nothing, but Freddy could see his concern. The girls were together on the bow seat "chatting mindlessly to keep in practice" as Freddy would have said had he been in a mood to jest.

Before long they were well past the two boats. They passed the outer channel marker and headed toward the sea buoy and a short time later they were five miles farther out at the reef. There was a moderate breeze and a slight current.

They found a good spot and Freddy went forward to drop the anchor. He dropped the fluked Danforth and watched it settle in a sand patch nestled between some rocks. Wayne backed the boat slowly until the anchor bit. The scope was good, about eighty-five feet of line with the boat in twelve feet of water on the inside of the escarpment. The boat swung around as it aligned itself with the breeze out of the northeast.

"Freddy, swim down and check that anchor, would you please?" called Wayne. Wayne was being extraordinarily cautious, it seemed to Freddy. Freddy was about to ask what for when he decided that it would be easier to humor Wayne. Freddy would be getting wet eventually anyway. He pulled on his gear and swam down to the anchor. It was securely entrenched in the sand in the center of the rocks, the flukes deep in the sand. It wasn't going anywhere.

"It's ginger-peachy, Wayne," yelled Freddy as he came to the surface, "anything else you'd like me to check?" Instead of a funny answer or a retort of any kind Wayne remained silent. Ok, Wayne, be inscrutable, see if I care.

They swam upwind in front of the boat. Ahead of them was a short swim in the shallow water and a massive stand of elkhorn coral whose tops were only eighteen inches under water. There were areas of sand where they could stand. They paired off and swam toward the shallower water where they might find some lobsters around the edges of the big islands of fire and staghorn coral, patrolling around these islands, working systematically, circling one then another and watching for antenna protruding from the lobster's hiding places. A good number of barracuda also patrolled the area, either swimming from side to side, making the esses of a small slalom course, or hovering, stationary, with jaws agape, opening and closing slightly as they breathed. Even the small ones two feet long had jaws the size of a large dog, filled with needle-shaped teeth pointing inward, razor sharp, to tear flesh quickly. Though they never attacked, they could be intimidating at times.

Pamela was nearly over her fear of barracudas. Freddy told her it was good to have a healthy respect for them, but they would not attack unless lured to strike by the flash of a ring or watch or an ornate piece of jewelry. The flash of the sun on the face of a watch in silty water is a signal kindred to the silver side of a herring presenting itself for the 'cuda's supper. The diver sees a flash, and then a motionless barracuda inches from his wrist. Sleek as a 50's racer at the salt flats for speed trails, it is suddenly there faster than the eye can follow.

****

The main things Freddy feared were not barracudas and sharks. The unseen things lurking in holes and caverns, the nurse sharks and the morays, easily provoked quite by accident if a diver was not careful, were the things he was a little wary of. A man-of-war floating above a diver ferreting for lobster or intent on shooting a fish could also teach a painful lesson if the diver was too enthused with his sport to look up as he ascended.

Sea urchins were another thing to be careful of. They will puncture fingers. They will even go through a rubber bootie and break off in a foot. Their carbony spines break and shatter when gripped with fingers or tweezers. Once impaled, they sometimes have to grow out. At that time they were abundant; now there are none.

Being restricted to the edges of the coral stands, as they were by the shallow amount of water above the coral tops, Pamela and Freddy, Wayne and Annie had to extract what lobsters they could find from the convoluted intricacies at the edges of the entwined coral colonies. If a lobster should make a run deeper into the coral maze they would not pursue it. To swim over the reaching abrasive arms would have them foundering onto the tops of the coral each time a tidal swell buoyed them up and then deserted them and dropped them. Swimming carefully without even attempting a lobster capture would at best be a test to see if the swimmer could get over the coral without receiving painful stings and burns that the rocky barnacles 18 inches below the surface would bestow upon them. Severely limited as to maneuverability, limited by little water available to accommodate the conventional propelling kick of fins, more technical swimming methods would have to be employed. Mindful also that coral burns are slow to heal because calcium particles and organisms get under the skin, that cement poisoning or blood poisoning can result, and that doctors and antibiotics are expensive, the four of them made an extra effort not to spook the little devils into the coral maze.

Now and then they would come upon a ledge under which there was a group of lobsters. This late in the season there was usually one legal sized one at the back of the group. The senior lobster used his or her smaller counterparts as a protective screen before him or her, like an underwater quarterback trying not to get sacked. In this case, the sack was Freddy's yellow nylon mesh game bag.

Absorbed as they were in what they were doing, no one had looked up to check their position relative to the boat in quite some time. The motor sound of an approaching craft broke Freddy's concentration, caused him to look up across the water out of curiosity. He found that they were farther from the boat than they should have been. If it had not been for the other boat they would have found themselves still farther away. Normally they would reposition the boat, staying within range of the dive flag flying from the radio antenna within which other boats were not supposed to approach. They would also be able to get back to the boat quickly if there were sharks in the water or some emergency occurred.

Freddy clinked his knife to the metal rim of his net, and the long-ranging of the sound underwater got Wayne and Annie's attention. When they looked up he called to them. "Wayne, Annie, let's start back, we're getting too far from the boat." Even if they did not hear him his hand signals let them know what he said. They were even farther from the boat than were Freddy and Pamela. Wayne looked sharply in the direction of their boat and at the other craft, which also flew a dive flag. It was obscured for the most part; Freddy's boat was in the way. It seemed suspiciously close to Freddy's boat. The dive flag Freddy's boat flew should have warned the newcomer to stay clear.

The two pairs started swimming back to the boat. After several minutes Freddy and Pamela were two-thirds of the way back to the boat and Wayne and Annie were getting closer to Pamela and Freddy when the other boat left at a high rate of speed as suddenly as it had come on the scene, again keeping to the far side of Freddy's boat. "Look over there," said Wayne. The haze in the northeast was darkening. "There's a storm brewing." It would be one of those rare ones that come from nowhere. It was a good thing they had started back.

They kept swimming toward the boat, but it did not seem to be getting any bigger. In fact, it looked as though it was getting smaller. It looked like it had been anchored with too much line tied off for the depth of the water it was in. The angle of incidence of the anchor line to the water was very small, although Freddy knew this could not be so - he had deployed the correct amount of line - about eighty feet. Now it looked as though twice that length had been played out.

Wayne called out, "Freddy, the boat is drifting. It's slipping the anchor line. Make a swim for it."

Freddy knew that the anchor line had been secure, yet the boat was drifting away from them as surely as the sun was shining, in one direction, anyway. In the other direction, the direction opposite that of the boat, the sky was turning black. Wayne was too far from the boat to make a go of it, although he had on the long, Italian racing fins that were right for the job. Freddy was in a position where he could possibly reach the boat, and he would have to do it with his over-large jet fins. Powerful, lots of control, but not built for speed over any length of time. The energy spent using them in a sprint was disproportionate to the sustained speed they were capable of; they would tire a swimmer fast.

But the boat was getting farther away. Freddy dropped the bag of lobsters he and Pamela had caught, knowing that the others would retrieve it. He started kicking for the boat.

He was no slouch in the water. His body rose up as the force of his fins pushed him ahead and the strokes of his arms pulled him along. The downward component of his stroke also served to lift him higher in the water. From his blurred vision of the boat through the mask as he made his way rapidly through the water, it seemed that the angle of the anchor line to the water was getting even smaller. The line could not have parted - it would have gone limp if it had. The line was playing out from the line locker through the chocks.

Ridiculously, a half-formed thought occurred in the back of Freddy's mind: it was a long swim back to Key West and the girls would be angry with him if he let the boat get away. There was nothing between the boat and the Dry Tortugas. He had already guessed somewhere in the back of his consciousness that the others had concluded that he had managed somehow to make a mistake when he anchored the boat, as ludicrous as that might seem. He had to catch the boat and exonerate himself or he might as well not come back at all. If the storm caught the boat first he would not have to worry about it - they might all be lost. Small consolation that.

Freddy was making up some of the distance. Wayne and Freddy both knew there was three hundred feet of brand new one-half inch nylon anchor line coiled in the bow, because they were too lazy to cut what line they had in stock when they replaced the old line which was gnarled and bent with age and frayed where it had chafed on rocks and coral.

The line was now at a very shallow angle to the water. Perhaps the cleat was damaged and Freddy hadn't noticed it. Perhaps it had simply broken loose. Freddy knew it was not so. The line continued to play out and Freddy continued to make up distance.

As the line played out it snagged and pulled its way out of the line locker in the bow and through the chocks and helped to slow the boat's rate of drift. Offsetting this, there was the increasing force of the wind from the storm forming behind him which was trying to make the boat drift faster.

Freddy was tiring. His legs were beginning to burn and his arms ached. Ironically, had the old anchor line still been in use it would have snagged solid in the chocks by now. The un-abraded, newer line was smooth and nicely coiled. The snags undid themselves with the pull of each gust of wind on the hull. Freddy was closer, but there could not be much line left in that locker and when it was gone there would be a mad scramble to overtake the boat before it took off with the wind toward the Dry Tortugas.

He was breathing heavily, explosively, through his snorkel. Because of it he was not hampered by the extra motions and inherent timing problems of a swimmer not so equipped. He was not limited to when he could take breaths, which was fortuitous because he was taking as many long, deep breaths as he could muster and still he was already deep in oxygen debt. His lungs felt as though they were ready to burst.

A cramp developed in Freddy's left arch. His foot wanted to curl up into a ball. He did not want to think about the other two and his Pamela being stuck out five miles from shore with ever less chance of a passing boat as the day wore on and the storm moving into the area. Make that "forming right over" the area. Night predators, sharks that could not be seen to fend off, would be around. If that threat did not get them, the elements might. He gave no thought to his own position should the boat get away. In the coming storm he would become disoriented and not be able to see three feet - scant would be his chances to find water shallow enough to stand in should nightfall come before the storm abated.

No chance of retrieving his friends.

The wind continued to pick up signaling the approach of the storm.

His heart was racing when the bitter end of the line slipped over the bow. The current had been helping to a small degree in preventing the boat from running off at high speed, but now even that slight impediment was not enough in the face of the rising wind. The boat turned, making more efficient use of the wind as the windscreen and the Bimini top became a sail. The boat speeded up as it turned away from Freddy and started to run with the wind. It was turning away at an increasing rate and moving away from him as he made a swipe for the side of the hull, knowing full well it was a futile act even before his hand slid from the sleek fiberglass side of the boat. The pressure of his swipe actually caused the boat to swing away quicker than before. The low part of the transom would be out of reach before he could get a grip on it. Kicking violently despite the pain in his legs, windmilling the water with his arms, he reached for the boat's side once more and stretched to reach a line hanging over the side of the hull that should not have been there. It was a line on a cleat on the gunnel near the rear of the boat used for tying up dock-side, normally stowed on board. It had been in its proper place as they motored out. Now it dangled almost within Freddy's grasp. He shot his hand out like the last crawl stroke of a racer reaching for the edge of the pool. He grabbed for the line and felt it in his hand. He pulled the boat and himself closer together.

He was gasping for breath.

With the line clenched in his right hand he lunged upward for the top of the gunnel with his left. Letting the rope fall free of his right hand, he threw that hand across the gunnel also. With every ounce of strength he had he kicked the big fins and propelled himself out of the water as far as he could while pulling himself over the gunnel with his arms, an aquatic gymnast mounting an imaginary bar. The movement sent a stab of pain up his arm from his recently injured wrist. He twisted in the air and sat on the gunnel facing out, rolled backward and sideways and let himself sprawl onto the deck. Now he had to try to keep the others in sight, get back before the squall swallowed them up and get them safely back into the boat.

Start, you bastard!

It did. With a roar and a rooster tail, a rear onto the stern and a mighty "Hi, ho Silver", the boat's nose rose and swung around as it lurched upward into the wind. Freddy opened the throttle, still sailing on adrenalin, high and giddy from oxygen starvation. He headed dead into the wind, reversing the course of the boat's wind drift. That course should lead him back to Wayne and Annie and Pamela.

The sea was coming at the boat in short chops. The wind was coming up fast and the little wavelets hadn't had time to extend the period of their undulation. The sudden push of the brightening breeze gave the waves time only to wedge sharply upward before it knocked their tops off in a white cap of foam.

A steady trail of spittle came at Freddy horizontally from the froth on the tops of the waves. It tossed onto the windscreen like brushes on a snare drum. Out ahead vertical rain lines appeared and big drops made a percolating obfuscation of the sea tops. The air above the churning ocean surface was opaque. He could not see his friends. Their bobbing heads were lost in the chop. There was a danger that he could run them over...

He slowed and searched anxiously. Then he saw Wayne's signal, a bully net extended out above the water, and corrected the steering slightly to head for it. Just beyond the net was a solid line of whiter water, the confusion of wind and water churning and beating through the baffles of coral, a natural warning for him not to pile the boat up on the reef if he over-ran the place where his friends were. It would also have been the dismal signal to put about and start a grid search had he not come upon them on the first lucky try. Moments later three heads materialized below the bully net.

****

Wayne had the sense to retreat with the girls to the shallower water instead of trying to follow in the direction of the boat. He had been forty yards behind Freddy at the start of his swim and loaded with gear and lobsters and two females loaded with consternation. The girls were good in the water, but Wayne had the experience. Now they had a little more as well. He also had something more - an instinct, or maybe it was the presence of mind to make the right decision in a threatening situation. It was more than experience, or him being the male taking care of two frightened females - both girls were capable in spite of their fears - it was a natural thing, something inherent, exclusive to him. It commanded respect and deference to his judgment. How well Freddy would learn this lesson in the weeks to come. And Wayne would have to trust Freddy if he was smart; if that was not his one blind spot.

The sweet, sticky smell of the water being flailed and releasing its carbonation rode before the frenetic mix of white water. Flipping the boat into reverse, Freddy revved the engine to stop the boat's forward motion and cut the engine. Freddy cut the wheel and the gang grabbed on – to that same line Freddy had used to recaptured the boat. Freddy had tied it to a life vest and thrown it back over the side. If the three had tried to grab the boat as it was now pitching in the ever growing heavy sea state any false move would find the weight of the boat coming down upon them.

The boat drifted back off the shallows as the others climbed in carefully and with deliberately will timed movements over the transom, one by one; Ample Annie came up first, then Pamela. Freddy pulled the girls aboard. Wayne stayed in the water in case one of the girls should lose her grip on the line as it tugged and pulsed with the rhythm of the waves. Wayne came up last, timing the pitching of the boat to aid his boarding. He mounted the stern as it squatted and rode it up as the boat kicked its ass high in the air. He looked as though he bounded aboard "Glad to see you, Freddy," he said with a grin. "Pretty impressive swim."

"Yeah, I'm gonna try out for the Special Olympics next."

"Oh, my goodness, Freddy, what took you so long?"

"Sorry about that, Annie. This thing," meaning the boat, "must have drifted quite a bit after the anchor line parted company with the boat." Freddy and Pamela had been forty yards from Wayne and Annie at the start. After the others had doubled back to the more safe position of the shallower water with Pamela, another forty-five yards separated them. While Freddy agonized during his frustrating swim he put more distance between them, how much he could only guess, but it had to be at least another eighty yards. Drifting at a much higher rate of speed after the anchor line got away and Freddy got aboard and continuing to do so for the time necessary for some mandatory breaths on the boat's deck, the gap opened much faster as the boat ran with the wind. They were possibly five hundred yards apart in low visibility seas before Freddy got under power and turned the boat straight back into the wind. It was a more serious and suspect situation than Freddy wanted the girls to know.

"Looks like we lost an anchor and a whole lot of line," Freddy said to Wayne. He was putting up the side curtains as Freddy turned once more and spun for home.

"What happened to the anchor, Freddy?" Pamela asked.

"I don't know. I must have tied it wrong and all the line slipped over the side," Freddy lied, not wanting to get her worried.

Matters were getting too serious to let the incident drop. Wayne had heard Freddy falsely admit to the mistake of not properly securing the anchor line and seeing Wayne's head cock as Freddy spoke the lie let Freddy know Wayne was aware Freddy knew that there was no mistake made. They had both checked everything before getting into the water, as they always did. They both could see that the cleat was still in place and knew that the line had been half inch nylon, practically new, and securely tied off.

The rain and the wind began whipping the Bimini top in earnest, a sheet of water hitting the canvas with each gust. But now it was an annoyance, not a threat. As the ladies sorted things out, gear and lobster and the like — not easy as the boat plowed through the waves, Freddy caught Wayne's attention with a tap on the arm as Wayne came to fix the curtains nearest Freddy's position at the helm. Freddy leaned over toward him so that Pamela and Annie would not hear them over the masking sounds of the engine and the rain and the sea.

"You know I just barely made it to this thing in time. We got lucky." He gave no hint yet that he knew that there was mischief afoot; and that the incident wasn't born of any natural danger, predators, or the weather. None od those things had been the cause of their trouble,.

"Yes, Freddy," he answered, "that was an impressive performance. Clean living - that's what does it."

"What about you, Wayne? Are you 'clean living'? Or are you mixed up with druggers or smugglers or something?"

"What are you saying, Freddy?" It sounded like he was starting to drop the pretension. He knew Freddy was on to something. He did not know how much Freddy knew or suspected.

"Wayne, the boat was wet inside when I came aboard."

"It was raining."

"It wasn't raining yet. Somebody came aboard and untied that anchor line from the cleat, and I think you may have an idea who it was. The line on the rear cleat was hanging over the side. Somebody either knocked it over or used it to pull themselves aboard. I think that boat that pulled up before probably brought divers with scuba tanks; I think they first moved the anchor underwater to make sure they got a good bit of distance between us and our boat and then they slipped the line. It had to be more than one guy to do that.

They didn't expect us to get back in time."

Wayne paused for a moment, and then he said, "You're right. Someone is up to something, but it could have been your friends from the Mascot."

"I don't think so." He went on after a beat. "They wouldn't go to that much trouble. If they did try something like this, they'd cut the line. They're not subtle enough for this," he said, referring to the manner in which the deed was done. "There's somebody watching us, I think, maybe every day."

"Did you ever think perhaps that it might be a prankster? Or even a boat thief?"

"If it was a boat thief it was the stupidest one in the world. This thing isn't worth the trouble, for one thing, and the keys were in the ignition, for another. And pranksters probably would draw the line at a possible multiple murder. You know no one except the guys at the marina knows we're out here, and they wouldn't miss us for a long while, if at all. Sure, if I didn't get to the boat we might have been picked up - there are a few hours of daylight left - but then again we may not have been. Wayne, I *know* you are mixed up in something, but I don't know what it is. Are you going to tell me about it?"

"Freddy, I can't tell you about it. Not at this time, anyway. They're out to hassle me, not to kill anyone. They couldn't know the storm was coming, that was just a coincidence, I'm sure of it. It's part our fault 'cause we should have seen it coming." Freddy's resigned look showed he didn't buy that, but Wayne was right about the others not knowing about the storm. It formed too suddenly for anyone to predict. But the culprits could have seized the opportunity and took advantage of the situation when they realized that the storm was developing. "Give me a couple of days," said Wayne, "I'll straighten things out."

Freddy sighed. "Ok, Wayne, we'll wait a couple of days. But then I want to know what's going on."

They continued in and outran the storm and came into bright sunshine. It was as though the other event was not real. Freddy switched on the sump pump. A healthy stream of water ran from it. The cracks in the hull were leaking; things could be better down there. Those stringers in the bilge weren't healing.

Chapter Fourteen – Questions

Monday morning found them with nothing much to do but finish prepping a hull. Having no other work lined up at the marina, Wayne and Freddy were sitting in the living room, drinking coffee. There was no rush to get to work today. Pamela was working at the boutique-cum-junk shop and tee shirt emporium and Annie was out running and undoubtedly giving whiplash to every male driving down A1A. Probably some of the females as well. Even with her four wire bra she could not arrest the natural rhythm her strides imparted to her breasts. Freddy had researched this thoroughly. She moved with a joyous, wonderful bounce followed by a circular jiggle of each one in turn. She had asked Freddy to join her but he said, "No, thanks, Annie, it's too hot to trot. Let me know when the video comes out." She left and they were alone.

"So what's going on, Wayne?" They had talked about their lack of work, the weather, and everything else to avoid this uncomfortable subject until now. "Are you on the wrong side of some drug ring or something?"

"I imagine it does look like the classic drug setup - fast boats and a shrimper that could be a mother ship making odd movements, doing nothing remotely like shrimping. There is really not much I can tell you, Freddy."

"Wayne, there are some things you *gotta* tell me! Who are these guys and what do they want? Are Pamela and Annie in any danger? If they are, I wanna get them out of town."

"They're after me, not you or the girls. They are former "business associates" of mine. I have some information they want." This was not entirely true, but it was close.

"So why don't you give it to them?"

"I can't."

"And you can't tell me either."

"No."

"Funny way of doing business. Couldn't you be more cryptic? Did you forget who I am?"

"it's for your own protection," he clucked. "These fellows don't go through normal channels. They aren't too well liked by the law in this country. In most countries, for that matter."

"Great. Somocistas. No, wait. Sandinistas? I forget which ones are the good guys. It's so confusing down there; it's hard to know who to root for. Whose side are we on now?"

"It's nothing like that at all. Just some business associates from up north which have gone international." This was all new to Freddy. The information was sketchy. It left a lot to be desired.

"That's it?" he asked. "That's all you're going to tell me? Is it drugs?"

Wayne made a quasi-nod of acknowledgment. "Part of their enterprises is a drug operation, but I wasn't a part of that. It was another situation in another place and I wish I had never gotten involved with them. It seemed like the thing to do at the time."

"So why can't you tell them what they want to know?"

He sighed. "That would entail betraying a trust. But I will have to tell them something. I can't have them harassing Pamela and Annie and you just because *they* and *you* are with *me*."

"Don't worry about me; I'll help you out whatever it is. But I have to make sure the girls are OK."

Wayne assured Freddy that he and the girls were in no danger and that he would tell his friends enough to make them leave. Freddy wanted to believe that it would be that simple, and so he did. He hoped that this was the end of the matter.

The next two days were uneventful. Wayne took off Tuesday morning and went out to the shrimp boat and had a "talk" with the principals involved in his controversy. Returning later that day, he announced that all was well and the matter was resolved. The mystery people had some "business in another area" and would be leaving, for good, to do business from another location. Freddy was relieved. He was still curious about something. He asked Wayne Wednesday at work.

"Wayne, I assume the 'other business' these guys left to do is drugs."

"I assume you might assume correctly, but then again your assumption might be wrong. As I have said, It could be any of a number of things."

"How can they be getting away with *anything* when they are so obvious?"

"They are very clever."

"Obviously. I understand that they have already been boarded by the Coast Guard for a 'safety inspection', and the guards at the old desalting plant tell me that the feds have been watching from shore. I've seen you looking at them pretty intently, also."

He sent Freddy an annoyed look, then he offered a brief explanation. "That shrimp boat anchored out there has nothing to do with the actual logistical operation. That's a command boat. That's the way he works."

"Who?"

"None of your business. As I said before, it's not simply just your typical drug operation. I told you these guys had a lot of other interests. That boat out there is outfitted inside like a pleasure boat, I doubt that there has ever been any contraband on it, and I'm sure it hasn't ever had a shrimp on it that wasn't on a plate. There is a *lot* of electronics equipment on board. I don't know why the outriggers are still on it, but I imagine they are supposed to fool somebody, somewhere, to stay low-key. They may even be disguised radio antennas. You can be sure that the boss behind those guys on board is not about to be seen around here if he can help it. They probably rendezvous in one of their fast boats several miles out."

They had finished scraping a hull Freddy had started Tuesday morning while Wayne was away with his nefarious business associates. Tomorrow they would give the hull a bottom coat, finishing with another on Friday.

But that Wednesday afternoon the shrimp boat-command ship left as Wayne said it would. Freddy's tension over the matter was eased and he was glad it had not been necessary to trouble Annie and Pamela over it.

****

"Ok, Nick, I told Teddy are operations here are over. I think he bought it. He says he'll keep his clam shut."

"I don't think that will be good enough, Mickey. He knows too much. He should not have been snooping in the first place. He's going to have to go. Take care of it."

"I could have done it yesterday if Teddy wasn't packing heat."

"Yeah, well be that as it may, Joe wouldn't have liked for it to go down here on the boat, anchored right here and all. That would make us vulnerable. Joe doesn't like that much."

"How do you want it set up, boss?"

"I don't care. Make it look like an accident or frame it on his friend, whatever. You know what you're doing, and you're on the scene. I've had business elseware; I'm not up to speed on this situation locally, and I don't want to bother Joe."

"I'll take care of it, boss."

****

The money situation, or, more correctly the possibility of having a dearth of it during the coming weeks, was sorting itself out also. Wayne was to start Monday working a construction job on South Atlantic Boulevard where a motel was adding more units, an early harbinger of the nightmare of development which would hit Key West in the years to come. Freddy was to stay with the boat work for a while and generally get things organized so that they could carry on a limited operation until things picked up, and in case one of their customers should need something done. Freddy had a line on a job himself. UPS would soon be hiring temporaries and the job would probably last right through Christmas. The pay was good by

Key West standards. Wayne had tipped Freddy to the job opening - Wayne could not take the job himself due to his past dealings up north.

Pamela would be leaving her boutique job to help Freddy close out the boat work jobs, and to clean and straighten and store things. She would be the real organizational factor behind that project. She would then look for something more substantial herself. Annie would be picking up additional shifts of cocktail waitressing. She was also thinking of starting some type of cooking venture. For the next few nights, she was not scheduled. And so none of them had much to do on that Thursday evening late in October, nothing until Monday morning. This was fortunate in that a big holiday was approaching for Key West - Halloween. A kind of mini Mardi-Gras atmosphere would prevail. The household seemed back on an even keel. They all had work, and Annie's worries dissolved as Wayne became his old, former self again. Tonight they would celebrate their good fortune. They would attend a performance of a four-part play at the Waterfront Playhouse after getting some prime rib and baked potatoes at a place known for it near the marina. "Goody, real meat!" said Annie.

****

The play was only fair, but the food was good. Colorado beef, baked potatoes with plenty of butter, sour cream and chives, corn on the cob, and a salad bar. Annie was ecstatic.

****

The Casa Marina had been Freddy's latest local haunt, B. P. (before Pamela). It sat on the corner of Reynolds and Seminole, on the ocean between the swimming pier and Louie's Back Yard. The entrance was opposite the apex of the corner, in an outer wall section that faced the corner squarely, set back far from the street. The two streets bordering the property and the extension of the planes of the two wing's front walls off the center section of the building contained a roughly five-sided parking lot and canopied garden promenade to the hotel entrance. To the right of the entrance was the restaurant; to the left was a boutique.

Through the central double doors of small glass panes and white painted wood trim was the lobby; wood columns vaulted to the ceiling and a hardwood floor shined impossibly. Opposite the entrance, across the lobby from the street side, a wall of paired double doors looked out onto the grounds and the ocean. Those far-side doors gave way to a terrazzo terrace and a cloister of arches of wood and colonnades of cement block enclosing ceiling fans hung high under the eaves of the second floor balcony. Beyond the hedge-lined terrace wall was the pool and Jacuzzi surrounded by grass and sculptured bushes, then a Tiki bar and a barbecue, both of unfinished wooden decking and wood lattice work enclosures, then sand, then ocean.

As it was back then, there were two tennis courts far off to the left overlooking the water. They were built where scrubby Australian pines and land crabs over a span of years once presided when the hotel was dormant. The placement and choice of the trees planted around the courts were either carefully planned or a beautiful mistake. A bushy-topped one here, a smooth-barked one there, with horizontal limbs for pretty girls to sit on and perhaps have their picture taken. There were leafy trees and Christmas palms, flakey Gumbo Limbos and coconut palms, crawling vines and bougainvillea on a trellis, flagstone walks in the grass and flowers and fern-like bushes, and a wood-shingled roof over part of the decking, with a banister to lean on.

A pier far out into the water was on the right. It had a gazebo on it one-third of the way out. It replaced a line of rock that had been there as support for a previous pier which was long since gone when Freddy arrived in Key West, and which Freddy and the other patrons of the piano and beach bar next door gazed upon as they looked toward the shuttered and locked up property, as it was when Freddy first arrived.   Terrazzo walkways wound through the grounds. They were interspersed with the bushes and old-time black, metal lanterns. The Casa Marina was a picture postcard place with a red tile roof, built of the same cement Flagler used to build the bridges for his railroad.

The Casa Marina was where they were going next. They hadn't been there since Pamela's initiation to Freddy's dancing several months earlier. She must have forgotten about that by now, he thought.

Parking at home, they walked the two blocks to the hotel. Freddy said hello to the bellman and they stepped into the lobby. They started up the three steps to the lounge, preceded by a young lady with long, straight, blond hair in a short, white dress and high heels. The dress seemed much too short for her; she revealed much leg to them below at an enticing angle as her hips swung up the steps.

Wayne or Freddy must have gone Mmmmmm or Ahhhhhh or something because the sexy, leggy lady swung her hips and made a half turn toward them as she walked and smiled coyly with come-on eyes. She had slightly prominent upper front teeth, a pretty face and a slightly cleft chin. As Annie looked back to catch the perpetrator, Freddy quickly switched his attention to a potted palm. Pamela smirked at him as he admired the plant.

"My goodness, Wayne, you behave yourself," Annie scolded. He threw up his arms and let his mouth drop open looking completely innocent, wrongly accused of checking some other girl's merchandise. Freddy, still preoccupied with the plant, got a short tug on the arm from Pamela. Seeing Wayne's dumb show, Annie quipped, "I suppose you are going to tell me that noise was your stomach. It sounded like a hungry polar bear, for gosh sakes!"

This prompted Wayne to say, "She isn't my type, Annie." Zounds! thought Freddy, she was *anybody's* type! Freddy rolled his eyes behind Annie's back at Pamela and she laughed into her hand. "I'm not into white bunny rabbits," said Wayne, and with this declaration he stuck his top teeth out over his lower lip, pressed a finger to his chin, tilted his head and smiled goo-goo eyed.

"Oh, silly you," said Annie, slapping his arm and laughing. Pamela turned to Freddy.

"That was you, wasn't it?" she asked as she leaned to him so they weren't overheard.

"Yup." He wore a self-satisfied grin.

Annie addressed him. "Freddy, you are being strangely silent. I thought you always had something to say when it came to pretty girls. Don't tell me this is one you don't know."

"Oh, you mean that sexratery?" he asked. Annie frowned.

"What is a sexratery, Freddy?" Pamela was playing along to see where he was going to go with this.

"A sexratery is a female office worker, known for long legs and a curvaceous rear end."

Annie looked indignant. "Wouldn't you just know he would say something like *that*. Chauvinist swine."

"Pig."

"**What did you call me?!**" She spun on him, arms angled back at her shoulders and hanging behind her, shocked.

"Not you, me. Pig, not swine, Chauvinist pig." He feigned a hurt and dismayed look.

"Oh, Freddy, I'm sorry." He looked happy again. He was having a good time. Wayne cut in.

"You could be describing Secretariat, Freddy."

"*Who* is *that?*" Annie wanted to know.

"Secretariat was a race horse, dear," Wayne explained. "A fast one. As I remember, the horse had long legs and a curved butt, too."

"I'd better not catch Wayne running around after that legs and butt in there."

"There really are similarities, you know," Freddy instructed, "the better they are the faster they have to run. I like that one's decoupage."

"You mean décolletage," corrected Pamela.

"No, decoupage. Look at the sexy surface decoration and the transparent designs and artsy manner."

It is décolletage, though, that is getting her the entourage that is following her around this place," rejoined Pamela.

"Same thing."

"And now she has a pair of sniveling dogs waiting in the wings and drooling here as well," added Annie to Pamela like Oliver Hardy to Stan Laurel, nodding her head toward Wayne and Freddy.

The girls were looking good. Annie was wearing a red pants suit on the dressy side and Pamela had on a black dress with lacy material at the top you could almost see through. Wayne wore a tan shirt and brown slacks (Annie had called them "sienna") he had purchased at Annie's prompting and Freddy was in a blue velour shirt with a vee neck and gray pants. Very civilized. Freddy's attire had inspired many "Beam me up, Scotty," jibes.

They found four seats at the bar. Once seated Pamela asked Freddy, "How do you know that the girl in the white is a secretary?"

"It's Thursday night, right?"

"Right," she said tentatively.

"Tuesday night nurses get drinks half price. Wednesday is Margarita night. I guess Margueritas get drinks half price. Thursday is half price for secretaries." She glanced around the bar and sure enough, there were a number of women, alone or in two's and three's, sitting at the bar. Some were more than a little sloppy from drinking cheap since closing up shop at their law offices, real estate, and insurance brokerages. Some were good lookers, others had started to spread. There was a downside to free munchies. At the end of the bar a graying lady was waving to Freddy and smiling.

"Who is that?" asked Pamela.

"Jealous?"

"No, but---"

"Freddy is well known around here, Pammy," said her buddy Annie. "He used to support this place before you moved down here."

"That lady," said Freddy "happens to be a friend of mine. I'm *her* type. Old ladies think I'm handsome. I'm looking forward to my old age. 'Some enchanted evening...'"

"Here it comes," lamented Wayne.

"You may meet a stranger, you may see a stranger, across a crowded room..."

"Booooo..." Wayne again.

"And night after night, as strange as she seems, she will make you more miserable, than your wildest dreams. Thank you, thank you. Wayne you gotta wait for the message, there is always a message. Pamela, don't you just love the message? Annie?"

"I think you're silly, too, Freddy," said Annie, in giggly reply, and gave him a kiss. Pamela gave him a kiss, too.

****

They could have danced all night, but they didn't. There wasn't enough room on the dance floor for them to engage in their normal free-form Terpsichore, so they sat and chatted. Hugging Freddy, Pamela asked, "Do you remember the last time we were here? Let's take a walk, Freddy; I want to talk to you."

They walked to the Tiki bar outside, now closed for the evening, stood out on the decking and watched the night. There was a breeze. Pamela moved against him to ward off the chill. She felt good against him.

"I'm having a wonderful time down here, Freddy." She was nearly as tall as he. She turned, tilting her head slightly upward toward him. "Freddy, do you think you might like a more permanent situation?"

"Do you mean like a real job?" he said, although he knew where she was leading. She was, after all, a girl from a respectable Ohio upbringing. He was uncertain of what he should do. She looked into his eyes, those unconscious betrayers of emotion, and continued to press her case.

"No, Freddy, I mean like getting a place of our own and starting a family." She paused again. "I love you, Freddy." She said it softly, still looking up at him. Her eyes told him she wanted to hear the same words from him, words he had not used, except in passion. He'd been indolently independent for so long. He thought of how much Pamela meant to him as she watched his face work and misinterpreted his delay and facial contortions, thinking that Freddy did not feel as she did. Turning to her from his thoughtful, unfocused gaze, he saw her shrink from him in shame as her composure break. She tried to turn away, embarrassed by her tearful eyes.

Hugging her, his cheek against her hair, he said, "I love you. It just took me a while to get used to the idea." Pamela made a miraculous recovery. She shivered, and then made a breathy, relieved laugh through her sniffles. "We'll start saving," he said. "Maybe in a couple of months we can get our own place." Lingering a while longer, they kissed, sealing the resolution. Freddy felt giddy, light-headed, and scared. The prospect of putting himself in focus, pulling himself out of the ashes of the burned-out Freddy, a phoenix evolving out of Pamela's inspiration, excited and frightened him.

****

Back at the bar they came upon Wayne sitting alone. He picked up on Pamela's radiance and noticed the pride of ownership was reciprocal as Pamela let Freddy steer her by the arm. Soon they would all be respectable. Freddy had no doubts that Pamela's plans would include marriage, and that would be all right, too, at least after token resistance.

"Where is our favorite cheerleader?" Freddy called out to Wayne over the sounds of the band.

"Oh, she's inspecting the plumbing," he quipped euphemistically. Annie's drink was on Wayne's left. Pamela and Freddy regained the chairs they had vacated earlier, Freddy on Wayne's right and Pamela next to Freddy, nearest to the band.

Something made Freddy glance to the right and he saw Annie returning. She had started up the three steps to the level of the bar. Something caught Freddy's attention. A largish man with the look of a thug was following her. Indeed, he was headed right for her and was overtaking her. Freddy felt warning signals going off and became alert as his adrenalin started to flow.

The man accosted her, grabbing her rudely by the arm. He was trying to hustle her quickly out the side door before they saw him. She was trying to pull away.

Freddy was forty steps away. He started from his chair to Annie's aid, but Wayne was already whizzing past him. He had wheeled out of his chair, propelling himself from it with such force that he sent it flying ten feet in the opposite direction. It rolled and bounced into a glass-fronted cupboard next to a settee with a piercing jangle of shattering glass, then making shards of the sliding glass doors, perforating the noise of the band as a piccolo's trill is heard over an orchestra, turning heads the wrong way, toward the cupboard, until they caught the blur of Wayne's flight.

The man had pulled Annie out and away from the dance floor as Wayne had reached the top step. The thug was repeatedly trying to get hold of her other arm and hustle her through the crowd and out the side door. Annie was strong and athletic; she gave him more resistance than he bargained for with quick evasive moves to disengage herself each time from his grasp. As Freddy watched, Wayne hurled himself headlong from the top step. He went for the man's throat.

They landed on a table top, breaking glasses, getting cut, causing the couple seated there to recoil in shock. Wayne lost his purchase on the other man's throat as they fell to the floor. The man grabbed Wayne's shoulder to throw him off. Freddy caught a fleeting glimpse of Wayne's eyes and they were wild, wild as the night in the Mascot. Incredibly, instead of backing off from such close quarters, Wayne next grabbed the shirt of the thug in his left hand and balled it up in his fist. Using the grip for leverage he pulled himself so close to the villain that their noses were only inches apart. With his right hand tilted back, he repeatedly drove the heel of his hand into the chin, nose, and throat of the brute. The man's face was bloody and he was foaming and drooling. Wayne was glaring and fuming in the attacker's face as he made a pulp of it. He continued pulling the man's face, again and again, toward the heel of his onrushing right hand as they slid across the floor. The large man finally rolled free. Wayne regained his feet first. As his adversary stumbled to his feet Wayne did something astounding. It sickened Freddy. Wayne jumped into the air and kicked the other man's right knee. The knee had been supporting the man's considerable bulk. It broke with a snap. He came down on it with all his weight.

As he spilled to the floor Wayne set after him again and he might have killed the man if Freddy and a security guard hadn't pulled him off. That gave the man the opportunity to hobble far enough to join two others, unseen until now, who hustled him toward a waiting car.

****

Freddy felt vaguely confused by what had happened. It was as though he was watching a movie that he didn't want to see. Wayne had blazed past him with a speed he did not know Wayne, or anyone, was capable of, and showed hidden talents which lent themselves quite well to mayhem. As the man was half-carried from the building by his friends, he turned toward Wayne and said something. Freddy was close enough to hear.

"This isn't over yet, Teddy," he said in a gruff voice as he passed, bracketed by two others bearing his weight. The security guard was clearly in no position to confront these men.

"*Who is Teddy?*" Freddy blurted.

"The guy probably calls everyone Teddy," said Wayne, his breathing and his countenance returning to normal.

"Is there *something else* I should know, Wayne?"

"Not now." Annie was still standing off to the side. She had seen and heard everything. She was clearly very disturbed. The manager, an attractive lady whose goatee Freddy had thought about kissing on several occasions, had seen the man manhandling Annie and understood that this had brought on Wayne's reaction. She was shocked, as was everyone, at the tenacity with which stoic Wayne took after the man. But she did not want to involve the police. She suggested that they call it a night and leave the establishment. Quickly. As soon as possible. Freddy looked over at Annie. She was staring at Wayne. There was fear in her eyes.

****

They made the short walk home in silence. Walking rag-tag down the street, Wayne was in the lead, head on a swivel, Annie apart from and behind him, Pamela and Freddy together at the rear. Freddie kept a watch behind them....

****

Wayne was now in the bathroom tending to a few minor cuts and one nasty gash from a broken glass he had fallen on. It had sliced deeply into his side. When Annie, confused and frightened, timidly tried to help him mend his wounds he said he could take care of it himself. Wayne did not seem disposed to be in her company, as though it was her fault. It was as though he was rejecting her. Annie sat close to Pamela. She was tearful and very troubled.

"Pamela, did you see what Wayne did? Did you see his face? How could he do such horrible things, Pamela? He isn't mean and vicious, I know he isn't. At least I never thought he was. But where could he have learned to do those nasty things? And now he doesn't want me around. Pammy, what *ever* am I going to do?" A trace of make-up ran from the corners of her weepy eyes.

Pamela had her arm over Annie's shoulders. "It's all over, Annie that wicked man deserved what he got." Somehow Freddy didn't think Pamela believed those words. "Wayne is OK, he is just winding down. Wayne loves you, Annie."

Annie began grasping at straws. "If there are bad people here we should leave. Me and Wayne. I have a lot of money saved up, Pamela!" Annie said this in a way which seemed as though she was beseeching Pamela to support her desperate hope. "Wayne and I could get away from here. Maybe open a restaurant. That's what I've always wanted to do. I think Wayne could be interested too, given the chance. He's really interested in the cooking."

"He's is that," said Pamela as she thought of Freddy's seemly lack of interest in anything.

"It'll be a French restaurant. That's what I do best 'cause I like it the best. I'll – I mean *we'll* call it Le Tire Bouchon."

"I like it, Annie, "The Corkscrew." Pamela hoped that Annie would find her dream.

"Why did that man grab me? Who is he? What did he want? Whatever it is, it isn't my fault. I never did anything to anybody. Do you think Wayne thinks I did something to cause this?" Annie was confused, devastated. Pamela had no answer. How could anyone blame anything on Annie?

The questions stopped as Wayne entered the living room acting more or less like his usual self. "Are you all right, Annie?" he asked gently. She brightened a little, regained some color, and tried to smile for him. "We've all had a hard night. It didn't turn out so well. Annie, you go and get some sleep, honey, I'll be there in a little while. I have to talk to Freddy." That was also Pamela's cue that they needed to talk privately. She rose to go to the bedroom she shared with Freddy. She looked thoughtfully at Freddy and was solemn as she passed by. She would be expecting an explanation later. Annie rose slowly and followed Pamela toward the hallway to go to her and Wayne's bedroom. Wayne grabbed her hand and pulled her close to hug her. She buried her wet cheeks in his chest and cried.

"Cheer up, honey. We'll all go out on Big Frank's sailboat tomorrow, OK?" He held her head lovingly in his hands and bent down to kiss her on her lips and then each cheek. "Good night," He said sweetly.

"Good night, Wayne," she said, smiling at last. Freddy was touched and embarrassed for having witnessed the exchange. Two doors closed at the end of the hallway and Freddy and Wayne were alone.

Freddy waited for Wayne to say something. He walked to the kitchen and brought down a bottle of Scotch whiskey from the cupboard over the sink. Pouring two ounces into each of the rocks glasses, he returned to the living room and handed one to Freddy. Freddy remained standing as Wayne started to speak.

"I know I told you I could handle the problem with the harassment by those old associates of mine. Apparently, I was wrong. They told me Joe Sargento was dead. He was a man with a grudge against me, you might say. They told me they only wanted information on informers who had betrayed them up north. If I were to give them that information; those men would be hunted down and killed. I didn't give them the information, and they are still after me, although they had promised a truce if I remained silent. Joe Sargento must still be alive, and there is no telling what he will do to hurt me. He's a power hungry, twisted, psychopath, and one of his lieutenants is down here. I have no doubt that his arrival here to find me is at Joe's behest. He must have manufactured this incident I'm thinking Joe won't thank him for it. Joe would never pull a stunt like that in town."

Freddy remained silent and let Wayne continue at his own pace. He spoke haltingly as though it were difficult for him to decide how much Freddy needed to know. Staring at the ceiling, he went on.

"I knew that man in the lounge tonight. His being there, his trying to get at me through Annie confirms it - Sargento is alive. That man was one of Joe Sargento's private goons; I doubt that anyone else would put up with him. The stunt he pulled tonight was pretty risky. The idiot was probably acting on his own and trying to please his boss on the boat. Joe won't like that. He gave the fool strict orders not to think years ago. Now the man is dead weight with a broken knee and a security risk for the organization. He will probably be punished.

"They suckered me. I can't be sure what they're after, besides revenge. They have most of the information they were after, so maybe they think I have some money salted away that they think I raked off from their operations. Lord knows I was in a position to do it. I tried to convince them I don't because they can't afford to let anyone off easy in their line of business. People that cross them have to be made examples of."

Freddy asked him, "What can you do to get out of this mess?"

"I tried to make them think that I don't have anything of value to them. They guessed that they might get leverage on me through Annie. That didn't work. *I* need some leverage, something I can blackmail them with to get them off my back. That might not be so easy."

This time Freddy poured the Scotches. He wondered about this possibility of revenge. "Wayne," he asked, "what did you do to them to make them want you so badly?"

"I think that comes around to Joe and me, and that it really has little to do with the business dealings."

"You think it might be an honor thing, like a grudge? Was a personal thing?" Freddy asked, struggling to understand the scant information he was receiving.

"Yes."

"Yes, what? Was there a woman involved?" Freddy asked in a rare moment of insight. This brought a hard look from Wayne.

"Yes, a woman I loved was hurt because of her involvement with me. That can't happen again. Don't ask any more about it."

"All right, Wayne, tell me this, then. It they were out to, ah, - 'get you'," he said, avoiding the word "kill", "wouldn't they have done it before now?"

"That's why I think that there was something else they wanted. Now they know that I am not talking they are moving on to their primary objective, which is me. Joe won't like the fiasco tonight. I'm betting the boss on the boat acted prematurely. Joe does not have much tolerance for that. Joe will try to get whatever he can out of me if he captures me intact, but if he can't do that he will opt to take me out altogether. Joe will make it hard on me - he can play a brutal game - and he has no conscience. I crossed his brother."

"Is there any danger for us?" asked Freddy, referring to Pamela, Annie, and himself, in that order.

"Not so much for you and Pamela I don't think, as long as you stay clear of me. I kind of thought that you two would be setting up house before too long anyway. Now would be a good time to do it. I'll have to leave the house now; you might as well stay here. Maybe the old lady who owns it will sell it to you. I won't be able to see Annie anymore, maybe not ever."

"Don't you know what that would do to her, Wayne?"

"I can't let her be in danger because of me. I'll have to get her out of here tomorrow."

Clearly the situation was a good deal more dangerous than Freddy had thought. It was more than a case of Wayne being caught with a hand in the till. It was revenge, a vendetta, or at least Wayne indicated that it might be.

"Can't you just get out of here and run someplace with Annie?"

"I'm not so afraid for me, but I can't let them do anything to her. She can't stay with me or around me. I've run before and they found me, how I'm not sure. I've broken parole and kept clear electronic surveillance, haven't signed anything and still they found me. It may have been a lucky coincidence. They have a big contraband operation in South Florida. I could have been spotted by any of their operatives, at the marina, or anywhere else, for that matter. If I run with Annie they may not find us, But I can't take that chance. They'll know how much she means to me if I take her with me, and that will be even worse for her. She'll be better off by herself until I get this sorted out - if I can. I'm going to send her back to her folks tomorrow. She will be hard to trace from there, and there will be no reason for the bastards to do it anyway if they think she is not with me anymore. They won't figure I'd let her go if I still want her, it's not what they would do. If anyone asks you about it, tell them she got tired of Key West and split. You don't know where she ended up. Even if they were to find out by some chance; a remark by someone who knows where she's from, or checking by our mail, or whatever, they won't want to extend themselves all the way out to San Diego on such a flimsy chance. I'm pretty close-mouthed; you and Pamela know how I feel about Annie, but who else really knows if we are doing anything more than shacking up? And I'll still be here. Their first concern will be keeping tabs on me, if they can find me. Maybe I can buy enough time to put something together and use it against them to end this nightmare."

"When are you going to tell Annie?

"Tomorrow. I'll take her on Big Frank's day sailboat excursion. They won't be able to follow us easily and will have a hard time getting to us on that boat. I'll put Annie on the plane tomorrow night. I think I can lose them when we come back in from the sailing trip. Big Frank will put us off somewhere near the house if we ask him to, and return to his berth without us. They will be expecting us back there at the end of the day. I know I can trust Frank. Once Annie is away from me, she will be out of danger."

They sat up and drank late into the night. Freddy told Wayne that he and Pamela would go out with them tomorrow on the sailboat and then help Annie get a few things together and get off the island unseen. Freddy realized that Wayne had the expertise in this kind of thing, but Pamela and he could pack a few things, divert attention or do whatever else might be necessary. Wayne didn't want anything left behind with Annie's San Diego address on it, just in case. The one solid link to her last name would be the lounge where she cocktail waitressed. Everyone else in their circle of acquaintance in Key West was on a first-name basis.

If the others did start asking questions word of it would get back to the boys, and then maybe Wayne could take some action of his own. They would be after each other at the same time, a game of counterpoint instead of Wayne being an easy target. Any movements the monsters made had the potential to make them vulnerable - according to Wayne - and Freddy trusted that Wayne would know. Freddy wanted to help. Wayne said no.

Until Wayne came up with something, Pamela and Freddy were to stay clear of him and wait for a contact. Freddy went to bed.

Wayne stayed up all night.

Chapter Fifteen - Plans for Annie's Move

They were aboard the Blue Moon. It was a fifty-two foot Swedish built sloop run by Big Frank and his wife, Candice. Frank was big - six feet five with a lean, long build, dark hair, and a curly mustache. He had formerly worked up north as a diver out of Montauk, working construction in New York harbor and around Long Island and occasionally working deep sea wrecks off foggy Block Island. During this time, he apparently had a casual acquaintance with Wayne. He didn't talk about it much. Born of an academic family, he was a Harvard man and well-read, as well as being well schooled in the ways of mischief. This was not uncommon among Lampooners. A life on the sea rather than in ivy halls was his dream. After working as mate on other excursions, delivering sailboats from one place to another, and finally getting his Master's license, he became a Scuba instructor, then took a course in survival training for just about anything else that was likely to happen. Big Frank and Wayne had similar credits and had become friends of sorts. Freddy could see why. Each recognized in the other competence in unusual or difficult situations. They knew how to deal with the events as they occurred. As opposed to Freddy. The only thing Freddy ever had to deal with were the sexy models featured in the marketing shows space-aged rowing machines and key fobs made of chrome for Porches.

****

Candice was a lovely, intelligent lady. She was thirty-two, three years junior to Frank. They had met on one of Frank's Fort Lauderdale trips and started a commuting romance. She could not resist this rakish figure. When he had swept her far enough off her feet with the help of sailboat rides by moonlight, she found herself swept clean from her prospering career as a boat broker to become Frank's bunk mate.

She was not a little girl, five-seven with light brown hair, oblong, pretty face, round and robust figure. Good advertising when seen in a string bikini next to the sign touting day sailing excursions, eighteen dollars per person. She was not a little girl but next to Big Frank she seemed as small as everyone else did.

The group got special treatment and an improvement on the tourist price. After greetings all around and once they were away from the slip Frank and Candice offered their guests what there was handy to nosh on, Feta cheese and Greek olives. Coffee and rum cake also. The rum cake was good, Freddy's queasy stomach, rebelling at last night's Scotch, was hauling and stalling about the quay in concert with the gentle undulations of the sailboat on the mild swells entering the mouth of the bight. His nose got one whiff of the Feta and voted the cheese down.

The swells at the bight's entrance had been born of days of wind from a far-off storm. Inside the shelter of the safe harbor, they were much attenuated. Motoring out of the mouth of the bight, the sailboat was a huge, Swedish rocking horse, seesawing in slow motion across the long waves.

It wasn't so bad once the sails were up, out in the main ship channel. The ground swells were still there, rolling waves of long interval, the product of that steady wind centered two hundred miles away, but the boat was under sail now, reaching through the channel and out past the range marker, slicing through the waves the way the designers of the craft intended, instead of puttering slowly over them in a monotonous, fugal, rolling pitch to the tune of a 2 cylinder diesel engine.

They sailed around the tip of Key West's southernmost point, made a jibe to starboard, and skirted the lower keys for forty minutes before taking a turn out to sea. Once they were in the lee of Key West they left the rolling ground swells behind. The wind, often and recently out of the southeast, had veered through the south to the west because of that distant storm. The storm was big and the fetch for the ground swells was also large but as yet far off. The storm wasn't fully formed. The worst they encountered was a stiff breeze and a moderate chop on the water from localized wind swell. This same chop would make a ride in Freddy's boat uncomfortable, but the big Swede cut through the water swiftly and smoothly. She was pushing forward, running with the wind, sails hissing and flapping from time to time in a freak gust, her bow riding up on its own bow wave.

They made good use of the hours, sunning and sipping white wine. Even Freddy was drinking white wine. He didn't get a chance to buy any beer.

The morning wore into afternoon and Frank turned the boat and tacked closer to shore. In the shallower water, they lowered the sails, dropped the anchor, and got into the water. The buddy system was used - they went swimming in couples, each in a different direction. Freddy's buddy was Pamela, of course. He didn't know what the other guys were doing, but if they were doing to their buddies what he was doing to his, they were having a good time.

Too soon, they had to head back to the boat. Frank and Candice knew what was to happen since it was necessary for them to drop the four passengers off in the water close to home. Back at the marina there could be someone from Wayne's ex-mob watching for them to pull in. Frank knew as much as he had to in order to help them and he asked no questions. He and Candice could be trusted. When they were all on board they got the mainsail up and got under way. After the jib was up Frank trimmed the sheets and they beat into the wind, heading back toward Key West. Ahead the weather was clear, but to the southeast far off to their left a squall line lit by the low sun filled the sky.

Pamela was on the cabin top leaning against the mast. Freddy looked at the outline of her figure against the corona of the sun's bright rays, that body that he had come to know intimately, and had some feeling for what Wayne must be going through. He moved forward to speak to Pamela. Wayne had already joined Annie in the stern. Frank discreetly stayed at the wheel while Candice busied herself below.

"Why so serious, Freddy?" asked Pamela as she slipped next to him. She saw his face and the smile he was greeted with evaporated.

"Pamela, Wayne's got trouble. He's planning to move out and he's going to send Annie back to California." She looked as though her worst fears had been realized.

"Are things as bad as all that?"

"Wayne seems to think so. Some kind of a revenge thing."

"Freddy, can't we help them?"

"I don't see how, Pamela, unless somebody tells us more of what's going on." His tone showed his resentment at being kept ignorant of much of what was happening and what had happened in the past.

"And how do you know Annie will go? I don't think she will." It hadn't occurred to Freddy or to Wayne that Annie might refuse to leave. The possibility was a revelation to Freddy.

"We have to get her to go somehow, Pamela. For now, that's all we can do to help." That was all they were being allowed to do to help. Freddy found it frustrating. He was sure that Pamela did also. "Wayne wants to get her on a plane in about an hour and a quarter. Frank will drop us near the swimming pier from the seaward side of the boat and then he'll sail around for a while to waste some time. By the time he gets in to his slip Annie will be on the plane. It will be too late for anybody watching for our return to back-track to the house and find us there or figure out what happened."

"Oh, damn, Freddy, why does this have to happen? Things were going so well between Annie and Wayne. This ruins everything."

"Yeah, well, maybe not. Wayne figures to get at them, ah, his enemies that is, somehow, once he doesn't have to worry about Annie's safety. If it means getting Annie back, he'll do it." He hoped. Freddy was not convinced that he could.

"I hope it does work out all right," said Pamela. "Is there anything you want me to do?" He told her about helping to get

Annie packed and making sure her identity went with her as an added precaution.

****

They waited until they were close enough to swim to the pier. Freddy wondered how Wayne was doing with Annie. His thoughts turned to Pamela, the woman who left a job she had been training for, the seemingly naive girl in the street sense, but smart and good. It would seem she made a poor choice leaving a guaranteed future and friends and defying her family to join him here. But here she was. Freddy was lucky. Now she was drawn into this sorry mess, poor payment for all her sweetness. Freddy hoped they could get Annie off safely and Wayne safely away from the house without arousing suspicions of complicity between Wayne and the rest of them. Wayne hoped so too. Maybe then no more grief could come to them from the mysterious shrimp boat.

"Who are they, Freddy?"

"I wish I knew. Wayne only tells me what he thinks I need to know."

"I trust you Freddy. You are a good man. Wayne knows it, Annie knows it, too. And *I* know it most of all. Why do you think we put up with your foolishness? We're waiting for you to find out."

They saw that the weather had closed in.

And how would Pamela be repaid for her trust in Freddy? He would know before much longer.

****

Annie was in tears. Frank slacked the main sheet to drop them off when he was as near to the swimming pier as he dared go, but it was still a good distance out. The sailboat drew over six feet of water. That put them at about 150 yards past the end of the pier. There were a few lone coral heads here as close as four feet from the surface. Frank couldn't risk hitting one.

The four swimmers assembled at the rail and got ready to go over the side. Looking to the sea, the water was tepid and flat, green custard under four inches of the luminous purple sky. Over the seething line of purple, the towering clouds, lit by the sinking sun were bright, hot pink cotton candy above; in the lower reaches they were the texture of pink suede. The foreboding sky weighed heavily on the group. They were spent from last night even before going over the side for the swim to shore. They would be four exhausted swimmers after the swim.

It was a miracle that Wayne could function at all. He had been up the entire night before, after a fight at that, and drinking to boot. What hidden reserves kept him going Freddy could not guess, but he knew he would not falter while there was a chance of unpleasantness for Annie. The men from the shrimper were looking for Wayne's weak link. He had to get Annie away before they were sure of what was happening.

Wayne had pointedly told Annie to go visit her folks for a while. He was having problems with his former business partners and would no doubt be tied up getting matters right for the next week or two. Maybe longer. Although she had been mentioning not having seen her folks in a long while, this unsolicited prompting by Wayne that she should leave immediately was a shock to Annie, Annie who would rush to hug him when he came home from work each day as though he had been gone for a month. It was easy to see how she misinterpreted it. Wayne did not love her anymore. She knew something was wrong with the way Wayne had been acting lately, but why this? Why else would he tell her to go to the coast and no time like the present? To her, that meant the sooner the better, get lost, scram. It confused her. Why swim to shore? Why not take the boat in? They had to get the car, didn't they? Was something wrong? If Wayne had a problem she would help him with it. Surely he was over-reacting, unless he just wanted her gone. And Pamela and Freddy were going along with it; they were getting ready to go over the side, too. Why were they conspiring against her? They were her friends. She had to swim to shore with them, or they would desert her and she would have to return with the sailboat by herself. Then she would have to climb onto the empty pier, alone. She still had not fully come to terms with the frightening visage of Wayne's attack on that other man last night.

Sweet, stunned Annie climbed over the rail of the Blue Moon in disbelief. Face blank, lips parted and mind reeling, tears in her eyes, she slid into the water. Then Wayne urged her on to hurry all the way to shore. What was wrong with him, she couldn't swim as fast as he could, none of them could. What had she done? They were all tired when they climbed the steps near the end of the pier, but Annie was shaken and punch drunk. Freddy supposed she thought all three of them were crazy but it was Wayne she watched with baleful eyes, walking and stumbling and hunched as though it were she that Wayne had beaten up and not the man in the lounge. They started for home. They were in a big hurry to get her on the plane and get rid of her and they made her walk faster when she fell behind. Unbelievably, when she couldn't keep up they *grabbed her arms* and *pulled her along.*

****

They had stolen into the house like thieves through the back way. The car was not out front. It was tucked into a dead end on the street behind them. Now she cried her eyes out, sitting alone on the couch while Pamela looked on, painfully distressed at her friend's travail. Freddy and Wayne were moving fast in what was apparently to Annie some pre-conceived plan. Pamela could bear it no longer and joined her wounded friend. Pouring forth onto Pamela's shoulder, weeping in great sobs, beautiful chest heaving, she was as morose as she could be until finally Wayne relented and soothed her with whispered words as he held her in his arms and stroked her with a gentleness that belied his urgent need to get moving.

At this Annie's escape plan came to an end. Annie did not want to go, and Annie was Wayne's blind spot. She was staying; he would just have to work things out some other way. She would move out if he wanted her to, he was there first. But he couldn't make her leave town. In truth, she just wanted to be close to him, as close as he would let her be.

In the end, Wayne in desperation tried the truth - the partial truth - and told her there were men that wanted something from him that were dangerous, and she should leave for her own good. Both Pamela and Annie thought he was overreacting as to the seriousness of his dilemma, his concern for Annie's safety on the one horn of the dilema, and the settling of his secret dealings with autonomy on the other. Annie insisted that a bit of harassment was not going to kill her. She was a big girl now. Freddy called Big Frank later and told him the plan was off, but thanks, anyway. No, there had not been anyone snooping around that he could see. Goodbye.

Freddy had his share of distress as well. Of the three of them, the girls and himself, Freddy was the only one who knew Wayne could go to prison for violation of parole for some crime *he would not tell Freddy about!* If the others – Wayne nemesis's - got to Annie enough to prompt Wayne to give in to their demands, surely Wayne would embroil himself further in their machinations and foul enterprise. If Wayne did not give in, Freddy did not see any recourse for him other than to go to the authorities, as applicable. His disclosure of his identity would then put him under lock and key. Wayne was in a no-win situation, and Freddy was frustrated by his lack of knowledge of what game these others and Wayne were playing. Pamela thought Freddy was protecting her and pressured him for information he did not have. Had he been in possession of that information he did not know if he would – or should - tell her, but not knowing the who's and where's and why's and trying to bear up was difficult and for the first time Freddy felt friction between them.

And Annie, poor Annie. She was adamant; she would not go to San Diego and she could not stand to look towards Wayne because he would immediately avert his eyes and knit his brow. This furtive secrecy brought her time and time again to the brink of tears. It was not a situation that could be maintained for long and although Wayne wavered a little at his estimation of how much trouble his old cronies could cause, he still brooded about them bothering Annie in order to get to him.

It was decided that Annie would stay with a friend across town, one of the girls she had worked with as a cocktail waitress. Annie was still skeptical about Wayne's claim that she could be in danger, but she would go along with this. Annie joked lamely that it would be something of a change for the girl to have a female guest rather than the string of paramours with whom she customarily shared her couch, in what *she* considered to be the highest cocktail waitress tradition. It was the least she could do for a good customer, right?

Wayne would also be leaving, he would not say where to, but he would be in touch in a few weeks. If he left town he would let them know. This last he imparted to Pamela and Freddy so as not to unleash another torrent of tears from the one who he could not bear to see crying.

****

They saw nothing of Wayne from then on, and neither did Annie. She would call Pamela to say that she thought she had seen him lurking at night near the apartment that her girlfriend was renting, where she was currently staying. Pamela was alarmed when she heard this; it was entirely possible that someone *was* lurking and that it was not Wayne. Once Annie got a call from him and told her everything was going well and would be all right soon, not to worry. He didn't sound convincing.

Freddy finally did have a piece of information to keep from Pamela. A week after the sailboat trip there was an item in the lower right-hand corner of the Miami afternoon paper. It stated that a body had been found in the mangroves of an uninhabited island near the Dry Tortugas. It was a male Caucasian, about forty years old and as yet to be identified. The body was of stocky build and had been immersed for some time before floating into the mangroves on a high tide, where it came to rest on a platform of exposed mangrove roots reaching down into the water in a manner likened to being laid out on a funeral bier. Drowning was not the cause of death - foul play was suspected, and for good reason. There were two bullet holes in the body, one in the head and one in the stomach, the trademark of a gang formerly operating in the New York and Chicago areas, some years ago. The body showed signs being beaten some time before death. It had a broken nose and glass cuts on the back. It also had a broken knee cap.

Chapter Sixteen - Flotsam/Fantasy Fest

It must have been dumb luck that the body of the murdered man was found at all before it fed the animals and insects, dried to a collection of bones and fell through the chinks between the prop roots in its live wicker resting place of mangrove forest. The bones should have fallen unnoticed into the water to someday join the rest of the fossils. Whoever killed the man would not have cast him into the water off the beaches of Key West and trusted to the tides to carry him away. The killers had to dump him far offshore by boat. An extra high tide running in front of the storm forming in the Gulf must have flung him ashore and hung him up in the mangrove roots.

Freddy made an excuse to go to the marina. He hadn't used the boat in days and enough water must have seeped in through those hairline cracks under the broken stringers to make the boat sit lower in the water. It wasn't sitting low in the water when he got there. Maybe a friend ran the bilge pump for him. It seemed that the boat was tied up just forward of where he had last left her. On a hunch, Freddy checked the gas tank. He had left the boat full. It was less than two-thirds full now, and Freddy had humongous tanks. Someone had taken a long trip. There were no signs of the ignition being forced, and it would have been hard to jump shart, positioned as it was high inside the console behind a jumble of wires. Wayne had a key.

****

Freddy was more troubled than ever. Glass cuts and a broken knee cap. Did Wayne kill the man and dump him at sea? Wayne never went to bed that night.

Freddy vividly remembered seeing Wayne jump up and come down with frightening force on the knee cap of the man in the lounge, heard the snap as the knee cap broke. Would it be Wayne's solution to kill every one of the mobsters that approached Annie or himself? Freddy remembered how the man, who must have been in considerable pain, did not whimper or howl or anything, his face just closed. Freddy expected the police. There were none. As far as the lounge was concerned it was over, the man de-materialized soon after he was out the front door, and any additional notoriety was not in their best interest. The man himself had obviously not pressed charges, but Freddy did not wonder about that over-much. He certainly had gotten away from there with a minimum of fuss; no one had seen where he had gone. There must have been others with him. Or watching him. Or watching Wayne when the man blundered into the lounge. Only now, Freddy remembered the quiet walk home. Wayne had been looking around, Freddy thought, to avoid talking. He had not been keeping his thoughts to himself; he had been searching the area.

Freddy remembered the man's words - "This isn't over yet, Teddy," - and there had been something else, after the man was too far from Freddy to allow him to hear precisely what was said. It all happened so fast. Trying to piece it together, trying to remember, to read the man's lips from the stark memory of the bloodied man's exit, the only thing that occurred was something like, "we been lookin' for you since you left the nut house." Nut house. Could it have been "nut house?" A nut house is not a prison. A nut house is an asylum. Freddy did not want to think it, but the thought came. Maybe Wayne was crazy.

****

"Annie was over today. She seemed a little cheerier."

"That's good, Pamela," Freddy pronounced as he entered the room. He had just shaved and was now fiddling with his mask.

"The poor dear still is very upset, but of course she couldn't keep on the way she was, crying all the time."

"Has she seen Wayne recently?"

"She saw him yesterday but only briefly. He was angry because she came over here again. I don't see why. It seems that the bothersome men are not around any longer."

"Get dressed, honey, we wanna get a good spot."

Pamela went to the bedroom closet to put on her dress. They were going to see the parade. She continued speaking from the bedroom. "I know she wanted to go with us tonight, but Wayne insisted that she didn't. She says he's changed. And he's still being so secretive." Freddy was reminded of his thoughts on Wayne's sanity some days ago. In the days since he had seen the article on the dead man, his fears had been allayed by his own rationalization. It took him that time to convince himself that his first reaction to the news of the body in the mangroves must be in error. It could not possibly have anything to do with Wayne. Freddy knew him too well, he told himself. Annie had been bothered by absolutely no one since the lounge incident and suspicious boats were nowhere to be seen. Moreover, the creepy feeling of being watched was gone. But Wayne still laid low. Pamela, aside from her concern over Wayne and Annie and the whole affair of the boats and the thugs that might end those two as a couple, was in good spirits. Freddy and Pamela had decided that after the issue of their friend's problem was resolved, Freddy and Pamela would set a date for a wedding. Next week he would start training with U.P.S. They were scanning the Sunday paper for a house to buy, and even Pamela's father had relented a bit and was less inclined to hate Freddy, if the tone of his letters and calls could be trusted as a measure of his loathing.

The celebration on hand tonight was Halloween. They were going to see the Fantasy Fest parade. "Freddy, stop doing that to your mask. You're going to tear it or break the elastic."

"That's good, because I ain't gonna wear the stupid thing."

"Oh, Freddy, don't be such a party pooper."

"My, but you have a way with words." Jab to the ribs. As she turns away he makes a fierce face and brings his arm back to deliver a devastating roundhouse, but then she snaps back around quickly to see what he is doing. He snaps back into place. She views him with a suspicious scowl.

"Freddy, what are you doing?" He had already returned to his more or less casual standing position as fast as he could. "Nothing, dearest." She shakes her head, making her black hair jiggle, and walks away chortling. He thinks that this would be a good time to cop a feel, so he slips his hands up under her breasts from behind. There is a short intermission. The woman is an animal.

****

Every year around Halloween, there is a festival in Key West called Fantasy Fest. It includes several days of celebration and exudes a Mardi-Gras type atmosphere. It has various costume parties and balls, contests for short story writing, beauty contests, a foot race from the Atlantic to the Gulf down Duval Street, an open-air street vendor affair called the Fantasy Feast, and a parade. The parade was what Pamela and Freddy were going to see. Freddy parked the car at the Bottle Cap and they walked toward Duval. As they walked a guy in a pink tutu greeted Freddy. He waved and called "Hi, Freddy," and closed the distance between them at a fast mince.

"Hello, Peter," Freddy replied. As Peter approached, Pamela asked, "Who is that?"

"A guy who likes me."

"Is he gay?" He looked at her askance with a sarcastic eyebrow raised and said nothing. The man fell into step next to Freddy, taking three steps to Freddy's one, and peered around him to make a critical check of Pamela's dress.

"And *who* is *this?*" he asked.

"Peter, this is Pamela. Pamela this is Peter."

"Hello, Peter," said Pamela

"Hi," he replied. "You two are together?"

"Pamela is my fiancée."

"Oh," said Peter, his mouth compressing in disappointment at how Freddy was wasting himself. He bounced right back. "Is this your first parade, Pamela?" he asked vivaciously.

"Yes, I'm looking forward to it. There is excitement in the air."

"I couldn't have said it better. This event is a *huge* event for my folks. I personally have a penchant for peignoirs, a love of lace, a passion for high heels and the walk to go with it," he said bawdily.

"He always talks like that," deadpan Freddy said to Pamela."

"If you can't make fun of yourself, well..." He left it there, as if further explanation was not necessary. He warmed up to the subject. "You'll see a strong sense of gaudiness, tawdriness, tackiness and general proclivities toward doing anything there is to do to excess. We'll parade down Duval Street in lights, tights, fiber-optic wigs, silk, and chiffons, a bunch of grease-painted faggots and straight exhibitionists on pharmaceuticals and fire water, festooned in filmy foppery, flaunting, flashing and taunting the crowd with our frail frames as only flamers can."

"See what I mean," Freddy interjected, explaining Peter's flamboyant speech, "he gets carried away."

"Hyperbole," said Pamela.

"No, really," said Freddy.

They said goodbye to Peter and looked for a good spot to watch the parade. Freddy opted for a place atop a cement wall three feet high near the Atlantic end of the parade route, just after the parade floats would form up and start their procession. The other end would be much busier, a crush scene, and Freddy didn't care to have his pocket picked or have his pretty Pamela vomited on. Less chance of wearing someone's drink, too. They climbed up onto the wall. It was a foot wide at the top, backed by fill and had a chain link fence behind it that they leaned on to stabilize themselves.

Pamela had wanted to go the whole route - costumes, masks, and all the glitter, but Freddy said "nothing doing." It was bad enough he had to bring a mask. It was in his pocket.

When he had set Pamela on the wall, she asked him, "Freddy, why don't we go up to the front and stand on the curb?"

"Because then someone will stand in front of *us*, guaranteed. There are going to be some nearly naked ladies here, you wouldn't want me to miss that, would you?"

"No, Freddy," she said clutching his arm, making him feel adorable. It was a good feeling, even if it was a ruse. They stood there and watched the parade, adorable, mask-less Freddy and angelically beautiful Pamela Greer, perhaps soon to be Pamela Greer Taylor.

People were talking and milling around, with quick looks toward the starting point in anticipation of the beginning of the parade. Heads turned toward the Atlantic end of Duval as the first float rounded the corner onto the parade route. They watched raptly as the first of the floats went by.

Music from the floats drifted above the noise of the crowd. Freddy studied Pamela in that magic setting. She was wearing a simple white dress, cut low, of crushed cotton. It was lacy at the edges and very feminine. It was almost see-through and the frilly designs of her underwear made evident the lush, fullness of her breasts and hips. She was wearing "Joy" (a gift from her father) and smelled as heavenly as she looked. The white mask over her eyes pointed upward at the corners.

She wore exaggerated make-up of cream and pink and rose with an air of mystery. For several moments she rose up on her toes as a float's fog machine sent wafts by, misting the air. The smoke-ring haze around the gas-filled street lamp behind her framed her black hair, a halo imparting a texture to the night air, softening the look of all the harsh and garish things around her. In the spectral shadowed, vapor-lighted night, Pamela's soft-skinned, smoke-shrouded face was truly angelic and the image was etched forever in Freddy's mind and heart.

****

Six-gun totin' cowboys flanking a stage coach, shooting blanks into the air, filling it with the smell of cordite, passed by their vantage point. A person on stilts on the sidewalk before them stopped, blocking their view until Freddy said something rude in the extreme to him. Pirates followed the stage coach, dueling their way down the street. Native dancers. A grim Reaper pulling a coffin with a bicycle with a big front wheel. Two ladies Freddy knew walked by in their costumes of grease paint and "G" strings. Pamela scrutinized them in mock jealousy. She knew Freddy was in her thrall and that was that. Lots of other stuff followed as Pamela watched. Sharks chasing bathing beauties, a flasher here, a streaker there, the regular fare. They didn't do this sort of thing in Cincinnati.

Key West was a small town then and it was a little parade. The entire route could not have been much over a mile and a half. As the last float passed, the watchers dispersed, some following the tail end of the parade down Duval Street and others headed for their cars, bicycles or some ambulatory destination. Pamela and Freddy perambulated to the Bottle Cap, where the green machine was parked. They went inside for a drink.

****

"How you guys doin'?" asked Sally from behind the bar, more in the redundancy of a greeting than in curiosity.

"Well, Sal, so far we're ok. The hedges at the house need trimming. I suppose I should change the oil in the Olds. I'm going to start a new job next week---"

"Shut up, Freddy. Pamela, how do you stand him?" Some of her authority seems diminished by the fact that she is dressed as a tube of toothpaste.

"I *love* your outfit," said Freddy. "Does wonders for your figure. Wha's zat say, Preparation H?"

"PEPSODENT! It's PEPSODENT, dummy!"

"I'm fine, thank you. How are you, Sal? Pamela, how are you? Sally's not talking to me."

"I'm thirsty, Freddy, buy me a drink."

"Pamela, just what are you smiling at?"

"You're funny when you think you're being witty, that's all."

"Humph."

"All right, then," said Sally, "What'll it be?"

"I think that I would like a Grasshopper. It is an adventurous night and I want to try something out of the ordinary."

"I think this might be my lucky night," Freddy quipped. "Wanna rub legs and make noises?"

Sally said, "Is he always like this? Don't answer that, I know he is. You are in luck tonight, Pamela, we got vanilla ice cream. Tonight only. For the occasion, you know?"

"That sounds wonderful," she responded.

"If I throw a shot of Tequila in this thing, it's a Mexican Grasshopper. How would you like to try that?"

"Oh, why not, I'll give it a try." They watched Sally make the drink. It looked good, it smelled good, and from the expression on his date's face and her pursed lips Freddy took it that it tasted good also.

"And now what can I get for you, sir, would you like one of those?" asked Sally in the most professional manner she could muster dressed as a tube of Pepsodent.

"I think a beer will do nicely, thank you."

After the Bottle Cap they made stops at the Pier House, a Piña Colada and a beer; Louie's Back Yard, a Banana Daiquiri and a beer; and now they were back at the Casa Marina within walking distance of the house. They had not been back to the house yet tonight.

This night Pamela was the flighty one. It was good to have the tables turned for once. Although the reformed Freddy was drinking far less, he still liked his beer on those occasions when there was something to be festive about. Years of practice forestalled any actual stumbling and shuffling, but he did tend to become desultorily loquacious. Pamela was getting slightly tipsy.

Pamela expressed some curiosity as to Freddy's adoption of the Casa Marina as his second home during her absence, so he had taken her there the previous evening for the sunset and some people watching from the perspective of his favorite rattan chair. Over two cocktails that they sipped slowly they munched shrimps and oysters from the raw bar on the terrace. The magnetism of the place at sunset, something Pamela had not seen before from the relaxing spot on the terrace, spoke for itself.

Freddy's usual spot was the last rattan chair from the central doors on the patio terrace, just outside the lounge and overlooking the grounds, pool, Tiki bar, barbecue, and gazeboed pier just below the horizon. He generally faced towards the sunset, although it was not a religious requirement. He had pulled another chair next his on that evening and they watched the costumed people strut their stuff. The Great Gatsby masquerade ball was going on in the main ballroom.

From this vantage point looking to the right were the double doors paralleling the lounge, where they had danced on other evenings. The evening shows by the bands could be seen through the glass-enclosed lounge. When the weather was cool enough the doors were left open.

Their attention last night, the night before the parade, had not been on the band but on the natural show of the setting sun. From their dual rattan thrones on the red brick bordered terrazzo they could look down at the surrounding grounds four feet below the level of the wall. Blue-green, small leafed hedges circled the outside of the wall, hiding it from the view of those perusing the grounds from below.

The half-light at sunset made the wide wall top a light shade of beige. It angulated in a hemisphere of several sections around the terrace, the short vertical inner sides facing the chairs at various angles receiving varied amounts of light, making the segments variously brown and beige and gray. The shadows at the wall's foot were long, black trapezoids. It was a block design of soft colors and subtle lighting, an abstract painting in counterpoint to the lush, green landscaping, a fairy tale, surreal in the yellow lights of the paired black street lamps lining the promenades of terrazzo on the lower grounds. The grounds fell away past the hedges and shrubbery to the lighted mirror surface of the pool. The darkening sky was behind the line of tree tops. They still retained an element of dark green, more sensed than seen. The undersides of the trees were floodlit, green and yellow, after the sun had set, in concert with the selective yellow light of the street lamps falling on the growing things concentric to their brilliance. Shadows of the lighted palms close to the rambling building were black, mute mimes on the walls, standing motionless behind them and swaying to an occasional breeze.

To complete the fairytale image there were festive lanterns hanging from the trees in honor of the holiday, and the scene was framed into sections by the closer lamp posts. Costumed people seemed perfectly in place: and elven magic was afoot, a hobbit-like quality prevailed.

But tonight the sun was fully down, had been for some time, but the moon was up and full-bright, heightening the other-worldliness of the place. The haze-glow of earlier on persisted around the moon, the lamp posts, and the lanterns. On this night the stately costumes of the masquerade ball yesterday gave way to an abundance of much more avant-garde outfits, some wild, some funny, and a few scanty, sexy ones that took Freddy's breath away. He was for that. On the girls, anyway.

After hand-holding and walking a bit and leaning into each other, they returned to the patio. The band started to play and they danced outside - the regular way, slow dancing, but barely moving, heads bent together.

They were about to start for home. They were oblivious to all around them when something made Freddy look up and he saw them running. He guessed that even hobbits have troubles sometimes, so he accepted the fact that something was about to happen.

Chapter Seventeen - The End of a Beautiful Evening

He saw them coming fast across the front patio. One man in bib overalls and another dressed in mufti. They were in a near-run so Freddy didn't imagine they were going to ask the time of day.

Freddy strained to understand how this could be happening again. Why would they try again at this same hotel? The answer was obvious. The police were downtown tending to the drunks. A lot of folks were wearing eye patches and pirate vestments and brandishing swords. It was the perfect cover for chicanery.

Mufti had a short sword on his belt. Brilliant! No one would question that tonight. There were fake sword fights in the street, for Pete's sake!

Mufti's sword was on his right-hand side. He's left-handed, thought Freddy.

Freddy and Pamela were behind the shrubbery, mostly concealed from the few stragglers who were left on the grounds Freddy stepped in front of Pamela, separating her from them.

The overalled character, the larger of the two, lunged as though to try to get a big, beefy hand on Freddy's shoulder. It seemed that once again nasty people were trying to get one or more of the four of them to go somewhere. Perhaps they were keen on having a discussion, but their manners and methods could use some work.

Freddy realized that he had played right into their hands. They had waited for a night when the police were almost all downtown and a heck of a lot was going on. They could wear costumes to blend in with the crowd.

Freddy was not going to let them get to Pamela. He opened his left hand and spread the fingers like tines on a pitchfork and thrust the hand in the man's face, hoping to get a finger or two in his eyes. That didn't work, but it made him avert his head, converting some of his forward motion sidewise as his body followed his huge head's lead. A right hand shot with his knuckles under the breastbone to the solar plexus also missed its intended mark but landed well enough to slow, if not arrest, the man's forward motion. He merely grunted, a grizzly, coughing grunt.

"Come with us, we want to talk to you," said a civilized sounding voice with a trace of a British accent. It had come from the man in Mufti, stopping the action momentarily. He was circling left as his larger counterpart moved to the right.

"Where's Teddy, asshole?" inquired the bib overalls in a rough, thick voice. The costumes certainly seemed to fit the characters. Freddy could imagine the confusion Pamela was feeling as she wondered who "Teddy" was. Indeed, she was more perplexed than fearful. Freddy realized that it was the name that the man found dead in the mangroves had used to address Wayne the night of the previous altercation initiated by a large person at this ritzy hotel. Freddy had a ridiculous flash thought. If this sort of thing didn't stop immediately, they were going to get a bad reputation.

Freddy watched them circle and said nothing. There wasn't much to say. He didn't know where Wayne was and wouldn't tell them if he did. He didn't want to strike up a friendly conversation either. He hoped that they didn't take it as a snub. Sure. They circled calmly and continued closing in.

Not knowing how far these guys would go in the middle of the street in front of this busy hotel, Freddy finally broke his silence. "You guys have been noticed. Security will be here any minute." He hoped. They glanced around at the walkers and sitters who were now potential watchers.

"I'm afraid a minute will be too late," said Mufti in his clipped accent. "And at any rate we are well concealed here. Now, your friend has created a problem for us. Now, you are going with us, and I mean now, and quietly. I think that you would be surprised at how quick I am with a blade. We are anxious to bring this matter to a conclusion." He meant their interpretation of a successful conclusion. They gained ground.

Now the larger guy was very close to Freddy on his partner's right. Freddy circled left and bought some time, putting Mufti behind Overalls. Pamela stayed behind Freddy as he moved, as he had indicated with a hand motion. They were all in a line. Only Overalls could reach Freddy at the moment.

For some undefined reason, Freddy feared Overalls less than he feared the smaller man in mufti. Pamela remained behind Freddy as the bigger man bore down again moving rapidly, reaching out with his right hand. He had Freddy by forty pounds and would bowl him over unless Freddy got tricky.

Freddy stepped back quickly getting him wrong-footed, then stepped back in. He stuck his right foot behind Overalls' ankle as he pushed Overalls' right arm away with his own left. He pushed at the center of the large man's chest with his own right hand, causing the man to stumble backward. For a short part of a second the bigger man's own left arm was behind him, toward the outside of their circling and useless. With all of the upper body rotation that Freddy could muster, he punched Overalls in the throat, hurting him, forcing his head and upper body back. Overalls' weight continued to carry his torso forward in spite of itself.

Freddy drove his shoulder into the chest of the big man and set the rest of him moving backward as well. With his foot still behind the big man's ankle Overalls buckled at the knees and went down hard. Freddy's right knee, already chronic with tendonitis from years of feet flapping on hard surfaced tennis courts, ached dully as the man's weight rolled over Freddy's leg. There had been no time for a warm-up. Knee, don't fail me now, thought Freddy, one more to go and then we run for it.

Mufti was much smaller but cagey. He got in a good shot to Freddy's ribs as he dodged the falling "Mr. Greenjeans". Mufti faked left, an obvious move, then very quickly and subtly to his right. Freddy cleverly countered the move. The only trouble was that the subtle right fake wasn't a fake at all and Mufti came in low to the ribs and knocked the breath out of Freddy with a "woof". So much for running away. The big guy was already getting up.

"Oh, darn," said Freddy. Mufti let him have a short, painful jab to the face, squashing his nose but not breaking it.

"All right, let's *go,* or you are going to get hurt." Going to get hurt? Freddy's ribs were sore and his nose felt very big and flat. He could see white light as his knee flashed with a spasm of pain and threatened to go out. He had probably re-injured his wrist. Maybe he could get another chance. Maybe, if Mufti died laughing. Freddy was out of his league with these guys.

Freddy tried anyway. His ex-girlfriend - the one who ran off - three blocks - with the Brazilian - she was a karate freak and had shown Freddy a couple of things. One came to mind. Freddy flipped his arm quickly under Mufti's guard and whipped his knuckles into Mufti's temple, sort of a backhand snap shot with his knuckles into the temple above and behind the eye, intending to blind that eye.

Mufti looked surprised and held his hand to his right temple while appearing to try to focus on something. Maybe Freddy had done something right. "Pam, let's get out of here, hurry," Freddy urged. She was looking at something behind him. Too late. It was Overalls, looming over Freddy with a malicious grin, clutching something in the bib of his overalls. Just then, Wayne came from nowhere and premptorily smashed a glass ashtray into the back of the man's skull and Freddy never found out what it was that the man had in his hand. It made Freddy ill to think it might have been a gun.

"Let's get inside and call the police," said Pamela. For the first time Freddy noticed she had one of her shoes in her hand, high heel pointed forward.

"No, let's go. Conners' 'muscle' is unconscious. We're at a stalemate right now; it will buy us some time." Wayne said, almost politely, but forcefully. Freddy had opted for the flight response, was going to take Pamela's hand and run, flee, with no thoughts of where or how far, but Wayne sounded as though he had something definite in mind. Freddy paused only a split second, long enough for the chill to go away that had shivered through him when he saw that bright, keen insane look of violence in Wayne's eyes, the look he had seen in the lounge the night of the fight, and in the Mascot bar months earlier.

They followed Wayne out through the inner and outer lobby doors and out over the grass of the gardened area around the parking lot. Pamela protested but went along. Freddy and Pamela started to curve off to the left, inland, to where the house was, or to where the car was parked. "No, not that way. You can't go back to the house right now, and the car is being watched. That's how they knew you were here."

Pamela had stopped. *"Who?* Wayne? Who is after you?" She said in exasperation, imploring him to give her some idea of what was happening.

"That's the same thing I've been asking for weeks, Pamela," said Freddy.

"It's not the time," said Wayne.

"When *is* the time?" she beseeched him.

"Pamela, I know I've been taciturn---"

"Taciturn!" she cut him off. "You've been treating me like a child!"

"I'll explain later," he said. "We can't stop here. We don't have time for this now," and he urged them on with the gentle nudge of a hand on the small of each of their backs. They ran.

They stopped two blocks away, near the ocean and in the shadows of an ivy-covered wall, Pamela and Freddy feeling the headiness of too much oxygen on top of the alcohol. It did not seem that they had been followed. Anyone doing so would have had to do it on the run. Wayne stopped them abruptly and listened. They heard no one running. Wayne continued to stand silently. He appeared to be listening for something and looked in all directions, methodically and carefully.

"I'll explain everything later," he told them. "Now we have to move," he said, stressing the first and last words and then pausing for half a beat.

"We don't have a tail. First we have to go back to the car while there is still time. We're going to need it. It should take a while for Connors to get his unconscious friend out of the Casa Marina. He can't leave him there, that's for sure."

Regretting the need to ask, Freddy did anyway. "Why can't he leave him there?"

"It wouldn't be neat. It would leave a loose end. Connors has to get him out or get rid of him, and that latter option would be hard to do in the middle of a crowd."

"Maybe the police will get them," Pamela ventured.

"Not likely. Connors is good - the best they have. He'll talk his way out of there if he has to; pretend his partner drank too much; he has the time. The police have more than enough to do on a holiday night like this. Most of them are downtown."

So Mufti was Connors. Freddy and Pamela could hear the respect in Wayne's voice as he spoke of the man he had called Connors.

"If they *do* come out while we make a try for the car they'll 'make' us right away. They've seen how each of us is dressed and they know what we look like. Then I'll have to handle it as it happens. But the guy watching the car may not have gotten that good a look at you, and he hasn't seen me yet. Put these on." He handed each of them a pull-on over-the-head mask. Wayne had one too. He was a pirate, an apt choice of mask for him. Pamela was a bunny rabbit and Freddy almost smiled in spite of himself and his very nervous condition, aching wrist, knee, ribs, and a nose that hurt when he put the mask on. Freddy hadn't thought to look and see what he was. He wondered if he was also in character. It seemed ridiculous to ask, and too late. Wayne continued with his instructions.

"The guy staking out the car is at the wall on the end of Seminole street. He will be looking for a guy and a girl. He may recognize your clothes, but that's all right. I want his attention fixed on you, trying to recognize you as who you are. What I want you to do is walk naturally toward the car."

"What if he tries to do something to us, Wayne?" Pamela inquired in a weak but committed voice. She didn't know what Wayne had in mind, but had accepted that this was not the time for lengthy explanations. She waited for Wayne to tell them what to do.

Freddy's heart was heavy at the evening's turn of events. Pamela had been wined and dined tonight, had enjoyed the parade and the whole mystical evening and now this. Violence. Mayhem. No apparent rhyme or reason to anything that was going on. And Wayne there for guidance while Freddy felt helpless, not knowing what to do. His heart ached for all of them that this should be happening.

They waited there for two minutes as Wayne had told them and then started walking from the beach along the Reynolds street side of the resort's boundary. As they turned the corner onto the

Seminole street side and walked clear of the shrubbery, they caught sight of the car. It was where they had left it, just past the center of the two blocks distance to the street's end. Past the street's end was the water.

Looking carefully, Freddy spied a man at the far end, shadowed from the street light by a tree behind the wall he was leaning on. The wall surrounded the property adjacent to the dead end street. The street light was blinking on and off intermittently giving the scene an even more eerie setting on what was already a strange night. The man saw them and straightened. He had "made" them, as Wayne would say. He shrunk back against the shadowy wall, deep under the canopy of the tree. They walked on, trying to look normal, in spite of the weak, timid steps Pamela took and Freddy's stiff-legged, limping gait, like the scarecrow and Dorothy walking lightly past the witch. In the dim light Freddy thought he saw an arm go around the man's throat from the other side of the wall. The man's body jerked twice. It body jerked again, this time lifting his feet slightly off the ground. The jerks continued, each one elevating the body a few more inches off the cement. The head and shoulders curved back over the wall, and then into the shadows, jerking and moving upward and into the gloom, as if being pulled into the maw of some giant snake, a pig being swallowed whole by a hungry python in the shrubbery.

The shoes flipped up and over and the body was soon out of sight on the opposite side of the wall. Freddy felt sure that Wayne had killed him, as he had thought he had killed the man found in the mangroves. Freddy turned away from Pamela and ripped the mask from his face in time to be sick.

Wayne was over the wall. "Freddy, get in the car." Freddy recovered as best he could. "Where to?" he asked, still looking pale.

"Drop me off a block from the house, on the next street over. Then drive around slowly to the house and pull in. Don't get out of the car until I tell you to. Leave the lights on, and keep the engine running. If anyone but me comes out or approaches you, leave fast." Freddy did as he said. They were to be a diversion again while Wayne went in the back door to do the dirty work - if there was any to be done. Wayne appeared at the front door in a few minutes. "Come inside, hurry. If they catch up with us here, I don't want you to be sitting ducks out there." Made sense to Freddy. Nice of him to think of them.

****

Wayne was packing a few things into a blue canvas bag, the bag that was Melinda's single piece of luggage as she hitched a ride with Freddy three and a half years ago. Freddy approached and looked into it. He saw a big, mean, revolver. He was sure it was a recent acquisition. "Freddy, don't tell Pamela about the gun."

"Ok, Wayne." A moment passed silently but for the sounds of Wayne's packing. "Wayne, did you kill that man at the wall?" He looked up from the bag with a sad, amused smile and shook his head. A low laugh actually escaped his lips.

"No, Freddy, I didn't, but he's going to be asleep for quite a while. When the people living in the house on that property find him there in the morning, he is going to have a lot of explaining to do. The police will find the dope I stuffed in his pocket. The pressure should be off you guys once one of the gang is in police hands and they run him through their computer for priors. Then the heat will really be on them. The gang will pull out of town, probably by tomorrow. All I have to do is get you through 'till morning. If they make another grab for either of you or if they try to get me, it'll have to be tonight. Soon even the federal boys will be down here. Freddy, watch the front window, would you, please?"

"One thing, Wayne."

"What is it, Freddy?"

"What was I tonight, a clown or a pig or what?"

"You mean the mask."

"Yeah."

"It was a clown."

"Thanks."

"It was all they had left," Wayne said apologetically. "I wasn't going to be the clown."

"Certainly not." Freddy went to watch at the front window as he was told. Pamela was seated on the couch by the window and he joined her.

"I don't like not knowing what is going on." Putting his arms around her, he tried to rock out some of the worries that were evident in her trouble-twisted face. She shook herself free.

"Freddy, I feel so helpless! Is Wayne leaving town?"

"I think so, honey. I have a feeling we'll know what has been happening around here lately, very soon."

Wayne came into the room from his bedroom. "I know I have some explaining to do. There isn't much time left. Let's get out of here while we can and I'll tell you as much as I can in the time remaining, then I have a couple more favors to ask you. Let's go to the park."

Chapter Eighteen – Explanations

Chloroform is a clear, colorless, mobile liquid with a sweet, pleasant, ethereal odor. Inhaled, it induces deep anesthesia in a few minutes. The margin of safety is narrow; the mortality rate is high.

****

Connors had a propensity for chloroform. No fumbling with needles, no gun's loud report or the mess made by knives. It took more time, but was in some ways surer than a blade that missed its mark on the first thrust or a slug unexpectedly obstructed by a last final effort by its target to protect his vital organs. A bad bounce from a bone could cause the lead capsule to tumble and carom doing much damage and leaving the victim impaired but alive enough to talk.

Sargento often was annoyed by Connors' methods. He disliked having to wait while Connors patiently sent someone to a sleep from which they would not awaken. Connors preferred killing with the sweet fumes from the cloth laced with the heavy liquid to more violent methods.

Connors was as exacting and meticulous as Sargento was bold and brutal. Both were ruthless in achieving their ends, but Connors would go to great pains to keep things neat and orderly. He leaned toward psychological tactics. paradoxically, Sargento was impatient and impetuous. He was inclined to use scare tactics and terror, caring little that his methods were crude so long as they got fast results. Connors was not squeamish; he would use any means necessary when time was at a premium or safety was a factor. But generally the two men tempered each other. To Sargento, Connors was a restraining influence; to Connors, Sargento was the impetus to get things done.

Sargento was the mastermind. He decided what ventures would be tried and was the strategist for his own campaigns. Connors was his eccentric second man, the major-domo, field marshal, and seer, a psychological tactician with a penchant for neatness; the supreme organizer who implemented Sargento's plans.

****

They parked well back in the trees. Wayne was in the back seat, sitting as though he were totally spent. Freddy and Pamela waited to hear what else had happened tonight. Briefly Wayne explained to Pamela as he had to Freddy that the men he was involved with had interests not only in drug trafficking but also in many other areas of organized crime as well. She had heard about the southern drug operation from Freddy. They had been "big time" up north until a police investigation and crackdown had shaken them up and started their fall. They smuggled art, both fake and real. They were precocious harbingers of technical skullduggery dealing in stolen hardware and software, both corporate and military. Precious metals, fine gemstones... whatever was in demand.

They lost their northern "holdings" in the north as the North through the work of a few key operatives who had infiltrated their inner circle.

The remainder of their operation was in the Southeast, the Gulf coast, Central and South America. They retained these operations and adapted by becoming brokers for any entity which would provide them a cut for their expertise in moving product. Money was never a problem for them - they had taken enough of the profits from their northern holdings to live well for the rest of their lives. They were sick for power. They wanted their northern holdings back. They were working with their southern organization as a base of operations so that they might rebuild their empire and regain what they thought was rightfully theirs. Wayne claimed that he had only been involved in the northern part of their dealings and that that was a thing of the past.

"Then why are they after you, Wayne?" asked Pamela.

"At first they told me they only wanted information on some of my contacts up north who had crossed them, snitched or turned state's evidence. I was reluctant to do this because they surely wanted to use the information to track those men down and reap revenge. Kill them or depose them. They are a very vengeful bunch. They can be very nasty." From what Pamela had seen she had to agree. Wayne went on.

"Now it seems they think I have a stash, that I raked off money from their northern scams, ran down here, and now I'm holding out on them."

"I can see how they might have gotten that idea," said Freddy,. "At times we must look like we have no visible means of support. But you said they didn't need the money. Why are they going to all this trouble?"

"It is a matter of principle for them. They don't like to think that there is a chance anyone got away with stealing from them. They don't want anyone else giving it a try, so they make examples out of those who do.

"There is one other thing they might be after - and this worries me the most - they might be out to get revenge on me for another reason altogether. Freddy, you're right in noticing how much trouble they are going through to get me. It's a lot of trouble even for them, all out of proportion to anything I could have taken." He paused for a moment and then continued without further preamble.

"I was in love with one of their women. She belonged to one of the two top men. Both of those men are supposed to be dead now. I know one is, because I was there when it happened. The other, Joe, hasn't been seen since their operation folded up north. The ones out there on the shrimp boat are supposedly running things now. They told me that it was true, that Joe took a bullet while they were making their escape and died of it later, but I'm not so sure they're telling the truth, Lord knows they've lied before. I can't help but think only Joe would be so maniacal as to chase after me to this extent, especially so close to the U. S. authorities. If he is found alive around here the best he can hope for is life imprisonment.

"And there is no reason for them to harass Annie and yet they are doing it. I can't believe that they think she knows anything about my past - they know me very well and they know I wouldn't confide that sort of thing to her, both to keep her safe and to prevent her from running away from me if shw knew the truth. But they were after her again tonight. Somebody wants a lever to get at me with, and on a personal level. I think it must be Joe."

Pamela's mouth dropped open; she was struck with alarm. "Annie's all right, isn't she, Wayne? Has anything happened to her?"

"She's safe. Yes, something did happen to her, though. They tried to grab her again. Now she's back at Susie's where she should have been all along. I don't know what they were planning, but they almost got away with it. That's what brought me over to the Casa Marina. They failed with Annie; I thought they might be after you guys as well."

"You thought right," said Freddy. Clearly the story was not over. Taking a deep breath to collect himself, he then told them how he had been collecting information on the gang's activities. He related this to them and then told them what else had happened that night.

"Aside from my research into finding a solution to the problem of getting the goons off my back, I've been keeping an eye out around Susie's apartment house after dark to see that no one is bothering Annie." Judging from Wayne's haggard countenance Freddy guessed that he must have been watching the house all night every night. He didn't appear to have had much sleep. "Annie was alone and lonely," he said to Pamela. "I imagine she tried to call you several times. I saw her on the phone through the window and there didn't seem to be any response to her calls. She left the house, and I assume that she was headed over to our place *–your* place, that is. I told her not to go over there when she went to stay with Susie. That was the whole point of it, to keep her clear of the house. If she had waited a few more days I might have had enough information compiled on Sargento's southern smuggling ring to either blackmail him into leaving us alone, which would have bought some time while he re-organized, or to take to the feds, and try to put him away for good."

"How did you get this information?" Freddy asked.

"I know where to look," he said with a sad, self-mocking smile. "I'm a professional." "Wouldn't it be better to go to the - uh - 'feds?" asked Pamela. "I would think that you would want those people put in prison so that they could not bother you again."

"But then I would have to do some time myself, and I might not survive that. Sorry, Pamela that's too long to go into now.

"They know I'm on to them. They saw me last night while I was watching them make a drop. I must have been careless, or tired, or something. Their time has run out here, and anything else they try in the short term will happen tonight. They're desperate men, and this is the second time I've crossed them. I just want to make sure you guys and Annie are going to be all right before I take off, so no more questions. Let me finish."

Wayne explained that the men who had accosted Annie earlier that night were thugs hired locally - probably part of a small-time satellite ring in the area - to either abduct Annie or harass her in some way. Wayne deduced that the mob, Sargento's men, as he had alluded to them, had limits as to manpower. His operation was a small nucleus of organizational minds directing the fiscal and logistical aspects of a network smuggling many kinds of contraband, attended by a small coterie of thugs who had been part of their "army" up north. Wayne suspected that they had a low-key hidden island base somewhere in the southern waters. No high profile island drug depot would it be; no marinas, no airstrip in or near the States, nothing to lead inquisitive eyes to an over-confident drug lord, unlike the places his Colombian, South and Central American counterparts funded as they flaunted their wealth and power. It would be a place to which it would be difficult to gain access, probably with physical barriers as well as seclusion. Sargento kept his operations and the number of his key personnel small and secretive. They farmed out some of their dirty work. This was again evidenced tonight be the choice of a chemical used by the assailants. A rare mistake by Connors, who should not have equipped the hired help with a tool they had no experience with.

Three of Sargento's own men had been assigned to Freddy and Pamela this night. Whatever they had intended, it was a trickier task to surprise Pamela and Freddy out in the open on this party night than it was for the hired ones sent for Annie. She was a lonely girl in an empty house. The local boys should have been able to handle that. Had she stayed at Susie's apartment she would have remained in safety, and the two hired villains would have waited in vain for her to return to her former home.

Of the three mobsters that went after Pamela and Freddy, two of the miscreants were not yet neutralized. If all went as expected, one of their number would soon be in police hands, and this was exactly what they did not want. It compromised their position.

"You see," said Wayne, "many of Sargento's men would be in serious legal trouble and subject to long prison sentences if they were caught in the United States. They might be tried here, or worse, they might be extradited to a place where they had little influence over the authorities and get lost in a squalid prison cell for years before they even came to trial. Joe Sargento himself, if he is alive, would do well never to set foot on this county's soil again. But I think he is alive and has done just that, and he is far from being stupid. He must want me very badly.

"They sent two men to get Annie, young Latin types, probably chosen to miss direct blame. I'm sure they had nothing to do with Sargento's mob. They were just hired for the job. Sargento's men would know where to look for such men. I saw Annie leaving the apartment and getting into the Scout. I guessed that she was going over to our place. I told her not to go over there, that the house might be under surveillance. But I imagine sitting alone at Susie's house was finally too much for her. But tonight of all nights, for Christ's sake, with all of the noise and confusion for cover. It was the worst night she could have chosen to go over there."

Pamela said to him, "Don't blame her so much, Wayne,

everyone is out celebrating tonight and she was stuck at Susie's. You know how she must miss you, don't you?"

"Yes, Pamela, I know, I'm just regretting what happened tonight. I was so close to putting a stop to all this. I knew their drops, I knew their couriers, and where the money was coming from. Now they will leave the area for a while when they learn one of them is in jail. They will set up new drops, a new operation out of another location. I'll have to start all over again. If I don't, they will eventually get me. I can see that now."

"What happened at the house?" Freddy asked.

"I ran the eight blocks across town. There was a van I didn't recognize parked around the corner from the house so I cut through the Currin's place. I jumped the block wall in the back yard. The back door to the Florida room was open. I stopped there and listened. I heard a muffled excursion of breath, like the sound someone new to snorkeling might make after taking in a little water. I went through the Florida room to the kitchen and looked around the corner and saw Annie looking wild-eyed, with a hand over her mouth, trying to breathe through a wad of gauze that was clamped over her face. She was in shorts, kicking and struggling with her bare legs to fend off the pressure of the hairy legs of the guy trying to pin her against the counter. The guy had straight, black hair, smallish build but wiry. He had her arm pinned up behind her. There was such a contrast between my beautiful Annie and the ugly guy that it turned my stomach.

"The guy saw me and he dropped Annie's arm. He was pulling a French knife at least a foot long from the kitchen rack when I came down on his wrist with the edge of the heavy metal serving platter we have, or had, hanging on the wall. It probably fractured the bone and of course he dropped the knife and Annie spun away. Then somebody hit me from behind with something hard and stunned me for long enough for them to run away. I guess I must be slipping."

"How do you know they were not Sargento's men?" Freddy asked.

"Sargento's men wouldn't have run away."

And how many people, thought Freddy, would have thought to

swing the edge of a heavy metal serving platter as a weapon against the wrist of an assailant with a fourteen inch French knife? It certainly sounded ruthless, vicious, and must have been done with a speed, force, and precision of someone who could react without taking time to think, someone sure of himself and able to commit himself fully to a course of action with no hesitation. If they were to come to grips with these people again, it was Wayne who would get them safely through it. If that could be done.

Chapter Nineteen - Departures - A Last Vigil

"A low pressure system starting to form off the Yucatan in the southwestern Gulf of Mexico centered at 24.6 degrees north latitude, 89.2 degrees west longitude is drifting north-northeast at about 5 knots. It is expected to strengthen as it continues to move out into open water.

Offshore waters forecast for the Gulf between 81 and 85 degrees west Longitude. Tonight through Sunday night generally southerly winds at 10 knots, gradually strengthening and shifting towards the west. Seas will be 5 feet or less through tomorrow with widely scattered showers and thunderstorms throughout the area.

At midnight Key West was under mostly clear skies, the temperature 84, relative humidity 80 percent. Southeast winds at 9 miles per hour. Water temperature 85 degrees. This is NOAA weather radio station WXJ95 operating 24 hours a day on an assigned frequency of 162.4 megahertz."

****

The mob had to get out. Connors, Sargento, and company were astute in the ways of subterfuge. They were intuitively brilliant in judging what Wayne might be doing. Spurred to action after Wayne had gone to ground, they made attempts to make him surface and failed; Wayne had foiled them each time. They had drawn too much attention. One of their henchmen was presumed captured. They had made a few mistakes, but they speculated, correctly, that Wayne had been working to undermine their empire, and had something on them that could damage them. Any last desperate act of retribution would be tonight. Then they would leave.

Wayne would follow. He couldn't watch out for Annie, didn't want her easily accessible to them later. She must be kept under wraps until either he won or they did. He would get her out with little fanfare, hoping it appeared that she was just a shack-up, was fed up and left on her own. He would not contact her again until this was all over, if ever.

Wayne had brought Annie back to Susie's and told her to pack. This time he would make sure that she would leave town. Realizing that the situation had come to a critical pass, he then rushed back to rescue Freddy and Pamela. Now he would make his private plans to achieve dissolution of the mob, even if it meant that he would have to go to prison where he would constantly be in danger of them.

Annie was woozy. The gauze pad clamped on her mouth by the Latin man had been laced with chloroform. Wayne had recovered the bottle of chloroform from the aftermath of the scuffle at the house, and he used it to subdue the man in the shadows by the wall who had been standing watch over Freddy's car. The man went limp so convincingly that Freddy thought Wayne had done murder by garrote or some other equally evil weapon from the movies.

Now Wayne was to go back to Susie's for Annie and drive her in the International as far as Marathon, forty-seven miles distant. After making sure she was away safely and headed back to her folk's home in California he would then make his way back to Key West as best he could. He knew that the man in mufti - Connors - found out that his plan to take Annie failed when the hirelings did not return with her. Connors would be too late to pick up her tail; she would be driving through the Everglades by morning, headed for home.

Pamela and Freddy were to stay out of sight and keep under cover as instructed, on the point of land across from the marina where they normally worked. They would park in the trees near the electric plant. Wayne hoped to be back in three to four hours, well before daylight. He would maintain a vigil with them until he was sure they were safe. When the mob left, he would follow Connors to Sargento. To Freddy, it sounded like a suicidal plan.

Connors would have two loose ends to contend with. One would regain consciousness with a headache from a knock in the head by Wayne. The other would have a different kind of headache, a chloroform headache, and unless things went awry would awake behind a wall, a trussed turkey with a note pinned on him alerting the residents that the man was a dangerous criminal and by no means should be undone by anyone but the police. The note was a precaution Wayne had taken in case he was not able, for some reason, to alert the police of the man's whereabouts by other means. Wayne had made acquaintance with this felon years earlier and so he provided a list of names he had used and of his associates and victims, as well as mentioning that he was wanted for murder in New York State.

With all three of his easy targets vanished and not knowing the whereabouts of his goon, Connors would have to deduce that the man was killed or in custody. Killed wouldn't be so bad, but either way police and federal pressure would be on and Wayne expected the mob to vacate the area before another day passed. They would bide their time and keep tabs on happenings in Key West until Wayne surfaced again somewhere, and then formulate another plan to get him. The present plan had failed. Wayne had won the round, but the contest was not over yet. Wayne was not going to let it end or give them time to re-group. He was going to stop them. The set of his face convinced Freddy he was committed to a course of action, and he was equally sure he was not going to tell them what it was. There was nothing to be done but to do as Wayne directed. Freddy and Pamela drove to the dark and lonely point of land. Wayne set off on foot for Susie's house to get Annie.

****

They sat in the Olds under the sparse overhang of the scrawny Australian pines. The shallow bay separating the point of land from the marina faced them across the unpaved road. The Oldsmobile's top was down, as always, and Pamela was close by Freddy's side in the back seat. She dozed fitfully as he looked up through the thin boughs at the stars. They peeked through the branches, dodging from one space between the twigs to another as the branches rustled in the breeze. It was quiet. Freddy was aware of Pamela's warm body where it rested against his side. He stroked her hair and felt her move. He looked down and saw that she was awake.

"What time is it, Freddy?"

"About four."

"Wayne has been gone a long time. Do you think he will be back soon?"

"I hope so. We got out here at a quarter to eleven, give or take a few minutes. Wayne should have been to Susie's by eleven-thirty. If Wayne left Annie at Marathon, he should have started back by one at the latest. It's forty miles back from there and he has no car. He might have trouble getting a ride. I don't think he'll be relying on hitching a ride, though."

"What else could he do at this time of night?"

"Take a cab, if he has money. Or else steal a car. Probably." They pondered this for a few moments.

"Freddy, what will we do? I mean after this is over? I don't think things are going to be the same as before all of this started happening. Maybe it's time we should leave here, for a while at least."

Could he leave here now? He had thought that he would spend the rest of his life on this island, the last link in a chain of islands separating two seas, and now instead he saw a string of bad memories becoming a heavy necklace. As each black pearl was added he felt his spirit for the place sinking lower. His shoulders stooped to bear the growing weight. Surely, Pamela must feel it, too. They were bearing albatrosses they did not put arrows into.

"Freddy, where do we go from here - I mean right here, tonight? Do we have to hide?" Good question. Freddy was waiting for Wayne to tell them.

"I hope Wayne has the answer to that one, Pamela, 'cause I don't know. I hope he can resolve all of this somehow, and soon."

"I think Wayne is going to chase those men. The police will have arrested that man Wayne tied up on Seminole street and the other men will run away. If Wayne doesn't go after them they will get clean away, but Wayne isn't going to let that happen. He already lost his chance to have them arrested and if he doesn't stop them they'll come after him again someday. They found Wayne down here. Sooner or later they could find Annie, too, and Wayne must know that. I think that he is either going to kill those men or they are going to kill him. But I don't want to lose you, that's the most important thing, so don't go with him. He won't ask you, so don't offer. If anyone can stop those men, Wayne will do it. This will be over for us soon. No matter who wins, the bastards won't be interested in us anymore, and we can get on with our lives." She sighed, and they sat and waited in silence until Wayne's return.

****

Wayne was walking up the decrepit, pitted road. Something was different in his walk; by his stride he seemed oblivious to all around him - a dangerous condition for a man in his position. Pamela was aware that Freddy had tensed and followed his gaze to Wayne's approach. "Oh, no, it's Annie..."

"Stay here," said Freddy as he got out of the car and walked toward Wayne. Wayne approached Freddy with scrapping steps, shoes grinding in the gravel one slow foot at a time, dust devils trailing at his heels. Freddy could almost feel the effort Wayne made to lift each leg in turn, as though exhaustion finally caught up with him.

Freddy couldn't see him very well until he got up close. The light of the moon a day past full lit his face softly but evenly except for the dark caverns of his eyes. His mouth was set in a line, lower at the left and crooked up at the corner. Sallow cheeks showed the fatigue he must have felt; - if indeed he felt anything - made more sunken and pallid by the greenish moon glow. Stubbled chin, eyes, and sockets dilated, curly hair matted and curled tighter in sweat curls, he looked eerie and disconnected.

"Freddy, I need your boat. I don't think I'll be able to get it back to you." There was no need to ask why he wanted it. Freddy waited for Wayne to tell him what went wrong.

****

Pamela got out of the car. She started forward, but Freddy motioned for her to stop. Whatever was coming would come slowly and painfully. Wayne tilted his head back and looked defocused into the sky. Upon turning back to Freddy he at last registered some emotion. Freddy saw his eyes clearly now. The moon had caught them, and they showed a hurt deep within. "Wait here, Pamela," he said softly, and they turned away and walked toward the end of the point on land. As they walked down the dirt road toward the ocean Wayne began to relate to Freddy as much as he knew of what had happened.

****

Annie and Susie had been in the bedroom packing Annie's things when two men burst into the apartment. These were not hired assailants. They were a little older, perhaps in their early or mid-forties. One looked like a turtle in some respects, - mannerisms, face, posture, but was of lean build and sinister. Evil and intense, Susie had said. That would be Joe Sargento, still alive, driven by such a hatred of Wayne that he had become involved personally with the dirty work. The other was different. He didn't look all that dangerous. His hair was ridiculously blond, cut short, receding at the temples. Under cold, pale blue eyes reposed a longish, thin nose, to which a pair of framed, dark glasses were affixed once he entered the brightly lighted room. That would be Connors. Susie said he had a habit of peering over the glasses, as one might do if he needed bifocals. It was an odd detail to stick in her memory.

When the men entered Annie was at the side of the bed. Susie was halfway into the little closet, removing some of Annie's things from wire hangers. On hearing the men burst through the door,

Susie prudently ducked unnoticed further into the shallow closet and wisely pulled the door nearly closed behind her. She watched from there.

Annie took one step away as they came into the bedroom, but there was no place to go; they were upon her too rapidly. Connors stood close on one side of her as the turtle took her arm. The most disconcerting thing about him was not his unusual appearance; it was the large automatic in his left hand. He looked around the room, released her and sat in the stuffed armchair in the corner of the room, letting the grip of the gun come to rest on his leg. It was out of place in the serene surroundings of the conch house bedroom, set with female trappings, as was the collar-length hair on the otherwise well suited and well-manicured man Susie had described.

As Wayne had maintained, Sargento was far from dead. Susie remembered him very well, but this was no surprise when it came to Sargento. His malevolent, psychopathic intensity riveted her attention. She said that he spoke calmly, but still she felt that he was slightly crazed. He looked around absently at the flouncy yellow curtains with white frills on the bottom and from there to a framed print of a white baby seal with disarming, big black eyes. "Cute," he said. He sounded ambivalent, bored and impatient as he addressed Annie, speaking like a busy desk clerk dispatching trivial business.

"Now, Miss, ah, White, is it?" He had somehow found out her last name. "Maybe you can help me out with a few things. We're pressed for time. When we find out what we need to know we'll leave you to your, ah, flat, as my friend here would say, and be on our way. It's really kind of nice, in a cheap, chintzy kind of way." Connors, still standing, prim and proper, remained impassive.

"We want to know where your boyfriend is," he continued flatly. "If you try to protect him we will have to be unpleasant. He's not the hero you think he is. He's a killer, like us, so tell us, and we'll leave."

"No need to be nervous," Connors clipped at last in that close-to-British way he had of speaking. "We know you've had a trying day. Now, where's McLaren?"

Annie was confused and frightened. She bit her lip.

"Well?" he screamed suddenly, shocking her so that she cowed momentarily, then squared her shoulders again and answered.

"I-I haven't seen him for days."

"How many days?"

"Since... Tuesday. Three days. I've been staying here with my friend---"

"Stop it," said Sargento. "We know you've seen him tonight. He has something we want, and we're pretty persistent when it comes to - ah - business." Annie started to look wobbly, as though the floor was rotting away and collapsing beneath her. She was perspiring and knew that she would fail to convince them she would not be seeing Wayne soon. She had seen these evil men, she knew about them now, and she would not give in to them. They had her; they only had to wait until Wayne showed up and they would have him too. She was lost. She knew that they would never let her go. Maybe she could save Teddy - Wayne.

"I would help you if I could but I don't know where he is. Sorry," She said liltingly. She tried to sound calm, like a receptionist in an office building, but her voice sounded shrill to her and her and her words came a half beat too fast.

"We think he will turn up right here. We don't have much time, thanks to him. We're getting exposure we don't want. There's gonna be some cops nosing around and we got to leave soon. We aren't happy about that. The sooner he gets here, the better it will be for you. He don't know we know about this place. He's in for a surprise. If he don't show, you could be in for a nasty time. But he'll show."

"He's probably gone already," Annie said hurriedly, "He said he was going to Washington, D. C., to see the federal agents or something. My goodness, you don't think that he was going to let you keep bothering us, do you?" As she said this her pride in her Wayne showed through her fear. "He was on the plane to Miami Friday - morning."

"Look, lady," Sargento snapped, "There's no meeting with no agents - they'd lock him up. Nobody's that stupid. And he wasn't on no plane Friday. I got to give you credit for trying, but it was a lousy try."

Annie broke and ran for the door. It was still partly open, a few short running strides from her across the tiny conch apartment, and

Annie was a runner. But Connors had lost none of his speed or agility from his eye malady and was around the bedroom door jamb and upon her before she was halfway there. He wrestled her back into the bedroom where Sargento still sat.

"Please let me go. I'll help you. I'll tell you what you want to know. I'll - I'll take you to Wayne - I mean Teddy..."

"This ain't working," Sargento spat. "She isn't going to tell us anything and we don't have any more time to persuade her, and she might get in the way later, when Teddy gets here. Do it. This will settle the score. Teddy killed Nick, and now we're gonna kill his woman."

Annie was in hysterics. She was struggling furiously but nothing seemed to be working for her. Sargento got up from the chair to help restrain the strong, beautiful woman. Now the terrible game was over, she fought to no avail. Connors produced a bottle from his pocket and poured some liquid onto a cloth, being careful to hold the bottle and cloth at arm's length. He held the cloth over Annie's nose and mouth. She shook her head frantically until her bouncy, blond hair no longer hung smoothly to her shoulders. It had somehow frazzled.

It was a sweet smell; pleasant really. Annie held her breath. She tried to wriggle away. She was strong, but Connors was stronger and moreover, he took perverse pleasure in the struggle. Finally, she had to breathe. She understood what was happening, kept struggling, desperately, with no hope of escaping whatever they were going to do to her. Annie's hands went numb. Her mind started to wander and she relaxed

She quieted and was reduced to nervous, mumbling incoherence as she voiced her last words into the cloth. She was talking to Wayne, one last time. She wet herself. "Get down onto the bed," growled Connors with some disgust, and Annie meekly proceeded to recline, half falling, onto the yellow butterflies on the bedspread. Connors guided her fall. The chloroformed gauze was still clamped to her face. A stuffed panda bear perched on the tucked-in pillows rolled against her neck and seemed to kiss her there, good night. She slept. He continued to hold the cloth to her face to make sure that she would sleep endlessly. Annie slipped away. Her last dream was a hope that these men would not get Wayne. She loved him. He was three blocks away.

Chapter Twenty - The Point

Susie, watching through the louvered closet door, saw it all in horrid fascination. She was transfixed and afraid to move or even breathe by the spellbinding, gruesome scene. Seeing Annie being killed finally triggered the realization of her own peril should the intruders decide to search the place, as well they might. Susie did not want to be there, whether they searched or not, when the two confronted Wayne. He should be there any minute now.

Connors was still holding the rag over Annie's face when Susie sprang from the closet and bolted out the still-open door and ran for her life.

Connors was occupied, but Sargento wasn't. He bolted from the chair by the bedside and nearly got around Connors and the bedroom door jamb in time to catch her. But he didn't. She got through the outside doorway and slammed it shut just as Sargento lunged for the back of her belt. It was luck for her that the two men had made the glaring error of failing to close that door. She barely made it. She made it out into the street and ran toward the center of the Halloween partiers. Wayne was in the street. He saw Susie running toward him and caught her by the arms. It took a little time for him to calm her down and realize that something was terribly wrong.

"I left Susie there and ran on to the apartment." Wayne had continued relating the dire events of the evening.

"They were gone. Susie's escape made it impossible for them to stay any longer. Annie was there on the bed. Her hand was in her hair and it pushed up a silly cowlick. It was absurd - clown like. She just lay there silently. She trusted me."

Susie had straggled back in and, shaking and crying, told him the rest of what happened.

"You couldn't have known they would come for her there," Freddy said quietly.

"I ought to have known. I've had enough training in that sort of thing." Freddy had no idea what that meant. "Then I stayed with her as long as I could. It wasn't long enough."

"I'm so sorry, Wayne." There was nothing more to say.

"I know."

"What will you do now?"

"I'm going to take your boat and go after them. I don't know if I'll make it back. It doesn't matter anyway, Freddy. I don't think I can get your boat back to you, in any case."

"I'm not worried about it, Wayne. Take it. What else can I do? Do you want me to come with you?"

"No, just take good care of Pamela and have a good life. And if you can, try to see Annie's folks and explain. Goodbye, buddy."

"Take care, Wayne." With that he started wading across the shallow bay. He would swim across the deeper channel to the marina and to Freddy's boat. From now on Freddy imagined that it would be all water travel for Wayne. Freddy wished him luck. He noticed that Wayne held something above his head as he slogged through the mud and the grass and the gunk. Of course, he had to keep it dry. It was his gun.

****

Freddy's thoughts were in an abysmal turmoil:
Oh my goodness, Annie. Oh, Annie, who would want to kill you? Could there have been a nicer, kinder, person? Ok, Wayne, what will you do now, kill them all? It won't bring Annie back. It won't clear your name. Maybe you can do it, maybe you have to, 'cause you know they won't stop chasing you. But maybe they'll kill you.

****

There was nothing for it. It was out of his hands. He still had Pamela and somehow things would eventually be all right. Not here, somewhere else, perhaps, but they had a chance. Wayne's chance was gone.

Freddy was surprised to find that he was near the end of the point. Wayne and he had walked and talked longer than he realized. Then there were motor noises and Freddy's pulse quickened. A fast boat was coming in. It appeared that it was too far to the right of the channel - it was lined up with the end of the point, some sixty yards from him. An awful feeling hit him. He had known that the evil men would soon have to make a hurried departure from Key West due to a dawning awareness of their presence there by the police. The heat brought on by Wayne and his repeated thwarting of their covert assaults and abduction attempts, their fear that he had amassed information to imperil their operations, and the capture of their man had compromised them. Could they be meeting here, on this point of land? It would be a brazen move; there was an armed guard at the deserted desalting plant close to the end of the point.

Pamela was alone, waiting for him, well down the road. Freddy had to return to her as quickly as he could.

Behind him was the rumble of tires and the sounds of loose stones popping from under the wheels of a fast-moving car. Freddy turned from the approaching boat and saw a car's headlights rounding the turn two hundred yards down the road, trailing a cloud of dust. Susie's escape must have precipitated an even earlier departure than the one Sargento had planned. Of course - she had called the police.

Freddy knew he'd strayed too far - the car would overtake Pamela's position at the roadside before he could get to her. The gangsters were returning to their mother ship, the shrimp boat so often seen anchored at the mouth of the channel in the past weeks. The need for speed had changed their plans. The fast boat had been sent to pick them up.

Freddy saw no lights out across the water. He didn't expect to, even if the shrimp boat was close enough to shore to see. They intended to make a discreet departure.

Why had none of this occurred to Freddy before? Wayne might have thought of it if he wasn't so out of it. Wayne might have seen something, with his way of looking so intently, searching the shadows for a glint of the moon on metal, looking for a silhouette not of natural origin in the bushes or on the horizon. Wayne might have anticipated this moment if only for his own dread purposes, except that he had been going on mindlessly since finding Annie. Freddy hoped it wasn't them, but he knew it was. He felt dizzy. Maybe they wouldn't see Pamela. That hope sank as he heard the car slow and crunch to a stop, wheels locked and sliding on the loose scree. Freddy stopped and listened. "Freddy..." he heard Pamela's voice calling his name and his mouth went dry. Standing, swooning, legs rubbery, he was caught from behind by the searchlight from the boat as it probed for a place to land. He saw his shadow stretched out long before him. The beam flashed around him and continued down the road.

Sixty yards down the road three figures suddenly flashed briefly into view seemingly larger than life in that narrow shaft of light. It seemed to stop their motion like a strobe and for a moment they were like three stark figures in a grainy photograph, frozen in the beam of the light, struggling in a cloud of diffused glare from the unsettled dust.

The light went out and Freddy broke into a headlong run for Pamela. When last he saw her in the frieze-frame she was on the water side of the road, her white dress flanked by two dark figures, clutching her arms at either side of her. The Olds was farther along; parked where it had been in the trees on the road's other side. Pamela had been uneasy at Freddy's long absence and was wandering in the direction he had gone when they saw her.

Freddy strained his eyes, but he was still too far away to see what was happening at the darkened roadside. Then he had to dive headlong for the bracken near the water's edge as the car they had come in lurched forward and the lights came on. He laid there near the water, settling in time to avoid the swath of the vehicle's headlights as it swung back onto the road. It moved slowly up the road, presumably looking for him.

He tried to think clearly. He was halfway between the bastards in the boat and the ones in the car. Pamela had called his name, so they knew he was there, but not in which direction. The people on the boat had might have seen him, too, but they could not let the others who arrived by car know this unless they were in radio contact. Unlikely. This event was, for once, unscripted and unplanned. They were on the run.

Once the two factions joined they would compare notes and come back for him. The important thing now was for Freddy to find Pamela and try to get her out of there.

The car was past him now. Freddy edged down the side of the road, staying low. Now he forgot his ills and injuries, wrist, knee, ribs, nose - it didn't matter how he felt. Eyes strained ahead. Short running steps in a low crouch. He moved rapidly; it took forever. Then in front of him was a patch of white on the ground at the roadside. There was a sweet chemical smell in the air.

****

She was lying there, halfway on her side, white shoe on her right foot off, strap broken. She was in the weeds at the side of the road like a broken bird near the Goose Pond of Freddy's youth. She looked vulnerable and innocent. She was the sweetest thing ever to visit Freddy's life. He settled down beside her.

Her hair was in her face. Her dress had ridden up revealing her pretty legs and a little bit of her panties at her hip. Bent sideways at her waist, she clutched her tummy. There was a red stain where her hands covered her stomach, and her head was at a bad angle. Stabbed. No time for the chloroform to work this time. Pain touched the gentle face that only deserved to smile. On his knees at her side, Freddy touched her hair and pulled it back off her cheek... traced the cheek softly with his fingertips. It was warm. He pulled her dress down to cover her legs and straightened her head. He held her and kissed the side of her mouth – If she was breathing it was too shallow for him to notice.

Something was moving in the grass nearby. A harmless black snake had come upon their still figures. It had sensed the warmth and approached them as it would have approached a hot rock. Freddy in his anguish took it by the tail and hurled it with furious violence against a boulder set at the water's edge. Then he felt guilt for having done that to the innocuous creature.

The car that had passed earlier had been gone for many minutes now. If they had started looking for him, so far they were looking in the wrong place. He knew one place they would check first, the guard shack at the desalting plant. They would not want Freddy to get to that shack. He could call the sheriff from there and let him know what was occurring. He knew place they would check first, the guard shack at the desalting plant. They would not want Freddy to get to that shack. He could call the sheriff from there.

Freddy needed to get help. First, he had to get Pamela out of here. Leaving her in the bushes with the ants and the animals - Freddy didn't want to do that. And he could get these fiends arrested if he could get the sheriff here in time. But he didn't want to exact justice on them by bringing them to trial. He knew a hate such as he'd never know before. He wanted them dead.

He heard sirens. He would not have to call the Sheriff, at any rate. The deputies were coming, barreling down the dirt road, flashing lights and sirens in the billowing dust. He jumped bask into the bushes as the searchlight on the cop car lit up her white dress. They would be there in seconds. At least that meant that Pamela would get medical attention very soon. Freddy's car was parked yards away; Annie's murder had been reported, and Wayne was gone. Sargento and company had gotten clear of *this* scene before the arrival of the Deputies. And that left Freddy as the fall guy for all of the recent mayhem. He had to make a choice, stay here and become embroiled in an investigation which would render him useless to help anyone, or get to Wayne and the boat and seek revenge and restitution for his friends. The world misted over. And Pamela... all he had done was to bring her trouble and pain. She would be in good hands now. He had been too late even to say goodbye

He headed toward the open water and ran...

Part Three

No Place to Stay, No Place to Go

Chapter Twenty-One - Open Pursuit

He stopped running. He was aggrieved, but he tried to think. Freddy knew there was danger at the end of the point. He had to assume that someone had been left to watch the other end of the road as well to cut off his escape. He must move while there was some time left. As he ran past the Olds earlier, thinking to bring it to where Pamela rested, he saw that the hood was open. They had pulled off the distributor cap and taken the rotor. But when? The two men who assaulted Pamela could not have had the time. Then he had the answer.

Stealth is hard on a quiet night away from the city. There were pebbles shuffling as someone tried a silent approach. Turning, Freddy saw two of them. They were not so far away from the last of the street lights farther down the road that Freddy could not make the appropriate assumptions from their movements and their stance. They were forty yards away and had guns *and radios.*

Freddy took a runner and jumped on the chain-link fence behind the trees enclosing the electric company property. There was nothing beyond that property but the old desalting plant near the end of the point. He climbed the fence and made a graceful fall to the other side, his hurting wrist balking at the event. Running feet followed him. What to do? He heard someone scramble over the fence farther up the road. Having underestimated them once, he would try not to do so again.

He skirted to the right, past the fuel oil tank before him to avoid other watchers that might be on the road and made for the channel on the other side of the peninsula. His ultimate goal would be to find Wayne and join forces if Wayne would let him. If not he would go alone, all the way to the *"Big Nick's"* home port of Turbo, Colombia, the port he had seen painted on the trawler's stern, if he had to.

He made good time running silently on the mat of needles dropped by the Australian pines that proliferated on the property of the utility. It was probably half-past five by now and dawn was not far off. They couldn't waste much more time on him, the deputies must be close. If Freddy could get across to the water on the other side of the point, he might find help in time to stop their escape. Maybe Cap'n Walter's boat was docked at the ice house, in for repairs or supplies, or maybe he could find someone he knew at the bar at the base of the promontory, the last stop for alcohol before heading back to the boats. Maybe somebody had a gun he could have. One with no registration.

Meanwhile, as he was silently running on the pine needles and contemplating these imponderables, was the awareness and guilt that Pamela's body was lying at the roadside with the water lapping at the rocks only two feet from where she lay. Thoughts of insects and crawlers in shells, marauding rodents and reptiles made his mind black with despair in frustration that she should lay in state there among nature's wild things; but she would not be unattended for long while he ran the other way. The deputies who were rolling up would be far better equipped to help her – if she could be helped – than he would be after being riddled with bullets by the men who were chasing him now and who had come close to coming upon him in his anguish at Pamela's side.

All at once, moving north to south, there were the onrushing sheriff's deputies who would soon come to the aid of Pamela, and next up the point in the direction of the open water were Freddy's pursuers who, while chasing Freddy were actually pressed for time themselves and on the run from the law, a contingent of which whose arrival behind them was eminent and would soon work its way up the point toward the old desalting plant, where Sargento's fast boat and crew were waiting for *Freddy's* pursuers so they themselves could flee to the mother ship. And farther still down the point there was Wayne, swimming across the channel with the object of soon pursuing Sargento's mother ship in Freddy's boat.

Sargento's mother ship itself was offshore waiting for the crews from the point to arrive by the fast boat, and, to close the loop, Freddy who hopefully, eventually, would rendezvous with Wayne and join in the pursuit of Sargento. It was a dynamic situation wherein each constituent party was running to or from each other. But the immediate reality for Freddy was this: If Sargento and his men could pick Freddy off as they escaped that would be bonus points for them.

He suppressed thoughts of grief in order to address the problem at hand, the need for survival. He found himself thinking, calculating on a higher plane. He would *have* to survive if he was going to get them.

The trees thinned and he was standing in the open, a trawler's length from the sea wall of the shrimp boat channel. There was a crack - not loud, not like a gun, more like a cap pistol - and a sapling behind him shivered and splintered four feet above the ground, bent and swung down at the point of the schism, but did not fall. The wound gaped, white wood flesh at the laceration in shards, angling out from the bottom and top halves of the obliquely bent tree, stark, sharp, fish-like teeth jutting from a wooden maw like a shark attacking from below. One of the two pistol-packing radio men had out-maneuvered Freddy by running around the sparse copse of trees thus avoiding unseen obstacles under the matte-black canopy of pine boughs. Even as shots landed around him, Freddy was aware of the changes in textures - hard packed marl instead of the cushion of pine needles underfoot. Open air, sea smell and unfathomable sky instead of the damp, resiny dimensions of the sweet-gum smelling pine wood glade with its cartoon-like animation, more distant trees moving more slowly past him, the closer ones whizzing by, like Bambi running through the woods distressed and enraged at his mother's loss and realizing he had horns. Adrenal flow lubricated joints and peaked senses to a new awareness. His perception of all things was clear and he had a purpose, knew each course of action without deliberating on what to do next, and was moving toward another fence to jump. What's one more fence, right? You jump one, you've jumped them all.

His escape to the base of the point was cut off. The fast boat and crew had landed there. The other man of this couple who were gunning for him was no doubt picking his way toward him through the woods at his back. The boat that had landed to pick these men up was waiting in the same direction as the fence he was headed for, but there might be enough working room that he might elude them. At the moment there was no pain - not even for Pamela. That couldn't be, but it was. It would surface again, perhaps many times. Now the fence was upon him. He leaped upon it, over it. There *was* pain; from his wrist, his knee, and yet there wasn't. He wouldn't let it be, so it remained detached from him, as though someone else was feeling it. He landed lightly on both feet and ran to the guard shack.

****

The guard on duty had been Mike. He was off duty now, a simple bump to the head. One of his adversaries had beaten him to the guard shack. The phone lines were cut, as Freddy had expected.

Now there were lights wavering back and forth behind him and in front of him as well. Freddy would surely be spotted if he tried once again to get to the water on either side of the point. He would be an easy target out in the open in the moonlight. The best course of action was to hide. They would have to leave soon and would be wise to do so while still cloaked in darkness. He could out-wait them if he could remain out of sight a little longer.

Freddy was on familiar ground,. He'd worked at the desalting plant and knew his way all around, and the inside as well as the outside, of the old evaporator. There were fifty stages, separated into top and bottom halves. Fifty compartments on top, fifty on the bottom, all four feet high inside. Stages one through forty-eight were fourteen feet long. Numbers forty-nine and fifty were fifty-five feet long. Each compartment had at least one "manway" or manhole cover type opening into it on the bottom, either on the sides or under it, and as many hatches on top of much lighter construction. Some had two or more. Lots of holes to hide in. Even if they should think to look inside each one, it would require strenuous climbing under and over the evaporator and a hard flashlight search in each one of the holes in the time before daylight. The odds were in Freddy's favor. Unless they got lucky, Freddy felt that his chances were excellent.

Choices. Top or bottom? The bottom stages offered easier entry and were closer, but it would be easier for them to see him getting in. He ran up the two-story metal-grate stairway to the top of the evaporator and jumped four feet down to the steel plating which was the roof of the evaporator. Where to hide? One of the smaller stages in the first two rows? Good cover of machinery and a heat exchanger there. Too small to hide in. The next two rows were larger stages - not longer, but wider, with two holes in the top of each of them. They were too much in the open if Freddy should have to bolt from the hole for some reason and make another run for it. A big stage would be best - hardest for light to penetrate. They would have to come inside looking and ferreting for him. Hiding among the tubes and debris, he had a fighting chance to take them as they came.

Number forty-nine, or fifty? Forty-nine it was. It didn't have them damn gasifier baffles in it and might not stink as bad.

As he climbed down into the hole at the southern end of the chamber the dank smells of sulfur and old rust came up to greet him. There were several inches of standing water at the bottom of the compartment. Scurrying in the fetid water, hunched over to accommodate the low ceiling, he moved into the total darkness away from the hole, toward the end wall of the stage, brushing stanchions, rubbing rust-scaled walls and wire-mesh vapor passages on his right and the outside of a horizontal bundle of three thousand tubes on his left which used to carry sea water to the big brine heater on the top of the evaporator. Freddy was not being overly clumsy; the space between the wall and the tubes was less than a shoulder width.

His slacks were taking a beating, smeared on the left with the reddish oxide on the copper tubes. The caked rust on the wall on his right side - inches thick in some places - came in reds, browns and blacks depending on the heat and acidity it had been subject to. It tore at his clothes. Freddy felt his shirt rip and tore the skin on his arm as he brushed a stanchion made of a thick-wall four inch diameter pipe used for structural support, now eroded to a razor-sharp dual edged crescent by the flow inside the evaporator. He had only snagged it. Hitting it squarely would have parted his arm to the bone.

He reached the end wall and laid down supine in the few inches of stagnant water and rust chips he had been slogging through and then slid under the tube crossover gallery between stages where the watercourse made a one hundred and eighty degree turn from the preceding row of stages. The four foot wide, six foot long space was high enough to leave just two inches of clearance over Freddy's chest. Spooky and claustrophobic, in the depths of the dark, steel box, it was still better than the alternatives. Freddy let the back of his head settle into the dank, standing water, saturating his hair with the putrescent liquid.

The metal of the evaporator held the heat of yesterday's sun well and the water was not as chilly as he expected. He thought back to his days working inside this thing in one hundred and thirty or forty degrees, ventilator blowing on him through the hole to the outside. Climbing from the vessel into the one hundred degree heat sizzling from the sunlit top of the metal box he would shiver uncontrollably. Now it was silent and cold and his joints began to congeal.

Several minutes into the inactivity Freddy thought of floating, the games of tag in the water, treading water silently under the raft at the Goose Pond of his youth long years ago, head in the dark air space below the wooden decking, hands clutching the rafters, hiding from his little friends. Grown now, he was playing a game of tag again, hide and seek with men with guns. He would soon find whether his skill at the game, the elusive prowess unused for so many long years, was still with him.

****

He must have been lying there for ten minutes or so, guessing on how long it might be before he could get out. His diver's watch was on his wrist, and it had a light in it, too. Trouble was, he could not move his arm in the too-tight enclosure and get the watch in front of his face. How was he to judge time? Maybe he would see a glow from the manway when the sun was up far enough if he waited that long, but by then the area would be crawling with gendarmes.

The time went by predictably slowly until he heard the first clang. It was followed by others. He knew the sound; they were closing the manways. He hadn't thought of that.

****

The clanging continued. It might well be his death knell. He imagined he would be entombed in the skulking dinosaur. He wondered whose idea that was - it seemed like something Connors would think of.

Closing the entire evaporator, every manway, would be a major effort. It couldn't be done before dawn, even by people who knew what they were doing. They didn't have time to wait that long. The ones on the bottom and sides were two inch thick steel circles and thirty inches across. They were heavy, but it would only take two of the thirty-six bolts on each to keep someone inside, the one that the manway hung on and swung around on, and one other on the opposite side to keep it in the closed position. The top holes were covered by convex hatches with dogs to secure them. One dog on each would keep the cover closed. A man inside could not get to it and would never get out.

It was a big job; they were going through a lot of trouble for him, and he was duly impressed. He doubted that the thugs, although tough, were up to the job physically. But this course of action would take less time than searching inside the box. It was a crap shoot. They may not get to him, but they could harry him until they made their escape. With any luck, they might even kill him. The dangerous substances, flammable liquids, machinery, and valuable metals on the plant site were the guard's major concern, not the steel hulk of the evaporator with its hard-to-extract tubes. If he was sealed inside, and no one thought to look for him here, here he might stay. He envisioned his skeleton sitting here in years to come, sitting with its back against the wall.

Sooner or later someone would venture within shouting distance on the other side of the thick, steel wall. Who was he kidding; no one would hear him through the steel. He had nothing to bang on the walls with but his hands, wouldn't know when someone was out there. He decided he was not going to let them get away with this so easily.

At least *some* luck was going his way. It sounded as though they had started on the other side of the evaporator first. He extricated himself from the crossover and rubbed the circulation back into selected areas of his body he would need and started back to the hole. He could wait for a face to appear at the hole and make a grab for it and get immediately shot, or he could run.

Getting out was a combination of pommel horse and contortionist skills. It could not be done gracefully or quickly by a man of Freddy's years. Or so he had always thought. Then again, the bad guys wouldn't be expecting him to come out and face their muzzles. Or their guns either, for that matter. It was all so sarcastic, silly, sick, funny, and he was out and rolling on the top of the box before he knew it. Things were picking up again, no more rest and relaxation. He saw that his clothes had become a camouflage suit of reds, browns, blacks, and tatters.

"Hey!" the man closing the manways on top shouted as he saw Freddy, and he went for his gun. Freddy rolled further, under a pipe gallery running along the outside wall of the box which was facing the sea. Horizontal pipes, from two inches in diameter to over thirty inches separated most of Freddy from the gunman. Another silenced pistol report and a loud clang of a bullet striking a metal pipe prompted him to run along the outside edge of the evaporator toward to the 6 foot high brine heater on the opposite corner. His old Florshiems, serving so long as his premier dancing pumps and party shoes were ill-suited to running down a six inch wide metal path at the edge of the evaporator three stories above the ground. Their hard leather soles, already having had their noses bear the insult of being thrust into chain link fences on this night, petulantly slid and turned on the loose rust on the box top as the two-by-four runner fixed to the very edge of the steel box tried to trip him.

Then he was "safe" for a moment behind the sixty foot long metal cylinder of the brine heater. He looked down and saw a man on the sea wall by the shrimp boat channel, looking up at him and making an all too familiar move. Before the man brought his gun to bear Freddy was clambered into the end of the heat exchanger. The bullet hit the side of the vessel and the resultant bell-like ringing inside was deafening.

Now his confines were a three foot long end section bolted onto the main body of a long cylindrical chamber bearing one thousand and eighty tubes whose ends faced him. Hot brine once had passed through them, heated to 240 degrees by steam circulating around the tubes. This time the men outside knew where he was.

He heard clacking footfalls approaching on the metal gratings. They soon would be poking guns in the manway and shooting. One bullet fired in here was bound to get him sooner or later as it bounced round and round.

Again he had an "advantage." He knew what was in here and they didn't. At his feet, at the bottom of the end bell was a hole about thirty inches wide which had made the climb into the thing awkward. A fall down that hole would have been grievous to flesh and blood. It was a down-tube to the bottom half of the first of the fifty stages that the heated brine once coursed through. Freddy slithered and slid down this escape course as it twisted forty-five degrees, and another forty-five degrees again out over the side of the box. Another two such turns, like segments of the large intestine, brought the pipe back into the side of the box at the bottom half of stage number one.

He bumped into stage one after a laundry chute-like ride, adding more bruises to his beat-up body, and was already climbing out of the manway in the side as more pursuers clanged along the grate work above. He dropped five feet to the ground into a crouch, concealed behind steam turbines and pumps, hoping that the camouflage of the turbines and his rust-darkened clothing in the shadows would allow him to get to his next objective. It wasn't far.

The effluent of the plant had been hot brine; super-saturated salt water. The discharge flowed to a concrete pit at the southwest corner of the evaporator and down an underground pipe to the channel about five feet below sea level.

He made his way to the pit and moved under the remnants of the grate-work for concealment. There were two feet of water in the bottom. He had countered all of their moves so far, except for the one that took Pamela. Now he would try again to outwait them. He looked at his watch and was surprised to see that it was only five-thirty. Still over an hour and a quarter until sunrise.

Voices approached. They had traced the pipe to stage one.

"He in there?" a voice asked."

"No, it's empty" answered another.

"He has to be close by." That was Connors. "Guido," ("Guido?" thought Freddy, as he mouthed the stereotypical unfamiliar name. How cliché). "Go out to the sea wall and see that the idiot doesn't try to make a run for the water. If he does, shoot him. Don't miss this time."

"Yes, boss." Guido departed. Freddy was insulted at being called an idiot. They had failed to get him so far. He deserved a little respect.

"Charlie - stand just off the corner of this thing, whatever it is, and watch down the lines of these two sides. I've looked into the side of this confounded thing and he isn't in this little section that the pipe empties into. Joe, get in there and make sure he doesn't have himself wedged up in that pipe somehow." Very thorough. Freddy did not like all this. "The rest of you search around the machinery the way I instructed you to search. And no one without a silencer fires. But be ready to go. We have little time left. We're out of here as soon as that boat is loaded."

Around the box there were twelve steam turbines and pumps, two compressors, a tank with one thousand gallons of caustic soda in it and two large tanks, each containing seven thousand gallons of ninety-seven per cent pure sulfuric acid. They were still full. Two boilers were housed in a building off to the marina side of the property, a forty-three foot tall fuel oil tank stood in an overflow pit.

Past that there was only the open section of landfill contained by the sea wall surrounding the end of the point. It made for a lot to search. Freddy hoped they would overlook the pit was he in.

Three minutes passed, then four. Footsteps got close and a stray beam of light raked the grate above him. They passed by. They were very methodical. Another pass and they would be on top of the grate over Freddy's pit. He would be hard to see, but not impossible. He could jump out and run, but he would not get far, only as far as Guido on the sea wall. There was only one more thing to do now, and he *really* did not want to. He waited until they were close at hand.

He breathed deeply to hyperventilate and tried to relax his pulse rate down to somewhere below two hundred and fifty beats per minute. At the last possible moment and ducked his head and shoulders under the water and into the effluent pipe. He would do the one thing he knew he could do well - hold his breath.

He had his hands out in front of him as he crawled into the pipe. Now all was dark, cold, and silent. He could back out with a major effort if he didn't get in too far, but he knew nothing of what was going on above him. If they shot him while he was backing out of the pipe they would probably die laughing. Freddy couldn't stand the thought of that. Idiot, indeed. He started down the pipe.

At first the high salt content seared his wounds. Kicking was impossible in the narrow space, and Florshiems are not swim fins. He kicked them off. Goodbye, old friends. Farther down slimy vegetation had taken hold where the pipe became diluted with the tides. There was no way to judge distance or time, or even forward motion. He might merely be slithering in place. He kept going, trying to slither farther along, inch by inch. He swallowed once, to resist the urge to breath. Something slid past him, maybe an eel who had taken up residence in the pipe. Freddy hoped he wasn't hungry. The encounter increased his anxiety and pushed his pulse rate a little higher, causing him to burn oxygen faster at a time when he needed all of the breath he could get. He thought of how Pamela had been beating his breath-hold dives and bottom times. This time he had to perform flawlessly; he could never hope to slither back up the slippery pipe in reverse.

Then he swallowed a second time and then a third, and now his chest muscles were contracting involuntarily in spasms as he fought with them not to do so, not to give up. There was no purchase for his hands to pull him along; the slime came away in his fists. His feet slid on the slimy pipe insides. All he could do was rub and scrub and fan at the slime hoping the scant friction he could create by stroking the slick sides was moving him forward.

The tunnel vision of pre-blackout sought to render him unconscious.

Finally, he saw a dim light ahead. The night sky filtered through five feet of water. Then, his knuckles hit something. A grate. There was a grate on the end of the damn pipe! What for? To stop lobsters from getting into the factory?

Freddy was enraged and dismayed. He could not turn around; even if he could he would never make it all the way back, up the slope of the pipe, he doubted he could get two feet. He had an image of a frightened boy in a submerged railroad car as he started to black out. If he died here no one would ever find his remains, except crabs. Panic tried to take hold of him, but his frustration forced it down.

At least the grate was in poor shape, nearly rusted away. What would Jean Valjean do in the Paris sewers? He clutched the rusty grate and felt it rip the skin of two fingers. Converting all of his angry power from his violently convulsing lungs to his arms, he shook that grate. He pushed back and forth with all his might until it began to give way a bit, then more, and then it was falling to the channel floor. Freddy left the pipe, gratefully, pulling himself out with his arms and then kicking off the concrete sea wall into water that felt clean, leaving the pervasive darkness of the shaft of slimy water where he thought he might bloat, decompose and come away from his bones in small pieces of chum. He was desperate for a breath but he imagined Guido with his gun stationed somewhere above him. The effort sent small spurts of bubbles from his lips.

He swam a little further and surfaced in the center of the closest of the dolphins that the fuel barges had used to tie up to. They were pilings, like big tepee frames in the water driven into the bottom of the channel in a circle and drawn together at the top with steel cable. He could surface, concealed in the wooden teepee, unseen. Once inside the dolphin he knew he was safe, Sargento and his men if he chose to be. It was only a respite until their next meeting. He would see them again, for Pamela. Breathing long, deep draughts as quietly as he could, fending off the last vestiges of the blackout that had tried to overcome him, he regained his breath and then swam under water to the next dolphin in the line of dolphins flanking the sea wall.

The dolphins were not twenty yards apart. He easily made his way farther and farther from the fiends, swimming five feet below the channel surface. When he was far enough away from the plant, he breast-stroked up the channel, making no wake, no splash, causing no ripples they could see. He struck out for the shrimp boats.

Chapter Twenty-Two – Wanted

Freddy swam up the channel, small and insignificant as he bobbed along doing his breast stroke in the channel chop. He had heard the siren of the ambulance coming for Pamela. They would be caring for her right now, if she was still alive. He then heard Guido shout, "Let's get out of here, boys, we're outta time."

He swam past the floodlit electric plant four stories high on shore, its stack towering up into the dark sky. The musical gurgling of the choppy water against the sea wall had given way to the splashing sounds of the water on a stretch of pebbled shore. He heard the high-low horns of an ambulance, and then distant siren wailed, then got closer, merging with and then drowning the lapping sounds of the water. Then the horns dopplered off and grew faint after if passed and Pamela was on her way.

Freddy was looking for the *Southern Lady,* Cap'n Walter's boat. He could have walked to the dockage, could have gone ashore at the electric company property, but some feeling within him told him it would be safer in the water.

His approach to this next meeting with Walter must be handled carefully. It would not do to have escaped the hands of Sargento's men only to be shot as a burglar on the shrimp boat docks. He knew that wet and disheveled as he was, he would attract attention if there was any to be had.

He was also shy about his ravaged clothes and filth that would not wash off - the slime would need scrubbing and the rust of the evaporator would probably stain the skin as it used to years ago. He felt it would be prudent to exercise caution. Whether it be the sheriff or security guards, or anyone else, Freddy did not wish to be hindered. Those he would prefer to confront were Sargento and his murderous men, but on his own terms.

The siren had gotten much louder. It was a patrol vehicle, a sheriff's cruiser answering a call for backup on the Point, most likely.

It seemed too soon for anything to have happened in regard to the discovery of Sargento's activities by the authorities. Freddy suspected that would change by morning light, and that was soon approaching. He assumed that Connors and company had already left the point. The clubbed security guard was due for a shift change; daylight was somewhere around seven; Freddy's disappearance and the siren's night-piercing wail would have advanced their departure in any case. They were old hands at disappearing. Anything that delayed Freddy now would make it harder for him to catch up with them later.

****

Walter's boat was tied up at the end of the second pier. Freddy swam to the side of the boat. With an effort, he climbed a tire hung as a fender on a piling next to the dock. He peered cautiously over the top of the weathered two-by-sixes into the shadowy incandescent light, saw no one. He put his hands on the dock and hauled his torso up and over, flopping onto the dock and swinging his legs onto it. He stood up next to the boat.

Bushy fenders were on her nose, tires hung from her sides to prevent bruises to her white, lap-straked wood hull from naked pilings, docks, and other boats. Rust lines streaked down her sides from rusted chains and fittings. The smell of new grease came from her running gear.

"Walter," he called trying to direct his voice down into the boat and nowhere else. Had he stepped aboard unannounced, Walter might be prompted to greet him from the other side of a barrel, shoot first and examine the remains afterward. Freddy knew he looked horrible.

"Walter, are you down there?"

"Who in the hell is it?"

"It's Freddy."

"You sure as hell got a nerve, considerin' the last time I ran into you and what your friend did to my crew." The steps creaked as he made his way up from the galley. As his head cleared the hatch he looked once, did a double take and looked again with face twisted and eyes squinted in close and curious scrutiny. "Uh, what you been doin'?"

"Taking a swim. Mind if I get inside? I don't want to be seen if I can avoid it."

"Whew! I don't blame you. We gotta stop dumpin' the shit from the boats into the channel. I don't like the smell of ya, but this don't look like a merely social call and you ain't drunk. Are ya? Better come inside." A twelve inch black and white TV set in a recess in the bulkhead rendered a dance number superbly executed for the ten thousandth time by Fred and Ginger. They danced and Walter waited. He showed some signs of apprehension when he thought Freddy was about to sit in his chair. Its cushion was upholstered in a print cloth which once could have been blue. Or green. At any rate far be it for Freddy to ruin Cap'n Walter's decor. Freddy dropped to the floor and slouched against the bulkhead.

"I'm in a bit of trouble."

"Figured that." He shook his head and shut the TV.

"Is there anyone else here? I don't want to be overheard."

"No," said Cap'n Walter. He turned on the radio, moderately loud. "What do ya need? He asked with an upward inflection". Good ole' Cap'n Walter had offered his help - to a point, Freddy gathered by that inflection, and nothing more need be said about the Mascot Bar Fiasco.

"I can't tell you much - it wouldn't do you any good and you're better off not knowing."

"That's fine with me. Those sireens for you?"

"Very likely. Or at least everything that has happened is going to point to me. My car is down there and..."

"No, it ain't."

"What do you mean, 'no it ain't'? It's sitting out near the point with no rotor under the distributor cap."

"Well, maybe it don't have no rotor, but I saw it go by from where I was sittin' in the bar down the street."

So they replaced the rotor and drove the car away to where Freddy couldn't get to it unseen. Why? Were they afraid he might get back to it and go for help? Were they trying to limit his mobility?

Both seemed plausible. Or maybe they thought if the car was found on the point with its rotor *missing* it would be a lead for the police, not back to Freddy but to them. Tucked away under suspicious circumstances, somewhere along the road to the point and intact, perhaps with some clues planted in it by one of Connors' flunkies, it would appear that Freddy had tried to murder Pamela. "I think I'm being framed for murder."

"Who's dead?"

Freddy almost couldn't bring himself to say it.

"Maybe Pamela. I don't know"

"I'm sorry. Freddy."

He waited for his composure to return. "I'll need shoes. Sneakers, if you've got them."

Wouldn't wear anything else. 'Cept sandals, a'course, if I'm partyin'."

"I'll pay for them."

"Damn straight, you will." He turned to get some things near his bunk. "I'll get you a sweatshirt and some jeans, too. If you don't mind me sayin' so, you better wash. If you have to deal with anybody you'll do better if there ain't slime on ya."

"Good point." He washed quickly. He needed the remaining forty-five minutes of darkness to cover his movements to his next planned stop.

He would stay away from the marina on Stock Island where they worked and where Freddy kept his boat. Wayne was probably long gone by now, and someone might be looking for him there. He was sure Connors had left some hints to help them along in that direction. He would head back into Key West, away from the action.

Later, he must not be detained by whatever authorities held jurisdiction over whatever Wayne's vague satanic nemesis, Sargento, was involved in. He wasn't in the mood for it in any case.

Freddy was cleaned up considerably when he came back out into the galley. As he sat to lace the sneakers, Walter said, "Listen to this." The local station had been reporting the party night's news. There had been a few fights, and, this just in, a stabbing. A woman had been found murdered on Stock Island out past the shrimp boat docks. They had found a knife near the body. The sheriff's department had a suspect in the case, the owner of a car that had been anonymously reported as moving suspiciously in the area. A local man was being sought for "questioning".

Freddy had to give Connors credit. He had quickly implicated Freddy as the number one suspect. He probably had made the report to the Sheriff about Freddy's car himself. But Freddy was learning. He saw no choices now. He couldn't go to the marina to find Wayne, he had known that already, and he couldn't stay in Key West. He had to get across the island and to the other side of Key West. He wasn't sure yet how to go about what he must do next, but maybe Big Frank could help him. He and Wayne were of a type, able to find a way around any problem, at their best in adversity. Freddy had to get to the marina on the opposite side of Key West, Because now there was only one way out.

He had to steal a boat.

****

There wasn't much time. Freddy's first obstacle was the shrimp boat channel. He could stay close to shore and skirt around it, sneaking past the boats, trailer parks, a few houses, and the junkyard, or he could take Walter's dark grey rubber dinghy and risk the open water. The dingy was quicker and safer. Clouds had obscured the moon and odds were good he would not be seen. Finally some luck. It looked like they might be getting some heavy weather.

Something big - like a murder - would see a roadblock set up on the highway headed north. He was not headed that way. The terminals and marinas would also be watched before long. He must move, before the world awakened, before the manhunt started, and steal a boat.

It was not likely that the search had gotten this far yet. It had only been a few minutes since the sirens started, the report had just come across the radio, and the sheriff and police were spread thin dealing with the revelers. Freddy was in the water again, kicking along in back of Walter's dinghy. At least it wasn't a department store cheapo of high visibility yellow. His sneakers and clothes, recently borrowed and donned, he had removed again after barely getting them warm. They were in the boat to keep them dry. Naked and cold, he swam behind the little yellow boat, and not inside where he would present a higher profile and a beacon for any who would see it with white skinned Freddy in it. He emerged on the other side, left the boat in the bushes where Walter could find it and ran quickly to the trees. He regretted leaving the little boat there. Much as he would have liked to take it along for the next water portion of his journey, it was too cumbersome for the overland part of it. He realized the sweatshirt that Cap'n Walter had given him was white. It *would* have to be white! What was wrong with black? Or gray? He felt slightly aggravated at Walter.

Crossing Cow Key, staying close to the water, he soon faced Key West. He had run the short, desolate half mile at full pace. He caught his breath and looked across the water.

The lights of the airport and the street lights on South Roosevelt Boulevard looked at him from the other side of Cow Key channel where the boulevard curved around the airport and then behind the public beaches. Freddy had hoped to find another little boat, preferably black, to "borrow". He did not. There was nothing there. Now he was wading and swimming to Key West as the water became deeper and then more shallow, in much the same manner as Wayne had done when he left for the marina in the other direction. He looked at his watch, found that he had about fifty-five minutes to go until sunrise.

His conversation with Cap'n Walter and the channel crossing took sixteen or seventeen minutes. He'd had to make an arc well away from the community of permanently anchored boats sheltered in the broad mouth of the channel, a no-rent, floating, mobile home park of erstwhile sailors who never went to sea interspersed with a few half-sunk wrecks, so as not to give them the impression that he intended to board their boats. Then he had to make his made his way past those same beaches he drove past each morning while musing about visiting faraway places.

At first he ran, plodding in a few inches of water at the bottom of a three foot sea wall which maintained the adjacent road's integrity against stormy weather making the best speed he could while lamenting the futility of keeping his clothes and shoes dry earlier. Wet though they were, the shoes were a must. To step on a sea urchin recessed in the rocky niches they favored now that his first aid options were nil would be courting failure and arrest. He slid his feet into the water at a sharp forward angle, a maneuver he devised to minimize the chances of stepping straight down on an urchin or a wobbly rock. He had no doubts that an urchin would penetrate the sneakers if he hit one squarely; nor would it do well to turn his ankle.

Once he got to the beginning of the beaches the wall and the boulevard fell away from the shore and that danger lessened. The annoying thing then, what he truly did not like, was diving headlong into the shallows when headlights approached. He could now be seen running; the wall was no longer there to hide him. There were grass clumps, low ledges of cap rock, smelly accumulations of festering weeds and morasses of brown mud. By daylight he had seen birds here, standing far out at low tide. He imagined the tourists thought the birds had very long legs. What insensitive creatures birds must be.

The grass moguls and rock ledges pre-destined Freddy for bruised toes and sore ankles. The shallow dives gave him cut hands and a butt as wrinkled as a prune and as pallid as a casaba. It felt as wet and clammy as white, chilled fish flesh, and he burned with the chaff of salt water and denim at the crotch. He kept plodding and sloshing until he came to the main beach.

The main beach was clear unobstructed running with the road falling away inland still farther until it skirted the coast some one hundred twenty yards back from the shore behind a curtain of foliage. He ran flat-out, unseen on the hard marl surface, high and dry between the weed line marking high tide and the brush growing on the uncleared property, past mangroves and bushes and salt ponds in the low spots, nesting egrets, frogs, turtles, and estuary areas. It was good cover. One day soon there would be a string of condos here. Who needs nature, anyhow? Fortunately, Freddy would not be there to see it.

About ten minutes later and winded, he had gone almost another two miles. He was back to the road's tangency and across it, riding on the momentum of his sprinting in a forward-leaning canter. He was diagonally across a large lot, past the ship-to-shore radio tower, past a few sleeping bums who would not tell anybody anything, no less who was running at what hour and where, and finally past the darkened tennis courts at the park near his house.

Soon he was slowing to a sneak to attempt entry into his domicile so that he might grab what cash he had and something in the nature of a weapon.

****

It was his dad's knife, given to him many years ago. His father had it made out west someplace thirty years ago. A Bowie knife it was, the top edge a scimitar shape from the tip to three inches back, the crescent at the top ground in a sharp-honed, deep cut bevel. There were rust discolorations on the blade, but it was good steel and had been in its oiled sheath for years. It kept its edge very well. Inscribed on its blade near the top was JOHN TAYLOR, in block letters. The knife was intended for skinning game and for general purpose outdoorsy stuff. It looked menacing and deadly never the less. Freddy was not the woodsman or hunter that his father was, but he had shown him how to throw the knife, as hard as he could throw a football, with a reasonable chance of hitting a target, with the point.

It was time for Freddy to get out of the house. He doubted that any of Sargento's crew had remained on the island, but just in case it was still being watched, the watchers would be out front. Freddy would leave the way he got in, very carefully, out the back, over the wall, through the Currin's and along the bushes for several houses. A lesson learned from Wayne. As an afterthought Freddy had grabbed one last item, one which Wayne had warned him could get him in trouble. He removed the brass replica Walther PPK water pistol from its drawer and stuck it in his pants under his sweatshirt.

****

There were twelve minutes left, no more than fifteen, before the scheduled rising of the sun. A thick line of clouds had begun to form on the eastern horizon. That was good, it would stay dark longer. Freddy had been in the house only a couple of minutes. If any blue uniformed guys showed up, he did not want to be there. It would take them a while to figure out where he lived; the address on the registration for the Olds was two residence changes old.

He had crossed part of Key West east to west. Now he would do it south to north, at the narrowest part.

After backtracking the way he had come, south through the park, across the field and part way back up the coast he started north across the overgrown fields adjacent to the high school, bringing him roughly to the center of the island, near a residential part. Well back in the brush and moving north, he came to the salt water creek he was seeking. The creek fed salt ponds and tidal areas on the island and separated the north side of the island into two halves where it flowed through culverts under the two main roads. All other roads stopped at the creek and resumed on the other side. Freddy scurried through the creek, keeping low to stay out of sight of the residents at the dead end houses. It was slow progress, sloshing past old tires and shopping carts, crawling through the culverts, trying unsuccessfully not to be heard by barking dogs. The moon had set and the sky was devoid of stars. The sky filled with crepuscular light He moved faster.

He passed five double dead ends, then was flanked by open ground at the island's northern limit at its waist. Time had run out. The cloak of darkness was gone. Early workers were on the road and the sky showed a barely perceptible glow in the east. Freddy had a sweatshirt, he had sneakers. Sodden but proper attire for his next gambit. He became one of those early morning fanatics who care little for their arches, ankles, knees, and lower backs. He did what sweet Annie had so often asked him to do. He became a jogger, making plodding, lumbering, stumbling progress that could be called running. The easily discernible squish-squish of the sneakers was not audible to the motorists. Freddy hoped he looked like a runner and thought that he must look like an incredibly sweaty one. He was sure that the agonized expression on his face closely approximated the pained, contorted expressions of other runners he had seen. Annie was the only happy runner he ever saw.

Less than a mile and eight minutes later and very tired he was at the marina, and now his planning was running out. He needed a boat, soon, before the marina opened, so that he could get out of Key West before being arrested for murder and perhaps find Wayne and help him go after the mobsters. He did not want to involve Big Frank and Candice in the whole mess, and did not want to leave any more of a trail than he had to, but he could see no other way. Whatever he was going to do, he had to make his move now or maybe not at all.

The piers ran perpendicular to the road and had fish names, Wahoo, Snook, and so on. The Blue Moon was tied up at the Kingfish pier. He walked down the pier to Frank and Candice's sailboat, no longer hiding or sneaking around. That would have made him too obvious. Theirs was the seventh boat out.

Freddy slowed at the sixth boat and approached the Blue Moon cautiously. He tried to peer through the slit in the curtains hung at the windows of the Blue Moon's cabin. Then he heard his name called.

"Freddy." Surprised, he spun and saw no one.

"Down here, Freddy." And there was the battered bow of his old boat nestled under the pier just before the Blue Moon. The boat was mostly under the dock. There was a shadowy figure seated in the boat, who in silhouette against the dim light reflected from the water Freddy recognized as Wayne. Glad to see him, Freddy smiled a grim smile.

****

The dock was still in pre-dawn half-light on this slow-starting mournful morning. The sun's rise was repressed by clouds in the east; it was climbing on the other side but had not yet scaled them, and so Wayne's concealment in the darkness under the dock was near complete. He had no head room and the windscreen was down, the engine didn't fit and was hanging out the other side. "I thought I might find you here," said Wayne, "get in." Wayne to the rescue, again. It appeared to Freddy that the boat was sitting very low in the water.

"Wayne, is the bilge full of water?"

"No, the bilge is pumped down."

He walked the boat out backward with his hands and Freddy jumped in. He started the engine and pulled away from the dock, wasting no time heading out the mouth of the bight. Freddy then saw why the boat was so low in the water. It was heavily loaded. The most striking items on board were 6top side gas tanks, resplendent in red plastic, 18 gallons each, three to a side strapped in with the heavy rubber keepers they generally used for SCUBA tank storage, along the gunnels toward the front of the boat for balancing the load. Freddy thought he saw the curtains move briefly on the Blue Moon.

Explanations would come later. For the moment, they kept their eyes open for trouble. They left the safe harbor and Key West together for the last time as the sun shone through and struck their backs.

Chapter Twenty-Three - Going South

It was a windy morning. It could have been worse - far worse. The storm that had been far off several days ago was closer now, stronger and organizing into a menacing counter-clockwise blow.

The sea can be a real charmer, a placid thing for photography and water sports, blue and shimmery under the sun. A marketable thing, something chambers of commerce use to entice fun seekers with funds of "disposable income" to spare of within the range of the purveyances those chambers are touting. Instructors sell lessons on what to do in it, on it, under it. Stores sell what to wear while doing it. What board, which sail, which watch, what lotion. The sea is a wonderful thing, but it can be awesome and uncontrollable, too.

On this morning, it was windy, just windy. That storm was still far enough off to allow the sun to shine, unhindered by clouds after the morning's low eastern array had dissipated. The threat of rain was, for the immediate future, non-existent. It was November 1st, a month from the end of the hurricane season, but the water was warm yet, warmer than normal at this time of year, and the warm water is where the storm was drawing its strength. The sea was green, greener than it was when they left the harbor. An emerald green, but lighter. It was not too bad. On a day like this when the waves are rolling and the wind blows from far off, mild discomfort is the general feeling for those who should not take to the water in a small boat. Should the breeze freshen, the light emerald becomes a watery jade and the rollers sharpen. Tops fall forward before the wind. They can't wait for the bulk of their massifs below, powerful but heavy and too slow to keep the pace. Too impatient to wait, the tops tumble out ahead over empty space and too late realize their folly; they have left their bottoms behind. They land angrily, falling forward and becoming froth on the face of the wave. An angry slap and sizzle mark the displeasure of the wave so scrambled. Disarrayed, it fizzles, literally fizzles, like a broken bottle of soda pop on a cement floor. The froth breaks up and runs down and across the mass of the wave in lattice patterns and lacy white doilies, shawls on the shoulders of huge dowagers.

With each increase in wind, there is more white on the green and in the shining sun the ever-changing patterns of sliding green and bright splotches of white can hold a sailor transfixed in terrible fascination. Below the designs, beautiful and complex in scope and intricacy, lies limitless power.

Nearer to the storm, clouds overhead dull the interest. It turns into apprehension and disquiet. The flat light makes the puzzle not intricate but infinite, miles of maelstrom waters now, not bright green and white in the sun but gray-green grunge in the gloaming. The sea no longer slides, sluices and glides, now it throbs, surges and pulses. As matters worsen the sea begins to grow out of its troughs. Time of day passes unnoticed as a master-brushed sky keeps the illumination constant, the heat and position of the sun a secret, closed out by low-slung clouds.

On a small boat in a heavy sea there is little time to see much of anything. Tons of water could crush the craft asunder. Something large enough to stay afloat on the fringe of a major storm would roll down troughs so deep that all that can be seen is a solid wall of seething, fuming, bile-green sea overlain with white foam lattice facing to the downward side of the roll. Straining to look up from the other side would still not give sight to the top of the water mountain without a dizzying bend of the neck. To guess the distance to the top of the wave is sheer folly. The constant roar, the pressure of the wind, the sting of the spray, and the depression of the mind that comes when the barometer is low all contribute to a distortion of the senses. The mind reels, unable to fathom the real proportions of the elements, and the dimensions of the situation. This is a sea that pounds and lunges, lurches and plunges silly things like little boats into one watery abyss and then another, thrust up in a moment to the top of the monster, for a brief second of giddy weightlessness to see more monsters on all sides, then a terrifying drop to the next cataract where one wave meets another. Again, there is nothing to see but water.

But that morning it was not too bad. They were heading into the weather, and that portended a deterioration in sea conditions, but it didn't matter to them. They were in the same boat. Freddy could not go so far as to say that the sea held no fear for him, but in his dulled emotional state what fear he did have was pushed back somewhere inside him, not enough to deter him from his shot at retribution. It was silly for him to think that he and Wayne had any chance of success against that mob, but being aware of that aspect also changed nothing. One Halloween night had changed his whole life, his entire outlook on life. On most things he had no outlook at all. The sea, the ocean, the water, so long a part of his life, was very different for him now. It had been a training ground in Bucks County at the Goose Pond, then a vacation spot for him up north during his formative years, then the beach-and-bar scene at the Jersey shore on weekends as a disgruntled corporate entity. In Key West it was it had been sport, exercise…therapy; an alternative to indolence, a way to sober up and stop the onslaught of years for a few hours in that quiet, colorful world, alone on the water and under it. With Pamela it had been best of all, his aquarium, a playground that he could share with her, show her its mysteries, a place for love in the sun. He could still see her smile, and her lovely, smooth body. It was a world that ended yesterday, abruptly and with a finality that was the only emotion he had left, except for vengeance.

The sea held finality for him, too, a conclusion. It was not pretty; the water looked like it would be brutal over the next few days. It was an adversary put between Freddy and the men he would destroy, fates willing. Freddy and Wayne would follow the shrimp boat, so much better suited to the heavy weather, across the sea to where Sargento had flown. After it was over, after the chase, after the confrontation, it didn't matter who was left. Nothing mattered except the need for destruction.

****

Freddy and Wayne looked out ahead. They knew they were heading into the weather. It was still a good way off to the southwest, and many owners of small boats going out for a ride today would be unsuspecting of the change to come in the next few days. Freddy knew it, and Wayne knew it, as did anyone who spends enough time on the water. It was coming, and the direction they should not go to avoid a bad time was the direction they were headed.

They had been aware of the course of the storm for days, its location, direction, what the barometer was doing (dropping) and where the squall line was, and the organization into a counterclockwise flow, from TV weather and the ubiquitous color radar. They listened frequently to NOAA weather radio forecasts, the National Oceanic and Atmospheric Administration broadcasts on 162.4 MHz. At this point in time no forecasting was necessary. They could feel the wind and see the wisps of high clouds, gauge what was happening far off by what the waves were doing here. They could feel the change in pressure. A blind sailor could sense what was happening.

After clearing the bight they ran past Fleming Key, the narrow strip of Navy property, and turned left into the harbor and shot down the main ship channel. The sun had come up and they were highly visible and so spent little time there. They sped past the restaurants and resorts of the downtown end of Key West, past the spoil area at the beginning of open water, and then turned right after Christmas Tree Island, out of the channel, roughly west. Sand Key was in a haze seven miles off to their left, the mangroves of Ballast Key before them in the distance were a curly head hunched down low behind a restless, rolling sea.

Freddy's eyes hurt in the inescapable glare of the low sun after the long night of partying, running, the tour through the evaporator, his trek across Stock Island, Cow Key, Key West and the swimming in between. They were irritated, too, from the too-salty water in the discharge pit, the rust and rusty water falling and dripping in the chambers, inevitably finding its way into his eyes. He squinted and put on one of the pairs of junky sunglasses they kept in the center console. Wayne was squinting, too. Freddy had no idea how long he'd been awake.

Wayne had picked their direction. He seemed to know where they were going and was disinclined to talk about it for the time being. They were both somber, their recent losses keeping each locked in his own dread thoughts. Conversation would start again after they wound down emotionally. Physically, they were spent. They were well out of Key West harbor, out of sight of Key West, before Wayne spoke.

"Glad you're not dead, Freddy," he said with a mirthless smile. He was grim, and there was sadness in his eyes.

"Thanks, me too, I guess. I'm sorta glad to see you, too. I thought you'd be gone. What did you do, stick around to get me out of trouble again?"

"Something like that. I saw the light on the cigarette hull when it came in to land on the point, and then the headlights of the car coming down the road toward you. I was watching from across the bay. When the car stopped where your Olds was parked I figured you were in trouble. I realized they were pulling out from the point, and that took balls, and I knew once they found you they would not leave you there to tip their escape to the cops. I couldn't get there in time to help you. If they got you it would probably have been in the first two minutes after they saw you. If we hadn't wandered so far, and you were near the Olds when they came, they wouldn't have had much of a chance to get you at all."

"How do you know that?"

"I have faith in you, Freddy." He made a real grin, but it didn't last long. It left his face again. "I'm sorry about Pamela. I heard about it on the radio this morning."

"I wasn't there just when she needed me. There was a radio report, but it was vague. No names. But somebody's dead. If I had been there I would be sure she was alive. Or if she's dead, at least we'd both be dead."

"You'd both be alive. You would have thought of something. It was just bad, bad luck that you were separated when they got there. It didn't work out that way, so try not to blame yourself."

"Thanks for coming back for me."

"I had to make some arrangements. Fuel, food, water. Big Frank and Candice helped me out. If things had worked out better -

for you and Pamela - I wouldn't have stayed as long as I did. As things are, I figured you didn't have anything better to do. You're still alive and so am I. There isn't anything left for us here, no place to go. I thought you might like to go after Sargento with me. They made it out of Key West, but that only means it will take us a little more time to catch up with them. They won't get away with what they've done. Not unless they get us first."

"Right." Freddy said nothing for a while, just stood next to Wayne at the console, now and then shaking his head. He made the attempt to think about what Wayne had said and found he couldn't do it. "I suppose you're right, it's done, from now on it's just you and me. Tell me what you plan to do, and we'll get them. You *do* have some idea where we're going, don't you? Do you know where they are, or where they are going, or are you just taking a wild guess?" Freddy didn't really think that he was taking a wild guess. Wayne's face was smitten with sarcasm when he answered.

"Certainly I know where they are, and that's where we're going. We're going to catch up with the shrimp boat."

"How?"

"Because I know where it is. They had to stop to make a few repairs." He looked smug.

"Are you going to tell me what you're talking about, or are we going to keep up with this question and answer format? Eric Severide I ain't, you know."

"Did you get up on the wrong side of the bed this morning?"

"What bed? I haven't seen a bed in a lotta hours."

"So take a nap. We're going to have plenty of time on our hands."

"I'll take one later. So tell me what's going on."

He did. "I had to make a choice when I knew you were in trouble on the point. I could have come back for you and taken a couple of them out, but that would have tipped them that I was close and after them, left me with some bodies to get rid of, and it wouldn't have done you any good if you were already dead."

"That's true," Freddy agreed. "Coming back I could have blown my chances - our chances - of getting Sargento. That would mean looking for him in his home port in South America. I took the boat out, without lights, as slowly and quietly as I could. Then I swam in to the shrimp boat from the seaward side. It was out quite a ways, almost to the sea buoy, farther out than I've seen it before. I had a fifty," he said, referring to a small scuba tank, "and a weight belt and regulator with me so I got a bearing on the shrimper and came in underwater. When I needed a course correction I came up enough to get a sighting and I got to the boat with no trouble at all."

"Sargento?" Freddy interrupted.

"He was long gone. He doesn't hang around when things get critical. Anyway, I tied the tank off to the anchor chain and climbed aboard."

"Just like that. Wasn't there anyone on board?" asked Freddy.

"Of course there was. They wouldn't leave the boat unguarded. There was a lookout. He was on the bow, watching for the return of the boat from shore. There was plenty of noise on the shrimper as the boat rocked in the waves. Gear was banging around and the hull was creaking. And they had everyone else on shore looking for you. Noisy boat, lookout on the bow. That couldn't have worked out better because I wanted to work on their radar in the wheel house. I had a couple of tools with me and I took the radar set out of the cabinet and re-arranged some of the things so that the set won't work, and they would not have found that out until they got under way. They were not about to hang around and have it fixed anyway. They won't even suspect it was tampered with."

"Why fool around with their radar?"

"Because we are going to tail them. *They* will lead us to Sargento. He took a cigarette hull out of the area when things got hot, is my guess. I'll bet that really pissed him off. That trawler is really posh inside. I'll bet he doesn't much like losing the Key West operation, either. He is going to have to re-organize. But I don't think we're going to let him get that far."

"Do you have an idea what their destination might be?"

"South. In a couple of days their boat might be linked to what's been going on. Their best chance to keep from being noticed is to head into the storm."

"That's crazy."

"Connors is crazy, and he's on that boat."

"How do you know so much about what he's going to do?"

"I've worked with him before, and also I've spent the last couple of weeks, and actually a long time before that, snooping into his business. I've done this kind of thing before and I know how to go about it."

"I'll bet you do. How are we going to find the shrimp boat again?"

"It's on the other side of the Marquesas. It broke down. I told you, they have to make some repairs."

"So what else did you do to make them break down?"

"I pulled a couple of the injectors far enough to cut the ring seals on them. Made it look like they were damaged when they were installed, I hope. I loosened the head bolts on one end enough to make that give them trouble, too, especially if the head gasket goes. The boat was smoking a mite when they passed Ballast Key, and that draws too much attention to suit them. I have a sinking feeling they are taking on some water, too. I found a pry bar in the engine room and worked it around the shaft seal to get it to leak. I figured they would stop once they got clear of Key West to stop the injectors from leaking diesel fuel into the bilge, and to tighten down the head, if it's started to leak fuel or oil or water. The shaft seal was just for good measure. Fixing the ring seals won't take long, if they have spares on board. I'm betting they do. The leak in the bottom of the boat may take some jury-rigging, though, more than enough time for us to get back to them. They probably won't get a permanent fix until they get back to their home port in Colombia. Their man will jury rig something, there is always a way. Well, almost always. It's a good thing you came along when you did, though, I couldn't have waited much longer. You almost missed the boat.

"How long were you out there?"

"Half an hour."

"And the lookout never found you out?"

"Freddy," he said as though talking to a child, "I have a lot of experience with this sort of thing."

"Where did you go to school, Leavenworth?"

"You've got it all wrong, Freddy. I was one of the good guys." Freddy's face betrayed his surprise at this news. That thought had never occurred to him.

"I knew it all the time."

"Liar."

They continued on the course Wayne had set for Ballast Key. It was too rough to take a nap, and now there was no time. Freddy looked around the boat and realized they were well prepared for this venture, at least in the material sense. They were both exhausted, yet Wayne, with the help of Big Frank and Candice, had somehow come up with fuel and provisions for them and had a fair supply of a commodity they would need most - water. From the amount Wayne had on board he must have thought that they would be out for a long time. There was a string of one gallon collapsible water bottles in front of the steering console with a nylon line through their handles from one side of the boat to the other. There were more stored in the engine well at the back of the boat. Freddy could see six tanks of gasoline, eighteen gallons each, to supplement the fuel in the enormous gas tanks in Freddy's boat. They were along the inside of the hull toward the stern, just before the bench seat which ran the width of the boat. Wayne had fixed them in place with the elastic straps and hook eyes they had mounted there to hold compressed air tanks in place. He had put two cans on each side of the boat to keep the weight distribution equal. They must have been heavy. Freddy figured that each tank must have been close to twenty pounds empty. Gas was about 6 pounds per gallon, so the fuel in each tank was 108 pounds or roughly 120 pounds for each full tank. Equivalent to having four additional big guys on the boat. Which is why the boat was riding low in the water. Freddy surmised (correctly) that the tanks had been filched in the early hours of the day by Big Frank in collusion with his best friend Kevin who ran the marine supply store. Reparations would, of course, some later, if that was possible. Neither of the men were thieves.

Freddy looked under the two wooden covers atop the bench seat into the lockers which normally served as cold storage and live bait well. Their Li'l Oscar six pack cooler was in there, and some bottles of juice, some canned fruit and another small cooler he didn't recognize.

"Wayne, where did we get this stuff?"

"What stuff is that, Freddy?" He was being impossible again.

"Well, the food and water, for one thing."

"Most of it is stolen, pretty much from our friends around the marina."

"You *stole* stuff from our friends?"

"Of course. It was easy. It's always safer to steal from your friends. I'll make it up to them and explain if I ever get the chance. They were all out partying and I knew the layouts of their boats and houses nearby, and even if they did catch me - highly unlikely, by the way - I doubt that they would have turned me in. It's 'stuff' they can spare, even if it does cause them a little concern and confusion. That's all right, too. They should be more careful about their places." Good. So Wayne was doing them a favor by teaching them a lesson. "It's for a good cause, after all. I assume that after a while if the story of all this ever comes out, they will realize who took their 'stuff'. I don't think they will be mad at us."

"What *'us'?*"

"Well, of course they will think you had something to do with it. Might even raise their opinion of you." Of course, though Freddy. Thanks.

"Don't you have any money?"

"What good is it before dawn, and what did you think I was going to do anyway, go shopping? I have some money, but I want as few people as possible to know our movements. Big Frank knows, those are his water bottles. He helped out with the gas, too. It couldn't be helped, though, we'll need water and fuel, and he'll be our eyes and ears back in Key West, to watch over things. But somehow I don't think we'll ever make it back there. Our odds are not good. As for the food, you don't have to eat it if you don't want to."

"Let's not be drastic," said Freddy hastily. He changed the subject. "Look at all this water. You must be thirsty." He looked in the L'il Oscar. "Hey, where's the beer?" Wayne smiled a real smile for an instant. "Sorry, Freddy, I must have forgotten to put it on the list. We will have to do without it for the duration. We're tired already. There is no sense getting dehydrated as well, if we can help it." Everything Wayne said made sense. His planning was well organized.

"Freddy."

"Yes, Wayne."

"What is that stuck in your belt? I hope it isn't your brass water pistol. Tell me you didn't bring your brass water pistol."

"Ah, well, I thought maybe---"

"You thought you were going to bluff Sargento's men with that thing, so you've been lugging it around all night long."

"All *morning* long."

"Wasn't it hard enough sloshing and slinking through stinky backyard creeks and culverts?"

"Well, now that you mention it'"

"Can't you be happy with the chaffing you're going to get from salt water drying in the clothes you're wearing? Freddy, bringing that thing was a waste of time. You risked a trip back to the house for it, didn't you? I know you did." Freddy was insulted by Wayne's chiding and that he might be finding some humor in Freddy's having brought the water pistol. "It *looks* like a real gun!"

"And as soon as one of those guys sees it he is going to shoot you without preamble. You will be summarily deceased, dispatched from the land of the living before you even get off a squirt." Freddy could feel a flush coming up. Wayne was teaching him another lesson. He was getting red on the neck and behind the ears.

"Ok, maybe it was stupid to bring the water pistol, and to go back to the house at all. But I got a knife, too." Freddy said, showing him the Bowie knife strapped to his leg. Wayne smiled. "I know it's a little big," Freddy went on, "but---"

"Freddy, you did good. It could come in handy. Perhaps not as a weapon, but if we need a survival knife, that will do nicely."

"*Survival* Knife? What in hell are you talking about, Wayne? I thought we were going to some place to shoot crooks and murderers, not live out in the mangroves. You may be a cross between Marlin Perkins and Jacques Cousteau, but I sure as hell ain't."

He smiled at Freddy in a condescending, pitying way, so as to tell Freddy he was being naïve. Again.

I'm going to shoot crooks and murderers, I have a *real* gun, and I know how to use it. Perhaps you can get them to stand still while you spray them with that thing to soften up their tough hides so my bullets will go in easier. You may be distressed to find that we may have to spend some time in the wild if they don't lay down and die for us, but you will be happy to know that I brought ample sunscreen and bug repellent."

"Who'd you steal that from? I don't know if I'm psychologically prepared for this jaunt you invited me on."

"Having doubts, Freddy?" "You know better than that, but I woulda liked it better if we just shoot 'em and get it over with."

"It isn't going to be that quick a deal, I don't think. And I wouldn't call it a jaunt, that makes me think too much of a pleasure trip. And we aren't marching across a desert of anywhere else, so it isn't a trek. Call it a crawl and a scramble through mangroves, maybe, some swimming, too, interspersed with some short sprints. I see it as sort of an aquatic triathlon."

"I did that already," Freddy spat shortly. "Last night."

"That may have been just a warm up. Maybe the marathon comes next. But imagine that it will be more cat and mouse. We chase them, do some damage, they chase us, and we run. And so on."

Silence.

"It may not come to that, Freddy, not if we get them the first time around."

"Or if *they* get *us* the first time…"

"But if we bungle it, we will need every bit of supplies we have, and probably some of theirs."

"MacArthur would have been proud of us. Think he'll bail us out? Do you think we'll get lucky and miss this storm? Do you think our chances are good?"

"No, no, and no"

The Marquesas were not far now and Wayne slowed somewhat. He said he wanted to approach from the opposite side of the atoll where the shrimp boat had been anchored, using the outlying islands for cover as they got closer on the odd chance that there might be a lookout posted on the shore, though it was unlikely that they had put someone ashore on the other side of the island from the anchorage – there was little solid ground and the growth was too dense for easy repatriation. Also, the repairs they required were not time-consuming enough to warrant sending a man there. Still, Wayne was scanning the island very carefully anyway, though Freddy doubted he could have seen anyone in the clutter of mangroves and vegetation. He must have been looking for signs, a glint off a windshield, or field glasses, or metal. Maybe he thought he would see smoke or something, like when the cowboys spot the Native Americans. Freddy didn't know. He was not initiated in Wayne's type of hide and seek games.

Maybe it was force of habit which kept him so vigilant, though he had not slept in a long time, far longer than Freddy's own lack of sleep. Freddy remembered that Wayne had advised him to take a nap and felt guilty that he had not realized Wayne's need for rest must be much greater than his own.

****

They were now close to the island hiding the shrimp boat. Wayne eased the boat forward slowly with the engine engaged at idle speed. He parked the boat in the mangroves of the nearby atoll, nosing its tired bow onto a small sand bank for some reason not yet not overgrown. Freddy looped the bow line through the mangrove roots.

The foliage was sparse enough to see through. Freddy moved a bit more to the right of where he had been standing and his foot contacted something. He looked down. Next to the console at the right rear corner, strapped carefully to the fire extinguisher with a piece of electric cord (whose house had *that* come from, Wayne?), was a single ball mason jar three-quarters full of an opaque liquid.

"Wayne, what's that stuff, grapefruit juice?" (Freddy liked grapefruit juice). "Sulfuric acid."

"Come again?"

"SUL-FUR-IC AC-ID." Freddy wasn't thirsty anymore.

"Where'd you get it?"

"The old desalting plant. While I was there I dunked into acid tank. There is still seven thousand gallons of sulfuric in that tank. I didn't think that they would miss a quart. Not even a quart." Every time Wayne spoke it seemed to Freddy that he had been busier than he could possibly have been. He had a knack for efficient use of his movements, anticipating what would happen next, what he had to do to counter it, and what he could get away with.

"When did you do that?"

"After a surveillance of the shrimp boat a couple of days ago."

"What do you intend to do with it?"

"I don't know. I took it purely on speculation. It might come in handy." Freddy shuddered. At least there was this one thing Wayne had done that didn't fit neatly into place, something he might not find a use for.

Freddy hoped he wouldn't find a use for the acid. It was nasty stuff and hard to handle. Freddy knew of guys working on the production of the acid who had been injured or killed. Some had been burned and scared by small quantities that had sprayed on them from a defective pump or dropped on them from a leaky pipe overhead. Some died. One man he knew of fell into a sulfuriic pit up north. It must have been horrible to be standing waist deep in the sulfur slurry knowing what it would do to him. In his anguish he wailed as he waited for someone to pull him out, withered by the knowledge that even if he survived the acid would penetrate his flesh and permeate his bones and soften them to formless links between muscle, incapable of supporting his weight. Fortunately, the man died. Wayne didn't have enough to immerse anyone in, but he had more than enough to get sadistically nasty with. The passion for revenge that had sent them on this quest, bent on causing the death of those who took Annie must have been a mental aberration of a sort, even if it was understandable. Freddy hoped that Wayne was not so crazed as to do something fiendish. Unless it was to Sargento and Connors.

""I wanted to go back to the desalting plant after I saw Connor's goon squad leave, to look for your remains, if any," said Wayne, "But there was no time for that."

Freddy shuddered at the thought, remembering the discharge pipe and the thought of crabs eating his decaying flesh.

"Wayne, we're carrying an awful lot of gasoline." The boat was unusual in that it had two fifty gallon tanks in the hull, and an eighty gallon tank with a floatable cushion on top which served as the seat behind the steering console. Then there were the six extra gas cans strapped in on the inner sides of the boat. If they took any hostile fire they would be a floating fire bomb.

"That we arrgh, Freddy, that we arrgh."

"I love it when you talk nautical. Why do we need so much gas? We can't possibly be going far enough to use it - you don't think it's going to get us to South America, do you?"

"Bombs, maybe. Or arson. We'll play it by ear."

"Bombs?"

"And maybe a little arson."

Goody. Freddy was going to learn a lot on this trip.

Chapter Twenty-Four - Rough Weather

After they skirted the island where Wayne had last seen Sargento's boat they pulled in behind the mangroves. They got out of the boat and walked up the small sliver of beach to find a place to spy on Sargento's men and wait. Freddy asked Wayne, "What if you are wrong, what if they already made their repairs and are gone?"

"Then you can take the day off," was his curt reply. Freddy followed Wayne as he cautiously made his way around the tiny curve of beach, watching all the while, until they caught sight of the shrimper. No one was in evidence on shore. She was sitting some thirty yards out from the island where the water was deep enough for her to anchor. The small dish of deeper water she sat in was in a shallow curve of the shoreline, a saucer scooped out of the island's southern side. The concealment was good, offering shelter from the open water. As far as Freddy and Wayne knew there had been no hue and cry for the craft at the time they left Key West. If she was spotted by a passing boat, there should be no cause for alarm, although that might change later when investigators pieced things together back in Key West. They might look for it later, around the Gulf Coast, but they would never expect it to be heading into a major storm, a decision probably owing to Connors' vulpine cunning. It was obvious to Freddy that these people were as cautious as Wayne, just as furtive about their movements. Now Wayne, or Teddy, had started forces in motion to unsettle their complacency.

****

They settled comfortably into the bushes where they could watch unseen through the chinks in the mangroves. Freddy finally got all of the questions answered that he ever could have wanted to ask about Wayne's involvement in the whole mess. For the greater part of the next hour he listened as Wayne related his life story as pertained to his acquaintance and association with the gangsters.

****

Wayne Talbot was formerly known as Theodore McLaren, a reddish-brown haired male of six feet two inches. The hair was curly. Of Scottish descent, Teddy was the last of three children born to a couple in upstate New York, later to move to the "sticks" of New Jersey - that little-heard of area of wooded hills above the urban confusion known as the greater New York City area. Teddy was born much after his siblings, when his parents were on in years, and had not shared many associations with his brother and sister before they were of age to move from the family home, whereupon their own marriages took them out of state. Teddy's mother was thirty-eight when he was born and her health deteriorated not long after. She died when she was relatively young, just after Teddy's ninetieth birthday, at the age of fifty-seven. The loss was traumatic to Teddy's father whose health also began to decay after his wife's death. Teddy's father was seven years older than his bride had been. After Teddy was old enough to get by on his own his father went to California to live with his daughter and her family until his father died also.

There were sixteen years between Teddy and his sister. His brother was fourteen years older. He was only about five when they each married and moved away and he was raised almost as though he was an only child. He obtained self-sufficiency and independence in spite of it, or perhaps due to the wisdom of his remaining parent in his waning years. At twenty-three and alone, with no desire to become closer to his two estranged remaining blood relatives, Teddy put himself through the remainder of his last years at Rutgers, working and taking courses over the next six years.

His connection with organized crime stemmed from a move to the city and an interest in law and criminal justice. One thing led to another. He took courses at City College. His professor of Criminal Psychology was aware of his interest and his intellect. The man had worked with high-ranking police officials at their request, and later with the district attorney's office, infiltrating the mob families in New York and Chicago.

The Professor was a wealthy and influential man in his own right. His friends were prominent statesmen and people in the business world on an international scale. He moved in influential circles and had a network of contacts and underworld operatives on both sides of the law.

An opportunity arose for the New York police to track down a lead on a drug-related aspect of the Sargento family's operations in the north. They needed an agent who was not known to the money men. Teddy was enlisted to run a briefcase full of cash to a drop. He did well and started moving his way up the chain of command. Subsequently he became familiar with the "wife" of Nick Sargento, one of the two kingpin brothers of the family. Her name was Moira; she was a young and beautiful dark haired, street-wise Italian girl with an Irish name. Teddy felt that she should not be involved with the Sargentos'. He became protective of her. His unchanneled emotions at last had an outlet. He fell in love with her. Nick, and his brother Joe, were both jealous, possessive men. It was a dangerous situation, one that could not last. If it could be said that an expenditure of emotion such as this was a failing for a man in his position, then Moira was Teddy's weakness.

Teddy had learned much. He worked himself up to a relatively high position in the mob for an outsider, in part to stay close to Moira, and was responsible for the incarceration of many mobsters before his affair with Moira was found out. When Nick learned that Teddy and Moira had become lovers, Nick killed Moira brutally. Nick had backed her into the bathroom and pushed her through the sliding glass doors before he beat her to death. It was Teddy who found her battered body.

Teddy searched out Nick. He found him in his den and killed him viciously with his hands, shocking the court at the hearings to follow, and almost jeopardizing the convictions of the felons. Sargento's highly-paid legal battery of defense con men used the brutal execution to swing the mood of the jury to sympathy for the crooks and outrage at the methods used by Teddy in his employ as an instrument of justice. During a melee that followed in the courtroom Joe Sargento was spirited away and left the country, a very timely departure, amid federal bullets. He reportedly received a fatal wound during the getaway. It was not so. He swore revenge against the network of agents and informers responsible for the downfall of his empire. He still had clout with the other families, who also wanted an example made of those who had worked the destruction of the Sargento's northern holdings'. It was a thing too close to home to be ignored.

Joe Sargento had all the cash he would ever need. His small band of gorillas, the core of his organization, accompanied him in his flight. And the South Florida smuggling ring was still untouched by the not-long-enough arm of the law.

Teddy's vicious vigilante act and seemingly wanton lust for blood, as portrayed by the sleaze-legals in the Sargento family employ, caused a public outcry demanding that the court take some action against him. The public faction decrying Teddy's actions were those misguided persons who, if their litany could be believed, would sue for the rehabilitation of the killer of their own mother and return him to society. Fortunately, prudent heads more often prevail.

The district attorney had made a good case for Teddy's actions on the premise that his close association with the mob and Moira's death made him crazy. In actual fact Teddy was as sane as anybody. Saner than most. The execution of Nick Sargento by Teddy was an un-pre-meditated, violent act.

Rather than sending Teddy to prison where he was sure to be executed at the mob's behest, he was sentenced to a period of observation and whisked away to the state hospital at Marlboro, New Jersey, a spread-out group of very old buildings used variously in times past as a detox home for anonymous senators, a place to hide prominent people, and an asylum for the criminally insane. He was to be incarcerated there until he was deemed fit to be returned to society. After his release Teddy was to be on parole.

News of the deaths of informers turning state's evidence and officers in the investigation of the Sargento family reached Teddy through a friendly attendant at the institution of his incarceration, and Teddy realized that it was the work of Joe Sargento's mob.

Teddy knew Sargento to be a dangerous and unpredictable psychopath, a trait he apparently instilled in his followers. Acting on the knowledge that Joe or his followers were eliminating witnesses and agents who had worked against them, Teddy prevailed upon the attendant he had befriended to release him. The man let him out a side door, directed him to the maze of catacomb-like tunnels underlying the facility. By candle light he found his way through the labyrinth of shafts delved beneath the hospital's grounds, past the walls hung with shackles installed there for inmates in a more unfortunate time, and with the attendant's instructions to an ending of a tunnel not altogether blocked, out of the facility. And then Teddy disappeared, not to be seen again, just when he was soon to be let go anyway. Wayne had in effect broken parole. The attendant who helped him was killed in an automobile accident soon after, a fate which had almost befallen the Professor a year prior, but the tough old bird wouldn't die. So it was that Freddy came to realize that Teddy - Wayne, to him, had gone through this enormous grief before. He had lost two women he loved. All of his reticence about the past, his taciturn manner and general demeanor were now understandable. Annie had almost snapped him out of his solitary ways. It was hard to understand why one individual should have to bear so much. Surely one would think that there was more fairness in the world than that. Apparently not.

Another thing explained during this interlude was Wayne's competence in dealing with the unique situations Freddy had seen him in and his frightening performance when violent measures were necessary. He had been highly trained, mentally and physically, to cope with these people he had been sent to bring to justice, as much for the sake of the operation he was involved in as for his own self-preservation. His professor had chosen wisely, Wayne was just the type of person they had been looking for. He was out there alone most of the time with no one to rely on but himself. With his natural self-reliance and his intense training he was the perfect person for the job. His trainers had done the job well.

After Wayne finished relating his story they slept for a while in turns. Freddy implored Wayne to take the first sleep shift - he needed it more than Freddy did. The watch would rotate every two hours. Freddy let Wayne sleep for three and a half hours before he woke him up at noon and then went to sleep himself. There was nothing much to be seen on the shrimp boat anyway.

The outlying mangrove hedge screening them from view was distant enough to require them to use field glasses. One man paced the deck; two others were snoozing or lying about indolently as they waited for the *"Big Nick"* to get under way. A half hour into Freddy's sleep he was awakened by Wayne's foot rocking his leg. "Freddy, something is happening. I think they're going to put to sea." Sure enough, they pulled the anchor. Freddy went to start the boat but Wayne restrained him. The boat's starter could be heard a long way off. They needed the shrimp boat to be farther off before Wayne and Freddy pursued them. They would follow after the others were well away and making lots of their own noise.

Soon enough they were far back in the shrimper's wake. Wayne's objective was to stay low on the horizon and dead astern, the last place the others would be looking. Their boat was much smaller, much lower in the water than the trawler, and they could probably remain unnoticed with the sea's help. They were pitching about quite a bit as the now not-so-far-off storm's influence increased and dark clouds could be seen on the horizon they were pointing at - southwest again. Off to the left the light between the clouds and the sea on the southeast horizon was a day-glow purple line. It was part of a line of squalls at the edge of the storm. They were on the rim of a violent, spinning pinwheel of cloud and precipitation, headed toward a storm sky that looked like vapors in a smoking, boiling flask of dark and stormy liquids.

On a clear day they might have been spotted, had the others been looking in earnest. The men aboard Sargento's boat had not seemed too concerned about pursuers at their anchorage in the Marquesas, so they must have known from monitoring the radio that a search for the killers of Key West and Stock Island had not yet followed in their direction. With the little boat bobbing up and down, in and out of the line of sight, obscured by mounding swells of sea water, Freddy's boat would be next to invisible. Freddy had a tarp over the windscreen to stop the sun's glare from signaling their position to their prey. If they could keep the shrimper "hull-down" in relation to them until nightfall, bobbing just high enough to catch a glimpse of the shrimper's lights on the rigging on each of their porpoising leaps forward in the rolling seas, they could close the distance this evening and follow the shrimper's running lights, leaving their own boat darkened. Unless the shrimper kept *its* lights off as well. But why would they? One thing at a time.

Freddy wondered why Sargento had chosen a shrimp boat as a command vessel. He questioned Wayne about it.

"Wayne, why did they take all of that trouble outfitting a shrimp boat with all that electronic gear and staterooms and all when they could afford to buy anything they want?" Wayne mused on the question for a moment.

"It's hard to say, Freddy. His father was a fisherman; his family up north were poor people. Who knows what made him turn in the direction he went in? Or why he chose the trawler. Could be that it fits in better where he's going. Maybe it's a link with his past. I don't know."

Long, dirty clouds formed a line before them, joined, and soon became a smoky ceiling above them. Circling winds brought wetter clouds over them and gray rain fell straight down around the boat at one moment and sideways the next moment. They edged closer to the trawler in front of them and stayed in its wake. Soon they could see nothing around them save the wake of the other boat. The wind freshened and visibility improved and the shrimp boat materialized once again, and they backed off once again, but the rain turned cold, small, stinging drops pelted them, driven by the freshening breeze.

It certainly looked like those aboard the trawler did not fear pursuit, and Wayne assured Freddy that the shrimper's radar would not be working right, as the captain of the *"Big Nick"* must know by now. Their screen would be completely blank, no islands, no passing boats no nothing. If Wayne had indeed left no trace of his presence on their boat they must assume that the failure of their radar was an electronic problem. Which of course it was. They still had Loran, and star sightings if they were lucky enough to find some clear sky. They were better off than Freddy and Wayne who were clinging to the shrimp boats coat tails.

The situation continued on this way for the rest of the day. The rain stopped and they continued on towards the dusk.

The weather was hard on the hull. The bilge pump was running often and this caused some concern as to whether or not it would continue to function. Bilge pumps on boats such as Freddy's were prone to failure, a throw away item, a nuisance you could count on having to replace every two years. If the thing quit now, it would add the burden of bailing to annoyance of the vexatious undulating they were doing. It could be worse. The waves were long and regular combers and they were matching the shrimper's slow speed, so they were riding up one side and down the other of each one, jockeying the throttle as necessary. It was making the hull work, but not so badly as would a moderate chop, which would slap the hull and push water past the hairline cracks under its damaged stringers. Still, they had been at sea a long time for a boat of this type in these conditions, and the hull's bending up at the ends on the upswings and humping down the down sides was causing the leaks to run freely, if not yet in great quantity. The motor, a half year old, was working perfectly.

They ate, beans, and peaches, canned, same as the beans. They shared a bottle of orange juice and Wayne put the empty under the console with some rags he was trying to keep dry for some reason not made known to Freddy. It was no doubt some devilishly reprehensible part of Wayne's master plan.

Wayne hadn't mentioned Annie, and Freddy hadn't mentioned Pamela, except for mumbled condolences. Pamela and Annie were there, though, at the backs of their minds, behind the grim, hollow humor, the exhaustion and the rigors of a sea already too rough for their little boat.

Now the sea was just beginning to rage. They talked little now about anything. The wind was starting to howl, the engine's note lightening and yowling in rhythm to the waves each time the stern tipped up to follow the bow as the boat slid into the next trough, and it was too hard to talk. They said no more than was necessary to run the boat. They listened perforce to the flapping canvas of the Bimini top which they had put up against the weather, wind and spray, to the wraith-like shrieking of the wind, and to the monotonous change in pitch from the exhaust discharge each time the stern became light and the discharge gargled and burbled as the water over the discharge port became shallow.

Evening came and the shrimper put her lights on. Freddy and Wayne could see them well enough, but they closed up some anyway, hoping that the larger boat's wake would ease their way. The shrimp boat's hull was a deep vee and cut the water nicely. Freddy's modified vee was a planeing hull and nearly flat on the bottom. She was made to run fast in smooth water, not cut through this. She didn't like this at all.

Now they had zipped the side screens into the Bimini top. Freddy kept watching them. He didn't like the way they were whipping about in the wind. The engine noise changed to include some cavitation sounds as the propeller caught air when the waves got higher and the stern came farther out of the water each time up and down. Each time the prop caught air an egg-beater growl came after the yowling engine sounds trumpeted from the exhaust discharge into the air behind the boat.

The uncomfortable tedium went on through the night. They tried to sleep, to little avail, took turns at the wheel and made the necessary efforts to evacuate body wastes as periodically called for by their systems. That too was inordinately difficult. Halfway through the night the wind shifted, or the shrimper made a course change to the south. The sea was now coming at them from just right of the bow and their forward motion picked up a diagonal pitching element. The noises were the same, with the addition of an insane engine flare when the propeller occasionally failed to keep its bite on the water, only now they were also being rocked from side to side in a series of corkscrews, added to their tedious carousel-horse up and down. What few stars there were, flickering through the scudding clouds, went out and stayed out one by one. The clouds were getting thicker; the ceiling was dropping. The change in barometric pressure was apparent, it was dropping, too.

Toward morning Freddy checked the radio. The ambient noise in the boat was too high for any intelligibility to be made from the crackling emanating from the speaker with the volume at full. No matter, they were resolute, numbed. They would follow the shrimper to Sargento where ever the trail took them. They would follow the shrimper also simply because they had no other choice; they would be lost without it. The trawler had loran, a low frequency radio transmission guidance system, they knew where they were. Freddy and Wayne didn't.

So far everything was still working, which is to say that nothing as yet had been wet badly enough to stop functioning. They still had the engine, bilge pump, radio, depth finder, and maybe some lights. They were not on, and they were not going to be turned on while the shrimper could see them.

They had been at sea now, since the Marquesas, for fourteen hours. The high speed run from Key West to the Marquesas took about forty-five minutes. Their normal fuel consumption was less than six gallons an hour on average, in fair weather, and on plane and properly trimmed. Fuel economy would be far worse in this stormy sea, waddling like a duck through the waves and popping up and down like the head of a pigeon. The poor boat had to travel a lot more miles up and down the waves than it would have done on a flat sea. Faster and on plane meant better fuel efficiency, but they could not do that in their current situation. Add to that bucking a head wind... But the bottom was clean, the fuel filters clear, and there were no dings on the prop. Wayne estimated that they were using well over six gallons and hour when he switched tanks from the second fifty in the hull to the eighty in the seat sometime near dawn. Unknowns were the amount of sludge in the tank bottoms and the accuracy of the fuel gauges, a weak point in fuel systems that gets worse as the tank approaches empty. He did not want to run the tanks too low. The 80 gallons in the seat tank would last them a while yet. After that there were still the six gas tanks. It meant perhaps another twenty-four or twenty-six hours of sailing at the present rate.

****

With dawn past due and the two of them enduring the weather, trying to move with it and not fight it, there was little to do but think. Visions of Pamela visited Freddy - wondering what her fate had been, wondering if he should have stayed, and intruding on the dark privacy of pre-dawn. With the visions were the knowledge and a fear that the image of her face would fade with time. If there was to *be* any time left after this adventure. Freddy was aware through the mists of memory taking him back to Pamela that his prospects for coming through this alive leaned toward the unlikely. The prospects were fading with each hour they were at sea. If the sea did not get them, probably Sargento or Connors would. But maybe they would get them as well, and that would be a win. They might even live through it all. Then all they had to do was get back somehow. Freddy inclined his gaze to the darkness and Pamela's image formed on that nebulous screen in front of his forehead. They had been together on this boat, in the water, at Sand Key, Pelican Shoals, Eastern Dry rocks, Cay Sal bank. They were making love. There was the day the boat nearly drifted away in the wind, the taste of her salty lips. Finally a few tears came, as they had the night he left her – it was just last night - lonely in the bushes at the roadside by the water. The salt spray on his face was met by streamers of warm salinity streaking back from his eyes and over his cheeks. Fortunately, it was dark.

****

Freddy didn't know how long the reverie lasted, but now they were being wrenched up by the port bow and flung down as if something had grabbed the stern on the starboard side and yanked it into the air, tipping the boat's nose into a void. It was a wild peristalsis of plunges and twists squeezing them forward. Either the trawler had changed course again or the sea was attacking them from a different angle. It was hard to say because the compass was spinning crazily over one hundred and eighty degrees in its liquid bath. One thing was sure, the seas had steepened and the rollers were now bone-crushers. The waves were now hitting them exactly wrong. Instead of being off the starboard quarter they were now hitting at twenty degrees ahead of the port beam. They were not humping through them - this sea was so high that they could not do that without being swamped - and they were not pitching back and forth as they would if it were dead on their beam. The sea was trying to tip them over catty-corner. It had a considerable way to go before that happened, but it was most disconcerting. Wayne was sure Connors was on the trawler. He was perverse enough to make the trawler stay on this course, when anyone else would have steered a more forgiving one. The men on the boat would probably be sick inside the boat, and not be in any condition to be looking for anything or anyone.

Sometime well after putative dawn a couple of inches of greasy, grimy gray illumination slid up over the horizon in the east and graduated to black where the night sky tried to hold its ground in the other direction. The black rolled back slowly like a hemisphere on hinge pins, and shades of gray, devoid of color, were universal in the sky for three hundred and sixty degrees of horizon. Blotches of black smudging the sky's gray complexion indicated that moisture would soon be precipitated out of the gloom, that this lack of light was not an unscheduled solar eclipse, that they were not in an opaque world domed in thick crystal on a planet of Assimov's imagination, that Freddy did not have some progressive eye disease - Wayne confirmed this - indeed, it was going to rain.

They'd gone through this before, the wind, the spattered top, frying water, sheets of liquid hurled at them from the sky. But this was worse, the worst they had ever been in. Wind-luffed fumaroles were caught in violent gusts; swirling plumes of water were wrought from the waves. Any sane person didn't want to be there, it was miserable, that goes without saying. Freddy said it anyway, but then he complains a lot. As for the sanity of it, well, they were following Connors.

The extra added bonuses, both bad as Freddy saw it, were two-fold. On one hand, they kept losing sight of the shrimper. They had backed off previously so that they would not be spotted when the sun came up (ha!). Riding in the trawler's wake was not smoothing their ride anyway. The water roiled right up again after the trawlers passage. Freddy and Wayne had to try to stay on course and close the distance again enough to maintain sight of their lead to Sargento. They had to do this several times. On one of these occasions they found themselves not fifty yards off the trawler's stern starboard quarter when a wave larger than most set them up high for all to see. Freddy didn't expect that anyone saw them. Even aboard the bigger boat with its hull more suited to the open seas, life must have been miserable with everyone on board except the helmsman strapped into their bunks.

The second thing was that the hull was leaking badly. The pump was running each time Freddy looked over the side at the overboard discharge. Which was not often. "Wayne," Freddy yelled into his ear, "I think that pump is running continuously now." Wayne nodded to acknowledge that he heard Freddy. "Why don't they put into port somewhere on the Gulf coast until this blows over, instead of heading into it?"

"They won't, Freddy, thanks to us. Connors does not take any unnecessary chances. By now an investigation must be under way in Key West, and it might connect the trawler with the smuggling operations in the area. The man I tied up behind the wall, that present we left for the Key West police, will help fill in the blanks. I left a list of names and places of the drops of the runners that I had been working on where the cops could find it. Once they tie Sargento into this whole thing and get their computer working on it every law enforcement agency on the coast will be looking for that boat. Sargento and Connors don't know what else I've got on them, but they know how I work - I ruined them up north. They must have known I had something on them when I kept upsetting their plans to seize - Annie." He clearly was done, if only because he would soon be hoarse, so Freddy clapped him on the shoulder. There might be a search under way later in clearer waters, but not in this weather.

Freddy and Wayne had no way to navigate in the storm. They were trusting to the shrimper's loran "C" navigation to keep them both from getting lost. The direction of the sea was an indicator for them, and they could make a rough approximation of their speed, but the margin for error was great. There was no sun, none. If they lost the shrimper they would be lost themselves, heading where the storm wanted them to go. They would lose Sargento as well, and probably drown. The thought of getting away uncontested from the grief they had caused bore heavily on Wayne and Freddy. Freddy didn't have to ask Wayne his thoughts, he knew them. They mirrored his own.

Those on the shrimp boat would not be a lot cozier than they, lashed into their bunks in weather like this, save for one or two on watch. Freddy and Wayne tried to rest in shifts, wedged between the base of the bench seat/storage compartment and the base of the console seat/fuel tank. They closed their eyes and tried to relax, but sleep was impossible. It was even worse with eyes closed. The day wore on, seas remaining about the same, keeping the shrimp boat in sight still a strain. They had taken the floatable cushions off the bench seat and laid them in their rest area. The deck was wet, and the cushions did little to keep them drier, but it served to save them some bumps, aches and pains from the buffeting of the boat. They were banged up all over, and had aching backs from staying bent-kneed, and badly bruised hips from bouncing off the console and gunnels. Straightening their backs or locking their knees as the boat fell off the wave crests transmitted the shock of the jarring hull slap throughout the length of their skeletons. It was a damn fine course they were sailing. It was time for Freddy to take a turn at the wheel. He got up from the wet deck to relieve Wayne at the console and assumed the bent-standing position he had to assume at the helm to absorb the shock of the bounding boat. They changed positions.

"Having fun?" Freddy yelled at Wayne with a fake ear to ear grin. Wayne turned his head slowly to look at Freddy and then turned it back again slowly. "Here," he said, offering Freddy the wheel.

"Anything new, anything I need to know?"

"Yes," he said, and turned away and lay down without expounding on the matter any further.

****

Wayne rose as it was getting dark. "I don't like the feel of this thing," he said. It seemed that the boat was "bending" now as it labored up and down the waves. Of course it was impossible that they could have been able to detect something like that, with all of the motion going on and it being so hard to hear anything - like a groaning hull - it would undoubtedly have been disguised by those things, but still, there was a feeling that Freddy felt, too, that something was going very wrong with his little boat. Then the engine stopped.

"What happened?" cried Wayne.

"The engine stopped," said Freddy. The boat rapidly lost its heading and swung broadside to the weather. They would lose the shrimp boat quickly if they did not get the boat re-started right away and back on course. And another small matter, they would founder and drown.

It was getting dark now and the shrimper was sailing away. Freddy cranked the starter. "Sounds like it's out of gas, Wayne."

"Can't be, not yet."

They had gone through the tanks in the hull and were on the seat tank. If that was out they had already gone through one hundred and eighty gallons in the twenty-nine hours of this sea chase. Freddy unscrewed the filler cap.

"It's empty, Wayne." They were losing the shrimp boat, and taking on water as they sat dead in the water, lolling broadside to the heavy seas. Without headway they would sink. Wayne disconnected the fuel line as quickly as he could and hooked it up to one of the gas tanks on the port side. He worked the rubber bubble in the gas line to re-prime the engine. "Try it." He kept working the bubble, waves breaking over him as he crouched low in the stern, outside the protection of the Bimini top, as Freddy cranked the starter.

Those same waves were falling on the engine as well, wetting it, cooling it down. It continued to crank. The longer it took to start the more likely it was that it wouldn't. They had plenty of battery, the problem was the waves. The engine was cooling rapidly and salt water was getting to the ignition wires. The heat of running had helped keep it dry. Now that heat was being carried off to sea.

This wasn't good. Now they were sitting lower in the water. The small bilge pump in the battery well was not meant to keep up with the volumes of water coming into the boat over the side. A wave hit them hard and spun them. The next one completely engulfed the engine, And Wayne. Freddy strained to see through the water whether Wayne was still there. But he hung on, was not washed over the side, and Freddy saw that he was still there squeezing the rubber bubble when the water subsided.

Not that it would make much difference if the thing wouldn't start.

It sputtered, then it shook and caught on three of the six cylinders as one of the magnetos did its job. Not to be out-done, the other tried hard and soon they had four, five, all six cylinders firing. Freddy headed the boat back into the sea, approximating the same heading as they had been on before. He looked at his watch. They had been drifting for six minutes to the left of the shrimper's heading, at an angle of about one hundred and thirty degrees to it. Wayne climbed out of the engine well and over the bulkhead which formed the back of the bench seat, into the relatively safety under the Bimini top. Now they needed luck.

"Get the time, Freddy?" Freddy answered "Yep."

"Think you can work out a parallel course?"

"Yep, in theory." Freddy had thrown a can over the side before the boat lost its head and guessed that the sea was running at four knots. The wind would have the boat drifting a bit faster once it turned broadside to the sea. The limiting factor was the size of the waves - the wind would have to push the boat up those slopes, and the hull would tend to stay aligned with the troughs. Freddy guessed at eight knots drift. Eight knots for six minutes. About eight-tenths of a nautical mile, nine-tenths of a statute mile. The sea had been thirty degrees ahead of their port beam. Freddy didn't worry about sines and such - it was a simple three-four-five triangle. Nine tenths is to five as X is to three, they should be five and a half tenths of a mile right of the shrimper's course.

"Wayne, if we take up the same course as before we should parallel them at about a half mile to the right, or maybe a little more."

"That's what I like about you, Freddy, such precision." He was only kidding, I think, thought Freddy. Freddy gave him two possibilities.

"We can try to overtake them by staying parallel and looking for their lights. The weather is clear enough that we might be able to spot a lighted ship a half mile off." He paused as their knees bent in compression as the boat's plummet was brought up short at the bottom of a wave. They flinched as the windshield was inundated and the Bimini top sagged a little more. "But if my navigation is too far off, or we can't keep right on our heading, or the weather closes in some more, we'll miss them."

"What else did you have in mind?"

"Turn right, into the sea for six minutes. Try to run at sixteen knots. Turn back onto the shrimper's course and make a theoretical run right up the stern 'till we see them. We'll probably still find them way off to one side or another."

"Ok, Freddy, sounds as good as anything else to me. I hope they don't turn. What's our compass heading after we make up for the drift?"

"As near as I can make out, the compass was swinging back and forth through two hundred and thirty degrees." Wayne took the wheel and they stormed back at the sea, trying to make sixteen knots dead into the waves at a time when the prudent thing to do from a survival standpoint was run with the storm. It felt like white-water rafting.

They had been at twenty-eight hundred rpms before running out of gas. They opened up the throttle as far as the little boat could take it for now. They knew they had to catch up, but if they pushed the boat too hard they would sink before they caught sight of the shrimper, and with too much throttle and no chance of getting on plane they would run out of gas that much sooner, bucking the waves but not going much faster. After six minutes Freddy turned back on to the course the shrimper had been on when they last saw it. After he made the turn back to the course that they hoped they and the trawler had been on before he pulled back on the throttle.

They were riding low in the water. The saving grace was that the boat was actually much lighter than it had been at the start of the trip because it no longer had the weight of the 180 gallons of fuel in the hull and in the console tanks. Wayne had done his turn in the engine well, now it was Freddy's turn. Grabbing the bucket, he climbed over the bench seat into the engine well and removed the cover to the batteries and the bilge. He started bailing. He had to squat, hold on to the cleat at the stern with one hand and reach down with the bucket into the bottom of the boat with the other. He tried to help the bilge pump catch up with the volume of water that had come over the side and added considerably to the problems that the overworked little bastard had with the leaky hull. At least Freddy felt right about one thing - he had made a decision in this nightmare of choices. He picked a course, a course of action, and Wayne was following them both. Maybe there was hope for him coping with the ridiculous dilemma of sea and Sargento after all. Freddy hoped that they could spot the trawler, hoped more than that that Sargento's boat would stop soon. Wayne figured that they had enough fuel to keep them going no later than noon tomorrow. Now they were using it faster than they had been before.

So there was Freddy, throwing buckets of brine back to Neptune when he noticed he was making no headway in reducing the amount of water in the bottom of the boat. He looked over the side. The bilge pump's discharge was not spewing forth the effluent of oily ocean water and grime from the boat's bottom. It should have been running constantly. It had finally failed, and bailing would be a continuous operation from now on.

Wayne's eyes were better than Freddy's; there was no question that he should keep watching for the trawler. That left Freddy to continue bailing while Wayne stayed at the wheel, maintained course and speed, and watched the water ahead of him for the stern light of Sargento's command craft. It was going to be a long night. Freddy hoped.

Chapter Twenty-Five – Roundabout

It was four o'clock in the morning and Freddy was still bailing. Wayne had assessed the situation and knew what had happened when Freddy remained in the back of the boat to bail for so many hours. The ocean had become more lenient with them by small degrees and Freddy could take breaks now and then, twenty minutes bailing, then back to the cover of the tattering Bimini top for a few.

They had been going through squalls during the night and Freddy stayed wet. Each time he came into cover to say a few words to Wayne and see what progress they were making he did so in a caveman stance because he could not stand up straight anymore. His back ached from the constant squat he maintained while shoveling water. His knees were even worse. The ligaments were stretched out and loose feeling from being over-stretched in the deep knee bend imposed upon him by the task. The right knee, the weak one, was hitting him with sharp spasms of pain, traveling from the joint, up and down like lightening. As Freddy came forward to take a turn at the wheel Wayne asked him a question. His voice had become hoarse owing to the volume of speech that was perforce necessary to maintain operational communication over the whistle of the wind and the din of the roaring sea.

"Freddy, I don't like where this is headed. Ever been down here?"

"No, and I wish I wasn't down here now. We must be somewhere in the vicinity of the Yucatan channel, and that's bad news. Ya got the Yucatan current flowing north offshore of the peninsula and the Cuban Counter Current flowing south on the other side. Two wicked currents goin' opposite directions over submerged rises of the sea floor in a so called channel that's too short to be a channel and too narrow to be a strait. I gotta say this, but you probly know it already. This little boat wasn't made for this. Wayne just shrugged, Freddy did a short shift at the wheel until he recovered somewhat, and then he returned to the bilge. Wayne's eyes were better than Freddy's and better than most people's eyes for that matter, and so he was the logical choice for their best chance to spot the shrimp boat.

Wayne tried to overtake the trawler at three thousand rpms for as long as he deemed they could stay at that speed without passing it, then he settled the boat back to twenty-seven hundred again, about what they were doing before they lost sight of the other boat. To have any hope of spotting it now they would have to wait until daylight if their lights were off.

The sea's lessening fury was saving them some fuel over the rate they had been using it for the last day and a half. It was easier on the boys, too. The top had started to rip, unfortunately, but although the hull cracks must have gotten worse, the flow of the leak had slowed somewhat in the smaller, less terrifying waves. They slept an hour each. It got gusty and some stars could be seen every now and then. They were on the fringe of the storm.

After six o'clock, with not much night left, Freddy had to forgo his next sleep shift, or at least postpone it. The little boat was once again riding low in the water, burdened by sea water in her belly. It looked as though they would have to start a zig-zag search for the trawler, or for land, whichever came sooner. They didn't entertain much hope at this point of finding either.

Now it was merely blustery. The storm had passed them by or had lost its identity. The radio crackled and sometimes said something in Spanish but there was no hope of getting a weather report. Freddy climbed into the engine well again and pulled back the cover. Water was sloshing around half way up the batteries. Dip, lift, and splash; dip, lift, and splash, as he poured it out, a bucket at a time. For the first time since he started Freddy was able to hear the splash of the water he had been throwing over the stern. His cramped left fist held on to the cleat, although he did not have to hold on so tightly anymore. His right arm hurt along the biceps and the bottom of the upper arm from lifting hundreds of pounds of water from two feet below the level of his feet in the classic bailing crouch, up to the level of his knees to clear the height of the transom. He was going to have a hell of a serve next time he got onto a tennis court.

He admitted it to himself; he was weary. Something flickered in the edge of his vision and caught his eye behind them as he looked over the transom. Two lights, one above the other. They had come up out of a trough and there was a red and a green light flashing alternately below them, side by side.

They were almost directly in front of the shrimp boat, and not too far in front, either. Its lights had come into visual range as the sea subsided, and sneaked up unawares as they searched for it ahead of them. The thought of squeaking past that ten foot bow at the height of the storm sent shudders through Freddy's bones the way his boat would shudder if the heavy wooden hull of the trawler creaked, groaned, and splintered his fiberglass boat. Freddy preferred to think that they passed the trawler during the night and then the improving weather let it catch up with them. He already knew it was stupid to think they had been steering a perfectly straight line. He had to talk to Wayne.

"Wayne!"

"What!"

"Look behind us." Wayne spun and saw the lights of the trawler and the dim outline of Sargento's boat in the gathering light.

"Good grief!" A flicker of Annie must have ignited those words in his surprise at the sight of those lights. He seemed to realize he had borrowed the words from his poor dead lover and snapped back to the present. "Damn," he said, it's getting close to daylight and they're practically on top of us."

"Be a bad time to run out of gas again, huh? We'd have to stand up and wave our arms so they wouldn't run us over. Then they could shoot us." Wayne didn't like that too much, Freddy could tell.

"Why don't you make yourself useful and remove the drain plug from the stern. I'll crank this thing up and we'll get some of the water out of it." Freddy knew that. Wayne turned left and opened the throttle as Freddy undid the drain plug. Their acceleration lifted the bow and the water in the hull moved back toward the stern. The boat was not designed to be self-bailing, but it was bailing itself now as the inclination of the bow and the acceleration forced the water to the stern and out the drain hole at the bottom of the shallow vee of the hull.

The boat was sluggish at first, but soon it was up on plane, getting lighter as the hull emptied so that it rode still higher. The boat was more fuel efficient at higher speeds when it was on plane, but the throttle was now wide open to force the water out, and the gas consumption was enormous. But they had to get out from in front of the shrimp boat before there was enough daylight for the trawler to see their darkened boat. The moon was down, and a well-timed gathering of clouds made the darkness more complete, for the moment. The sea was still rough enough to disguise their wake and their noise.

"Freddy," Wayne called back from the wheel, "Did you intend to let them run us down before you said something to me?"

"Well, how did they get past us, eagle-eyes?" They would never know what happened, and they both knew that.

They were moving at thirty-five knots in fairly rough seas, running up the long waves, or what was left of them - just giant swells, actually - and slapping forward as they flew out onto the upward sides of the next ones. The top was flapping around, torn in several places. "Freddy, take the wheel. I'm going to get this top down." Freddy took the wheel.

"Might as well toss it over the side, Wayne, it's ruined. If we hit any more weather it is going to rip right off."

"No, we'll save it. The canvas might come in useful for shelter."
"Pardon me, Wayne," Freddy said to himself.

They ran off to the left for a couple of miles and Wayne replaced the drain plug when Freddy throttled down and put the engine in neutral so the water would not run back into the hull. The last thing they wanted to do now was shut the thing off. They drifted as they watched the trawler's lights pass. The boat seemed to coalesce before them as individual parts of it became visible as though they had been scattered in the dark. The seventy-six foot trawler took form as those parts came together out of the darkness, materializing wraith-like under the haze of its range lights in the gray gauze of rarefied early morning light. They sat, mesmerized, for a moment. Then it occurred to them that it was at long last time to dine.

Wayne produced two cans from his store of stolen goods. He looked at the labels and said, "Freddy, what would you like, asparagus tips or baked beans?"

"I like asparagus, but it turns my pee green." Wayne thought about this for a moment. After deliberating about it, he said, "You've got the next shift at the wheel, Freddy, I've been doing it for most of the last twelve hours. If I have to sit behind you, you're not going to be eating a can of baked beans on an empty stomach. Take the asparagus."

"Hmmmmmph." Freddy was insulted. Well, not really.

"Not as good as Annie's pork tenderloin in plum sauce... sorry, Wayne I..."

"It's OK, Freddy," he said with a grim smile.

They had been drinking water all along their voyage so far so as not to become dehydrated. Wayne had seen to that. Now, at the onset of this feast their stomachs were empty. They treated themselves to another course. Wayne had snow peas, Freddy drew creamed corn, which he usually hated. It was surprisingly good. Everything is relative.

It got light. The sun came out, and it was good to see. Freddy said he bet it was surprised to see them as well.

They trailed the trawler as far back as they dared on the flattening seas. They were far more vulnerable now, much more visible in the improving conditions. They kept the boat on the edge of sight and trusted to Wayne's long vision.

Freddy thought that if Sargento's men were searching for them with field glasses they could have seen them, although he tried to stay so far back that only the top half of the rigging of the trawler was visible. This nonsense went on for three hours, until about ten a.m. The plan was to pursue the shrimper for as long as the fuel held out, in the hope it would make port and give them a lead to Sargento. If that hadn't happened and it was eminent that they would run out of fuel Freddy and Wayne would try to board the shrimper rather that than risk a slow death adrift in Freddy's small boat. They were on the last of the six portable gas cans now. If that got too low, that was it, bonsai. They would be forced to confront Sargento's men at sea. Confronting the shrimper directly could be suicidal, but they would get results quickly.

During this time each got a little more sleep. Freddy hadn't had a beer in two days. Well, he had been wanting to cut back anyway. Then something happened. Wake bumps on the horizon to the west led their eyes to another boat coming to meet the shrimper.

****

Someone or something was being transferred from one boat to the other. Probably the trawler to the other boat. It was ludicrous to think that this was a mid-sea meeting on the heels of that storm, so they must be near the base that Wayne suspected Sargento had somewhere in the Gulf or the Caribbean. Now they had a fighting chance.

"I'll bet the shrimper is going on to Sargento's Colombian headquarters," said Wayne. "That other boat is small and fast, lower in the water. Probably working out of an island somewhere close to here. Freddy deferred to Wayne's judgment; he knew more about it than Freddy from the information he had pieced together while working undercover for the last two weeks. Wayne had suspected the existence of just such an island. They would follow that smaller boat to wherever it was going. They couldn't follow the shrimper any further anyway; they were nearly out of fuel. They waited.

Soon the trawler left and the smaller boat headed back in the direction it had come from. It was moving fast, so Freddy put on some speed as well. Sure enough, ahead of the fast craft's course was an island sitting in the haze. "Slow down, Freddy, it's shallowing up. We don't have charts for these waters." Freddy acknowledged him with a nod. Of course they didn't, they were possibly hundreds of miles from home, it was impossible to gauge how far they had come bucking the heavy seas or have any more than the vaguest idea of the direction. They didn't even know where "these waters" were. They had to assume this island was picked for two reasons; it was out of the shipping lanes and remote, and it had some natural protection to keep boats away.

"Maybe that's why they went to the trouble of an exchange in open water," said Freddy. "The shrimp boat probably draws too much water and can't get in there."

"Good thinking, Freddy."

"Arf arf."

"What is that supposed to mean?"

"Thanks for the bone."

"I'm sorry Freddy, I've had a lot on my mind."

"Woof woof," Freddy consoled him.

They saw brown water dead ahead. There was a shoal between them and the open water to the right, where the other boats were. They ran around it and got closer, straining to make out where the other boat was going to land and trying in vain to see if he wove his way to shore indicating reef or rocks, or current cuts through shallows.

They got an idea of what side of the island he was headed for, and cut the throttle. They dared not get close enough to be seen. They were more vulnerable now than at any other time during the trip so far.

Circling back the way they came, they approached the island from the other side. Both Wayne and Freddy instinctively were searching for signs of danger, natural danger. What they saw was a small white line running from the lip of a cove on the north shore of the island which was facing them. The line of white water traveled outward from the shore line several hundred yards from the beach enclosing the cove, then skirted the island in a southeasterly direction. The west end of this face of the island ended abruptly in a ninety degree corner. The island was not volcanic; it was flat and overgrown.

There were shoals behind them, a reef in front, and uncharted shallows all around the island. They did not want to come upon their hosts unexpectedly in broad daylight without knowing in which direction it was safe to run away. Since they were already in the least likely direction to be spotted by any of Sargento's men, Freddy put on a mask and jumped over the side to inspect the hull. The hairline cracks seemed wider, but the hull was intact. Something on the bottom caught Freddy's eye. Three cannons, 6 to 8 feet long, probably 3 tons each, most likely unearthed temporarily by the recent passing storm. Someone else, perhaps three hundred years earlier, had gotten lost in a storm and had found themselves at this un-navigable place. Freddy returned to the boat. They dropped anchor to wait for the early hours. Wayne explained his next plan.

"We'll wait until around three o'clock in the morning, and if this thing re-starts we'll pick our way in slowly. Then we'll hide the boat and search them out on foot." Freddy had a suggestion.

"Shouldn't we take one slow trip around the island and map out all the obstacles and outcroppings and see if we can learn anything?"

"We can if you like, just be aware that we will be burning more gas." Freddy lifted the gas can that held the remainder of the two hundred eighty gallons of gasoline they had started with.

"There's enough for a look around. And we're not going to get out of here without stealing some of their gas, you know that."

"That I do, Freddy, that I do. But I like the way you're starting to consider these things."

"Arf arf."

"Stop that. You know there is an element of risk involved in poking around this unknown island at night, even though the moon is close to full and we are *supposed* to know what we are doing." Freddy nodded that he knew. So that was settled, and Wayne was treating Freddy as though his judgment in "battle situations" was on a par with his own. Freddy liked that. The night was still and clear. The stats were out. Wayne was studying the sky.

"What are you looking at, Wayne?" asked Freddy, deadpan and tired.

"Ursa Major"

"What?"

"The Great Bear. Arthur's Wain."

"What are you talkin' about?"

Wayne cracked the merest of smiles. "No jokes, Freddy? Wain and Wayne? No pun?"

"I don't feel like it anymore. I'm tired of doing that. So what is Arthur's Wain?"

"Celtic Mythology, Freddy."

"Where do you get this stuff, Wayne?"

"It ran big in my family"

"Oh, yeah, right. McLaren. But that's Scottish!"

"The Celts were big time. They covered a lot of ground at one time. To Modron!" he said in a toast to the sky.

"Who?" asked Freddy, Mordred?"

"Close, but no cloak. Modron, Welch goddess of fertility."

"She's on our side?"

"I hope so."

"Who's on their side?"

"Afallach, god of the underworld."

They had nothing to do for a few hours, except bail now and then, so they had another feast from Wayne's larder, set the alarms on their watches, and went to sleep for the next eight hours on a gently rolling sea. The artichoke hearts were delicious. Woof!

****

Freddy's indefatigable old Casio watch beeped him alive at one o'clock. He was still tired but infinitely more rested than he had been in two days. Wayne heard the watch's alarm and was up as well, already heading forward to haul in the anchor. They had allowed themselves two extra hours to check out the physical characteristics of the island and surrounding waters.

Starting the boat and letting it warm up a bit, Freddy switched on the depth finder to make sure it was still working. It lit up, the trace was working, and he had a bottom indication of twenty-five feet. The engine settled out quickly and was running evenly after starting on the first four cranks of the starter motor. All seemed well.

It was a lovely night. Freddy slipped the engine into gear and nosed the boat toward the scalloped shoreline. Well, one scallop. A cove. They quickly got to within four hundred yards of the shore, running slowly and quietly, looking for lights that would indicate habitation of this portion of the island. They thought it unlikely, felt safe that they, whoever "they" were, would not have their landing area on one side of the island and part of their working and living quarters on the other side of what was probably a very densely overgrown piece of real estate. Privacy was what they wanted; there was no ingress to the island here.

Sargento's compound would be hidden from the open sea; Wayne didn't imagine that the operation was a James Bond nemesis type of island fortress replete with underground bunkers and a garrison of private army troops. That wouldn't be cost-effective. What Wayne expected to find from his spying missions on Sargento earlier in the year was a mid-ocean clearing house for smuggled goods, some of his own trafficking, but mostly contraband being handled by him for other concerns, for a fee. Sargento had the organization in place for smuggling things into the United States, and he sold his services to other factions in the criminal world. He was a very innovative criminal, Sargento. Wayne figured to find a bunch of mean guys with guns and evil dispositions, maybe six or eight fellows, watching over and handling tainted goods in mid-shipment, assorted contraband, drugs, maybe some money to be laundered, food and fuel.

There would be no watch schedules and guard dogs and uniformed patrols with assault rifles, or so Wayne told Freddy, to put fetters on his rampant imagination. "God, I hope not," Freddy said earnestly. Wayne assured Freddy that the gangsters would be relying on natural concealment and would not be expecting anybody, especially after that storm. Freddy was placated enough to be singing quietly as the tranquil, innocent-looking cove, the sandy beach and the tall, stately palms behind it grew larger as they got closer. It reminded Freddy of the opening sequence of Gilligan's Island.

"This is the tale of the cast-a-ways, lost on a deh-sert isle," from there his knowledge of the lyrics went sketchy and after a few lines he trailed off to bits and pieces of the song filling in the missing parts with "da da da's until he got to the stirring last line - "The *Minnow*" would be lost," and then again, to himself in higher harmony, "The *Minnow*" would be lost---"

"Don't get the idea this is going to be easy, Freddy. Even with surprise on our side we have to get them, get their fuel, and find out where Sargento went. We can't just go in and shoot them all and burn the place down.

"We're not going to shoot them?"

"Yes, we're going to shoot them…"

"But we're not going to burn the place down?"

'Yes! We're going to burn the place down! And even that won't be so easy. These are career men, Freddy; four-letter men, lots of experience. Remember Connors?" Freddy thought of his ribs and nose, and his hands automatically went to those places. "How could I forget?"

"I have a hunch he's ashore. He left Key West after Sargento, stayed a little longer to clean up loose ends (Freddy shuddered) and failed. But I'll bet he's in charge of this operation and stops by to check on things whenever he is in the area. I bet the shrimp boat dropped him off."

"He's a bad one, isn't he?"

"Don't underestimate him, Freddy; He's one of the few people I fear."

They moved toward the cove. It looked like a good place to put ashore but for that reef in their way. No boats would be trying to land on this part of the island. Unless they were nuts.

At the western end of the reef the white water line stopped just short of shore near a rock promontory at the cove's lip. At the eastern end of the cove the reef was three hundred and fifty yards from the sand of the beach and guarded by treacherous shallows. From there the island curved around, east and then south, where they had seen the fast boat put in to what must have been a bay or at least a salt creek facing south.

They approached the reef until the depth finder indicated less than fifteen feet of water. Freddy turned right and headed west following the tell-tale line of foaming white water to where it was closest to the beach. They might have piled up on it yesterday if the water had been flat calm instead of having the long, foot-high rollers, residuals of the storm, sending visual signals of the reef's location as they broke upon it.

Soon they were where the reef curved in closer, toward shore at the cove's west end. The depth was about eight feet. They stayed in close to the trace of white indicating the line of rocks and coral lurking under the water, until it ended abruptly at a brief gap between the reef's end and the outcropping of cap rock jutting from the island. Where the water near the rocky point had been light green jade in the distance by daylight now they saw it was milky where the limestone slurry of the backwash from the beach spent its energy oozing through the chinks and spaces between the rocks. A swimmer just might get through into the cove - a very reckless, foolhardy swimmer - but there wasn't room enough for a boat to get over the rocks at the end of the reef line, and there was no place to tie up a boat outside the cove. Inside the cove there was enough water and a sandy bottom. They were not more than twenty yards from the island when the bottom started coming up.

"I'm going to take her out a little, Wayne, we're too close, it's getting shallow," said Freddy. He turned away toward the deeper water. "Besides that, even with this light wind left over from the storm, we might be heard on the beach from this close if anyone is on this side of the island." Freddy turned north just in time, because just as he had done so the bottom came up still more. Three or four feet of water now separated them from the smooth bottom of sand or grass. It was too dark to tell for sure, but Freddy thought it was grass because of the indistinct trace on the depth finder. The bottom kept coming up. They kept running out to sea until they eventually had a comfortable eight feet again, perhaps seven hundred yards from shore.

There were flats - extensive shallow expanses - off this side of the island. They had to keep their distance and swung south-southeast to follow the hard left turn made by the island's shore.

There was nothing to see there, mangroves right up to the water. Several feet out into the water, actually, impassable by foot. Circling the island at this distance, the trip was taking longer than Freddy had anticipated, but there was plenty of night left. But not so much gas.

Something nosed the boat away from the island. A narrow current was flowing from the direction of island. Freddy corrected for it and brought the boat back on its heading. He looked down and saw moving water making swirling eddies at the bow and stern.

"Wayne, we've got a trace of current here."

"Tide is going out. Should be starting to change pretty soon."

"Probably running off the flats."

"Could be, Freddy, or it could be a salt creek from the island." They passed the sluice of water draining from the flats and continued south.

That west side of the island proved dull and uneventful. More cautious now, they turned east to patrol the island's southeastern exposure, where the bay and the criminals were supposed to be.

In a few minutes they could just barely make out lights far off across the water, recessed back into the bay, and maybe even further back, in the woods or on a canal or salt creek. The lights were only there for an instant, and then they went out, now behind some bend in a waterway or hidden by tropical forest.

They could see smooth-topped currents running in several tendrils, tidal cuts braided through the silt and sand below the shallow water. At tide changes water moving rapidly over the flats had grooved several natural channels to the island, weaving, winding paths with smooth, glossy tops, running through the ripples over the shallower water.

Freddy looked at his watch. It was 3:45 a.m. Moving slowly so as not to generate a luminous wake and to spot sudden obstacles the circuitous course dictated by having to stay wide of the shallows made the circumnavigation of this lonely land mass more time consuming than Freddy had anticipated. "Wayne, it's getting late. We either have to start back now or get in to shore.

"Well, Freddy, we've got a few choices. The cove is far enough away from their headquarters to be reasonably safe, and the bottom is sandy from the looks of it. I don't think the boat would be discovered there. We can go back the way we came, hope we don't run out of gas and try to bring the boat in to the cove somehow at the western end of the cove, but even if we make it back on the gas we have left, we'll almost certainly pile up on the reef or the rocky outcrop if we try to make it in, and we can't leave the boat anchored outside of the reef because it would be too easy to see the next time one of their boats is out and about. Or we could keep going this way, turn up the other side, after we pass the mouth of this bay near to us now and look for possibilities. Or we could turn around and try to find our way into the cove at its east end, through the flats between the shallows and the eastern end of the reef. At least we know there's a place to hide there if we can get into the cove and we wouldn't have to fear running out of gas on the far side of the island where there may not be anywhere to hide the boat. But then we'd have to pick our way through the shallows between the reef and the headland where the east lip of the cove comes back out close to the reef again. We don't know how big this island is. We can't chance going any further because we don't know if we have the gas for it. Or, if you feel gutsy, we can try to find our way in to shore right here across this shallow bay by taking one of these natural channels in. We already know there is at least one way in to shore across the bay because their boat had to take one of these cuts in. We don't want that one, or we'll have a reception committee when we turn into their hidden boat basin. But maybe there's another way in. We should stay away from the central channels. Some of these cuts are run-off from the flats and go nowhere, but maybe there is another one that will take us all the way to shore on one side of the bay or the other. We can hide the boat in the underbrush. I'd try one of the cuts toward the east, on the right side of the bay." Freddy made a face showing he thought the idea was chancy. Wayne read his mind.

"We're taking a chance, no matter what. We could be discovered at any time."

"Ok," said Freddy. "You're right, we've been taking chances since we started; I guess there is no getting around it. Let's sneak in here on the right, try to land well to the right of where we saw their light, and hide the boat. That last channel in the shallows just before the eastern tip of the island looks like it might go all the way in. Should be pretty comfy. We won't have to carry stolen food and gas so far, either." Freddy could see Wayne's grin in the moonlight.

They started down the last channel on the right. It curved from side to side, meandering past acres of silty water ten to twenty inches deep. The tide was starting to run the other way, flowing toward the island to fill the bay beyond to its high tide level.

The channel was a tidal cut, a creek through the flats. It could be likened to a fast-flowing aqueduct filling a vast, shallow reservoir each time the tide came in. At the height of the exchange the rushing water might travel at five knots or better. When they were on the other side of the island the tide was going out. Now it was coming in again.

They were proceeding nicely, moving right along with the incoming tide, staying in the center of the moon-shimmery surface glaze of the moving water and getting closer to shore, when the channel ended. Up ahead only two hundred yards and off to the right was the reef's end and what looked like a way into the cove on the far side of the shallows. But they couldn't get the boat across those shallows. It weighed over a ton. They couldn't leave it there to be sighted, either. Their error would leave the boat well out of the water with the outgoing tide.

The current tried to push the boat farther up onto the shallow area ahead of it where the false channel's bottom had come up and the moving water fanned out across the flats. Eddies formed at the sides of the boat as the water went around past the stern. "Freddy, the current is picking up," said Wayne. "I knew that," thought Freddy. They mustn't let the boat get too firmly entrenched. They could not to gun the engine to back the boat because of the noise that it would cause.

"Hey, Wayne, I think it's time to get out and walk." They were aground in the sucky silt. They had to get out and push the boat off backwards.

Straining, pushing and lifting at the bow, they got the boat off the silt, but it took a major effort, a lot of back and leg muscle. No sooner were they afloat when they came to a place where there was slimy grass on the bottom growing on bottomless mud - or so it seemed, as they sunk into it up to their thighs, afraid to let go of the boat for fear they would sink in too deep to get out. They struggled through it, panicky in their anxiety that the perverse suction would pull them from the boat and swallow them.

Finally the boat was floating free again and they were on good footing. Wayne stayed in the water and held it where it was while Freddy jumped in, started the boat – something they would never do ordinarily with someone in the waste - and put it in reverse. Freddy backed the boat slowly down the channel, which wasn't easy to do with the current pushing past the stern. When there was room enough to turn the boat around they did it by getting out again and turning it by hand, rather than make several back and forth maneuvers.

There was no thought now of going all the way back to the other side of the island. It would be light by the time they got back, and the chances of being seen too great. Now they knew the end of the reef was off the nearby southeast corner of the island and knew that the cove lay beyond that. They had seen the hint of a channel to the cove from the position where they had gone aground. They headed for it. Watching the depth finder carefully, they made their way into the cove through the deeper water between the shallows and the reef. Wayne stood on the bow to try to watch for sudden obstructions in the narrow, tricky channel, calling out directions when he saw rocks or coral heads rising from the bottom. Freddy was at the console, alert, intent on steering the boat. It was only by chance that they got into the cove. Had they not chosen that false channel and gone aground, they never would have seen the true channel into it.

Once inside the cove they put the boat in a handy swatch of mangroves standing twenty yards or so out from the shore midway between the eastern and western ends of the cove and rigged some of the canvas tatters of the ruined Bimini top between the mangrove branches as a canopy against the sun. It was six-thirty. They went to sleep for a couple of hours. They weren't going anywhere else in the boat that night. They were out of gas.

Chapter Twenty-Six - The Woods

Twenty hours had passed. Freddy moved now along the mangroves as stealthily as he could, making every effort to keep his footing on the irregular bottom. Behind Freddy, the watercourse by which he had come here was lost in vegetation by anyone who did not know the telltales, the clues to finding such and overgrown creek system snaking its way back into the island, branching off in several directions, thick, green wild, and overgrown, covered by encroaching foliage, the branches of the creek eventually terminating in a maze of small feeders to tidal pools, salt ponds, strangled watercourses and billabongs. Which is to say that they went nowhere. Freddy's passage through the salt creek's main flux was what he imagined to be the only cut that traversed the entire island.

Finding its entrance was something of a bit of luck; whether it existed at all and where it was located had been just a theory - based on a push of current on Freddy's boat flowing outward from the west side of the island during the reconnoiter they made the night after their arrival - as the indication that a salt creek flowed from one side of the island to the other. Its start was just where Wayne had postulated that it would be, and its existence had helped him elude the searchers he knew they had sent out. Wayne was no longer there to help him, so now he must continue to elude their search if he was to have them think that Wayne had come to this island alone.

Freddy had snuck off before those following him were far into the underbrush. He slipped from under a tall stand of sea grapes he had taken refuge in and retreated silently before them in as the buffoons blundered into the woods. He profited from the flagrant ineptitude that the encampment bound goons displayed in the mangrove forest.

The men turned to the north and then west to begin their circuitous route of checking the shoreline from the bay side and around the promontory from which Wayne and Freddy first had spied upon them. When they were clear, Freddy took the shorter route through the woods, as he and Wayne had done several times before.

After he left the small patch of woods near their "path" to the compound he had stopped at the boat's hiding place only briefly enough to "arm" himself. He had cocked the spear gun's three rubbers and put it back in its rack on the side of the boat as a fallback. It was too clumsy to take through the woods into the island's core. He left the cove and ran through the ankle deep water near the shore, looking back often to see if pursuit was close at hand. It was rough going, but he had to stay ahead of them if he could, and he had to avoid leaving a trail. Then he set out around the shore line on the north side of the island and rounded the corner to the western aspect – no shoreline here, just mangroves, shallows, and the tidal cut which fed the creek - where he plunged into the tropical forest at the creek's start. He ducked under the leaves of the mangroves at the entrance of the creek, an entrance which would be invisible from seaward and hard to find up close even by someone as highly experienced as Freddy.

Some places were so tightly overgrown that it was a struggle for Freddy to get his body through, too thick with mangroves, clogged with ferns and thistle-like bracken, interdicted now and then in a hammock of higher ground by horizontal limbs of huge, big-leafed banyans and ancient small-leafed ficas trees, each with vertical trailers like bars on a cage spanning ten feet or more around their bases. When relegated to negotiating the creek bottom for passage, which was most of the time, he was required to push through brush, duck beneath reaching mangrove arms seeking access to the sun, bend double and climb over mangrove limbs and climb out of the water altogether to walk on the roots of the mangroves, trying not to turn an ankle. In open places he could make better time on the creek's shore where the ground was a muddy, black compost of countless fermented leaves dropped by small-leafed trees, ironwoods, guavas, gumbo-limbos; or the spongy mat of dried, small brown broken bits of branches and flinty gray corky pieces of weathered, fragmented twigs in the respite of an occasional glade. But the open spaces were few and isolated to small hammocks of trees where the ground was high enough to harbor them. Down at the creek, surrounded by salt water, only the mangroves could survive. At the center of the creek where the current carried away the silt there was hard bottom. Some of the worst going was when he was forced to the sides of the creek where there was nothing but soft, methane-rich muck.

It was over and around crooks and nooks such as these that he had spent the last several hours since his escape from the cove and his flight around the island, crawling on faltering legs, clawing with tired arms through the weird, contorted wood, getting challenged by bristling land crabs, bruising his shins and rubbing them raw on mangrove roots in knee-high water. Gnats swarmed over the bogs and pools. Water bugs darted across the surfaces, alarmed at his passing, sprinting straight-away then abruptly turning on a tangent, making a pattern of many diamonds of the hundreds of diagonal etchings on the water's surface. Hydroids like horseflies in the brackish water fed on his fuzzy calves as he pushed past the sticky pull of spider webs brushing his face and arms. The webs matted in his hair as he broke through them. He was sheened in sweat, gasping as he drove himself forward, paranoid, glancing over his shoulder for pursuers who were not there.

He'd been traveling through the woods for most of the night, trying to find a way through to the other side of the island. In the desperate, tired, early hours close to morning flashes of silent heat lightning high in the clouds far to the south lit the trees around him, making them look evil. In the tropical forest the humidity was oppressive, but no rain fell. The flashes got closer and great crashes of thunder split the air, lighting every branch and frond. The darkness was filled with overwhelming noise and sudden light stark on leprous orchid trees, their flowers shone in ghastly reds and purples. Smooth-barked sandalwoods and blollys with green and yellow molds and blotches on their gray skins were sickly sentinels in the forest. Here the venerable banyans now seemed entlike, bent at odd angles and hung with long, incredible beards of twigs, lichens, and moss. Strange, macabre straight-trunked trees at angles to the ground had limbs only on their topmost side, lines of reaching arms in the opposite direction or radiating from half-fallen trunks like spokes on a wheel, throwing sharp evil shadows on the ground with each flash in the sky. Austere ironwoods had sickly green and gray lesions. Psoriatic gumbo-limbos with barks peeling like onion skins. Shiny smooth trees, others straight as ship's masts but ringed in segments. The disturbed images flickered on and off, leaving Freddy to blunder onward with night blindness after each pyroclastic barrage. It was a sinister, startling counterpoint to the gala Halloween bacchanal only a few nights ago.

****

The lightning stopped and the water gap began to widen. Moving more slowly now, he caught glimpses of open water through chinks in the jungle. He slipped down lower into the deeper water, sensing that he had come upon the back end of Sargento's lair.

Finally he felt a breath of air ahead of him. It struck his face and brought the smell of the sea, whisking away the dank odors of the tropical forest. Gradually the vegetation before him opened upon the still waters of the scooped-out basin. Before him was Sargento's compound. The narrow natural channel wound outward in an ess to the bay from his vantage point back in the bushes. It first went to his right and then his left out into the basin where they had their dockage, the wooden pier on the salt water estuary on the bay.

To fall and make a splash on such a quiet night might mean discovery. It would then be a simple matter for the guards to trace the radiating ripples on the still water's surface back to Freddy. He knew he could make it back around the bend and into the salt creek and into the dense tropical forest before the guards got across the water; he had seen the difficulty they had moving through the growth, and he was sure he could move through those thickets more quickly than they, but there would be no second chance to take the guards by surprise. He would be chased and they would post a watch. Without food and fuel he had the choice of being shot or starving.

****

Now he rested, watched and listened for a long while until he was sure of everything on the opposite side of the basin, twenty-five yards away.

Two men were outside the shack on a dock that was their sleeping quarters. One sat in a chair, reading a book by lantern light just outside the door of the shack. He would be easy. The other milled about, restless: perhaps on this island too long and wanting to leave. There seemed to be no method to his actions, he wasn't doing anything but pacing and fidgeting. He would be unpredictable. He walked off down a path farther inland.

It seemed that they were not aware yet that Wayne had brought Freddy with him to the island. The men sent out to search the shoreline for any other unwanted guests on the island must have given up and returned to base. Inside the cabin Freddy dared not guess what was going on, but it was the only likely place for Wayne to be. If Wayne could buy just a little more time Freddy might be able to get to him.

There was some activity farther into the woods. An engine started. Someone had started the generator. Freddy could see them now as lights came on around the compound - if you could call it that - the main building, the transmitter shack, and the storehouse on the pier. Two men at the generator. Now they headed for the transmitter shack. Judging from the size of the antenna tower standing over the transmitter shack and its obvious power requirements that wherever Sargento was, it wasn't close.

Two boats had been here earlier. There was only one now, forty yards from Freddy, tied up at the dock near the mouth of the basin before the bay with the bow pointed inland. The boat which had been closer to the back of the inlet was gone. Maybe looking for him, if Wayne had talked, or perhaps meeting another craft out in the Gulf. Whatever it was doing, it was bad news for Freddy. At least six men were living here, the four Freddy had seen and probably another two on the boat that was out. Freddy had hoped that somehow he could get them all at once, although he admitted to himself it was going to be hard to do with a knife and a water pistol.

He must get Wayne away from here, now, he couldn't wait, and there would be others returning who would pursue them. Assuming they got out.

Freddy was ready and alert and would never be more rested for what came next. Tired though his body was, it would only get worse from here. They might kill Wayne at any moment. He might be dead already, unless he bought time somehow. Wayne had told him not to try to bluff these people with the water pistol, but what else could he do unless he had a real gun? He had to try something.

He studied the dock. Rickety. Bolted four by fours framed the structure to which a deck of one inch planks were nailed. He looked at their boat. If he tried to escape in that it would take time to get the thing turned around, enough time to get shot. First he would have to make sure he disposed of all of them at this base and worry about the others later.

Getting to open water was another potential poser. Freddy had already gone aground on this island once. First he would get to Wayne, and then he would worry about the fine-tuning.

****

The two men in the transmitter room came out. They exchanged a few words with the fidgety one, and went into the shack. The restless man returned and walked out onto the pier where the boat was tied up and sat on one of those round, red, plastic, quick-disconnect auxiliary gas tanks similar to those that Wayne had appropriated for their pursuit. Good, he was a little out of the way. Why was he staring out to sea? Expecting someone? Was the other boat coming back?

Freddy had a rough idea of what he was going to do. He relaxed and breathed deeply to ready himself for the twenty-five yard underwater swim to the near end of the pier.

A shot cracked through the still of the night. The man in the chair started. He had looked close to being asleep before the shot was fired he had set his book down and leaned the chair against the shack on two legs. The man on the gas tank far down the dock turned his head briefly in the direction of the door of the shack, where the shot had come from, and then looked back to sea. Freddy's pulse quickened. Perhaps he had waited too long.

Maybe not. Nothing seemed to be happening. He calmed himself as well as he could and breathed out heavily several times, forcing the air from his lungs, suppressing the urge to breathe by driving the carbon dioxide from his body. He inhaled deeply and started out underwater for the other side.

Chapter Twenty-Seven - Sargento's Place

They had awakened at nine-thirty the previous morning when the sun's heat permeated the mangrove thicket in which the boat was nestled and its brilliance was no longer filtered and suffused by the low angle of attack of te sunrise the through the foliage. If there was any breeze to be had the foliage was preventing it from reaching them. The dawn birds hunkered down and had stopped chirping and darting through the leaves. The cloying air was close upon them, their clothes sweaty and sticking to their bodies.

Freddy stood and parted the branches where they were thinnest and looked out from under the canvas shards strung across the mangrove branches. Beyond the green leaves edged with the gold of the sun's brilliance a cormorant was swimming in the cove. Its body was below the surface of the water, its head held aloft by a long, curved neck as its alert eyes searched the water. The bird dove for a fish. Freddy watched for ninety seconds until the bird surfaced forty yards from his dive. Freddy smiled at the bird's diving prowess.

Wayne was up in the bow. Freddy spoke first as he plucked his clothes away from his skin to let some air between them.

"Ok, Wayne ol' buddy, whaddiya wanna do today?"

"Have breakfast," he said, moving from the area in front of the console where he had slept to the back of the boat. He rummaged through the stores. "We should go shopping soon." The supplies were going faster than Freddy thought they would. They still had four gallons of water, but they were about to finish the last of the orange juice, and the canned goods had to provide them with nourishment for the entire day. Freddy's previous thinking was in tune with providing provisions for day trips. Breakfast and dinner were never a factor for consideration. Wayne set some things on the console seat.

"We got crackers, we got liver pâté, we got some orange juice, and a can of crushed pineapple."

"In water?" Freddy asked, concerned that a fruit packed in syrup might be harmful, what with all that sugar.

"Yes, it's in water," Wayne was annoyed. "What are you worried about, your health? How good do you think beer is for you? "

This was too much, Wayne attacking his favorite beverage in this manner. "It's got plenty of food value," Freddy responded, which it did. "And magnesium and potassium."

"Freddy---"

"It's made from barley and corn---"

"Freddy, just eat the damn pineapple. You may need what sugar it does have for energy very soon." Wayne opened the cans. He insisted that they did not ration themselves. In his words: "If we get off this island alive it will be soon, we're not outfitted for a long siege against a well-fed, well-armed mob. If we don't succeed in neutralizing them right away we'll be dead anyway. We won't need the food. Might as well keep our strength up." Freddy was tired of arguing about such things and had long since stopped. They ate their pâté. Freddy never dreamed that they had such ritzy friends. He never dreamed he would be eating pâté in the wild, either. What a picnic this turned out to be. They discussed what they would do next. Freddy listened intently.

"Well, Fred, I figure it this way," said Wayne with a thoughtful look on his face, pâté and cracker poised at his mouth, "there are several things we have to do. We have to find out where Sargento is. We have to make sure these guys don't get off this island. And we have to find out where the hell we are." He finally put the cracker and its load of pâté in his mouth. Jaws working, he continued. "But what we have to do foremost, is steal some gas and fuel this thing up. Ready? Let's go."

"Go where?" Freddy asked. He had assumed that they were going to wait for nightfall, and diffidently inquired about the prudence of leaving the confines of the mangrove-shrouded boat and going out in broad daylight, footloose and fancy free, to borrow some gas from the neighbors. Maybe they had coffee ready also; Freddy would have appreciated that. Wayne, however, obviously was serious. He strapped his knife to his leg and got the gun from the dry storage area under the console.

"Well, come *on*," he exhorted, and gave Freddy an impatient look. "We have to do this now," he continued didactically, "Or it's going to drag on forever. Time is our enemy. Our best chance is to get this whole thing over with as soon as we can." He grabbed one of the eighteen gallon tanks and unstrapped it from the inside of the hull. "Get one on the other side, Freddy, let's go steal some gas."

"Wayne!" Freddy wheezed, "Do we have to *carry* those? It must be a mile and a half!" Of course they did, as Freddy knew. If they could get the console tank full they might have enough gas to get somewhere. And they would need the daylight to see what they were doing on this island whose layout and vegetation were unknown to them. They couldn't very well push the boat over to Sargento's lair and help themselves to their gas.

"Never mind." said Freddy.

"OK, Freddy, let's take two tanks each. If we can take four empties in we can conceal two in the mangroves on the side of the creek opposite their camp while we hustle two full ones back to the boat. That will stretch out our logistics, but it will limit our exposure in their camp. We don't want them to be aware of us before we're ready to deal with them."

****

Wayne walked in front. They walked in the water, to hide the tracks, and made their way east and south toward the others. To try to get through the woods inland for the whole distance would be senseless - the birds and the snakes were having a hard enough time.

Freddy followed Wayne several yards back. His job was to watch the water and keep looking behind them, and Wayne was to watch out ahead and make sure there was nothing but woods to their right. Wayne was carrying the heavy and cumbersome tanks by a piece of nylon webbing in one hand as he walked, gun in his belt, seven or eight feet of mysterious quarter-inch flexible hose coiled in his other hand. Where he had gotten it Freddy did not know, although he suspected that Wayne had used it before. Freddy kept changing the tanks he carried from one hand to the other, sometimes carrying them with both hands. They were heavy, and carrying them was not comfortable. How they would get the full cans back Freddy could not guess, even if they left two of them behind for another trip.

Freddy was also in charge of the binoculars. They hung around his neck, and the strap chafed at the skin above the collar-less sweatshirt he got from Cap'n Walter. He now wished Walter had given him something lighter.

They continued this way until they reached the right curve that brought them to the island's southeastern shore. The bay was a couple of tenths of a mile away. Wayne motioned to slow down, then signaled Freddy up beside him. "Tracks," he said. There was a pair of footsteps in the sand. They had come this far, turned around returned to where they had come from.

"Do you think it could be somebody just out for a walk?" Freddy asked.

"No. The walk is too purposeful. The track is too straight. They must patrol the beach now and then, but they obviously don't go too far from camp. We have to consider the chance that they may know we are here. It doesn't seem likely, though, if they only came this far." They went up to the edge of the woods, walking lightly on rocks and shells to cover their trail. From this point on they moved through the not-as-dense cover of the edge of the woods, just inside the line of scrubby trees and brush. At some point they would spot the compound, and they didn't want to be seen first.

It was quite a while of slow going before they saw it, although the actual distance wasn't far. Their vantage point was a place where the shore stuck out into the bay enough to give them a glimpse of Sargento's setup. There was a basin where two boats were docked, one behind the other. The basin, deeper water fed by one of those natural channels like the one they had been in last night, was set deep into the center of the bay. The channel that fed it was one that went all of the way into the island without ending prematurely, unlike the one they found last night.

They saw why the basin and encampment would be hard to see from the sea. It was angled in to the west and south of the channel's approach from the open water, a tight switchback. Freddy looked through the binoculars. There was some activity in the clearing beyond the dock, two men were opening crates and packing small items in them. Past the men, almost at the limit of the clearing and before the start of the dense greenery was a small, wooden building with a radio transmitter's antenna behind it. A few yards from where the men were working was a larger wooden building which must have been their living quarters. Closest to them was the dock, a pier of wooden planking with a shack erected on the end nearest to them. The two boats at the dock were identical sleek-looking craft with Cutty cabins. Wayne took a turn at the binoculars. "Now where do you suppose they would keep extra gas for an emergency?" Wayne asked rhetorically, peering over the binoculars with a thoughtful squint. "Near the dock and away from the living quarters, of course! Freddy follow me and look sharp. Stay in the woods and don't go near any footpaths. Try not to break any branches, we're going to look inside that shed by the dock. That same tucked-away basin that is giving them cover from being seen from the sea is going to cover our approach. As long as we don't jump up and down on the beach we should not be seen."

They swung inland, enough to make their way toward the dock and shed. Sure enough, as Wayne had foreseen, there was a foot track a small way inland, for what purpose they did not know. Perhaps it went to an outhouse. They had to get inland enough to where the strangled watercourse at the shallow end of the bay was narrow and an easy crossing. The fuel dock was mostly unattended, but should someone venture in the direction of the shack two men pulling floating red fuel tanks would be a dead giveaway, like shooting ducks in a barrel. Floating the tanks under the cover of the vegetation overhanging the far side shore would find the two at their most vulnerable for the whole of the refueling operation. The hard part physically would be humping the full tanks back to the near side over the spit of land and close to their cove.

Wayne was good at this. He said nothing, moved well, was agile and adept at not banging the gas tanks into everything he passed. Freddy felt clumsy and inept. He hoped that it was just his perception of himself with his senses in an overly sensitized state.

The apex of the narrowing triangle of underbrush ended up ahead at the ingress of the footpath which parted them from the more vast central island growth. No one had as yet used the path since they had arrived. They crouched. They were still far from the workmen.

"What now, Wayne?" Freddy whispered.

"See what those guys are doing, Freddy?" he said, gesturing to the two men packing crates. "Those white bags could be coke. What they're doing is putting the stuff into crates with something else in it, something smelly, like coffee or perfume. Then they ship the stuff with other crates of the same thing." Freddy was about to ask him how he knew that but he decided it was a silly question. Wayne went on. "I'm betting this island is placed just far enough from some convenient spot or the Gulf coast of Mexico or South or Central America to be remote from sea and air traffic, and near enough for their small boats to bring the contraband here. Pretty clever. It cuts them out from the operation at the other end - persons or agencies checking ports of export would find nothing wrong that would lead them to this place. Hard to trace where the goods are going from either end. No exchanges of contraband at sea in places where a radar screen might catch two blips together. If the guys he deals with down south or in the States get infiltrated or busted they can't easily follow the trail to here, nobody knows where his operation is based, and he does his transfers here. And I'm sure he has other gambits and fail-safes to get his goods into the States."

"Do you think they are dealing in other things besides cocaine?" Freddy asked.

"Certainly. Sargento likes to diversify, to run as many gambits as he can. Think of him as a broker, for any type of drugs, art, whether its black market pre-Colombian or fake Chinese jade. Gems, pearls, stolen goods, technology, - anything. He delivers and takes a percentage. He'd like to spread out into other areas again. He wants to be a conglomerate in the criminal world. He seeks power and influence; a God damned turtle in a business suit, just like the corporate heads of big business. Only difference is that his brain took a wrong turn; he learned the ways of the mob family early in life, and the power scrambled his brain. He could quit right now and be well off for the rest of his life, but he doesn't want to. It's part of the way he is, the way he is made. He's a fanatic, a psychopath." Freddy believed him. It saddened him to realize the changes in Wayne that his association with Sargento had caused.

Again, following Wayne's lead, they moved closer to the dock. Staying low to the edge of the woods, they crawled through the brush that grew right up to the water's edge at the shoreward end of the dock. They slid like snakes silently into the water. Not for the last time. There was enough daytime activity to mask what little sound they made. They worked their way carefully out toward the camp and stopped under the dock, gas tanks floating. The supply shack was above their heads.

The door of the shack faced outward, toward the boats and away from the compound. Wayne intended to go in and look around. Instructing Freddy to keep his gun dry and handing him the coil of hose, Wayne reached his hands up onto the dock. Using Freddy's shoulder for a step, he went up and edged his way forward on elbows and knees to lie on the pier with the shack between him and the shore. "Wayne, what if it's locked?" Freddy called up softly. He could here Wayne thinking.

"Freddy, don't be silly, why lock it out here in the middle of the Gulf of wherever we are?" Freddy had another question.

"Wayne, what if somebody comes onto the dock?"

"Shoot them. Now shut up." Freddy did. Freddy looked at the gun with displeasure. It had a slick feel and a sharp, oily smell to it. Not at all like his water pistol. Its weight felt dangerous.

Wayne stood, staying close to the shack, opened the door enough to get in but not so much that its swing could be seen from the compound, went in and closed the door behind him. Time passed.

"Freddy.... Freddy."

"Here I am, Wayne."

"See my finger?" He had stuck it through a chink in the back corner of the shed. "Pass the end of the hose through here." Freddy did so and waited. There were dull metal sounds, the hollow reverberation of the movement of empty steel drums, the muted timpani of others partially filled with liquid. Then most of the hose pulled through the chink, up into the shed. Wayne emerged and returned to the water as furtively as he had gone up. He looked at the end of the hose and frowned. There was less than a foot of it hanging below the bottom of the dock. "What we got here, Freddy, is a shed with some tools and spare parts, some "C" rations and five fifty-five gallon drums. The three nearest the corner above us are gasoline. I don't know what the others are, and I don't care; the ones in the corner could not have been placed more perfectly."

"You mean to say that something actually went right?" Freddy asked.

"Had to happen sooner or later. Anyway," he continued, "I rotated the drum over us until the smaller bung, the vent bung, was facing the back corner of the shed, and then removed it and stuck the hose in - it was a tight fit - and I threw a tarp over the back of the drum so the hose can't be seen and I loosened the bigger bung. If the wind doesn't change and blow the gas smell to them, maybe we can siphon off some of their gas." He was right about the gas smell, it was pungent. If the wind changed the others might notice the smell of the vapors. The weather looked good right now, but in the tropics at that time of year, you never could be sure what the weather might do.

"Wayne, that hose is awfully high, don't you think?"

"I know. I stuck the hose more than half way down the drum, maybe two feet. Then it had to go three feet to the floor and then out the chink and down here. It was only eight feet long to begin with. It's not right for this application."

Freddy assumed the application Wayne meant was stealing gasoline from boat docks. It must be the way he fueled Freddy's boat before the outset of this adventure.

"So *that's* why there's only a foot danglin' down!"

"Boy Freddy, you sure are a quick study."

"Well, how can we fill the cans?" Freddy didn't like the look of the smile on Wayne's face. He opened one of the big cans and placed it on Freddy's shoulder so that it would be high enough to reach the hose. Then he drew a suction on the siphon hose until gas came out. "That's kinda slow, Wayne, this will take forever." There wasn't enough difference between the high and low end of the hose, but it was the best they could do.

Freddy sat in the water with the tank on his shoulder and his hands on the sides of it to steady it as it filled slowly. "Are you sure this is unleaded, Wayne?" Wayne was out of retorts. He smiled maliciously instead of answering.

Freddy's arms and shoulder ached as the can got heavier. They breathed the musty smell of wet vegetation under the dock as it mixed with the gasoline vapors while slats of light burning through the cracks in the shrunken planking above them moved slowly across the dark water.

In about an hour and a quarter Wayne deemed that there was enough gas in the can. He did not want them totally full for some reason. Still, close to 18 gallons of gas is very heavy when it's in a tank cutting into your shoulder. Then it was Wayne's turn. Freddy waited and kept watch while another tank filled. One time somebody came out onto the dock and went aboard one of the boats. They both hoped the wet spot Wayne left on the pier had dried enough in the tropical sun to go unnoticed. Shadow steps sounded above them as dark footfalls moved over the interstices in the deck. Freddy and Wayne remained very still. There was a flush of the boat's head, and then the man left. "I was afraid of that," Freddy said, and he tried to judge if the current was running, and which way.

Eventually Wayne's tank was full enough, and he put the cap on it and tied the siphon hose in a knot. "I was afraid of that, too," said Freddy. Wayne inquired what Freddy was afraid of now. That you're going back up there to switch drums"

"Right! The drum we're in now is too low"

"And then what" "Are we coming back for more gas? How many trips do you think we'll need to make?"

He closed the vent on the gas can. "Only two more, Freddy. I don't believe that we are all that far from some major land mass. If we were they'd have more gas on hand. This trip and the next one to recover the two tanks stashed in the mangroves will get us seventy-two gallons, and that should take us pretty far, so long as we're running at an efficient speed on a not-too-rough sea and not bucking a storm. We're going to have to find their charts also, so we can get out of here with an idea of where we are headed. We have to tap into another drum up there, though, we can't siphon this one to the bottom, the hose is too short. Another thing - I want to move on them tonight. That will be the third trip. The longer we wait, the farther Sargento can be, and the longer we wait, the better their chances of finding us out." This last was with a nod to the compound. "They could find us at any moment; all it would take is a little bad luck."

"Wouldn't it be better to steal their boat then to steal their gas?"

"If the opportunity arises, we might be able to. You deserve a new boat anyway. That's the best case scenario, to get away in one of their boats intact, with charts, electronics, and fuel." The thought pleased Freddy and he grinned widely, but then he snapped back to the grim reality of the past few days. "Freddy, we can't count on being able to steal one of their boats, and we can't count on their boats surviving the conflagration I have planned for this camp, so we'll have to get yours gassed up." Made sense to Freddy.

They siphoned more gas. This time Wayne had to jockey the gas drum they had used previously out of its place in the corner and move the full one next to it into that position, the only place from which the hose was long enough to repeat the painfully slow siphon process they had done earlier in the day. They were done sooner than they anticipated and started back. The job went more smoothly now that they knew the terrain and were practiced in what they had to do.

"Wayne, how are we going to get these cans back? They must weigh a hundred and twenty pounds each!" "First we carry them through the woods. And don't break any branches!"

Freddy thought of doing this twice and then coming back to start a fight. They were never going to make it.

****

They floated! Wayne tied some cord he produced from his shirt pocket to the gas cans and he towed them along in the water behind them. The small air pocket in the top was enough to keep them upright. The hardest part had been crawling up the bank with the near-full cans. Carrying them through the woods until they were back to the water was no fun either, but the distance was short. Now they were wading back in the water. This part was not bad at all. Wayne insisted that they keep a good watch, so they could take cover if anybody happened by. The tanks might not be seen - they floated just above the water's surface. Freddy wondered how Wayne had known they would do that. Probably a lucky guess. They made it back to the boat uneventfully and dumped the gas into the boat's console tank. It was near three in the afternoon.

The first gas run was over, and it was time for lunch. They and ate the remainder of their stores, a large can of Dinty Moore beef stew - the label had come off but Freddy could tell what it was by the greasy looking thumb print on the top - and a tin of Vienna sausages. They finished the rest of the orange juice as well, and Wayne put the empty bottle with three other bottles he had saved into a musty, rotted shirt he found in the forward gear locker. It had been left on the boat and forgotten until it degenerated into a boat rag. He tied the four corners of the shirt around the bottles, making a pouch out of the shirt, and he tied the ends of the sleeves together, making a carry strap. By three-twenty they were headed back to for the other tanks. They were there by four. Wayne left the four empty bottles wrapped in the shirt under some palm fronds near where they had stashed the other two tanks they had stashed earlier at the base of a prominent palm not far from the path, one that had a horizontal run of several feet before it started skyward. Some time in its youth it must have started keeling over in a storm. It must have had the tenacity to resist being uprooted, and the temerity to continue growing at that crazy angle long after the storm was dead. The tree was at the edge of the woods, on the bank of the creek facing the camp across the water, and the start of their final struggle over the spit of land to their point of entry for the long walk in the water back to the cove and the boat. They dug out the tanks.

"Freddy, get me those juice bottles, would you please?" Freddy went to do as he was asked. He returned with the bottles and set them down in a small clearing bordering on a small stand of cypress near a tidal pond. Wayne asked him to bring a gas tank over. When he returned he saw that Wayne had torn the tail of the shirt the bottles had been wrapped in into four strips. Then he took his knife from its sheath strapped to his leg and punctured the top of each juice bottle with a narrow slash. He stuffed the strips of cloth through the holes he had made in the bottle tops, and filled each of the bottles three-quarters full of gasoline from one on the gas cans, with Freddy's help. "Cocktail, anyone?" he quipped. Oh, that Wayne was so smart. An idea of what he intended to do ignited in Freddy's brain.

"Wayne, what are we going to do after we finish gassing the boat?" He confirmed Freddy's guess.

"We have to get into their living quarters, find out where Sargento and Connors are, find out where we are, get some charts from their boat, and burn the whole place down. I don't think we can do it without killing them, and that's fine with me. They deserve to be dead." Freddy agreed in theory with his plan, but Wayne's grim bitterness scared him. Freddy didn't think Wayne would ever be the same. There must be other ways they could go about this without killing everyone here, less drastic ways. They could take a prisoner; this footpath would be a good place to do it. They could wait for one of them to come by on his way to the bathroom or something. Or they could steal a boat, disable their transmitter and the other boat, radio for help and then head for Colombia. The boat registration and the charts on board should give them an idea where to start looking for Sargento. Wayne said something and interrupted Freddy's thoughts.

"Freddy, I'm going to hide those fire-bombs back by the palm tree. Start back with one of the tanks and I'll straighten up around here, then we'll finish fueling the boat and come back here and check our options. I'm sure those cocktails are going to come in handy." Freddy finished speculating on how they should go about reaching their end result. He kept his thoughts to himself and started for the leaning palm. Wayne said he would be coming along soon, was going to make what he euphemistically called a nature call.

****

Freddy was almost far enough away from Wayne for the foliage to obscure his vision when he heard noises. Someone was coming down the footpath from the direction of the compound. Freddy realized too late that he had left Wayne with the other gas tank. It would be too much for one man to run through the woods with even one of them and expect to escape undetected. Freddy knew there was not enough cover next to the path for Wayne to hide with any hope that they would not see him as they passed. Freddy slid under the canopy of a tall Sea Grape tree whose big leaves extended right down to the forest floor and covered his bright red gas tank with leaf litter to wait until he could see what his options were to come to Wayne's aid.

Things were not all that bleak; if Wayne had wanted a prisoner, now was his chance. Freddy was sure Wayne could handle just about anyone Sargento could put up against him single-handed.

Freddy squatted low and looked through the bushes as best he could. Wayne was still there where he had been, near the salt pond where he had gone to relieve himself. This was puzzling, knowing how alert Wayne was. Why wasn't he doing something? Of course he was doing something; Freddy just couldn't see what it was. Wayne was low to the ground and appeared to be moving something - a tree trunk - into the salt pond. No, of course not. He was hiding the gas tank. He then crouched behind what little cover there was and waited for his visitor.

Whoever it was he was very noisy. He was making enough of a racket for several people. Then they rounded the corner in the footpath, four of them, moving clumsily down the narrow path through the woods, carrying crates. Freddy and Wayne had been very wrong, there was something more than an outhouse or signal post or observation point at the end of the path, and Wayne was in trouble.

****

Wayne had no chance. He did not even bother to spring on them. He stood.

Freddy could not see clearly, but by the way they stopped cold and the change in the set of their shoulders, the way their heads lifted and moved back, showed they were clearly surprised. Connors said, "Well, look who we have here! I was hoping that you might be dead. You're rather noisome, you know. If I hadn't seen you I might have smelled you. Rather careless of you to be caught short like this, Teddy. I expect that you found our little shack filled with valuables. The pre-Colombian art fakes are particularly interesting. They'll fetch a good price in New York. I expect also that you were thinking of stealing some of it, just as you stole that money to be laundered that we entrusted to your care." So *that* was what was at the end of this damned path. There was a shack down there somewhere containing their stolen goods and contraband. One more precaution they had taken in case somehow someone took the trouble to try to land a boat on this island with its forbidding natural defenses. They kept the "merchandise" out of sight when they were not working with it or transporting it "I admit you don't give up easily," said Connors as Wayne stood calmly by the side of the path, I thought killing your trollop might upset you enough to make you do something rash back on that damnable little island of the primitives of Key West." Wayne stayed calm. The gathering darkness hid the rush of red under Wayne's skin, already sun-reddened through the bronze of his tan, but Freddy could feel him seething. He kept his eyes steady on Connors.

"Who else is with you?" Connors barked. The sudden, imperious question shouted by Connors startled Freddy, but Wayne stood very still, then answered Connors almost casually.

"Who else is there to come with me? Everyone from our old school days is dead except me, and my friend went into hiding somewhere. He's a fugitive, and I'm all that's left, thanks to you."

"You will please accompany us back to our little domicile." Connors had returned to his civilized way of speaking. Freddy realized the previous outburst was merely a device Connors had cultivated somewhere along the line to browbeat people and extract information from them. Connors must have known it wouldn't work with Wayne. "We want to talk to you about the money you owe us. We want to talk to you about what you have told the authorities, and we want to know who else that you have been consorting with knows of us." Wayne had told Freddy there was no money. They would kill him, eventually, when they were sure they could get nothing out of him. They would kill him anyway, probably take pleasure in it. Freddy had to think of something while Wayne bought time painfully. Connors spoke again: "You two - patrol the shoreline. See if there is anyone else on this island." The two men he motioned to hesitated.

"But Mr. Connors, that could take---"

"I don't care how long it takes, do it now."

"Can we bring some food and---"

"**Now!**" They cowered, said no more, and left, leaving the path and plunging into the woods, thrashing clumsily toward the shoreline near the bay. They moved through the dense undergrowth as city men would do, unused to passing through the jungle. Wayne spoke, perhaps too quickly, although Freddy doubted that anyone but he caught it. The two men stopped to listen to the exchange.

"There is no one else here. Why would there be? And if there were what could they do, run around the island and get back here someway?" Wayne was giving Freddy instructions. "I suppose your waterfront resort has a secret back door. For Christ's sake, you've got an army here," he said derisively, as if to scorn them, imply that they were afraid of their own shadow. They were men used to power, used to bluster among their peers and meek subservience from their subalterns and subordinates. It was the diplomacy of their occupation. They were not accustomed to such brazen behavior from a captive aware of his impending doom. This conditioned in them a blind spot to such goading, so that they missed the message Wayne encrypted into his tirade and concealed in his bravado. Connors looked askance at Wayne, as though he hadn't entirely bought Wayne's speech. He nodded to his men to proceed with their search. He would make sure. Freddy was already on his way.

He left the gas tank concealed where it was under the Sea Grape tree and slipped silently through the woods toward the cove. Wayne had told him what to do. He had to find the back door. That was it! There was a back door, a way across the island. Why had he not thought of it before? With all of the shallows and creeks around this place, there must be a quite a current at changes of tide. He must look for a cut all of the way across the island for the current to run. They'd seen no evidence of one, but they had not made it all of the way to the other side of the island. The island was barely above sea level. A big storm could easily have inundated the place at one time and started a channel across the island. In fact it was a probability, it was the norm. Then he remembered. There had been a strong trace of moving water at the farthest extent of their proposed circumnavigation of the island, running straight from the island. That was the evidence of the cross-island creek, and perhaps a new ingress for Freddy's net foray against his foes. Freddy had to stay ahead of these men who knew this small part of the island better than he but were deplorably inept in the wilds. Freddy doubted that they knew much about the island beyond the area close to their encampment. He must run in the water to leave no tracks and still keep ahead of them, try to stay out of sight. And if they did pick up Freddy's trail, just let them try to track Freddy through the mangroves. It was a game of tag again, and Freddy was not going to be "it." Then he had to get back to Wayne before they killed him.

Chapter Twenty-Eight – Confrontation

After the long night traversing the island by creek and forest Freddy was poised for his swim to the dock. Freddy swam slowly to use less oxygen. It wasn't twenty-five yards across the water to the dock; it should have been an easy swim but the demands on his system recently and the sound of the shot made his anxious heart squander the air in his lungs. He must break the surface silently on the other side, it would not do to splash or gasp loudly as he came to the surface, and it was imperative that he do it under the dock, not in open water. The man seated on the chair at the other end was just thirty feet away....

It had been a hard trip the long way round, but he had found the other end of the salt creek which crossed the island. He found it 300 yards or so past the cove where his boat was nestled, in the direction away from the compound and away from the area they were concerned with; away from the area they had explored. The prudent course of action had there been time and resources enough was to study the entire island, but in their current capacity that had not been an option. Now Freddy was in the water yet again. The creek during his island traverse was clearly defined enough that it had not fizzled out into a sheet flow overtopping a substrate of mangroves, which would have made direction finding in the dark a guessing game, and was covered enough by a canopy of mangrove that is was wholly prohibitive for exploration by boat. It was not an excursion that the thugs would likely do unless under extreme duress. From their side of the creek, looking into the dark mangrove forest, the crooks no doubt thought that a traverse across the island was impossible. In fact, it was likely that the notion had not even occurred to them.

The light filtering through the water above him dimmed slightly. He reckoned that was close to the dock side of the little bay. Freddy groped for whatever lay before him.

Instead of touching the slick grass bottom sloping up at the far shore, Freddy swam into one of the pilings supporting the dock, hitting it with his left shoulder. He hoped that the hooligan hunkered down in the chair above him was enough of a dullard not to notice the inevitable slight shudder of the wooden deck due to his collision with the support for the platform. Striking the piling caused a short spasm of pain and a transitory increase in energy as he convulsed. He spun sideways, his legs went askew and he started broaching. His head was below his feet. With considerable effort he suppressed an impulse to kick hard to regain depth and he managed to avoid kicking his higher leg above the pond's surface. He walked himself down the piling with his hands, righted himself, and came up slowly, breaking the surface of the water with nary a ripple like a frog who rises just enough to get his eyes out of the water for a look around. He was back in Bucks County under the dock, playing tag at the Goose Pond. His childhood had come back to him. He rose until he could see the man at the end of the boat pier. He was still staring seaward. Freddy rose higher to look above the shoreline weeds. The man in the chair near the door of the shack was leaning on the two back legs. He seemed to be slipping back into sleep.

There was no cover between Freddy and the twenty feet to the shack door. Knife strapped to his leg, fake Walther PPK in what was left of his pants after the tearing journey across the island; Freddy slowly stepped out of the water and began circling around the shack toward the side of the shack facing island's interior, eager to be out of the direct line of sight of the sleeping cretin. As he was increasing the distance from the back of the man on the boat pier the man near him stirred in his chair but remained on the hind legs and rubbed his nose with the back of his forearm. He had only to open his eyes and turn and he could not fail to Freddy. Freddy drew the knife from its sheath and held it by the blade and stopped dead in a motionless crouch, ready to throw. The man settled back to sleep.

Freddy slipped the knife back into its sheath. He kept circling to his left until he was at the side of the shack farthest from the man on the pier and out of sight of the man in the chair. He was near a window. He heard a voice familiar voice talking.

"Teddy, we're gonna hurt you some more if you don't tell us where the money is. I got two bullets waitin' for ya, and my partner here gets to work on ya with his knife. I'll give ya the first shot now, the one that hurts. Tell me what I want, then you can have the other." Freddy had to make a move. First, he had to get past the man at the door.

The man sat, sleeping, facing the water. Sneaking behind him from the corner of the building, Freddy again drew the knife with his right hand and put it to the man's throat, clasping his left hand over the man's mouth at the same time. "Don't move," he whispered. The man did not heed Freddy's warning. Freddy could feel him start thrashing about and he bit Freddy's hand as they fought for control of the knife. The chair leaned forward on one front leg as they struggled and the man pulled a hidden knife from a scabbard between his shoulder blades.

Freddy had no choice. He pressed the steel blade into the flesh of the man's neck and drew the knife across the man's throat. As he eased the lifeless body to the ground the chair righted itself, its momentum carrying the back of the chair into the wall of the shack with a bang.

Freddy had to keep moving in the uncertainty of the moment while he still had the initiative.

He searched quickly for the dead man's weapon. Surprisingly, the body at his feet had **no gun!** Still, all Freddy had was a knife and a fake water pistol. With no time for hesitation, against Wayne's advice, and with more than a few doubts of his own Freddy drew the water pistol from his belt and kicked in the door.

****

Freddy burst through the door and found two men standing over Wayne. He was lying on the floor at the back of the room. A desk with a lamp on it was to Freddy's right, near Wayne's head. It had anchors embossed on a pale, brown shade that imparted a dismal glow to the room. The window was to Freddy's left, at Wayne's feet. He had been severely beaten, but there was no gunshot wound that Freddy could see.

There was one man on either side of Wayne. One of them was Greenjeans, the giant Wayne had cold-cocked with an ashtray at the Casa Marina. He undoubtedly harbored a hatred for Wayne. He stood at Wayne's head. The other, a normal-sized man Freddy had not seen before but seemingly dwarfed standing shadowed from the light by the bigger man, was at Wayne's feet. They looked up as Freddy made his entrance, water pistol at his side. They did not appear to be too frightened. Wayne took one look at the water pistol and sighed.

"Wayne, are you OK?" Freddy asked, not taking his eyes off Wayne's warders.

"Of course not, Freddy."

Freddy looked at the men's faces. They seemed amused. Greenjeans spoke.

"Looks like ya got the drop on us, *squirt!*" He laughed heartily at his joke. "What brought ya so quick, the shot? We din't shoot him yet. Not 'till he tells us where the money is. Then he gets one in the belly, and we cut a cupla' his fingers off, later he gets one in the head. That shot was just to scare him a little, ya know?"

The big, ugly brute didn't seem worried by Freddy's presence at all. Couldn't he see the gun? The two of them were poised to grab their own guns, real firearms, but they were in no hurry and Freddy was careful not to make any sudden moves that would force their hand. But Freddy's bluff wasn't working. They were making fun of him.

"Wayne, we're getting out of here."

"Why ya leavin' so soon?" asked Greenjeans. "Ya only just got here. I see ya got past that dummy at the door. Is he dead? I doubt it, you ain't got the guts." If Freddy had a real gun he might have shot them then, though he knew they thought he didn't have the nerve. Maybe they were right. Or maybe they had been right once, Freddy was not sure. It was the kind of thing that had to be put to the test.

"Stick around," coaxed Greenjeans, "let's talk."

"No, thanks, I don't talk to druggers."

"*Druggers?*" he said, "I'm hurt. We ain't *druggers!* Let's say we deal in pharmaceuticals, among other things."

"You own a drug store?"

"No, we're commercial. Wholesale, ya might say." Greenjeans was apparently amused with himself. Freddy let him go on talking as he tried to hide his nervousness and stall for time until he could figure a way to get Wayne out of there. Greenjeans continued toying with him.

"We sell to people who fill their own - prescriptions. Street vendors, achally, at the - uh - grassroots level, like hot dogs. In fact, some of those guys probly *do* sell hot dogs!" He laughed at his own joke again. This was great fun. And Freddy had thought that he was stupid. Freddy was feeling ill.

"Got any free samples?" Freddy asked, "I'm getting a headache. I need a couple of aspirins."

"Aspirins!" he echoed, as he tilted his head and gazed comically at the ceiling. "I don't think we sell that one." Then he turned a hard look on Freddy. "But I can get ya enough of something that will kill your headache - permanently."

"Gee, thanks no, I like to keep my mind sharp."

"You're already too late for that; ya lost your mind when ya came in here." He was getting more menacing now. With that last remark, Freddy raised the water pistol and aimed it at him. Who did he think he was fooling with, anyway? Greenjeans laughed.

"What are ya gonna do with that, squirt me?" So that was his big joke, he knew the gun was fake.

"We know that's a water gun, stupid. Are ya so stupid ya din't know we searched that dump ya live in?" He called *Freddy* stupid. Well, maybe he was. But he didn't live in a dump. This wasn't the Hilton Greenjeans was living in; he had no room to talk. Greenjeans continued. "You Joe College types think you're so smart."

"Who, me?" Freddy was genuinely astonished. Greenjeans grinned broadly, moving slowly and deliberately for the gun stuck in the top of his pants - a place Freddy would think twice about putting a gun, a real one, anyway. Greenjeans was relishing every moment of this.

"Fun's over, Now I'm gonna kill ya."

As his huge hand covered the grip of the gun stuck in his pants Freddy's eyes moved one last time to Wayne. He had that look in his eyes again, ready for unbridled action. There was nothing he could do. He did it anyway. Wayne reached for Greenjeans' leg in a last desperate effort to keep him from shooting Freddy. The other, smaller, normal-sized thug kicked Wayne hard in the shoulder, collapsing him to the floor. Greenjeans merely paused to look down at Wayne and shrugged disdainfully, as though the futile gesture was insignificant, and with this closed his big hand over the grip of the gun once more. Turning back to Freddy, he began to draw it from his pants. It kept coming out for a long time - it was a very big gun. Through Wayne's eyes, through his pain, Freddy saw final despair and acceptance of their fate.

Then Wayne noticed something. Maybe Freddy's look changed, got harder. As Greenjeans finished pulling the enormous piece from his pants Freddy raised the brass water pistol to hip level. Wayne became alert. Perhaps he saw the corrosive bubbles at the tip of its barrel and knew what Freddy was going to do. Freddy raised the barrel still higher and with a straight took careful aim. As Greenjeans brought his own gun to bear Freddy shot with his arm fully extended. The stream of near-pure sulfuric acid hit the outsized man's eyes.

Greenjeans wailed like a bear with his head in a beehive. As he did so his hands went to his face and he dropped his cannon. While the other man looked confused, not comprehending what had just happened, Wayne retrieved the gun and shot the smaller man twice, fast, once in the stomach and once in the head. Then he shot Greenjeans the same way. He looked at Freddy and for a brief instant Freddy saw Wayne's grim smile of approval of his course of action.

"Wayne," Freddy said, "there's another one out there at the far end of the pier, maybe fifty yards. He'll be here any second." Wayne said nothing, motioned to the gun in the shoulder holster of the smaller corpse and then to the door. Freddy understood. He took the gun and watched the door, hoping there was nothing he had to flip on the gun to get it to work. He found a do-hicky near the trigger and pushed it forward.

Wayne still lay where he was with the bigger man's gun pointed at the boards below the window sill. He was silent, immobile. There was a noise from outside, near the window. Still Wayne waited. Then, as the top of a head just started to rise over the window sill, Wayne fired. Wood fragments flew from below the window frame as four close-spaced shots angled upward from the floor passed through the flimsy boards to where what was left of the rest the man's head had to be. After a delay they heard the body fall. It must have been in the air for a time before hitting the ground.

"I think you got him, Wayne," Freddy said queasily. Freddy was damn sure he got him. As soon as this was all over he was going to be nauseous again. Wayne spoke for the first time since Freddy had asked him his condition all of three minutes ago.

"Freddy, where's the other boat. Is the other boat still out there?"

"It's at the far end of the pier where it was yesterday."

"Ok, then, that should be all of them here. I haven't seen any of the other four since they left on the closer boat last night. Connors was with them." He reached over and searched the dead men for something he wanted, then tried to get up and failed. "Freddy, I think I have some broken ribs. Would you mind helping me up? I don't want to puncture a lung." He handed Freddy the matches and a lighter he had taken from the corpses. "You are going to torch this place, Freddy. You'll need these. They won't miss them. They were smoking too much anyway. Might as well include arson to the things you are learning here at summer camp and make your training complete. Do you remember where the gas cans and the fire bombs are?" Freddy nodded yes. "Douse everything. Start with their cache of drugs and stolen goods at the end of the footpath."

"Do the transmitter next, then this shack. Make it back to the boat as quick as you can. We have to get out of here; I think the other boat dropped Connors off at sea. It will be coming back. Get me to their boat and I'll get it started." They started for the boat at the dock's end.

Freddy got Wayne to the boat and went to do as he said. He jumped from the dock and ran down the footpath. They should have known it wasn't an outhouse that was back there when the flushings from the boat floated past him earlier yesterday. Neither Wayne nor Freddy expected an armed party to be coming down the path and that was their mistake. A major mistake. If they had known better much of Wayne's suffering might have been avoided.

At the point where Wayne had been taken by Sargento's men Freddy turned off to the right and found his way to the salt pond where Wayne had left the nearly full tank of gas he had been carrying. It was still there, pinned under the fallen palm tree trunk Wayne had placed on top of them. Freddy then worked his way farther from the path and into the woods to retrieve the juice bottles Wayne had filled with gasoline from their place near the leaning palm. Lastly he brought the tank he had been carrying back from its nest under the Sea Grapes. Slinging the old shirt containing the juice bottle-bombs around his neck by its sleeves that were tied at the cuff, Freddy took one can in each hand and struggled, half running, half waddling, to drag the heavy tanks back to the path. From there he took one of the tanks and went as quickly as he could with the gas bombs swinging from side to side from his neck to the shack at the end of the path that went inland. He set the containers of the volatile liquid well away from the shack and went to take a look inside before he burnt Sargento's illicit stores.

The door was wooden boards, like everything else built on this island, secured by a simple cast iron latch. He lifted the latch and entered the shack.

Inside he found a double headed metal tool for opening crates, a square hammer at one end with a forked pry bar for pulling nails at the other. He prized open the closest crate. Perfume, and cocaine, in small plastic packets. In another were what looked like integrated circuits, chips, probably outbound from the US. He moved to the other side of the shack and tried another crate to find what looked like pre-Colombian art, Costa Rican jade, pendants, stylized figurines, earthen urns, Guatemalan Tikal masks. Genuine or not,

Freddy could not tell, but these things regrettably must perish in the flames that would soon engulf the shack.

In the next crate he came upon a vase. It was packed carefully and looked to be ancient. Curiosity made Freddy remove the vessel from its packing in the box. About 8 inches high, it was red and brown ochre, wide for its height, flaring gently at the top and bottom from a delicately tapered waist. The artistry was a scene depicting Mayan mythological figures, maidens dancing before gods on thrones. Leopards - or maybe ocelots - and birds perched on stone parapets below the red rim detailed with a thin, black line. There were scribes toward the flare on the bottom. They were rabbits.

He put the vase down. He had wasted too much time on curiosity already. He had no time for art treasures, fake or not. They would not leave anything that might possibly profit Sargento.

Freddy poured gas onto the crates inside the shack and then splashed some on the outer walls. He left the rest of the gas and the tank inside the shack. Backing off to his store of incendiary materials, he picked up one of the juice bottles and brought it forward. He set it down and lit a match. Holding the bottle at arm's length, he lit the taper of rag coming out the top of the bottle and threw the thing at the shack as hard as he could, ensuring that it would break. It broke with a splash of flame.

He could have lit the shack with a match, but this was much more satisfying, and the building certainly did catch fire quickly with this method. Wayne must have meant to blitzkrieg the compound with the bombs, but the resistance was now dead.

Freddy stared for a moment glassy-eyed at the roaring fire as the red light of the flames reflected across his face. He got a glimmer of the fascination arsonists must feel with their predilection for pyrotechnic peccadilloes.

The flames shot up and a plume of smoke sailed skyward. Freddy realized with a start that daybreak had come and the smoke of the fire would be visible for miles, a signal that would alert the other boat and bring it back in a hurry when those on board caught sight of the tongues of flame and billowing smoke. He regretted becoming mesmerized by the fire, letting that boat get that much closer. Urged on by this thought, he redoubled his efforts and hastily rushed back down the path with his now lighter load of combustibles to set fire to the transmitter shack. Then he burned the main building after dragging the half-headed man inside, and after he pushed through the doorway the man whose throat he has slit, cremating the corpses of the four murderous felons where they lay in their living quarters.

When he returned to the dock he saw that Wayne had pulled the boat away from the dock and deftly turned her around in the small basin to face the sea.

"Where you been? Let's get going." He had one more cocktail left.

"Wayne, what should I do with this?"

"Have some fun. Burn the dock, too. All that fuel in the storage shed should go up with quite a blast."

Freddy did as Wayne suggested. He lit the taper and threw the firebomb as the boat pulled away from the dock.

The gasoline-filled bottle broke on the dry wood of the dock and burst into flames. With no rain in days the cracked and weathered wood burned like tinder. The island slowly receded as the sun rose and Wayne steered the powerful boat beyond the basin and into the bay. The flames kept creeping toward the storage shed on the dock and the drums of gasoline. They watched the scene in their wake as the boat moved away, flames licking at the shack as the throaty rumble of its big inboard engine penetrated the dawn. Suddenly, as the flames caught the fuel drums the shack flew apart.

A fireball ensued, spewing and spattering flames from its edges, Boards and debris flew tumbling end over end like a quarterback's bad pass. An umbrella of planking oscillated slowly downward, fluttering like feathers. A black reek rose high into the sky as the materials more reluctant to burn yielded to the intense flame. If the other Sargento boat had not yet noticed the previous plumes of smoke, they could not fail to have noticed this explosion and conflagration.

Within Freddy a cheer went up. They had struck back at Sargento, here and in Key West.

"Where to, Wayne?"

"Didn't I tell you?"

"No."

"Turbo, Colombia."

"Ok, just tell me where to turn when I have to drive. I don't see any signs."

Chapter Twenty-Nine - More Shallows

Wayne had been listening while he was captive. Turbo, Colombia was where Sargento had gone. Connors had left yesterday to join him there with two other men from the island and some of the crates that were implanted with kilos of cocaine. They were making connections at sea to drop off the contraband and then continuing on to their home port.

They knew that a good part of Sargento's business was transporting goods into the United States for other parties. For this, he received a sizable commission and a good deal of resentment from those Central and South American organizations he was dealing with. Those foreign nationals had been doing this sort of thing for years, and could afford to lose a shipment now and then to U.S. Customs, Marine Patrol, Drug Enforcement Agency, and state and local agencies of law enforcement. They could afford to, but they would rather not. There were millions of U.S. dollars at stake. They did not like the fact that Sargento could come along and set up his apparatus out of what had been his own modest drug operation, by their standards, and do what *they* had been doing, and do it better, but the decrease in their operational losses was too good for them not to work with him.

All of this Wayne gleaned by carefully put, seemingly innocuous questions, dangerous goading which earned him several brutal beatings, and overheard conversations during his brief but painful visit with the lads. They weren't overly worried about him hearing because they considered him to be a dead man. They thought it would be Wayne who would be dead and not themselves. Imagine their surprise.

As Wayne had always said, Sargento was smart. And he was a psychopath. Well, Wayne was smart, too, and given equal circumstances Freddy believed Wayne would have had Sargento bested. They hadn't given up yet, and now it seemed as though there was still a chance to carry the battle deep into Sargento's territory.

Maybe not. They had been so engrossed in watching their fiery handiwork that they failed to notice what was going on in front of them. Wayne said, "Freddy, get up front. Let's find that channel out of here." Freddy climbed around the cabin and stood on the bow.

"Wayne, there's a boat coming." It was clearly visible well below the horizon, the sister ship of the one they had taken from the dock. They had no doubt that the men on board were armed and knew that they soon would be in effective firing range, as soon as they made the tortuous passage through the one and only inlet deep enough for a boat to get through from the open water unscathed and into sheltered the bay and basin.

"It's got to be them," Freddy said as his eyes searched for an alternative to returning to the cul-de-sac of the bay. Alone, Freddy might make it back through the woods, but Wayne was in no condition to come with him at the moment. "We'll never get past them; there is just no room to get by them in this narrow channel. Even if we could squeeze this boat through they would gun us down as we passed - they would annihilate us." The prospects were not good. Freddy turned to Wayne for guidance and encouragement.

"Wayne, what the heck are we gonna do?"

In answer, Wayne pointed the boat toward the vast expanse of shallows separating them from the entrance to the cove. He opened the throttle wide. "Oh-oh," said Freddy.

"Frederick, we are going to make a run on those shallows as fast as this craft will go."

"We'll go aground!!" Freddy blurted in alarm.

"Yes, I know. But maybe our speed will carry us up toward the beach far enough for us to get to shore. We'll shoot down that blind creek where we got stuck in the mud two nights ago. Of course it won't do the bottom of this boat any good. When this thing comes to a stop we run for the beach and then the cove and our boat."

"The one with enough gas to get half way to somewhere?"

"Exactly. They know about the shallows as well as we do. They won't try to follow us across by boat. After this boat crashes they'll think they've got us."

"What will they do?"

"What would you do?"

"Check the damage to their camp, drop off some men here to cut us off from returning to the bay, circle around back out of the channel and into the cove between the reef and the shallows, in the direction of the wreck of this boat, and past the way we entered it two days ago because they won't be able to see it without going aground in the false channel the way we did."

"Right." The goons providing the muscle are no good in the elements, but from what I have seen, the boatmen are very good.

"What will we do?"

"What can we do? We'll try to get to the boat and out of the cove before they get into it."

"Can you run?"

"We'll find out, won't we?"

The boat was just getting to top speed, throttle pushed hard forward, engines racing with a throaty, burbling, warble and riding high out of the water on plane over 20 inches of water, and then ten, when they started hitting the bottom. At first it was just a bounce here and a skip there, momentarily slowing their headlong rush. The bounces and scrapes became more frequent until they were bouncing and skidding across the flat. The prop was eating mud. The mud became hard bottom, rock, and marl. Soon there was nothing left of the propeller blades and they continued glissading and grating along alternately on the boat's momentum, hydroplaning on the thin layer of water and maintaining some speed as she swung this way and that and began to hit the bigger rocks close to shore. Then they hit a *big* one and her back was broken. The boat slid half-sidewise to a stop. They had made it almost three hundred yards from the bay.

They sloshed to shore, running like Clydesdales, as the other boat cleared the channel and broke into the bay. It rooster-tailed into the deeper water with a high pitched whine and headed for the basin. Wayne struggled along without complaint, as Freddy knew he would, risking a punctured lung or hemorrhaging. He urged Freddy to go on ahead.

Freddy refused to leave Wayne behind. Freddy had been saved by Wayne too many times for that happen. He helped him along as much as he could. They turned the island's corner onto the north side, where the cove was and made for the boat.

Now the others would land men at the basin. It would take them more time than they thought. Now there was no pier. A slower, more difficult approach to shore would be necessary now that the dock was engulfed in flames. A walk through the water to shore awaited their men on foot and they would be well behind Freddy and Wayne. Still, there was no time to spare. Freddy and Wayne pushed on.

****

At the boat Freddy climbed aboard first and then Wayne tumbled into it as well. Freddy warmed the boat up and they started out from the concealment of the mangroves. They edged out of the veil of green leaves and twisted hardwood and pointed the nose at the near end of the cove. They would have to make another run for it - there was no telling where the other boat was, or if it could negotiate the way around the shallows in time to cut off Freddy and Wayne's escape from the cove. They sped toward the hazardous passage that would take them out of the channel if they could get to the narrow chute at the reef's eastern end before the other boat entered it from the other direction.

They passed the end of the mangrove patch between Freddy's boat and the shoreline. There, in the water, were the men sent to cut off an escape along the beach, appearing so suddenly there was no time for Wayne to react fast enough. He managed to shoot only one of them before he had to duck, or be gunned down point-blank by the other man in the next moment.

A shot punctured the fiberglass hull above Freddy's head as he lay on the deck. When the boat passed the gunman Freddy would be an easy target for the man as he shot into the boat over the transom. Only seconds remained.

Freddy pulled the still-cocked spear gun from its rack, rose quickly and fired. It was a good shot, an incredible, unbelievable shot. From the speeding boat, the steel shaft leapt from the gun into the air and arched upward and then down, the trailing line curving behind it like a streamer, following the lead-time Freddy allowed for the boat's speed. The man watched the spear come at him in surprised and horrified fascination even as it went clean through his chest. The trailing line went taut and the gun was torn from Freddy's hands. He had no time to dwell on it; he went back to the helm.

"They don't know we're low on gas," said Freddy. That wasn't entirely true; they had nearly forty gallons, but that was not likely to get them anywhere from here. "Let's try to get out of the cove and stay on plane across the shallows north and west of the island as close in as possible. We draw less water than they do. It may be our only chance."

"It might work, Freddy. I doubt if we can keep ahead of them in the open water. If they can keep us in sight they'll get us when we run out of gas."

It dawned on them that the men who have given chase to them in the surviving fast boat had gone into the blind channel far enough before they broke off pursuit had probably discovered the true channel that Freddy and Wayne had discovered two nights earlier. The crooks now knew that they could not get across the flats from the blind channel to the open creek, so they would have to exit the bay and retreat to open water and double back to the entrance of the true creek. Freddy and Wayne had to turn the corner around the end of the reef before the other boat got to the narrow passage to the cove's entrance. It was risky; neither one of them wanted to run aground again, twice was enough, but they had to take that chance to put some distance between them and the other boat.

They didn't make it. Before Freddy and Wayne got to the east end of the cove the other boat came full tilt around the corner of the island from the other direction and spotted them at the mouth of the channel hitherto unknown to them, as though their anticipation of Freddy and Wayne's plans had been its cue. Freddy wheeled the boat and they turned and ran. They made some distance on the other boat as it picked its way through the channel, but once in the cove the other boat opened its throttles.

Four hundred yards and closing. Even at that distance Freddy recognized it, knew the sweep of its cabin, the sleek line of its hull, distorted, foreshortened, shimmering in the morning sun, most of its bottom paint showing as it came roaring into the cove. The hull was palpitating in the haze - the sides of the hull seemed to be quivering, like a cheetah making a high-speed run at its prey.

The front of the boat was out of the water as it leaned hard into the turn at the lip of the cove as though helmsman knew that tricky passage well although it had been his first time negotiating the passage. It seemed that Sargento's boatmen were competent. Water spewed in a high arc from its stern, misting into rainbow colors at the fringes as the early sunlight filtered through the spray. It came at them in giant strides like a greyhound. The other boat was clearly faster than Freddy's.

"Hold on, Wayne," Freddy called as he spun the boat around from its bearing back to the beach toward the open water beyond the other, western end of the reef. Wayne turned slowly and reacted dully in his pain, exacerbated by the run to the boat, but he got down to a half-seated position on the deck in answer to Freddy's exhortation. He locked himself in with his legs between the console seat and the bench seat over the transom in the back. He had his guns - the guns he had taken from the corpses - ready.

Freddy looked to where he would try to escape the cove which had been their sanctuary and now was a death trap. At the beginning of the reef, at the westernmost end, the water, rather than breaking over the rocks, was surging and oozing above the rocks with each wave. It was the low gap in the reef they had seen yesterday from the seaward side. If the timing was right there might be enough water there to get over the rocks as a swell passed over them to keep the hull from being torn apart.

He moved the throttle quickly to three-quarters. She would not get up on plane, too laggard from a belly full of sea water which had seeped through the hull as she sat in the night of their absence. For the hell of it Freddy hit the bilge pump switch. It worked! What providence had descended upon them at that late hour Freddy did not know, but he hoped it would keep falling. If their trials brought any assistance from a sympathetic deity, they would accept it.

Freddy opened the throttle full, directing the boat toward the end of the shoreline where the tip of the saber of off-white beach pointed to the gap between the rocks and the white water. Wayne watched steadfastly as the boat at their stern made up distance, two hundred and eighty yards and closing, driving forward high on plane so that her underside could be seen fully two-thirds back of her bow, running swiftly on a few feet of hull at her tail, light and responsive, sprinting through the water, turning deeper into the cove in a long, gliding arc. Wayne looked in the direction Freddy was headed.

"Freddy, what in the hell are you doing?"

"Trust me, Wayne, we're gonna try to get over the reef, we'll never get past that boat."

Freddy's boat still lugged along. Her bow was lolling up and down, she was tired, couldn't keep her head up. As the bilge pump purged her hull she got lighter, but it would not be in time to outrun the menacing craft behind them. And they needed speed and agility to get over the reef.

Two hundred and thirty yards and closing between the boats; several hundred yards yet to the end of the reef.

A single shot rang out. They were still well ahead. The shooting would start in earnest when the distance closed. With an effort, unbidden, Wayne moved his battered body across the engine well and let his hand drop into the stern. He knew now what Freddy was about to attempt and cut the throttle momentarily. Wayne undid the drain plug and Freddy hit the throttle. The water in the bilge pushed to the back of the boat flowed out of that orifice. Slowly, the rate of acceleration improved. Her head lifted and dropped back down. Next wave lifted her shoulders, too. She was getting lighter all the time and with the next leap forward she jumped clear and was riding above the water instead of pushing through it. Now they were a match for the boat in their wake. It still had a few knots on her, but Freddy might make up for that with brains and experience if he could get the boat out of the cove.

The other boat closed to eighty yards, then seventy. Wayne fired at them twice from his regained sitting position, trying to stay the other boat's pace, but it continued in hot pursuit, undaunted and unswerving. "Damn," cursed Wayne, "The only target I have is the bow and the bottom of the hull. Maybe I can shoot some holes in their gas tank."

The cyan sky above the blue water was dappled with clouds. A jagged line of white breakers above the rock and the coral reef were like a tear across the center of a picture postcard of a tropical vacation spot, lamination rent as though scored by a jagged piece of broken glass. The mounting wind was giving him a clear indication of where the reef was highest. Crossing the gap too far to the beach side would pile them up on the rock promontory jutting out from shore. Crossing too far in the other direction mean instant destruction on the reef.

They were closer now. Freddy watched the waves approach as they ran parallel to the reef. Their passage must coincide with the upward surge of water as a swell crossed the reef so that the mass of the wave would keep the hull from obliteration on the rocks.

Waves come in sets. In each set there is one wave which is the highest. The first couple of waves of this set had already passed. They would miss the next one, the high one. As it passed under them, the first wave of the next set hit the reef. He saw the wave that he thought could carry them over, the second one out of the two remaining waves of this set.

Wayne continued to put slugs in the bottom of the other boat's hull. Freddy slowed a little to get the timing right and Sargento's boat edged closer. There would be no practice run. Freddy slowed a bit more and the boat's nose dropped slightly - too much - the wave he wanted would get there first; it was beating them to the rocks. Sargento's boat kept coming at flank speed, making up the distance. They were firing again.

Freddy slammed the throttle forward. Wayne did the only thing he could do now, he braced himself.

Another wave glided over the gap. The next one was theirs. It seemed to surge forward and increase speed as it got nearer trying to beat them to the gap in the reef. Freddy continued pushing the boat full-tilt.

Now Freddy saw the wave grow and approach more slowly as it met the rising sea floor before the reef. Too fast. Too late. Freddy could see dark shapes just below the surface. There was not enough water over the rocks.

It was too late to stop, and there was no alternative, the other boat would be on top of them instantly. The wave was in slow motion, slowing and getting steeper as the bottom came up sharply. They were careening toward the rock promontory at forty knots. Freddy waited a fraction more for the wave and pulled the wheel around to nose his boat into the gap.

The boat swung in toward the reef and the bow started up at the last moment as the swell arrived. They reached the rock line and climbed up the wave and were almost over when they hit. The right side of the boat, lower because of the angle of the turn, smashed into the rocks recoiled and shuddered. A frightening engine flare shrieked as the prop hung in the air but for that the prop got through unscathed. The boat bounced over and kept going, throttle still wide open. A splat and a confident growl followed as the prop bit again and the bow thudded into the next swell.

The engine was smooth - the propeller got through had gotten intact, but the hull had been hit hard. Freddy made another hard right on the other side of the reef to avoid the shallows near shore west of the cove. As the boat turned right again, the other boat was suddenly much closer. They were going to try the reef crossing. They drew more water than Freddy's boat; they would never make it. Wayne rose to watch.

The boat struck the reef and exploded in a ball of fire as the gas in the hull that Wayne had perforated with bullets ignited and burned furiously. The damage from the collision must have yanked out some of the wiring and shorted out.

A lucky shot sounded a half second before impact. Wayne had lurched and fell just as the other boat struck the reef. Freddy and Wayne were home free, they had made it out of the cove and the others were all dead, but Wayne was shot, right through, no bones hit, above the left hip. The danger was sepsis. Freddy had to get help as soon as possible and get medical attention for Wayne. Freddy tried the radio. It didn't work.

Chapter Thirty - Last Rites

The adrenalin ceased flowing. They realized they still had major problems. Returning to the island was not an option. Sargento would certainly send men to investigate and check the damage.

They tried to put some distance between themselves and the island, but it was of little use to hope that they would make landfall in Freddy's boat, probably ever again. The bounce off the reef had finally done it; the hull was badly cracked, leaking at an alarming rate, and no combination of bilge pump and bailing could keep up with the volume of water in the hull. Fast-running-with-the-drain-plug-out was a fast way to run out of gas, and most likely would scoop even more water into the cracks that must have opened up in the hull. Freddy confirmed this surmise by stopping the boat briefly and going over the side with a mask on to take a look. What had been a hairline crack under the right stringer was now readily visible. The boat also had a nasty bruise toward the stern on that side where it had struck the reef. A more recent crack now flared out from the already weakened area under that stringer. High speeds would only push the crack open wider. The best thing they could do now was make all of the distance they could before they ran out of gas and sank. Perhaps they could find an island, or a fishing boat, or blunder into a sea lane. Wayne had heard the others mention "the run to Progresso" and so he had deduced that the closest thing to them was the Yucatan Peninsula. It was not, however, necessarily the nearest landfall. They steered south and west and hoped for the best.

Freddy still couldn't raise anyone on the radio, the transmit indicator light was not working when he keyed the mike switch, but he kept trying now and then anyway on the possibility that the set was sending but not receiving.

Any forward movement at all probably was adding to the amount of water they scooped into the hull, but again, there was no alternative but to sit out there and wait to sink. They had to try to keep running as long as they could.

There were bullet holes in the bench seat and marks of glancing bullets elsewhere on the boat. The chance shot that found Wayne went through him on the left side of the abdomen. The bullet came out the other side with a lot less damage than Freddy expected, but the area was inflamed and tender. Freddy put a sulfa pad on each side of the wound. Wayne had both fever and chills. A clammy sweat was on his forehead and his eyes were sunk into their sockets, but his mind was clear. Freddy's concern was peritonitis, and that the internal damage inside him would cause his system to poison itself.

By nine o'clock Wayne started going in and out of consciousness. Freddy tied him in a sitting position against the console seat, facing aft, to afford him some protection from any spray coming into the boat and the rain of a passing squall. He did his best to adjust Wayne's lashings so that the nylon line would not chafe the skin off him as he moved in concert with the boat's motions. He fashioned the remains of his shirt as a head support, partially draping it over Wayne's face and tying it off to the gas tank filler cap as added protection from the elements. There wasn't much to see but water anyway, and it kept his head from lolling about. It rained a bit, and that was the worst of it. The weather was improving again.

By ten-thirty a.m. Freddy's ankles were sloshing in sea water. He tried to keep a heading and bail at the same time. He was now well-practiced in bailing, but after another three hours his arms and back ached again. He looked under the rag which had been his shirt at Wayne's face. Delirium. "I'd be unconscious too," Freddy thought, "if I wasn't doing something. Unconscious with sleep impenetrable." It was better for Wayne. He couldn't help, so there was no sense being awake and suffering.

Freddy would have to move him soon. The water was creeping higher inside the boat. The bilge pump finally died; Freddy couldn't blame it. By afternoon they had gone over eighty miles and still no land was in sight. Freddy had pulled the batteries up out of the battery well and propped them up in the transom as high as the cables would allow to keep them from being inundated by sea water. The batteries had been in the water for some time when the engine quit. There could not have been enough gas left to worry about anyway. Finally, they were dead in the water.

They were pitching slightly and helpless to prevent it, but the sea was flattening out. The sun was shining - a beautiful day. Freddy put Wayne supine across the width of the boat on the bench seat and tied him down to the "D" rings on either side of it, just in case. Wayne came to and asked what was happening. "I'm just putting you where you can get a sun tan," Freddy said. They were both sunburned and crack-lipped already from days of exposure. Wayne smiled, laughed softly and went back to sleep. A least his fever had broken.

Freddy disconnected the batteries underwater, cut the wires to the engine, and tried to pull the engine to life with the lanyard supplied in the engine cover. He thought perhaps he could get it to run on the magnetos. He couldn't. He threw the batteries over the side, useless weight.

When Wayne came to again it was late afternoon. The water was up over the transom and there were five or six inches of it in the boat. Bailing was useless now. Freddy was sitting up front on the seat before the console, his feet on the forward storage locker, when he heard Wayne stir.

"Freddy, where the hell are we, buddy?" Freddy moved to the back of the boat.

"Wayne, it's like this. I think we're lost."

"We're sitting a little low in the water, don't you think? What's that you're standing in?"

"It's the Gulf of Mexico. I think. Actually, I'm not even sure of that." Wayne laughed to himself and shook his head, smiling.

"I told you this trip might come to a bad ending. Sorry you came?"

"Not really. The water is my life. Besides, somebody had to do something about those guys. They killed two very good people." A momentary silence hung in the air, with only the sound of sloshing water slapping from side to side in the boat. "Then there's us!" said Freddy. "It looks like they got us, too, for whatever that's worth." They both smiled and laughed at that. It seemed funny. What comic figures they must be sitting in a boat full of water in the middle of nowhere. "I'm sorry we didn't get Sargento and Connors. If I'd been better at this sort of thing maybe we wouldn't be here sinking. Then again, I've made a pretty fair muddle of anything I've tried in the last ten years."

"Freddy," Wayne said earnestly, "You did just fine, and if you get out of this, you'll be all right from here on in. It isn't that you can't get things done right, it's just that you never knew you could."

Freddy was anguished. "So what, Wayne? What do I do, even if I get out of this somehow? There's nothing left."

"Do the best you can. There'll be someone else after a while. I lost Moira and found Annie, didn't I?" Yes, that was true, he did. What did it get him? He lost out twice.

All they could do now is watch the boat sink. It began to grow dark and they were left with nothing but their thoughts. Now, for the first time since he had left Pamela Freddy had nothing to take up his time and fill his mind, and she came to him in images. He thought of her trying to learn how to hit a tennis ball. Freddy would toss one of the six or eight balls stuffed in the grossly distended pockets of his stretch-woven tennis shorts in her direction. She would swing and miss, break into an Ohio cheer leading routine and totally distract the players on the other courts. They laughed a lot at that. Or the time taking her picture. She wore a black bathing suit with a zipper up the front. Instead of taking pictures Freddy unzipped her to her waist. Her face colored and the insides of her breasts blushed. They wound up making love. Or the way she used to look at him unabashedly, full brown eyes glistening, lakes of light with fire opal centers.

Wayne stirred again. Freddy told him to keep still, but Wayne was smarter, as usual. What for, he asked? To prolong the inevitable? He had some things he had to tell Freddy while he still had the strength.

"Freddy, that was a damn good shot with the spear gun. It saved us for long enough to let us get out of the cove, anyway. Sargento won't get the satisfaction of knowing his men killed us."

"Yeah, it was a good shot. It's about time I got my aim back. I'm just as good as I ever was."

"Well, you were a hell of a lot better just then than when you were shooting with a bent spear shaft for seven months."

"What?"

"Yeah, it was bent. Boy, you were hilarious."

"You son of a... you creep," Freddy said, laughing and angry at the same time. After the laughing stopped, Wayne spoke imploringly to Freddy.

"Freddy, there are a couple of things I want you to do for me if you get back home." Freddy started prevarications and mollifications of the "Oh, you'll get back; you're not 'gonna die" sort

"You can't know that..."

Wayne silenced him with a few words spoken so compellingly that Freddy found himself accepting Wayne's conviction that his doom was imminent. "Freddy, look at me. I'm beat-up bad enough to have some broken ribs. I'm shot, lost some blood, I've got a fever and internal infection. I can't swim, or do anything. Freddy, just shut up and listen to me. You *have* to get back. Somebody's got to get Sargento. Then there's a man in West Palm you have to see, and then you have to go see Annie's folks for me. The man in West Palm will give you some things, a few odds and ends he is keeping for me, and a little money. Keep the things he gives you; you're the only family I have. You keep half the money, too. You deserve it. Buy another boat if you like. If it hadn't been for me none of this would have happened to you. You're a good person, Freddy. One day you'll realize it. If you get out of this do something about it. Write a book, maybe. I think you could do something like that." He gave Freddy the name and address of the friend in West Palm and had Freddy repeat it back over and over again until he was sure Freddy had it, in case he lost the card he had told Freddy to take from his wallet. "The other half of the money I want you to give to Annie's parents. It's not enough, I know. How could it ever be? I took their daughter from them. Try to tell them how sorry I am." He paused. "Freddy, I'm sorry for whatever befell about Pamela, too." He fell silent, and Freddy respected that for a few moments.

"All right, now, Wayne, listen to me. You didn't put those evil bastards on this planet, so don't blame yourself. We had to try to stop them. I know it's bleak, but we, and I *mean* we, might get out of this yet." Freddy didn't know if he believed that himself. It was dark now and the boat was still slowly sinking. It was very low in the water, with three-quarters of a foot inside. "We have to last until daylight. A boat or a plane might happen by." Freddy started bailing again, knowing it to be truly ridiculous.

"I have a rough idea where we must be, Freddy, and so do you. Off the Mexican coast, far enough out of the sea lanes that it isn't likely we'll be seen. We won't be noticed from forty thousand feet, either. Our only chance is a fishing boat. We'll have to be mighty lucky."

"Maybe we will."

"Yes, maybe, but I doubt it. Stop bailing. You know as well as I do it's useless now. Talk to me while I still have the strength. Who knows how much longer we have together, Freddy, my friend."

"Wayne, whatever happens, I'm glad I got to know you."

They talked for a long while, rambling and desultory snatches of conversation, a few silly jokes, and some sad remembrances of the girls. Finally, Wayne started fading into that restless pain-sleep he had been in before. The sea was at last flat. After a while Freddy fell asleep also, too exhausted for even his wet, dirty discomfort to keep him awake.

****

Pamela was standing in the moonlight. She was wearing her white dress, the one she bought for the Halloween celebration. She gazed dreamily at the stars, and he walked up behind her until their bodies touched. He could smell her hair. He put his cheek to her hair and moved it up and down, feeling its silkiness against his skin. Turning his lips to her head, he kissed her. She turned softly in his arms and held him lightly against her chest, then she increased the pressure and raised her face to have her lips kissed. He kissed her. Their lips parted, and he tasted her mouth. The world was beautiful, everything was all right...

****

He opened his eyes. His hand was wet. It was hanging over the side of the seat in front of the console and there was water all around the console. It was up to the gunnels. Freddy pressed the light button on his watch and checked the time. Two a.m. Why were they not sunk? The bow was out of the water, and so were the tops of the seats, gunnels, console and engine top, but other than that he had an unobstructed view of the sea around him in the moonlight. The two remaining gas tanks were attached to their tethers and floating around within the confines of the hull's sides, plastic islands in a miniature sea within a sea.

The boat had flotation devices built into it - that was it. There was a foam liner between the inner and outer hulls, supposedly making the boat unsinkable, according to the manufacturer's claim. Other so-called unsinkable boats did - sink, that is, and so Freddy hadn't put much stock in that claim and eventually forgot about it. Apparently Freddy's hull was making an effort to live up to its credentials.

Freddy knew it couldn't last. Sooner or later the foam would get saturated enough that it would not be able to keep the boat at the surface. Freddy looked around. The stern was lowest, and that was where Wayne was laying across the width of the boat. The engine's weight was pulling her down by the stern. He worked fast. Being in the business of boat repairs, they had a better than average set of tools on the boat. Freddy knew where the bolts mounting the engine were, so, working with his arms under water by feel he cut away the electric and the gas line, disconnected the throttle, transmission and steering cable, and removed the mounting bolts. Freddy rocked the engine and shook the engine loose and pushed it off the transom, thirty-five hundred dollars of engine, a half-year-old, plummeting to the bottom.

With that weight gone she lifted a little, alleviating the immediate danger of having the water get high enough to wet Wayne's wounds. Encouraged by the improvement in buoyancy, Freddy set to work throwing everything overboard that he could break loose from the hull. The radio went first, with a curse for its failure to perform the one and only time he had ever needed it. Then went the depth finder. All that expensive stuff. The console seat/gas tank was empty. Good. Eighty gallons of air for flotation. Freddy made sure the cap was tightly sealed and crimped off the gas line so that the tank would not slowly refill with water. He reached under the console where the electric was routed through PVC pipes and pulled the putty around them loose. He stuck the putty in the tank vent. Last to go was the anchor. He cut the line and threw it over the side. Using sections of the anchor line, he tied off the gas tanks securely so they wouldn't float away. More flotation. They were a good five inches higher. Proud of his work, he went back to sleep. When he woke the next morning Wayne was gone.

He had cut himself loose during the early hours of the morning. One of the gas tanks was gone. He must have made the effort to swim away using it as a float because otherwise he would have drifted roughly in the same area as the boat in the flat calm sea. He was nowhere to be seen.

****

Wayne had left Freddy with what little water there was left. Of course, that was it. Wayne counted himself as dead so he took his leave, increasing Freddy's chances by twice, if he could stay afloat with the hull or on something. Freddy was mad at him. He owed him all over again, he just kept doing it to him, and just when he thought he was catching up, too.

There was nothing Freddy could do about it now. He lost the best friend he ever had, and now he had truly nothing left in the world. Nothing but a self-imposed promise to keep.

Chapter Thirty-One - Sinking Slowly

Another day and a half passed and the boat got lower and lower. It was on the brink of sinking with just enough positive buoyancy to keep it from slipping away. Freddy kept his head covered with some of the canvas from the ruined Bimini top, glad he had not thrown it overboard. The glare from a hazy sun bore down on him, made the horizon vague, hard to see. He was already very sunburned.

He couldn't stay dry. The water was washing over the seats now. It was hard to sleep, no matter how tired he got. He started slipping into and out of a sort of daze - he thought he had a fever. He was drinking too much water because he could no longer keep track of when he last had a drink. There was less than two quarts left. His mind rambled crazily:

> *Assorted stuff from the sea. Soon I will be joining it. What we got down there is a lot of round things that attach themselves to other things. Bivalves. All kinds of things in the mud. Small suckers, large suckers, extremely large suckers.*
>
> *Suddenly I'm swimming around a wooden pier, looking down at things in the grass. There's a marble, a room key, a quarter. A penny so thin from the sea's corrosion that soon it will make no sense at all. The world's thinnest penny. Call P.T. Barnum immediately. Look! The shell of some elongated cyclopean conical creature, now calcified and long dead, ancestored by giant primordial seashells. Now the shell is in space, on Star Trek. Real big, floating around eating planets. Captain Kirk is flying somebody else's starship into its mouth...*

He opened his eyes and looked at his wounds. Scratches from the mangroves three nights ago were doughy-white at the edges, thin and flaky like puff-pastry. Abrasions from coral in the shallow water were angry red burnishes with black and purple coronas. There were colorful bursts of blood poisoning on his left arm and leg.

Then he was lucid again, and something was different. The water all around him was a smooth, flat, silver-black mirror. He was standing on the edge of the windshield for the console and holding on to the remaining red gas tank can tied off to the boat like a helium balloon quivering and straining against its tether. He had tied off the last water bottle to the tank. He was wearing one PFD and had the others tied to the tank and water bottle assembly.

The flotation seat cushions were finally saturated and of no use. His boat was going down. With a sense of regret he unsheathed his knife and cut the gas can loose from its mooring on the cleat on the hull. He stepped off the boat as it finally fell away. Goodbye, old boat... Gone was his last link with the world he knew - last week. There was nothing funny anymore. Now he was shark bait. And *jellyfish! He hated jellyfish!*

More time elapsed, how much he didn't know. At the outset of this trip he had adopted a Churchillian attitude, taken drastic measures matched to recent events. He lost everything dear to him. Now he would leave the world with no fanfare. Insights and revelations on how things should be would go with him, no document or letter of lament for lost ones in praise of their love and loyalty, no loquacious and lachrymose entreaty of despair, no treatise on futility with the underlying hope that in posterity acts that must be done should not be judged in vain if they fail. His strongest images now were of her - on the boat with the wind in her face, blowing her hair straight behind her, naked, natural, free and smiling; a day of sailing pulling on lines; lying on her tummy on the sand of a secluded beach, a marvel of curves and roundness and soft warm places, worrying now and then about her "funny ass"; fussing over Freddy as he pretended to protest. In bed, asleep, the curve of her body in the larger curve of his own in the early hours before dawn.

****

A boat is coming. It is hard to see - his eyes are nearly swollen shut. It is floating out of the haze on a churning froth of bow wave above the black mirror surface of the sea's shiny skin. He still has his legs, as far as he knows. He doesn't feel anything at all down there. The boat is closer, coming to him, and he wonders why he didn't hear the engine. It is a shrimp boat. As it gets closer still. Freddy reads the name – "Big Nick". It is Sargento's boat.

Chapter Thirty-Two - Cliché Endings

He opened his eyes. The little room was bright. As his vision became adjusted to the bright light he recognized the now-familiar stucco walls, the simple wooden table at the bedside, the crucifix on the wall and the single, straight-backed chair by the door-less doorway. The strong, oblique light of the morning sun through the web of the woven seat of the chair made a crisscross pattern on the floor in front of the doorway. It was a pretty picture. Quaint. The thin, lumpy mattress was a luxury in this village, Freddy was sure, and to him it felt just fine. Antonio came to the doorway bearing a tray. On it was a glass of orange juice.

"Is that fresh-squozen, Antonio?" The man smiled, his faded eyes reflecting amusement from their deep portals in his lean, brown face, etched deeply from a lifetime in the sun. His gentle nature was revealed by the way he spoke.

"But of course, Senor Frederico, and where else would it be from?" It was a morning ritual, about the juice. There was not a real grocery store for many miles. He bowed politely and left the room.

The room faced east. It was someplace on the Yucatan Peninsula, on a slight rise above the small harbor where fishing boats were neatly arrayed on the beach in a two-tiered semi-circle. Men walked to their boats, carrying sails and trappings of their trade, preparing for yet another arduous trip into the Gulf of Mexico, where they and their forebears had fished for many generations. It was a simple life, a hard one, and the people here were open and honest. A person could depend on them once you won their trust. They seemed to like Freddy. Maybe because he liked them.

It was a story right out of an adventure novel: a man, lost at sea, rescued by poor fishermen, taken to the town mission. He is nursed to health by the parish priest. The priest is a humble man of modest means because his parish is a poor one, but none-the-less helps the lost soul.

Freddy first saw the hamlet from the sea. He regained consciousness long enough to catch a glimpse of the town in its sleepy setting as the fishing boat that had picked him up returned from its fishing trip. To the south was a primitive lighthouse on a rock promontory, falling away to the central, recessed village of thatched roofed huts of the fishermen and their families. The village was a few dirt lanes, a very rudimentary general store, and a communal pump in the very center of town drawn from one of the sinkholes typical to this area of flatland over soluble karst formations. In the foreground, at the sea's interface, were the boats, women fixing sails, and fishing nets set out to dry and be repaired.

The mission, Freddy's temporary home, was on the rise north of town. Beyond that was the cemetery. Here and there around the outskirts of the village the ground was cultivated in an attempt to farm the land, where the land would tolerate it. The attempt had been going on for centuries.

When he first awoke in the little room he hurt in many places, but he was alive. The priest was in the room. Freddy could see him sitting by the door in the dim light of a single candle.

"Where am I?" Freddy asked.

"You are in the mission of Santa Rosa." He spoke English with a pronounced Spanish accent. "You are in Mexico. The Yucatan."

"Who brought me here? Where is the trawler that brought me here?"

"There is no trawler," he said soothingly, "The men of the village are the ones who took you on their boat. They told me you tried to fight them to stop them from coming to your rescue. They said your blows were as a baby's."

"I thought a trawler picked me up."

"We have no trawlers here. Our boats have no motors. There is no money for motors, we have only sails." Freddy's vision of Sargento's trawler had been a delusion.

"My friend, the men of the village told me of how you talked. Or rather they told me of how you babbled. They speak Mayan, mostly, and some Spanish," the priest explained. "You are in trouble?" Freddy wasn't sure that was a question. Freddy didn't answer him and the priest saw something in his eyes that told him not to pursue the matter.

"Do you have a telephone in this town?"

"No, señor, no telephone is here."

"Do you have a radio - you know - two-way? Transmit and receive? Perhaps on one of the boats?"

"No, no radio. I am sorry. We have the telegraph." No matter, Freddy knew what he had to do, and he could get by without either of those things. More importantly, he knew that he was cut off; news of an American found in the sea would not travel from here fast. That was good. He didn't need anyone interfering with his plans. The priest blew out the candle and quietly left the room.

****

When he awoke some mornings later the small town with its little church outside Freddy's window was already awake. Fishermen were doing the same thing they had been doing for centuries, cordovan people whose faces were as cracked as the earth around their small houses. Their hands were as coarse as the sails on their boat. Hunched under the weight of gear and sails, they shuffled to the boats as Freddy watched from the mission window. One would think it was a miracle, or at least extremely unlikely for Freddy to have the good fortune to be thus taken in and taken care of, but there was no mystery about it. Who else was likely to rescue Freddy in those remote waters but the fishermen? And who would be able to afford to help him regain his health but the church? He would be too much of a burden for any of the households in the village. No one but the priest and his tiny mission could afford to take Freddy in. It was as simple as that. The other thing that might have happened, the likely alternative, was for Freddy to have died at sea, by exposure or shark attack. Or *jellyfish*.

After a week, Freddy was getting his strength back. Father Paul, the good priest to whom Freddy owed so much, was hinting that Freddy stay on at the village and work the fields or help with the mending of the nets until his recuperation was complete. Freddy had already declined an offer to have the villagers drive him the eighty miles to the hospital. The priest knew that there was something troubling Freddy, something that he had to do that might be unwholesome. Freddy demurely refrained from adding to his concerns. The village and its responsibilities were enough of a load for the man. Freddy told the priest only that he must leave soon, he did not tell him why.

In the three weeks that followed his rescue Freddy enjoyed his talks with Father Paul, realized his concern for Freddy and humanity in general, a far removed thing from so much of the commercial religion Freddy had come to know in the States. Further still from Freddy's own dark feelings of revenge and the unfairness of the world. He felt his own feelings tempered somewhat by the good priest's influence, mitigating his harsh perspective of humanity.

Freddy was grateful. He did what he could to help the village during his short stay, fixing the huts while the men were fishing, starting with the women's work and helping to mend the nets and till the fields with the wives and daughters of the fishermen.

One of the daughters was clearly interested in him. She had helped the priest tend to him when he was sick. Her name was Carlotta. She was a young, dark-haired Mayan girl with round features and full lips, and volatile peasant beauty. She seemed fascinated by the American stranger, intrigued by his strange and different looks, beguiled by his helplessness. She had taken it upon herself to share in taking care of Freddy, sitting with him, helping him eat, washing him when he couldn't fend for himself. Her touch was kind and gentle in that deliberate way that tells a man when a woman is interested in being courted. And she knew some English, thanks to Father Paul. She came and talked with him as often as she could. Freddy knew there could be nothing to it.

When he felt strong enough he started going out on the fishing trips with the men a few times in the final week of his stay. The men were surprised and delighted that gringo Freddy was good at it, a skillful boat handler and an able fisherman. It was not what they expected. The sunburned skin Freddy arrived with grew very dark. His hands cracked and bled and grew new calluses where they needed to. He was clad in peasant clothes and sandals furnished to him by the villagers. Only his blond hair and blue eyes distinguished him from the men he fished with.

****

Freddy had taken to walking in the village. He enjoyed watching the daily workings or the townspeople. They responded, their greetings were genuine, although at first they did not know what each other were saying. The children - he would miss them, running after him, trying to get him to help them with the English Father Paul was teaching them.

He would miss Carlotta also. He was attracted to her in spite of himself. She was shy and yet forthright at the same time. Her smoldering dark eyes showed her passion, but now Carlotta knew that Freddy would go. Compassion and affection in his own eyes told her that his heart was elsewhere. It was time to leave. Freddy had no way of knowing if he would still find Sargento and Connors in Colombia when he got there, but he had to start somewhere. He had yet to find a way to get there. What he did have, still in his wallet which somehow was still in his tattered pants in the one remaining pocket not ripped away in the mangroves, was forty-five dollars and a Master Card and the money from Wayne's wallet, four hundred dollars. He assumed that his credit card, a remnant from his years up north, was still good. The bank continued to take out the yearly fee, and Freddy had kept paying it for some reason.

Freddy had not used the card for a year. He dare not use it now, not yet, not without knowing what had happened back in Key West since he left and what authorities might be looking for him.

Freddy had the deliberate look about him of someone ready to move. Father Paul guessed that Freddy was preparing to leave. The priest came into his room the night before Freddy's departure.

"Frederico, it looks like you are going somewhere." Freddy had "packed". He put the extra set of clothes the village people had given him, along with Cap'n Walter's sneakers and some odds and ends, into the center of a piece of cloth and drew up the corners and knotted them.

"Yes, Father, I must be on my way."

"You will need money."

"I have some."

"American dollars?"

"Yes."

He smiled. "I am afraid that the people you meet on the way to the City may not take it. I will give you some Mexican pesos." Freddy took the money offered to him, promising to pay it back. Apparently the priest did not believe that Freddy would, or that he would ever hear from Freddy again. "Do not worry about the money, Frederico, it is a gift. Try for me to lead a good life. Carlotta and the children will miss you."

"I know." he said with a sad smile.

"I will miss you, too."

"And I you, Father, thanks for everything."

"How will you go?"

"I don't know, Father."

"The fishing has been good for once, much better than usual lately. You have brought us good fortune; we have much more than we need. There is a truck going to market in the city tomorrow. I will see that they take you." Freddy thanked him. He never saw the priest again.

Chapter Thirty-Three – Traveling

The truck was an old Ford. It had an ice box on the back and a radio in the dash playing Mexican music. The only concession to progress the small anachronistic village had made was to buy a generator and an ice machine to ice the fish so that it could be brought to market.

It was a bumpy trip. The suspension on the old truck was shot and the roads were deplorable. Freddy thought they must have gone fifty miles before they got to a paved road.

He sat in front between the driver and his helper. Both were stocky and very brown. They were in good spirits at the prospect of going to the city and selling the load of fish, running some errands and having an afternoon away from their small, dusty village. They talked animatedly across the truck cab in front of Freddy, but too fast. Freddy didn't understand much of what they said. All three were dressed alike in their white peasant shirts, pants, and sandals. In the city Freddy would pick up some "civies". He would save the peasant clothes. There would likely be a need to blend in with other remote local communities before this adventure was over.

It was hundred and two miles to Chetumal. By air. Their trip by truck was somewhat longer. They made it in ten and a half hours. There were closer markets for the load of fish, but Freddy learned from Carlotta on that last night that they could get better prices there for their fish and that these men had relatives there, and were going to incorporate a visit to them with the marketing trip. That was well-suited to Freddy's plans. In the city Freddy said his goodbyes, which consisted of handshakes, nods and smiles, bought a few articles of clothing and a pair of shoes, dark sunglasses, a nondescript cloth hat with a floppy brim, some black hair dye, a small suitcase, and a large cloth bag. He got a room for the night in a cheap hotel, paying for two nights, in advance. Guessing at the instructions on the package of dye, using the pictures on it as a guide, he dyed his hair black. Freddy knew fishermen and waterfronts, and he felt sure that's where he would find Sargento. His peasant clothes, dark skin and cracked and callused fisherman's hands would be his disguise when the time came. He would keep his eyes averted. It was too late to do anything more that night. Realizing he was taller than most of the people here, he minimize contact with them and avoid drawing attention to himself.

The next day Freddy cautiously canvassed second-hand stores and out-of-the-way bars. He had avoided the desk clerk that morning. He put the rest of his purchases, the cloth bag, and the knife, which had come so far with him strapped in its scabbard to his leg, even as he hung on to the floating empty gas tank, into the cupboard in his hotel room. The knife was the only thing left from his old life - last week. He left the hotel in his newly bought "American" clothes with the sunglasses on and his hair combed.

He found a bartender that he thought he might trust if he gave him a sizable tip, who directed him to a small sundry store on the edge of town. Freddy went there and discreetly asked the proprietor about the possibility of obtaining a false passport and visa. It was possible, fifty dollars. He took Freddy's picture. Come back tomorrow. He did so, and purchased some durable food as well.

The day after that, after spending the night in a different cheap hotel, Freddy put on his civies, picked up his passport and was on the Tica bus, the old bus line operated by Greyhound on the Pan American highway, heading toward Guatemala City. The sundry shop man had taken Freddy's forty-five dollars in American plus a lot of his pesos. He still had Wayne's four hundred dollars in the suitcase, but he did not want to appear to be rich, that could lead to a set-up and betrayal.

****

Plucked from the fishing grounds above the Yucatan, overland to Chetumal for 150 road miles, now Freddy was across the border into British Honduras heading south toward the Pacific. He had tipped the driver to secure a seat at the front of the bus, putting the activity of the polyglot of passengers and their pets behind him.

The coarse tarmac caused a low-pitched rumble to telegraph through the bus. Freddy sat back and enjoyed the ride. There was still the sadness about him, but there was also an inner calm found during his stay in the village with Father Paul. The other thing he brought away with him was a confidence born of the conflicts and hardships of his adventures since Key West. Bad things had already been done to him, and he wasn't dead. There were worse things than being killed by Sargento or the elements, and they involved the loss of others close to him. He would try his best to go on with what he thought he had to do and accept what happened, just as Wayne had done. For now, though, he could rest. He sat back and watched the scenery.

British Honduras, which would become Belize in less than a decade, and upper Guatemala were dense woodland. Freddy's bus climbed through British Honduras and then zig-zagged through Guatemala's mountains down to Guatemala City. It was a long day of traveling, distance made longer by steep inclines and serpentine mountain roads. Upon his arrival in the city Freddy made his travel plans for the next day and found a cheap place to stay for the night. Crossing borders so far was no problem; he still had his wallet and his I.D.'s, and his new false passport. If anyone suspected the strange American with his cheap clothes, weathered face and cracked hands, they said nothing of it. He drew no undue attention. Had they not seen these strange American expatriates before? Everyone had.

The next. day he made it through the lower-lying farmlands of Guatemala and up again into El Salvador and the most dangerous switch-back mountain roads of the trip, over rugged terrain with smoking volcanoes in the distance. Lower down he saw red and white flatbed lumber trucks hauling timber - massive trunks, some of them five and six feet in diameter.

Then he was into Nicaragua and through the still lower-lying farms, pastures, and brushy savannas as far as Managua. Another long day of more or less the same. The next two days brought bad connections, unusual on the usually on-schedule Tica bus line, and he made slow progress through agricultural Nicaragua. He passed Lake Managua just south of the city.

It was a six hour drive from there to Lake Nicaragua with its live volcanic island puffing smoke above the surface of the lake. Then another vertiginous climb, this time to Costa Rica, and a taste of the breath-taking beauty of the mountains there. Several times he saw passengers of the buses going the other way having to get out and walk behind the bus so that it could make it over the grades over the highest passes. Closer to the valleys women bearing huge bundles of wood walked along the steep inclines at the roadsides, their destination smoldering fires on the hillsides marked by thin, black, vertical plumes, which the women used for making charcoal.

During this bus ride Freddy reflected on all that had transpired to get him to this point, and he then thought also of how he might reap vengeance upon Sargento and Connors for the loses of his friends. He realized he had no clear plan.

The end of those two days found Freddy back down to earth at Panama City. Here he took two days rest and prepared for the final part of his journey.

****

He found a bank and at last dared to try his Master Card for a cash advance of two hundred dollars, and it worked. Now he had six hundred dollars total. He would be on the move from here on in and would try to change identity again; he would be hard to trace should anyone want to catch up with him. It should not be hard to find what he needed next in this city of four hundred thousand peopled by a mix of Spanish and Indian blood, spiced heavily with an international seasoning of Chinese, Italians, Greeks, Arabs and Blacks.

He traveled the diverse segments of the city until he found the pawn shop he wanted and bought a gun, a revolver. The proprietor was Chinese but spoke English. He explained to Freddy that the revolver would be more reliable and simpler to use that an automatic, showed him how to work it and sold him some cartridges.

Freddy asked the man if a bullet would go through a pillow or blanket. He assured Freddy it would go through walls.

****

The next morning, Freddy was on a bus again, heading toward the Darién Gap.

Chapter Thirty-Four – Turbo

Freddy had taken to the bars again in Chepo and found a ride to the end of the developed part of the highway system and into Panama's Darien National Park. He bought a machete also.

The park was adjacent to the Colombian border. He did not want to be found entering this country of drug lords and paid assassins. When he was well into the park, he asked the old man who had given him a lift in an old Chevy pickup about were to hire a guide. Freddy got out of the truck at the end of the road in Yaviza. Freddy walked into the woods and changed into his peasant clothes once again. He put the suitcase into the cloth bag. He left the sneakers on: He would be walking through the woods. With his hired guide who was now rich by Yaviza standards Freddy made his way through the park by hired piragua canoe and then on foot and machete. They avoided the police. He then covertly crossed the border into Colombia. Finally, he was in Turbo, Colombia, 4 days later, home port for the shrimp boat that wasn't a shrimp boat named *"Big Nick"*.

****

Freddy was headed into a place where he could expect no help from any corner. For Sargento and Connors, of course, Colombia was the natural choice for a home port. Many of their business contacts were there. It was a place where bribes would turn aside police scrutiny, where assassinations of court officials by the cartels had created a safe haven for their operation and for those of their ilk. They were on the level where they had money and influence enough that they need not fear Colombian justice, and their enemies could be expected to be treated harshly. If he were found with false papers and dyed hair that might be enough to send Freddy to prison for years before he even got to trial. And since the demise of the island camp where Sargento's vile minions and unsavory cohorts had plied their trade, Freddy was no safer in a Colombian jail than he would be in Sargento's hands.

He kept watch for official vehicles in order to avoid them, but he saw none. Only when he was well away from the frontier did he again try to get a ride. He got one, eventually, though there were few vehicles on the road through the wetlands near the border.

Turbo was a small city of perhaps ten thousand, on the Gulf of Darien, a body of water set back into the northern Colombian coastline, an inlet of the Caribbean Sea. It took a few hours of wandering through the town to get the lay of the land and then around the waterfront before Freddy spotted the *"Big Nick"*, Sargento's trawler. He might be in luck. The boat was in port; there was a good chance Sargento would be here as well. He had to find out when Sargento would be on board.

He knew it was not wise to ask questions in this town. It was too small, he would give himself away as American, and Sargento would surely find out someone was asking questions about him. Freddy had no illusions about his prowess in undercover work; that had been Wayne's forte. He would have to wait and watch.

He changed some dollars to Colombian pesos, uncomfortable with the scrutiny from the post office clerk as he falsified the change form, and found a room overlooking the harbor close to the wharf where the trawler was tied up after he bought some comestibles to consume in the room, all done using the system of communication he had developed during his travels. It consisted of grunting negatives and affirmatives, speaking a few Spanish words he knew when absolutely necessary, and letting the various clerks do almost all of the talking. They didn't detain him long, as though they were eager to be rid of him. Something about him had changed. Had he become more formidable or were they merely wary of this strange man before them?

Freddy watched from his room. Nothing the first day, nor the second. On the third day he saw them. He saw them both walking right beneath his window on their way to the boat. Connors was to Sargento's left, walking in that precise manner which mirrored the way he spoke, like a former British officer from a regiment of the

British Indian Army's cavalry before the great war, now in retired and in Mufti. Sargento was on the right, walking hunched over, head stooped forward, like a snapping turtle ready to snap. He would have been a perfect showcase for the talents of a plastic surgeon. The nose could be fixed, reduced, made less beak-like. The chin could be strengthened. Freddy didn't know if there was such a thing as an eye spreader in the plastic surgeon's bag of tricks, but Sargento certainly could have used one. Wayne was right, the man was a turtle.

Freddy's heart beat faster as he put on the peasant clothes he had been given to wear by his friends in the sleepy village of his convalescence. He had been in his skivvies as a hedge against the oppressive wet heat. He stuck the revolver under the drawstring of the loose white pants and put on the shirt of the same coarse material, letting it hang over the revolver in the loose manner in which the clothes were traditionally worn.

As Freddy dressed he watched them board. From the window of his room he could see there was another man there, evidently making preparations to get under way, and Freddy watched him at his duties until dusk. They must be waiting for something. Perhaps the tide. Or maybe the arrival of the rest of the crew. Freddy's chance, perhaps his only chance, came when that man left the boat on some errand or other. He could not be sure, but from his observations it seemed that the probability was that Sargento and Connors were alone on the boat. There was no time to wait. Freddy must get them now; he couldn't hope for a better opportunity.

****

There was little activity on the wharf. Freddy walked right down onto it, just another fisherman signed on from somewhere returning to one of the boats clustered around the dock. The revolver in the drawstring of his pants felt over-large, a conspicuous, enormous bulge. He thought he felt unseen eyes watching him as he walked down the pier.

He stepped out onto Sargento's trawler as if he owned it, without the slightest hesitation. But he tried to do it quietly, and slowly enough to avoid rocking the boat. He saw no one. Like other men of the sea he had known, the sailors were probably having some fun in town or sleeping on their boats before going out again. Cap'n Walter's sneakers trod silently on the wooden deck to the ladder going below. Freddy went down the stairs.

"Hey, Bruno, get in here!" It wasn't Connors, Freddy knew his pseudo-Brit accent. It must have been Sargento. The voice had been gravely and had an authoritarian timbre to it. Freddy expected no less. He continued toward their wardroom, taking care to utter no sound. He hoped they would think Bruno was heeding his summons. Freddy paused only to reach into a bunk and pull a blanket off it as he passed.

****

They were seated at a table of the plushly appointed trawler's ward room, for that is what it was, a place for the officers of this vessel and of Sargento's empire. Their backs were to him as he entered. That was good, very good. Freddy had the blanket behind his back in one hand, the revolver outstretched in the other. He stood there and waited.

Freddy had never killed anyone in cold blood before. He had never killed anyone at all until four weeks ago - the man at the shack with his father's knife, and the man in the water with his spear gun. That was different; they were fighting. Now he planned to shoot Sargento and Connors, and they were just sitting there. He was unsure of himself; he didn't know if he could do it. He'd never shot anyone before except with his water pistol and his spear gun. He could feel the hardness of the two men as he stood behind them. He was about to lose his chance to put an end to them.

Connors became aware of a presence behind him, but he thought it was Bruno. Finally, he glanced back and saw Freddy, and then looked at him more carefully. There was no fear; he was trying to think of where he had seen Freddy before. His hand went to his eye patch and his one good eye registered recognition. Freddy thought he might have seen an amused smile of greeting there also.

"Well, what have we here? I do believe that it is Mr. Taylor. My how you've changed." Sargento turned as well.

"This is the guy who blinded you?" he asked Connors.

"Yes, he hit me a clever blow which detached my retina temporarily and hence my eye patch. My vision will improve in time. You know, none of this need have happened. It is a pity that Teddy was a spy and not one of us."

"I'm surprised to meet you," said Sargento. "My pleasure. It's a wonder you aren't dead. Where is Teddy?"

"He's dead," Freddy answered.

"Good." He paused after his reply and then continued. "You're the one who doesn't have the guts to kill anybody, so what the hell are you doing here, trying to prove something? Are you going to try to take us in?" he asked sarcastically. "Don't count on it." He was the stereotypical successful businessman, suit and tie, clean and manicured. A turtle of a businessman, but that in itself was not unusual; there must be all types of businessmen, just as there are all types in every other vocation. Every so often his speech slipped, betraying his rough origins.

"What do you want?" he continued, becoming more animated and a bit annoyed. "You know you ain't gonna shoot us in cold blood, and we don't even have any guns on us." Freddy felt himself faltering. "You know, you're already in trouble. My friend here put enough coke in that heap of yours in Key West to point the finger at you." His anger rose as he continued. "Come on, get out of here, you're wastin' our time. Even if you did shoot that thing in here the noise would attract a lot of attention and you would never get away. We have a lot of friends here." Freddy had no doubt that his neighbors respected and feared him, but he doubted that Sargento's' neighbors were indeed his friends. Freddy took the blanket from behind his back and put it over the revolver. Imagine Sargento's surprise. Then there was concern, then more anger. And finally, at last, just a trace of fear. Sargento reached under the table for something. As Sargento raised his arm Freddy put a bullet into his head and it exploded. The chair went over backward and an automatic handgun fell to the floor. Sargento must have had the piece stashed under the table. Freddy gave grim thanks to

Sargento for releasing him from his conscience. He expected a move from Connors, but he just sat there, three feet away.

This was the man who was Sargento's general, the man Wayne had warned Freddy of. This man and his minions had gotten to Annie, bested Wayne in Key West. He was sitting there, unconcerned, apparently unarmed, upright and forward in his chair, sure of himself. Freddy knew he was still dangerous. He saw Connors tense, almost imperceptibly. He had some last words.

"Well done, old boy. Did you finally find the sense of the warrior in you? In the end, you will find this foolish, valorous act futile. You will fail; and you will fall, in the end. It won't change a thing."

Freddy saw the subtle fake to the left. He had seen that fake before, in Key West, knew it wasn't a fake at all. Somehow, faster than Freddy could see, there was a gun in Connors' hand. Connors managed a quick blocking thrust to Freddy's wrist, but it was not enough. Freddy got off the round. He had missed his mark by a few inches, but the round still found Connors.

He shot Connors through the neck. The body twisted in the air and was flung down to the deck. The head, with little neck left to support it, came to rest twisted halfway round.

Sticky red spatters were everywhere, and pools of dark red blood spread around each body. There was no satisfaction; he had merely done something that he knew he must do. The revolver's report had been much louder than Freddy had anticipated.

The blanket had not silenced the revolver as much as Freddy would have liked. Aware that the bark of the gun, even in the blanket, would attract attention, he hurried to the deck and then slowed and left the boat as calmly as he could. A head or two might have peered from below decks on the surrounding boats, but apparently the others in the area were too uncertain of what had happened to take any overt action. In this uncertainty Freddy walked off the pier hoping not to be challenged. He still could not shoot an innocent man, or one that might be innocent. The few faces Freddy saw expressed no desire to confront him. Perhaps Sargento had fewer friends than he thought.

Freddy knew he was conspicuous in that he was the only thing moving; he was suspect, and he knew that anyone close enough would see the blood spatters on his clothes, but he reasoned that a handful of faces on the pier would not take their chances on being shot. The hue and cry would go up as soon as he was out of their sight.

Freddy crossed the street and walked between the two closest buildings, turned the corner, ran for a block. He turned another corner and walked quickly back to the waterfront, hid in a shadow and wiped off the gun, then threw it in the water. He walked three blocks from the waterfront and then several blocks back in the direction he had run from, and then back to his waterfront room moving fast.

Freddy left the room darkened and looked out of the window. The alarm was out. Police units were arriving at the foot of the wharf. They would soon be canvassing the neighborhood. Freddy quickly washed and changed back into his street clothes. Again he was an American, traveling on modest means.

Leaving some money in the room, he left the building and started walking away from the sounds of the sirens coming to a stop at the wharf. He had killed two men in a strange town and spoke the language poorly. His forged passport had not been stamped coming into Colombia, and now he was almost out of money.

He was at the end of a chain of violence that begat violence. He had to break the chain; he was the last link. He must get out before the drug czars found him and set their armies against him. He must get out and leave no trail, because they could get him in South Florida almost as easily as in this country which was caught in the power of the drug trafficking Mafias.

Freddy had no idea what his next move would be until he saw the taxi. He took it. After a bumbling conversation with the driver he finally impressed upon him that he wanted to be taken to the best hotel in the city. The driver took him there and took most of the remaining money in pesos that Freddy had on him. Freddy did not protest. He was supposed to be another stupid American.

The hotel was... adequate. Freddy registered, showed the desk clerk his identification, something he would have liked to avoid, and hoped the clerk would not ask for money in advance. He had some pesos left, but he wanted to keep them in reserve for whatever might come next in his attempt to get back to the U.S. Most of the cash Freddy had left was in American dollars, which were not used in this small city.

Freddy told the clerk he would be staying for two weeks. The clerk took the proffered Master card and looked at it quizzically and then checked it by phone as Freddy waited, ready to run. He hadn't thought this far. The clerk made a phone call and wrote the numbers on the card on a blank form and gave Freddy a key. He didn't even ask to see Freddy's passport. Freddy went up to his second floor room wondering why on earth the Master Card was still good and why the clerk accepted it *here* in *Turbo* of all places, without the standard credit card machine. He realized in the heat of the moment that he had not been thinking straight.

Now there was a record of his being in Colombia, and he was sure there was a record of his being in Panama, the last place he had used the card. Wouldn't the authorities in the United States, where as far as Freddy knew he was thought to have killed his girlfriend and be involved with major criminals, use the card to track him down? There might be no extradition from Colombia, for all Freddy knew, but Freddy was in Colombia illegally, on a false passport, with no visa for crossing the border into Colombia from Panama. Maybe he had been cleared of Pamela's killing. Still, he was sure someone must want to talk to him about it, and the goings-on in Key West, and the drugs Connors had planted in his car. He had to get out of Colombia. He had to get out somehow without being picked up at the airport or any other port of exit. If he fell into the hands of the government, the drug czars would surely block his leaving and/or have him killed.

He couldn't stay here; not at this hotel, not in Turbo, and not in Colombia where he was in dire peril. He might be picked up and tried for murder, or killed by the mobsters. At best, he would be deported, to face who-knows-what. But then the fact that he had made it this far and achieved his objective was a surprise to him: he never had had much hope of living through this escapade. Then it occurred to him that the clerk may have called someone else and not the credit card number.

Once back in the States he could not become embroiled in the investigations he knew must be in progress there. He would be too visible; any focus on him would make him vulnerable to the mob. He had to get back; he had promised Wayne to do some things. And besides, he had no place else to go. He would try to get back somehow and discharge his duties, then, if he had no other choice, turn himself in and try to prove his innocence. But how was he going to get there?

He was afraid to try to use the Master Card to book a flight, but he still had that cash from Wayne's wallet. He had American dollars that he could use for a plane ticket, but he couldn't use his name at all; his visa hadn't been stamped coming into Colombia. He would not make it past even the most benign identification check.

Freddy decided to call the man whose name and address Wayne had made him memorize, the one in West Palm Beach. Wayne had told Freddy he could count on that man for help. First, he must do some things.

Freddy went to a nearby store, bought some cheese and crackers and returned to the room, staying abroad for as little time as possible. He unpacked his other set of peasant clothes and put them on. Removing the snacks from the bag, he put the blood soiled set of clothes into it. A covert departure out the back entrance of the hotel and another short walk brought him to a dark alley. He threw the package containing the bloody clothes into the loose rubbish there a considerable distance from the waterfront and in a place that he hoped that the police were not likely to look. Then he went back to the hotel and washed thoroughly. He made the call, collect, from the lobby of the hotel since the room had no phone, calling himself Teddy McLaren. The voice at the other end sounded like an older person, well metered and precise. There was a trace of a New York accent.

"Yes, operator, I'll accept the charges."

"Hello, Professor Sorenson?"

"Yes, speaking. You are not Theodore, who is this?"

"Professor, I'm a friend of Theodore's. I knew him as Wayne. He said you might be able to help me. My name is Freddy."

"Freddy, yes, I know of you. Teddy said you might call, he briefed me thoroughly. If you need help and he is not calling, he must be missing or dead.

"I won't ask anything else of you over the phone - I don't think it's wise. Give me the name you are using and the address of the hotel. Freddy supplied the information and his unfortunate use of the credit card. The Professor paused for a moment and then continued. "I'll send you everything you need. No, that might not be safe.

"Better yet, I'll send a package by courier. Go to the telegraph office in Turbo at noon tomorrow but do not go into the Telegraph office. Approach from the end of the street closest to the harbor. You will be intercepted by one of my people. It cannot be before noon. I'll need that much time for my people to get everything in place. My contacts can assemble what you will need, but they are not in Turbo and will have to make a trip of considerable distance to get to you and that will take some time. I am aggrieved that you tried to use a charge card there. That was an unfortunate mistake, but understandable given that you are a novice to this type of activity and are very fortunate to be breathing. I believe the clerk could be on to you and the call he made could have been to any number of concerns, but none of them are in your best interest. Gather what you need and get out of that hotel. If you cannot make the pickup for any reason call this number again as soon as you find a safer place." This begged the question where would that safer place be. Freddy wondered who "his people" were.

Freddy did not ask and he hung up the phone.

He went to the front desk to ask for his key. It was then that the clerk on duty, a woman that Freddy had not seen before, told him that his payment was not in order. She demanded cash. Freddy paid her for the night with the last of the Colombian pesos he had converted from dollars at the post office.

Now he knew that the hotel did not take charge cards, and in fact it was unlikely that any place in this city took them. He could speculate on who the last clerk called earlier that night, whether they be mob elements which might be in the town or had a distance to travel to get to Turbo, or the local authorities, or if he was merely the target of a shakedown, but all that speculation was futile endeavor. Now he must trust in the Professor and his people to get him out of Colombia.

Chapter Thirty-Five - Going Home

"In the marine forecast for the lower and middle keys just a few showers from the Bimini chain to the Dry Tortugas. We do have southeast winds right now at 10 to 15 knots. Seas beyond the reef 3 to 4 feet, inside 1 to 3 and there's a light to a moderate chop-chop on bay waters. Right now we do have a 20 percent chance of pre – cip – i - tation, mostly sunny skies and it's right now how many degrees? 80? Very good!"

****

They were turning for their approach into Key West International Airport. A flight plan filed in Sarasota said that their flight had originated there. They - John, who was the pilot, and Freddy, had left Puerto Rico four hours earlier. Freddy did not ask, nor did he care, what false flight plans had been filed there, or in Colombia.

This was the second flight Freddy and John had taken on their return from Colombia. They had flown very low both times. The first had been from a small field outside Cartagena, using similar deceptions, Freddy supposed. He wondered if a plane had actually taken off at each place to coincide with the flight plans filed to make sure this elaborate re-entry into the country of his birth would not go awry. Professor Sorenson seemed to know what he was doing. Seeing as how Wayne was one of his pupils for undercover work, Freddy guessed that he had taught more than English Composition.

Freddy stayed in the room the night of the executions, the night of the call to the professor, until the early morning hours. It had been ten-thirty pm when he made the call.

At 3 am he heard shuffling and footsteps in the corridor. He listened intently and heard someone try the knob.

What little furniture there was in the room that was movable in a practical sense, a night table, a chair and a lamp, was already up against the door. The only other piece was an old, ugly, white armoire. It looked heavy, would be noisy to move and may actually act as an impediment should he need egress through that door.

Someone had tried the knob, but this was a hotel sumptuous enough to have door locks, so they could not know whether he was inside the room or else ware. Unless the clerk told them that he had picked up the key. But then, if the clerk was aiding them, would not the clerk have given them another key to the room?

Whoever had come calling would perforce then use discretion before a frontal attack on a crazy gringo who had killed the two baddest brutes the city had known in a very long time.

He took his suitcase to the window and threw it into the softest looking shrubbery he could find and then climbed over the metal railing until he was hanging from the bottom rail with his feet seven feet from the ground. What an easy target he would make should one of the hallway lurkers choose to circle around to the back of the hotel looking for an easy and discrete way into his room!

He dropped to the ground landing as softly as he could, for once not hurting himself in the process, retrieved his suitcase and cleared the area quickly before future developments could be his undoing. He found a church and sat there cowering in the darkest corner for hours.

Before the next noon, less than fourteen hours after the call to the Professor, a woman wearing a shawl over her head and shoulders arrived with a package at the blind corner near the end of the street and close to the waterfront where Freddy was waiting for the appointed time to start for the telegraph office. She said nothing. She handed him the package and continued purposefully down the street without pausing or making eye contact. The package had Freddy's name on it and a message telling him to pick up a car that was waiting for him at the bus depot two blocks away. The keys were on the right front wheel. A map with directions in English was behind the visor. He was to drive it to an intersection outside the city of Cartagena. The package also contained some money in Colombian Pesos and a sandwich. The strange thing about the package was that it had no markings on it from any post office or delivery service. He picked up his things from their stash under a short flight of steps, retrieved the car, and drove to the assigned intersection, several miles outside Cartagena. He was met by an American about his own age. The man tapped on the window of Freddy's borrowed car.

"Freddy? How are you? My name is John." John was casual and likable, sandy-haired and lean. He looked taller, but Freddy figured he was about six feet.

They stayed overnight at a modest motel on the outskirts of town run by an expatriated American who limped pronouncedly on a stiff right leg. It was obvious that John knew the man, who settled them into a small cottage under the trees well back from the road. Freddy felt secure enough in that cottage to put his trust in John and was soon sound asleep for the first time since he left his friends at the fishing village, exhausted by tension and the rigors of his journey.

They drove to a small airstrip very early the next morning and flew to Puerto Rico, with John at the controls of the five-seater, two engine Beechcraft, and then on to Key West.

Freddy kept to his own thoughts for most of both flights. When he looked in John's direction, John would smile and go on with his flying. He seemed a competent sort, and he was sensitive to Freddy's not wanting to speak.

Most of the air trip was at low altitude. As they passed over the water, Freddy could see the patterns of color and texture change as their altitude and the water depth varied. Freddy reflected on how his life around the water had changed. He was far from his playground of chilly fresh-water ponds and streams as a boy in Pennsylvania. The teenager and young man on weekends and vacations in the more forbidding, cold Atlantic, with its short waves suited to body surfing, much beer, many baking bodies and the intricate caste system of the Jersey shore was also a thing of the past.

On his arrival in Key West years ago the water around his new home was first a warm, therapeutic medium, an embryonic, all-encompassing womb for a man running from the world. Then it became a place for Pamela and him to play.

Suddenly, it turned on him, became his enemy, as he ventured forth on it driven by dark and vengeful thoughts under dark and vengeful skies. It pushed him over its seething surface and tried to swallow him whole during the chase after Sargento and company.

That was all behind him now. Freddy looked down on the water under the wing on the approach to Key West International as the airplane circled in to the landing strip. It was now a key to unlocking memories of bad things. Freddy had lived at the water's edge all his life, and now he had to get away from it for a while, and leave this place, maybe never to return.

John parked the plane. Freddy waited there while he picked up a rental car and drove it back to where he could pick up Freddy with a minimum of fuss. Freddy did not care to be seen. He paused while passersby from a plane which had just landed had dispersed. When things were quiet Freddy crossed to the car and got in. It was nearly five p.m.

"Where to?" John asked cheerfully.

"First I want to check on things with a friend of mine on Stock Island. I imagine the police have stopped looking for me around here, but I would like to know for sure. Then, if it's all right with you and it looks safe, I'd like to pick up some clothes and things at my house."

"Fine with me," he said, smiling. He drove in a manner that would not attract attention. Freddy directed him to where Cap'n Walter's boat was usually tied up. He was in luck, it was in.

"I'll be right back, John," said Freddy. He left the quiet man waiting in the car as he walked to the pier.

There was not much going on at the shrimp docks; only a few boats were in. Cap'n Walter's was one of them. Freddy went aboard.

"Hello, Walter." He was on the fantail, fiddling with something or other. There was always something to fiddle with on one of those working boats.

"What can I do fer you...?" Walter looked up. At first he didn't recognize Freddy. "It's me, Walter...　Freddy."

" Freddy," he repeated, a half smile on his lips. He looked more closely. "No, it ain't, either. I'd have to say you're Fred now. I don't think there is a Freddy anymore. What happened to yer face? You gone native or sumpin'?

"I got a sunburn, I'm afraid."

"How'd ya get all chopped up?"

"Oh, a couple of bug bites, jellyfish, a few scratches. How are you?"

"I'm ok, but yer just skin n' bones an' ya look like ya got the weight of the world on yer shoulders." He looked at Freddy's dyed hair. "And yer roots 'er startin' ta show," he quipped. Freddy smiled at the joke. ""Jellyfish! What up with that?"

"Haven't you ever been stung by a jellyfish, Walter?"

"Hell no. Got a perfectly good boat right here and I stay *in the boat*! Ah'm guessin' you didn't stay in *your* boat."

"I don't have a boat anymore."

"Finally sank on ya, did it?"

"Yeah… I did lose weight though, thanks for noticing. Not too thin, do you think? A couple of beers will put that right back on. And the weight of the world, it's not on my shoulders anymore"

"That ain't exactly what I meant, and you know it. I know you've had a rough time, I can see it. How's Wayne?" he asked cautiously, as the weather creases at the corners of his eye sockets became more pronounced. Freddy said nothing. Cap'n Walter's eyes focused long and unseeing and the corners of his mouth tightened up. There was something in Freddy's face; perhaps it became even more severe, if that was possible, that told Cap'n Walter that Wayne had met his end. "Ah, well," Cap'n Walter said. He was never given to verbose oratories. Eulogies, apparently, were no exception. Freddy knew he was sorry, and that was all he would say.

"What can I do for ya, Fred?"

"Nothing too serious - I'm not going to ask you to go out on a limb for me again."

"Awh, don't worry about it. I liked you even when ya was a lush an' you useta make fun of everybody, remember? In fact, I think I liked ya better." Freddy smiled good-naturedly at the jibe, and then he got serious.

"Just a couple of questions, Walter. I assume that the police were around here looking for me."

"Ya got that right. First coupla days, there was cops all over the place. After that I went fishin'."

"They still want me?"

"Don't know. Hell, you been gone a month; more even, you can't be that hot. Be stupid if you stayed in town, though."

"I'm not planning to, Walter, I just got to get some things." Freddy realized he was slipping into Cap'n Walter's infectious idiom. "What have the papers had to say?"

"Don't know that either. I been out at sea and back twice, fishin's been good. Just pulled in and unloaded today. Yer lucky ya caught me."

"Did you ever find out what happened to my car?"

"Look over there." Freddy looked where Cap'n Walter had pointed across two piers to a lot. Freddy's car sat there. It was on a dead-end road near the water two blocks over. "After ya left *with my dinghy* I took a walk over an' cleaned it out. Later I went back n' got it and moved it over there where nobody'd bother it. I know about the screwdriver under the seat you use to start it with. That ignition switch is like an old whore, loose n' easy."

"What did you find in it?"

"They went and put lots a co-caine in yer car. I got rid of it for ya."

"What did you do with it?"

"I got no use for that shit. I dumped the bags out into the harbor. Figured it'd make the fishes happy. They ain't got much of a life." Freddy chuckled.

"Ok, Walter, do me a favor. Take care of my car until I come back. I'll sign it over to you in case something happens. I'll leave the title in my screen door at my house." He offered Walter five American twenties he got from John.

"There was a bunch a' hundreds in it, too. Three thousand dollars. Want 'em?"

"No, you keep the money, and thanks a lot for taking care of the car for me."

"Ok, Fred. Uh, when ya comin' back?"

"I don't know. Maybe never." They said their goodbyes.

John drove Freddy to his house. There was a "for rent" sign on it. Freddy went in through the bathroom window. He wanted to make it fast, and get in and out before dark so that he would not have to turn on any lights that would beacon his presence to the neighborhood. Luckily his things were still there. He got his bag and packed what few clothes were worth taking, and got a few important papers from his drawer. He looked for Pamela's things, but they were not there. Her family must have come for them. There were some photographs of them in the room, of them on the boat and around town, and Freddy packed them also after looking at them a little longer than was prudent. Noticing the gathering darkness, he took another moment to regain his composure and left by the front door to rejoin John. His neighbor, Mrs. Kupcha, was there to greet him as he left.

"Freddy, oh, Freddy, where have you been?" There was no avoiding her.

"Mrs. Kupcha, there has been some trouble. I have to go away, please do me a favor - you must know the police were after me, and I'll bet they still have some questions. Please don't call them until I can leave the Keys."

"Yes, I know they want to talk to you, but that's no reason for me to be calling them, not if you don't want to be bothered."

"What do you mean? Isn't there a warrant out for my arrest?"

"Heavens, no! It was in all the papers. Where have you been, South America? At first they were looking all over the place for you, then they found that man tied up at the end of Seminole street. They put him in jail. With all of that information they found with him he didn't have much choice, did he? The papers were full of it that weekend, and all of the holiday news, and the murders of those young women, and of a couple of criminals. The police wanted a man named Sargento and a crime syndicate. A day ago the man they arrested made a full confession to a lot of things that happened in the past when the news came out that two gang leaders who were fugitives from some famous trial up north a long time ago were found dead in a boat from around here. The boat was in Colombia! Your friend Wayne is a hero of sorts. They think he is the one who turned in the list of names and places about the mobsters and the drug ring and the smuggling. They are making arrests all over for smuggling and other things, too. They think Wayne killed some of the mobsters. I'm afraid they want to talk to him about parole and something about vigilantisms. How is he, anyway?"

"He's OK now, Mrs. K, he's just fine."

"That's good. If you see him, give him my best."

"Thank you, I will, Mrs. K..., when I see him."

John anticipated Freddy and popped the trunk with the lever inside the car. Freddy threw his things in and got into the car. Silently, they headed back to the airport.

The police did not want him, except for questioning. He would pass on that. The man at the end of Seminole had been taken in after the girls were killed, but he could have no knowledge of the murders. Fingerprints and forensics may have cleared Freddy of the murder within the first two weeks, but he couldn't have known that. Still he must stay clear of the police and the media, or they would draw attention to him and might make him a target for the mob as it now existed in its diminished state. The man at the wall did know of the untimely death of Sargento and Connors. Mrs. Kupcha had said that it was in the news. That news had spurred him to talk, and the weight of evidence against the mobsters must have implicated them in the murders.

He wondered that perhaps, in time, the news of his movements in South America during the time of the killings would filter down to the authorities, and then Wayne would get the blame. Or credit... He would be a legend - Freddy liked that. And the heat would be off Freddy; all he had to do is stay clear of the mob. He couldn't help thinking the story would make a good movie, but Freddy was the only living person that would ever know it.

Freddy decided he would find an anonymous way to send the police a rough position of the island smuggling center. Figuring from his probable position in relation to the island when the boat sank, his drift, and what his fishermen friends told him, but there was no rush. There were other things he had promised to do. It wasn't comfortable for him here, and he wanted to leave this place that had gone sour. They were taking off for West Palm.

"John, do you know Professor Sorenson?"

"I've known him all my life. He's my father." For the first time since Freddy had met him, John became serious. "I knew Teddy, too."

****

Professor Sorenson lived in a large one-level house set well back from the palm-lined street. It was situated on a long curve of beachfront property. Given the looks of the neighborhood, Freddy didn't have to be told that the property was expensive. John parked in the arc of the hedged driveway nearest the house, and they went inside.

"Coffee, or a drink?" the professor asked.

"Coffee will be fine, thank you, sir," Freddy said. John nodded, coffee also. They waited, seated in his den of hardwoods, books, and diplomas while the professor himself made the coffee. He soon returned.

"Sorry to keep you waiting. I gave the girl the day off. There is no one to overhear us; although it looks like that may have been an unnecessary precaution." He was a man in his late sixties, wearing his age well, standing straight and moving fluidly. He was starting to thicken in the shoulders, and would someday - yet far off - be slightly stooped. His hair and eyes were gray, as was his cardigan. His skin tone was healthy, a light yellow coloration. He began speaking, explaining his relationship to Wayne - Teddy.

"I was his instructor in Criminal Justice. I brought him along, got him involved in what he was doing to shut down the Sargento's and their cretinous minions. My son John worked with him.

"Everything went smoothly for a time. I never counted on Teddy falling in love with Moira Sargento, Nick's "wife". He produced folders which had been waiting for their introduction at the chair-side table near him. "Teddy wanted you to see this." They were records of his training, notes on operations and clippings of the accounts of everything to do with Wayne and the mob, and the scandal that followed in the courtroom over Teddy McLaren killing Nick Sargento after Nick beat and murdered Moira. Freddy read the history as they waited patiently. Freddy put the folders down.

"Thank you, Professor," Freddy said after he finished reading the chronicle of Wayne's career against the crime syndicate, "It looks as though Teddy was something else. It's too bad things went so wrong for him."

"I think so too. He showed great promise. And he was like a second son to me." He reflected on this for a moment and then went on to explain. "Teddy had no close family left. I had been close to law enforcement all of my life. My wife died of cancer twelve years ago, about when Teddy started school at City College, and I started teaching some courses in Criminal Justice to fill my time. He was a good lad. Smart, strong - he could think on his feet like no one I ever knew. He was my agent for infiltrating the Sargentos' - a personal grudge of mine. We were working with the District Attorney's office in New York. Wayne was the operative, John here ran him. He was the go-between, the contact, or, cut-out between Teddy and the law. For the most part Teddy was in there all alone. If I'd known that it was going to end this way I never would have sent Teddy in there.

"It took some doing to prevent him from being prosecuted and sentenced to prison instead of that asylum. After the incident I retired, moved here. When Teddy skipped parole he contacted me on his way to Key West. We've kept in touch ever since."

Then it was Freddy's turn. He told the two men the entire story, the involvement, the attacks and the murders, the chase and how he shot the villains. There was grim satisfaction sculpted on their faces when they learned of the two men's demise. Freddy felt none. He thought to ask how the professor had come by the false ID and the visa he obtained for Freddy, but then changed his mind. In his life, and with his underworld connections, there must be many things he could do. How he got it done didn't matter so much.

It was after three in the morning. They had been talking since early evening. The professor suggested that Freddy stay the night. His only assets were the clothes in his suitcases and the Colombian money that Professor Sorenson had sent him in Turbo. Freddy accepted the invitation.

The next morning Freddy wired for his savings and stayed for breakfast, then lunch. The professor, John, and Freddy talked a bit more, sharing remembrances of Wayne. The professor went off to his den to work on a book he was writing and Freddy caught up with the newspapers. John said his goodbyes and left to fly back to his home in Sarasota. Freddy's money arrived, all three hundred and ninety dollars of it, saved with Pamela's help. He made ready to leave. He caught himself thinking of what he must do next. He was doing a lot of that lately. Professor Sorenson approached Freddy with a briefcase.

"Teddy said to give this to you if anything happened to him." Freddy opened it. "One hundred and twenty thousand dollars," the professor intoned."

So Wayne had a stash after all. "I'll be damned - that rascal!" said Freddy. Freddy laughed at the thought of Wayne holding out on them like that. He had to grin when he thought of it. The professor did also, showing that he knew what Freddy was thinking. So Mr. Perfect was not entirely perfect after all.

"He took it the day Moira was killed, the day he killed Nick Sargento," the professor explained. "I think he thought they owed him. Perhaps they did."

"Well, thanks for everything, Professor Sorenson." The professor wouldn't take any of the money, said he had enough, had been well-off all his life. He wouldn't even accept Freddy's offer to reimburse him for his expenses. Freddy said so long.

Freddy was to keep half the money and give the rest to Annie's folks. Taking ten thousand of his half with him, he asked the professor to send ten thousand to Father Paul's mission in Santa Rosa and bank the rest for him. Freddy would not have known how to explain a fifty thousand dollar deposit to the tax boys, or to the narcotics boys either, for that matter. He had just made a suspicious trip out of the country without a visa, and his Master Card record in Panama would bear that out, should anyone start an investigation. The professor had said maybe he could quash the Master Card record in Panama. In the small city of Turbo there had probably been a search for a suspicious-looking American who had checked into a hotel for a two week stay the night of a double murder trying to use using a charge card and then left the next day after paying with Pesos and destroying the Master Card record. In Panama, there had been no need for such a search. The professor said he would work on it.

****

Freddy flew to San Diego and drove to the home of Annie's parents nestled in Chula Vista. He felt helpless. He had no good answers for most of their questions. All he could do was to keep saying he was sorry. When he offered them the money they almost didn't take it until Freddy asked them to do so for the sake of their two other children. At that point in time sixty thousand dollars could go a long way toward college or a business, or wherever their future lay. On the way down the driveway Freddy nearly walked into Annie's sister. He was bowled over by the striking resemblance she bore to Annie. Same hair, same figure but thinner, a younger version of his friend from Key West. He smiled at her. She smiled back generously with a curious look on her face. It would have been Annie's winning smile but for the sadness in her eyes. Annie's parents were doing something right. Freddy left feeling that they had ambivalent feelings toward him, and he could understand how they well might.

Next, the money being placed safely in the hands of Annie's father, Freddy flew to Cincinnati. He dreaded seeing Pamela's father, but he felt he must. On the plane to Cincinnati, he thought about all that had happened in eight short months. Freddy wondered if he would be changed forever, and then realized that he already was. It was not just the Sargento affair, either. It started with Wayne, who put him to work and made him regain a grudging self-respect. Annie tempered his sarcasm with her tolerant sense of humor and Pamela, who gave him a sense of purpose and filled him with love. The love was still there, but Pamela and the purpose were gone.

He started out in Key West with no goals or views, vestiges of morals but no morality. He returned, after seeing how good things could be, how good and worthy some people can be, honest, loving, dependable, and how evil others were. And how they could coldly end the lives of the good ones. He could not fathom the fairness of it. But now he knew that the evil ones, the aberrations, must be stopped. Even if it fails, the effort to stop them must be made. They have always existed and will continue to exist; they must not proliferate. Where they are extant they must be met and have their mettle tested by those who might stop them in whatever short time is given to them.

The difference in Freddy was one of degrees. It was difficult to provoke a reaction from him now. He got surprised but not amazed, irked but not angry, annoyed but not upset. He was frequently mildly intolerant and impatient though he had nowhere pressing to go. With all the time in the world he was anxious to get it over with; it was a nuisance, a bore. He didn't laugh much, but he smiled a lot. It was often the smile of a cynic. Now there was always time for thoughts of Pamela. Things were worse than before.

As for being free and easy-going Freddy again, perhaps some of that would return in time, with the right catalyst. Sargento had taken three of his friends, but what he could not take were their gifts to Freddy. He could recognize how bad the bad ones at large in the world's society of men could be, but he could also see the good in people as well, and he gained a habit of doing what he must for the sake of its rightness.

He looked down from the plane window. He could see the Southern Sierra Nevada below, rugged, snowcapped peaks through the gaps in the puffy, white clouds. He would have to decide where to go, what to do, now that life as he had known it in Key West was over. Maybe the mountains would be enough of a change to keep him from seeing grief in everything around him. In all of his life he had never lived away from the big water, the salty oceans of the

Atlantic, Gulf, and Caribbean. It was time for a change. Colorado might be nice. Or Lake Tahoe, it had a big lake. He had seen a picture in the airline's magazine of a skier jumping from a cornice with the lake in the background. The skier seemed to be hanging out over the lake, thousands of feet in the air. He could do that. Might even grow to like it.

The plane touched down in the dreary town as a light rain fell on the tarmac. The big wheels screeched and then rolled as the plane slowed. As they passed pools of water standing on the runway reflecting the bleakness of the sky, the engines reversed, sounding like four choked vacuum cleaners. It felt like they were sucking at the plane from behind, bringing its speed down to a less apprehensive rate. As it rolled along the ground and the engines wound down, their pitch declining as the turbines slowed and then flared again briefly as the pilot turned the plane toward the gate.

They had to wait while the ground crew attached the segmented inclined way to the plane's door. Baggage handlers moved in below and Freddy saw his one bag make it onto the cart. His only other luggage was the briefcase. Instead of the hundred and twenty thousand dollars it had contained at the start, it now had the ten thousand dollars of his own money Freddy had taken with him, less traveling expenses, sharing the remaining space vacated by the rest of the cash with his socks and underwear, three new shirts he had paid too much for at a store in the airport at San Diego, and a few toiletries.

Freddy shaved at the airport in a sink with only a tap for cold water, oblivious to the business suits' diffident looks of disapproval. He put on one of the new shirts. Picking up a rental car, he proceeded to the address of Mr. Greer, Pamela's father.

****

The house was big and square with large, long, wooden windows. Four wooden columns fronted a porch running the length of the front of the house. Each window had many panes in both its upper and lower halves, smaller vertical rectangles within the framework of a large, massive one. The house was of gray stone, two stories. It had hedges at the sides. The landscaping was severe, and the rain added a somber note to the dirge playing within Freddy as he dreaded the forthcoming confrontation.

He used the knocker and the door opened, answered by a woman, a maid/butler, sort of a female domestic factotum. She was neither pleasant nor unpleasant as she led him to a long, narrow room filled with trophies, mounted fish and heads of four-footed beasts. Freddy was to wait there for Mr. Greer.

He arrived presently, but he was not as Freddy remembered him. He was still rather portly but much more formidable now than he was in Key West. He was no longer in a floppy hat, outlandish shorts, and tent-like Hawaiian sports shirt. The sunburn was gone. He had reverted to his business mogul/paper factory tycoon mode of existence. He greeted Freddy.

"Hello, Freddy. I may call you Freddy, may I not?" Very proper and staid, face emotionless. His calling Freddy by his first name was a more familiar greeting than Freddy expected.

"Certainly, sir," Freddy replied. Mr. Greer was studying him openly, raising hackles on his neck, making Freddy especially alert to his behavior. Something seemed wrong. He had recently faced two of the most diabolically vicious men he could ever have imagined. Something, some sense he had acquired as a result of that confrontation, told Freddy now that something was not quite right here.

"My, how you've changed," Mr. Greer observed. "Looks as though you have had a good deal of wear and tear. You must have been through a great deal. Have a drink. Some white wine, perhaps? That is an excellent Johannesburg Riesling," he said, pointing to a bottle on the sideboard from the seat he had taken. Freddie was thinking that there was no such thing as a good Johannesburg Riesling. Well, he guessed it could be good if a person liked it, but Freddy was not that person. "Pour a glass for me as well, would you?" This was too much. The man thus far had shown no concern at all for his lost daughter. Had he no feelings? No anger, no remorse, nothing? Not yet one reference to Pamela, and yet Freddy felt that one was coming soon. It must.

There were glasses set out by the bottle. Could this be a pre-arranged set-piece? Freddy had pictured Mr. Greer as a Bourbon and Coke drinker. You never can tell.

Freddy poured the wine badly. The glasses were inverted, fluted parabolas. He dropped the liquid in from fourteen inches, down one side of the glass out up out the other. Freddy splashed his new shirt. He was so keen on observing Mr. Greer he hardly noticed the spill. He handed Mr. Greer a glass and paced to a window to look out at the rain. Mr. Greer moved to an overstuffed chair as Freddy watched and said nothing. With Freddy standing and Mr. Greer seated the window lights over the rotund man's shoulders shone down on him obliquely, highlighting his rounded features and leaving the rest of his face in the darkness of the shadows, making him a skulking, mysterious figure. Alfred Hitchcock. Sidney Greenstreet at the louvers in "The Maltese Falcon". They took a few sips each.

Mr. Greer said, "I'm sorry to see Pamela go, I'll miss her, but fortunately I have two other daughters. Perhaps you will meet them some time." Freddy blinked his eyes twice, he couldn't believe his ears, or the coldness of the man.   "Right now, we have some unfinished business, which I am sure you will want to get to right away." Something was dreadfully wrong here. "Come with me," he went on, "I have something to show you." Freddy hesitated. "Oh, come on. I won't let you get out of here so quickly, so you might as well come along." He led Freddy to an alcove near a door at the end of a corridor. In the small semi-dome was a vase, about 8 inches high, set atop an ornate marble column. It caught Freddy's eye. It was red and brown, flared at the ends, with maidens dancing before gods seated upon thrones around its tapered waist. Tropical birds and ocelots adorned the top. A rabbit with a quill pen was at the bottom.

He recognized it. He'd seen it before, or one just like it, in the contraband shed on Sargento's island. Mr. Greer saw that Freddy was interested in it.

"Do you know what that is?"

"Pre-Colombian," Freddy muttered flatly as he stood before it with cold detachment.

"Excellent, Freddy. I'm a collector. A friend of mine used to import the stuff."

"What happened to him?"

"He's not with us anymore." Freddy heard an alarm bell go off in his head. Could there be a connection Mr. Greer and Sargento?" Greer's hand went to the nearby doorknob. "The vase is a fake," he said with a short laugh. "Do you remember my Chinese friend and business associate? The one that accompanied me on my fishing trip to Key West? He makes them by the thousands. He recently returned to Taiwan. I keep this one here as a sort of a joke between us. About my daughter - you really must be more careful with her in the future." What? Freddy's mind was spinning. Mr. Greer was smiling as he swung the door open, and it was not a smile of condolence or grief.

As the door swings open inward what do you think Freddy sees but Pamela, lying on a bed with a frilly comforter drawn up over her waist. She is in a modestly cut nightgown with a frilly fringe and a string tie at the center of her bosom. As she turns her head to Freddy she smiles warmly in anticipation of his greeting, but the smile flickers on and off apprehensively and goes out. The door behind Freddy closes.

"Freddy..." He is fighting to understand, shaky, unsure of his footing. How can this be?

"Freddy," this time more beseechingly, "Freddy where have you been, don't you want me anymore?" she asks petulantly. He has been gone for a 5 weeks, she has had no word from him. She knows not what to think. Finally, Freddy is able to move and goes to her bedside. He crushes his head into her chest. He puts his arms around her. She is crying, and half-laughing, too, breathing in bursts and clutching his noggin to her breasts. Freddy doesn't understand how this was happening, but his heart has wings. He could leap into the air, he could fly. He could circle and swoop down and lift her in his arms, and they would glide through the heavens to a Mozart tune, a light and lively presto replete with continuo and lotsa, lotsa strings. They would fly away and slide down a mountain.

"Where have you been? I thought you didn't love me anymore."

"How could you think that? Of course I do, I just thought you were dead." She drew her head back with an annoyed frown.

"No, darling," she said, "they tried to kill me, and I was unconscious for a while from the drug they made me inhale, but I guess I didn't breathe enough of it for it to kill me."

"But how---"

"You always said I had great lungs," it was true, she was a marvel underwater, almost as good as he was. "I just held my breath for as long as I could! They ran out of time. Then they stabbed me. Isn't that cheating?"

He gently squeezed her warm, firm left breast to acknowledge her great lungs.

"But Pamela, the radio said you were dead! I heard the sirens, saw the ambulance lights!"

"Freddy! Are you going to argue with me about it? Don't you believe I'm alive?"

"Well, no, it's just that---"

"No, Freddy, another woman died that night. Her boyfriend got drunk and they had a fight at the docks at the base of the point. He stabbed her. I have a small stab wound, too, but it's only from where the knife they had at my side cut me when I started to struggle. I had some blood loss, and a twisted neck, and after effects from the drug, which didn't agree with me very well, I'm afraid, but I'm almost better now. I can travel. Are you going to take me back to Key West with you?"

"No," he said. She frowned, dismayed. He had burst her balloon.

"Why not?" She asked, as her voice rose peevishly. Her face went into a pout and she looked like she might cry.

"Because we're not going to Key West, we're going somewhere else, that's why," he said before the deluge started. She beamed, he basked. Presently, she asked, "Freddy, where we goin'?"

"Lake Tahoe. I've always wanted to learn to ski," he lied.

"I'll teach you! I'm an expert!"

"Oh, no."

They are smiling, laughing and tearful all at once.

"Freddy?"

"What now?"
"Kiss me."
"Where?"
"All over."
So he did.

Chapter Thirty-Six - A Little Town in the Midwest

There's a town in the Midwest not too far from the town where Pamela and Freddy live. It's a quiet town in a rural community where everyone has a pickup truck, an herb garden, tomato plants, squash, and a variety of fruit trees. There are no large stores and the tallest structures for 30 miles are the power line towers just outside of town. There are silos and fences. There are patches of forest, and a few hills.

A few years, or perhaps we should say a number of years after the events related previously, a man moved into town and bought the diner. The townies and the country folk were grateful because the lady who ran the diner previously was getting on in years and was anxious to retire.

The new owner operates the diner for breakfast and lunch, a good business model for a diner in a town where most folks are at home for dinner. He hires a couple of kids to help him and retains them until they are ready to move on to something more substantial.

The food is excellent, but the menu has some interesting twists which had not been seen before by the locals. They would speculate as to the origins dishes which were exotic to them. Were they South American or Caribbean, French or Polynesian? It made for lively conversation.

The man is amiable, but he keeps to himself pretty much. When questioned about the provenance of the menu items he just smiles and keeps working. He is quiet, but not timid. About six-two, or perhaps a little shorter with age and a bit rounder about the middle than he had been, but still in good health and good physical condition.

After lunch he goes with his dogs and walks the forest and the hills. Sometimes he sits by a pond and thinks as he watches the grasshoppers and butterflies in season, or alternately scans, which seems second nature for him, the critters who forage and flee from predation in winter around the icy pond or on and under the snow.

The next morning he is back at his diner, and he does this every day of the year. He is aware of Freddy and Pamela. Maybe someday they will stop in the town and find him here, who knows?

For now he has his dogs and his diner. It wasn't a French restaurant, it was only a diner. But what a menu! He thought "Le Tire Bouchon" was a bit hifalutin' for the name of a diner in this little rural town, so he just calls it "Annie's Place." He thinks that she would have liked that.

Author's Notes

There was no Traffic!

At the western termination of Flagler Avenue between Reynolds and White, a person had to wait for a while to see a car go by. Very few cars were parked on the street. At the top of the La Concha hotel downtown late at night a person could sit at the bar 7 stories above Duval Street and watch the street lights change. Nothing down there was moving. A person could park almost anywhere. As noted earlier, Freddy liked to park in front of Sloppy Joe's.

There were no cell phones!

There were no cell phones; no GPS readily available to the general public, and no one owned a computer except the people on the ground floor of the computer era who actually knew something about the way computers worked. No Graphical Idiot – so sorry, meant to say Graphical User – Interfaces.

My first computer didn't even have a hard drive. A ten megabyte – yes, I mean *megabyte,* hard drive in the early eighties was too expensive for me to afford.

Container ships would not get big and burly until the 80's and so port security was easier. Now, contraband is a lot easier to get into the country. Progress?

Of course, the males in the story are the active protagonists and the women are the romantics. That is the opposite of real life, but this is a story of fiction. And as far as *that* goes…

Freddy took Pamela to Lake Tahoe, where she taught him how to ski after he fell down a lot. Talk about being out of your element. Except for a small problem concerning Freddy's affinity for casinos things went pretty smoothly until Freddy decided to try gold mining. Pamela would have none of it. Then they moved back to Pamela's home state, away from temptation. They are probably going to be very happy. Pamela will have to handle that herself now that Wayne is gone. Or is he? Remember, they never found the body. Hmmmmm.

About Key West

I took some liberties with the moon phases relating to specific events in time (I didn't check at all), and minor changes in the time frame of Key West's growth and on-going over-development. Also, I altered some places, distances and water depths for my convenience. The basics are accurate enough for a yarn.

The tubes were not copper nickel when the desalting plant closed, but titanium. The plant did not close in the 70's, but by the early 80's but by then it was all but vacated and destitute. It was dead for all practical purposes by 1979.

The spring of 1979 was also when the Casa Marina re-opened after being dormant since the end of its occupation by the Army Hawk missile Battalion during the Cuban Missile Crisis. It was not open in 1973 when the characters visited. The first Fantasy Fest parade was also in 1979.

Modus Operandi

I did not want to write a book that was about drug smuggling alone; there were plenty in existence as it was. In Key West, most of the smuggling that I and everyone else were aware of was of "square Grouper". But I will say that the people I know and knew who had been smugglers were all fine fellows, and except for one friend who is now deceased, they went on to other things and have all achieved a degree of success, even the ones who did some time.

The bad guys in the book comprise a fictitious crime organization with a small but efficient core and with multinational connections with those who handle illicit goods from worldwide sources and transport them to floating delivery points on the gulf coast and the southern portion of the eastern seaboard of the United States. Their former ties with northeast operations had been severed by an equally elite squad of righteous dudes of whom Wayne was a pivotal constituent component.

Now, just prior to the opening of the story in 73, the Navy had just decommissioned the destroyer squadron and the submarine squadron, so Freddy wasn't here for that. There were however, numerous former Navy personnel still living in Key West to whom

Freddy was acquainted. They are gone now, for the most part. Freddy's initial character? He's flip because he's an insensitive but well-meaning buffoon at the beginning of the book.

As for the rest? The sea chase is a bit fantastic, but if it were routine there would be no book.

Key West, the un-natural key

As is mentioned in the book, Key West had salt creeks. It had more than that, if less is more. Filling of most of the salt ponds on the eastern end of the island doubled the island's size.

Key West's salt creeks existed back in the day when it was a not so big because the vast amount of landfill had not been perpetrated. A storm started the choking of the western creeks, which is to say that the next big storm could have flushed them out again, but landfill became the priority. That was when the island doubled in size with the filling of the creeks and of most of the salt ponds on the eastern end of the island. But this was back in the days of Flagler, and before that. Later, Fleming Key and Dredger's Key (Sigsbee) were made from dredged materials in the 40's by the Navy. Most recently, Tank Island (Sunset Key) was made by the Navy as a fuel depot in '65 from material extracted from the previously dredged Key West Harbor to make it deeper for the submarines, which had evolved into larger boats. The trolleys are gone; the ferries to Cuba are gone, too. Of course, I was not yet born and was not here to see them. As for the loss of the salt creeks; it is hard for anyone now to miss something they had no idea existed. I for one would have liked to see those creeks and the way the system of flows worked naturally. Here is my theory:

Geiger Creek

This one appears that it was truncated by the Navy runways and perimeter roads at NAF Boca Chica. There is still a flow by way of the quarries at the East end of the base, but it trails off into shallows as it approaches US 1 at the West end of Big Coppitt. The obstruction to free flow there has allowed sedimentation, progression, and the ensuing vegetation to restrict what I believe was once a free-flowing channel.

Sugarloaf

Sugarloaf and Perky have a good size system of salt creeks which are a lot of fun for kayaking. Here, too, some of the creeks are trying to close up or have closed up because the dredged cuts have diverted the volume of the flows necessary to keep them open.

Tarpon Creek

I have not been to this creek in a long time, but I saw its ocean end close up considerably in just a few years. Again, due to more human plumbing of waterways than the creek could compete with to survive in its pristine state.

Bahia Honda

This is a good example of how roads and insufficient flows can change things. The aerial photograph of Bahia Honda a few years back showed not only the salt lake at the interior of the key on the ocean side of the highway, but the portion of that lake which still lies on the far side of US 1 from the main body of the park. Traces of creek still could be seen leading into the far portion of the lake in this photography. I managed to cut and pull my way through these closing creeks in one of my kayaks to that body of water, which has a bottom of leaf litter.

The ocean side of Bahia Honda has a small creek leading to that larger component of the lake. It runs under a small bridge. When it runs that is; it does not always run. It becomes sand clogged at times. I do not believe that this would happen very often if there were natural periodic storm flows right through the key of Bahia Honda as there must have been before the highway. A reopening between the two sides of these now separate bodies of water would, I believe, facilitate rehabilitation of the creek system and an excellent kayak trail. More than that; a portion of the key which once was natural would be restored, which would benefit bird populations and fish. Culverts do not suffice to carry the volume of storm water necessary to return the system to its natural state. At high flow rates the water which cannot get through culverts fast enough piles up on the abutments and the face of these openings and then overtops and erodes the land. It would require a bridge and some digging to get the area back to some semblance of a natural state.

The Sea, the Beaches, the Reef

The reef has recently been reported as being 8 percent alive. It has been alternately covered with algae, bleached by excessive water temperatures, overcome by excessive nutrients supplied by agricultural and residential runoff, smothered by sedimentation, or killed outright by ocean acidification. To me, it looks pretty much dead, but then I saw it as it was decades ago. A dead reef makes for poor habitat for fish. Less fish and overfishing. Excellent combination. The reef is in urgent need of repair and there are people on the case trying to do just that.

Smathers Beach, along A1A (South Roosevelt) was formerly at the same level as the road. The wall had not yet been built, and the sand that the tourists now put in plastic bags to take home with them had not yet been imported from the Bahamas and other sources. The surface of the beach was hard-packed marl, which would remove the skin from your knees like sandpaper if you skidded across the surface while running or jumping. Forget sand castles.

Turtles, once a marketable food source, and now each of the five major species either threatened or endangered, have fallen prey to plastic bags that strangle their guts, by-catch, and loss of nesting ground; on beaches over developed, over-lighted, or walled next to the sea. There is an ocean of information on this for anyone who cares to look for it. It would be nice if our government would pay closer attention…

The People in the Story

Nationalities and ethnicities – I could not make one of each type of person, that is to say that if I had an Anglo villain and an Anglo good guy, as in Wayne versus Conners, they would offset in terms of offending or lauding one segment of the population over another, but this was not a practical reality for each nationality, ethnic, race, or cultural division. That would be too contrived.

Underrepresented in the book are the Spanish speaking population, and the black population. The reality is that the black population was not often seen frequenting the white areas, and vice versa. There were parallels; the water people, the fishermen and charter boat people of all types interacted amicably. Shrimpers came in all flavors. Politicos of relatively long Keys lineage were prominent and had a strong voter base among the older families in Key West before so many of those old time families sold their holdings decades ago and moved North as Key West became expensive and crowded. A large swath of waterfront land along Atlantic Boulevard procured by the City of Key West in 1950 for public use, as to which a small piece in the Key West Citizen accompanied by a Don Pinder photo attested, was then given up to developers who built – you guessed it – Condominiums! That public land could have been green space.

As another option, the salt pond area could have been purchased to avoid development there, but the voters would not approve the expenditure.

An excellent (in my opinion) history of Key West and one which I think is well worth reading is "The History of Key West" written by Jerry Wilkinson. He has also written about the history of the other keys.

The Book

I first wrote this book between 1976 and 1979 on legal pads. Then I typed it. On a typewriter! That was not fun. The original version came in at over 600 manuscript pages.

The book is fiction, a snapshot of the Key West that I knew back then. It is not a history; I took some liberties in the actual sequence of events of the time. The sources I used for the Mexican, Central American, and South American portions are long lost, but, again, the book is fiction.

Turbo is a real place, it is on the map, but the area described in the book is entirely contrived. I thought of making a fictitious city name but decided to use Turbo instead. I hope to get there someday.

Pictures

The way a lot of Key West Harbor used to look

Looking across the harbor toward tank and Christmas Islands

Land's End without the boats of today

The Bottle Cap

Sloppy Joe's

Mangroves and Salt Creeks

Sargento's Island

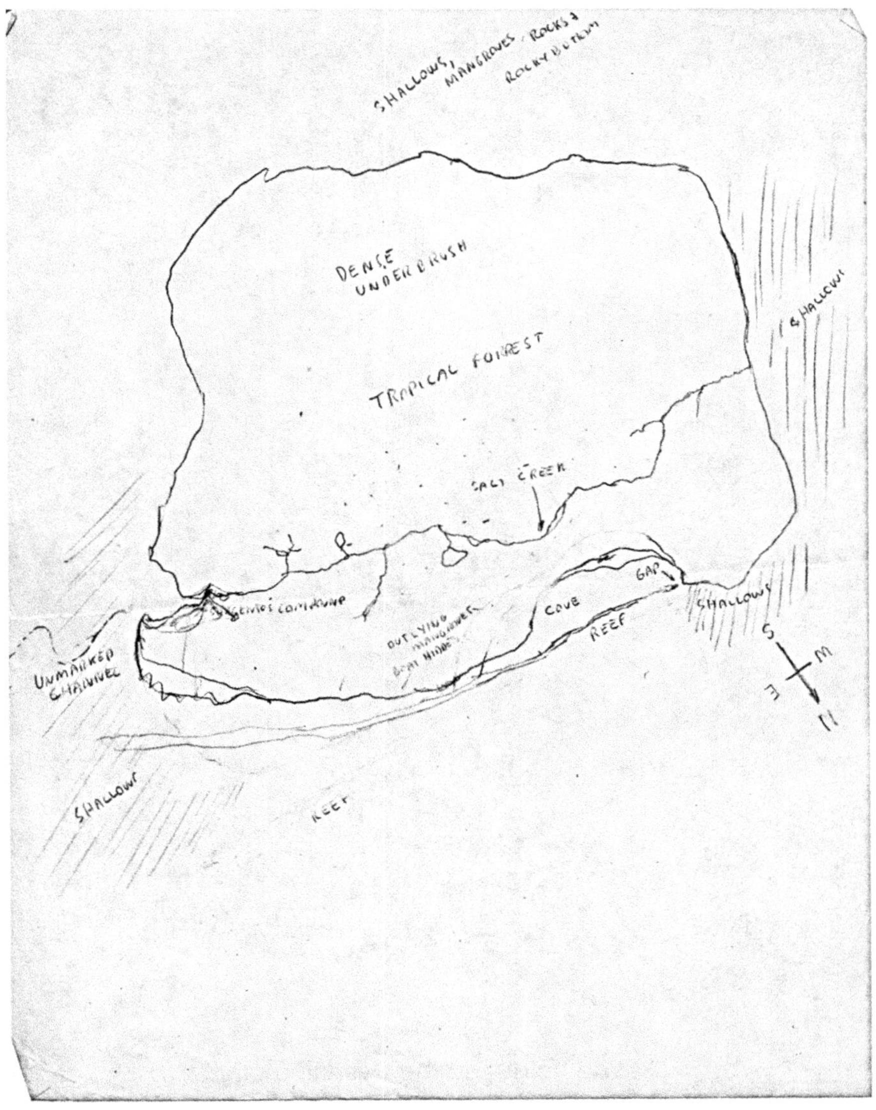

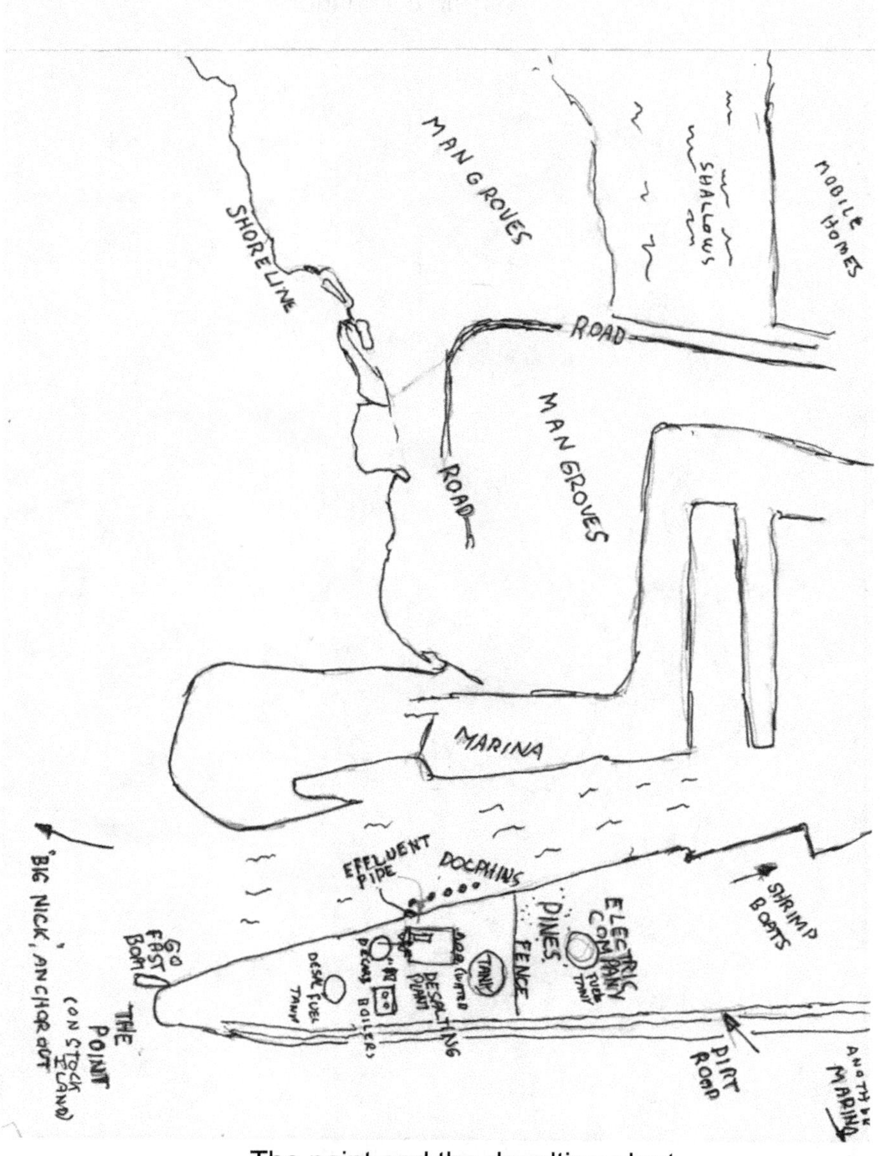

The point and the desalting plant

The old desalting plant